Nina Singh lives just outside of Boston, USA, with her husband, children and a very rambunctious Yorkie. After several years in the corporate world she finally followed the advice of family and friends to 'give the writing a go, already'. She's oh-so-happy she did. When not at her keyboard she likes to spend time on the tennis court or golf course. Or immersed in a good read.

Joanna Sims is proud to pen contemporary romance for Mills & Boon. Joanna's series, The Brands of Montana, features hardworking characters with hometown values. You are cordially invited to join the Brands of Montana as they wrangle their own happily-ever-afters. And, as always, Joanna welcomes you to visit her at her website: www.joannasimsromance.com.

Also available by Nina Singh

Miss Prim and the Maverick Millionaire
The Marriage of Inconvenience
Snowed in with the Reluctant Tycoon

Also available by Joanna Sims

A Wedding to Remember
Thankful for You
Meet Me at the Chapel
High Country Baby
High Country Christmas
A Match Made in Montana
Marry Me, Mackenzie!
The One He's Been Looking For
A Baby for Christmas

Visit millsandboon.co.uk
for more information

REUNITED WITH HER ITALIAN BILLIONAIRE

NINA SINGH

A BRIDE FOR LIAM BRAND

JOANNA SIMS

MILLS & BOON

First Published in Great Britain 2018
by Mills & Boon, an imprint of HarperCollinsPublishers,
1 London Bridge Street, London, SE1 9GF

ISBN: 978-0-263-26470-8

38-0218

MIX
Paper from
responsible sources
FSC™ C007454

This book is produced from independently certified FSC™ paper to ensure responsible forest management.

For more information visit: www.harpercollins.co.uk/green

Printed and bound in Spain
by CPI, Barcelona

REUNITED WITH HER ITALIAN BILLIONAIRE

NINA SINGH

To my parents—you always said I could.

CHAPTER ONE

SHE SHOULD HAVE known he would come.

The dark, commanding man at her back door was the last person Brianna wanted to see. Though she should have guessed. Marco Dirici had a knack for showing up in her life unbidden and unwelcome.

Brianna peeked through the side window again. She knew it was him. The voice had confirmed it. Still, she couldn't help but wish that maybe if she looked again it would be someone else standing there.

No such luck. It was definitely Marco, in the flesh. Not that she was surprised. He wasn't the kind of man to stay away.

Brianna looked down at the worn gray T-shirt she was wearing and swiped at the dark smudges under her eyes. Great. Six long months since she'd last seen him and he had to catch her on a morning when she looked her absolute worst.

But what did it matter anyhow? She no longer cared what she looked like in front of Marco. Except that he was immaculate as usual. The leather jacket he wore brought out the black of his eyes. His dark hair fell over his forehead the way she remembered. It hadn't been that long ago that she'd taken great pleasure in gently stroking that wayward lock off his face, only to have it fall forward again.

"Brianna, open the door. I know you're in there." His voice sounded from the other side of the door, dripping with that sexy Italian accent that haunted her dreams.

"*Cara*, open the door," Marco repeated. "I don't want to have to ring the bell. Little Enzo is probably still sleeping."

At the mention of her son, Brianna forgot all about her appearance and her apprehension. Two-year-old Lorenzo was the reason Marco was here.

Slowly, she unlatched the lock and stepped aside to let her husband in.

Marco brushed past her without so much as a glance.

"What took you so long? I had to go around the back when you didn't answer the front door."

She'd been in a deep sleep. Enzo had kept her up half the night refusing to go into his crib.

He gave her a stern look when she didn't answer. "I thought the little old lady across the street was going to come at me with a broom. I'm positive she thinks I'm here to commit some kind of crime."

Are you?

Brianna shoved the door closed and turned to face him. "What in the world are you doing here?"

"What do you think? I spoke to Nonna."

Of course. She should have never made that phone call to Marco's grandmother. But Brianna had been truly desperate for some advice from someone else who loved and cared about Enzo.

"You shouldn't be here," she answered.

"I grew tired of waiting for you to come to your senses," he said. "And I missed my son. What did you expect me to do?"

A small part of her wanted to hear that he'd missed her as well. But that was such a silly thought. He wanted nothing to do with her. He never really had. As she stood aching inside at seeing him again.

If it was possible, he was even more handsome than she remembered. Those dark eyes she'd lost herself in so many times in the past were as deep as always. She couldn't lose herself again. Not to this man. Not ever. She had given him too much of herself already.

"I didn't expect you to do anything." She walked over to the baby monitor on the counter and turned it up, just to give herself something to do. "Only to respect my wishes and give Enzo and me the time we need."

"You've been gone for six months."

"Nothing has changed, Marco. You've wasted a trip across the world for no reason."

"You want a divorce, *cara*. I am not divorcing my child."

Brianna stiffened. "That's not fair. You know that's the last thing I want."

He let out a laugh which sounded far from amused. "Is that what you call hauling him thousands of miles away?"

She took a deep breath. "Look, when I left I promised you we'd come to a fair agreement about visitation. Until we do that, you can't just show up here unannounced. You can see him at designated times or not at all."

He was in front of her in an instant, hardly an inch of space separating them. "I don't think so. You throw me crumbs and then have the nerve to threaten those measly bits. That I cannot allow you to do."

Brianna's heart pounded. She had to stand up to him. "Don't fight me on this, Marco. I need to make a clean break."

He took her hand in a gentle but firm grip. "I won't let go of my son, Brianna."

Any hope she had that Marco might have changed over the past few months evaporated. "And I don't want that either. I'm sorry you don't understand."

He sighed and dropped her hand. "You're right. I don't

understand it. I don't understand why your desire to cook for others in New York City overrides your desire to be my wife back in Italy. I certainly don't understand why you needed to leave."

He was certainly right about that. He never did understand. "I had no choice."

"So you seem to believe."

For the briefest moment, Brianna thought she saw utter weariness in his face. But the look was gone in an instant. Perhaps she had imagined it.

"No, you're wrong. I couldn't have been a good mother to Enzo being as unhappy as I was."

"And this." He gestured around the small house. "This is what makes you happy?"

Brianna crossed her arms in front of her chest. She didn't know how to answer that. No, she wasn't happy. Things hadn't worked out at all the way they were supposed to since she'd moved back to New York. Mostly, and to her utter horror, her son had so far not adjusted well at all.

But those last months in Italy, things had just been getting colder and colder between them. In fact, they weren't even pretending to be an actual married couple anymore. Simply two people living under the same roof. That was what happened when one tried to force a family into existence. She should have known better.

Still, she hadn't expected to miss Marco as much as she did.

He looked at her expectantly. His next words made her wonder if he'd somehow read her mind about missing him. "So tell me what makes you happy, *cara*." His dark, smoldering eyes fell to her lips.

He stepped closer. Brianna forced herself to look away. If she wasn't careful, she could so easily fall into the Marco Dirici trap again. His voice, that look.

"Do you remember being happy at least at first?" he asked.

And what kind of a question was that?

As if she could forget. Her mind automatically recalled the first time he'd kissed her. They'd met only hours before. Yet, she couldn't resist his charm and sheer magnetism. She hardly recognized herself that night and the following week after meeting him.

A small wailing sound from the monitor jarred her back and she glanced at the wall. "Now see what you've done? He's awake. It's at least an hour until his usual wake-up time."

Marco sighed then stepped away from her. Was that a hint of disappointment she detected in his eyes? Probably not.

"I'd like to see my son."

Brianna took a steadying breath and waited a beat for the pounding in her chest to slow. Then she made her way toward the stairs.

Marco watched her walk away and cursed himself. After six months without laying eyes on her, the second he'd seen her again he'd felt like a damn hormonal teenager. The same way he had close to three years ago. And just like back then, it had only taken one look at her. Her emerald-green eyes still blazed, just as he remembered. And her lips. Heavens, those lips reminded him of sin. Her nightwear left little to the imagination. But he already knew every inch of her. She was exquisite, she was stunning. And for a while, she had been his.

But never completely.

What was it about this woman that made him lose such control? The last thing he'd had on his mind when he'd walked in here was to travel down memory lane and reminisce about the first time he'd laid eyes on her.

He rubbed his brow. He couldn't let his attraction to her complicate matters on this trip. The attraction was merely physical. Same as always. He needed more from her than she was willing to give. He'd never begged a woman for anything.

He certainly wasn't going to start with his soon-to-be ex-wife. And certainly not to delay the inevitable.

He had only two reasons to be here: to tell Brianna she could have the divorce she so wanted and, most importantly, to work out final custody of Enzo. His son was all that mattered now. He'd never really expected Brianna to stay around. Women came and women went. But *familia…* He would fight to keep his blood.

He looked around the house he knew she rented. The kitchen was tidy, with a small round table in the center. Through an arched doorway he could see a living room with a center sitting area. A bay window overlooked the street. The house was small, modest.

There was nothing overtly wrong with the place, but it certainly didn't compare to the expansive mansion Brianna had lived in as his wife.

She preferred it here.

Not that he was surprised. His arrival in her life three years ago had served to totally derail it. At that time she had just landed a new job, was working hard to make a name for herself in the New York culinary world. Then he'd come along and disrupted it all. Before they knew it and to their combined utter shock, they found themselves unwed and expecting. He'd asked her to marry him and join him in Italy. For a while it seemed as if the union might work. But it quickly became obvious they were headed down a rocky road.

For one, Brianna had a difficult pregnancy. Passion, the one thing that bound them, had to be put on hold. And the expansion of Dirici Foods had hit snag after snag, taking him away from home consistently.

Still, Marco had hoped she would fall in love with her new home. That she would try to acclimate and settle into the new life she found herself in, regardless of how unexpectedly it had come about. But that had not happened. He never should have expected it. Foolish, really.

Something tightened in his gut. The time had simply come to cut his losses.

He had to finalize things with her in New York quickly, and then he had to get out of her life as best he could.

The hard children's book hurtling toward Brianna missed her head by mere inches. She rose from her ducked position as the book bounced against the wall with a thud and landed on the floor.

"Now! Now! Now!"

"Enzo, we don't throw things at Mama," Brianna scolded. A teddy bear hit her on the chest.

"Do you want me to start taking your favorite toys out of your crib?"

"Out! Now!"

Brianna picked up the screaming child and held him close, hoping to calm him down. Enzo smelled of baby shampoo and the delicate scent of talc.

Even during moments like this, Brianna couldn't believe the sheer wave of emotion that holding her child brought forth. She'd never expected to have a child at this stage of her life. But she was grateful beyond words to have him. Especially considering the terrifying touch-and-go moments that plagued her pregnancy. She'd prayed daily that her precious little boy would be born full term and healthy, so thankful finally when he had.

"Keech!" Enzo shouted in her ear.

"We'll go down to the kitchen in a moment," Brianna said. "But first I need to tell you something." She set him down.

Enzo ran toward the stairs, not listening at all. She followed close behind. He hadn't quite mastered going down the steps yet but that never slowed him down.

"Enzo, wait."

He was already pulling open the unlocked safety gate at the top of the stairs when Brianna caught up to him.

"Keech! Keech!"

"All right, all right." Brianna took his hand and slowly, carefully walked him down the stairs. "We're going down there now. There's someone here to see you."

As soon as they reached the first-floor landing, he ran to the kitchen.

"Joos!"

When he spotted Marco, Enzo came to a sudden halt. Brianna noticed the thinly veiled derision in Marco's expression as he lifted Enzo into his arms.

The baby monitor. Marco had overheard her and Enzo's little exchange.

"Hi!" Enzo said loudly, grabbing Marco's collar. "Joos!"

"Hey, little man," Marco said, rubbing his cheek against Enzo's. "Did you miss Papa?"

Her chest tightened at the scene and at Marco's words. She had no reason to feel guilty. She couldn't have stayed any longer in a marriage that wasn't working, one that had simply originated out of necessity because of pregnancy. Sure, it had been painful to take Enzo away from Italy and his papa. Not to mention the doting great-grandmother who adored him. But Brianna was slowly becoming a mere shell of herself there. That was no way to raise a child. Especially considering she was doing most of it on her own with Marco gone long hours for days on end.

"He likes to sit by the window and drink it while I get his breakfast ready," she said, handing Enzo a full sippy cup.

Marco sighed and put his son down. Enzo immediately scuttled to the love seat in front of the bay window.

"Do you suppose he remembers me?" Marco asked.

"I'm sure he does."

Marco looked skeptical. His eyes bored into hers. "I'm glad one of us is sure."

The implication was clear. There was no doubt in her mind who Marco would blame if Enzo in fact didn't remember him.

CHAPTER TWO

BRIANNA CHOSE TO try and ignore the tension in the air. Pushing her way around Marco to grab the bread off the counter, she dropped two slices into the toaster and stared at it, as if toasting bread took the utmost concentration. All the while she could feel Marco's gaze on her back.

"I have to get to the restaurant today," she said. "You'll have to find a way to keep yourself busy."

She moved to the refrigerator for the butter. Marco stood directly in front of it. He, of course, refused to budge. She brushed past him, the slight physical contact just enough to inflame her nerves.

"I'll stay right here with my son," Marco said.

Opening the door as wide as she could with him standing there, Brianna reached for the butter drawer. "I'm afraid not."

"I beg your pardon?"

"Enzo's nanny will be here any minute. She usually has the whole day planned for him."

He shrugged. "You can give her the day off."

Brianna slowly shut the refrigerator door. "It's too late to do that. She's probably on the train right now."

"So tell her when she gets here. I don't see a problem."

"I'm not going to tell her she's wasted a trip. Or that she'll have to miss a day of compensation."

Marco looked up to the ceiling and sighed. His expression made him look every bit the part of a man holding on to the last of his patience. "I'll compensate her for the commute and give her two days' pay for her trouble. A week's pay."

That was so typical of Marco. "You think you can solve anything with money."

"I've found very few issues money couldn't solve," he replied, his voice hard.

"Well, this is my home and I won't allow it," she declared just as the doorbell rang.

At the sound, Enzo jumped up and yelled "Ding-dong!"

Brianna barely caught him before he tumbled off the cushion onto the floor. He wailed in protest. The doorbell rang again. And again.

"I'm coming. I'm coming." Brianna set Enzo down gently on his feet. Marco gave her another amused smirk.

She scowled back and opened the door. "Mrs. Schelling. You're here."

Her nanny trotted inside and let out a loud "hmmph" before turning to her. "I only came for one thing, and then I'll be going." The grim set of the woman's lips sent alarms ringing in Brianna's head.

Not now, not today. She forced a smile, almost certain she knew what was about to happen. "Oh. All right. Why don't we go talk in the kitchen?"

"There's nothing to talk about. I've come to quit."

Brianna's heart dived. Somehow she kept her smile in place. Putting her arm around the other woman's plump shoulders, she tried to move her toward the kitchen. Away from Marco.

"Don't even joke like that, Mrs. Schelling."

Mrs. Schelling didn't move. "This is no joke, Miss Brianna. I refuse to tolerate any more from that young man."

Squinting, she pointed to Enzo. Enzo in turn stopped sucking on his cup long enough to give Mrs. Schelling a wide grin.

"I don't understand." Brianna dropped her arm.

Mrs. Schelling held out her palm. "I quit and I'd like my remaining payment."

"But why?"

"I can no longer take care of your son. Life is too short. And I'm afraid I've already lived the bulk of mine at my age."

Brianna didn't dare look at Marco. She had no doubt what he had to be thinking. In his eyes, she had failed him as his wife and now she was clearly failing as a single mother.

This was the last impression she would have hoped to give upon seeing him again. Rather than proving her independence and abilities, she was instead coming off as flighty and in disarray, unable to get her act straight.

All she'd ever wanted was a stable home, some roots. With the arrival of her son, that had seemed like a real possibility. But now it was all going to rot somehow. She may have ended up with a family but it had come about in a random and haphazard manner. Now even that was falling apart.

"I've been thinking about this all night. Agonizing over the decision," Mrs. Schelling was saying. Listening to her was like trying to focus as the walls crumbled around her. Brianna had tried so hard to lay the groundwork perfectly for her return to the United States. All to watch it implode now. And just her luck, Marco was here to witness the latest catastrophe.

The older woman paused to take a deep breath. "Your son is simply too much for me to handle. I dare say he's too much for anyone to handle."

Now that was a bit much. Brianna looked directly into

the older woman's eyes. "He's barely two. He just doesn't know any better."

Mrs. Schelling took a tiny step back. Maybe it was the edge that had crept into her voice. It was a small source of satisfaction.

"Nevertheless, I don't have to put up with his behavior. Not for any amount of money."

Brianna tried to steady herself and her emotions. It didn't help that Enzo was running in circles and shaking his spill-proof cup so furiously that he was managing to spill it anyway.

"Tell you what," Brianna began in a much softer tone. "Why don't you let me get dressed and we can discuss all this over a cup of coffee." She indicated Marco with a nod of her head. "He was just leaving."

Mrs. Schelling turned to look at him. Acknowledging Marco for the first time since she'd arrived, she studied him thoroughly. Apparently, she didn't like what she saw. Then she turned her eyes to Brianna's short T-shirt.

"I didn't realize you were entertaining a gentleman," she said with disdain.

Brianna's breath caught. That was probably the worst thing to say in front of her husband. She didn't have a chance to reply. Enzo, who must have sensed the tension between his mama and the nanny, whom he never really took a liking to, walked over and threw his relatively full cup straight at Mrs. Schelling's shin.

"Ow! Do you see?" she cried. "There are plenty of nice, manageable children out there who need looking after. I don't have to put up with—" She gave Enzo a look that could only be described as disgusted. "With this—"

"I am sorry for any trouble my son may have caused," Marco interrupted. His words were cordial enough, but they held a distinct undertone.

"Your son?"

Marco gave her a stiff nod. "Correct. And it just so happens, we no longer need your services. I am here to make alternate arrangements for Enzo."

Marco reached into his back pocket and pulled out a leather wallet. Removing several crisp bills, he extended them to the older woman. Brianna simply stood and stared. She would be hard pressed to match it.

Mrs. Schelling let out another "hmmph" as her pudgy hand closed around the bills. "I dare say I deserve it for all I've had to put up with." She gave Enzo a withering look.

Brianna sighed at the other woman's sourness. "I'm sorry our arrangement didn't work out, Mrs. Schelling. I know Enzo can be a handful, but he's just so young. There's a lot he needs to learn."

Mrs. Schelling pulled her coat tighter as she mumbled something incoherent under her breath. Then she stalked out.

Brianna shut the door and stared at it. What now? Behind her, Marco's sigh was clearly audible.

Brianna turned to him. "Don't you dare say a word. I don't want to hear anything from you right now."

He gave her a look a teacher might give a child who was having a tantrum.

"Listen," she continued. "I have made no secret of the fact that Enzo has been having some behavior problems since we moved."

"And what of the gentlemen you entertain?"

True to form, Brianna thought. "I do not entertain anyone. Mrs. Schelling just jumped to the wrong conclusion."

Marco's stony glare didn't change.

"In any case, I need to start getting dressed."

"Am I to presume that I will be given the privilege of sitting for my own son?"

"Only if I'm to presume that you'd still like to."

"Of course I do. But I have one question for you first."

She somehow knew that he would. "By all means," she said, not sure how much more conflict she could take in one morning.

"What exactly would you have done if I hadn't shown up?"

There was that hint of accusation in his voice again. "I would have figured something out."

"I'm afraid to guess what that would have been. Were you going to perhaps dump Enzo off on an unprepared neighbor? Or maybe you would have brought him to the restaurant with you where he would have been practically unsupervised."

Oh, he was just too much. "All the neighbors love Enzo, first of all. Secondly, I have a backup sitter."

"And how long would that have taken?"

He had a point. It would probably have taken long enough to make her late again. Enzo's antics had made her late so often in the past, Chef Ansigne had just about lost all patience with her.

"Are you going to sit with him or not?"

"Of course. Don't even pretend you have another option."

Brianna refused to take the bait. "Fine, I'm going to run upstairs and take a shower." She reached down to tussle Enzo's hair. He'd come over to hug her leg, seeking comfort, no doubt.

She leaned over to his eye level. "Enzo, you're going to spend the day with Papa. All right?"

Enzo shook his head and smiled.

Marco immediately went to him. "Why did he say no?" he asked Brianna. "I thought he remembered who I was."

"He shakes his head when he means yes. He's saying no when he covers his face with his arm."

Marco smiled but it didn't last. "It's been so long, I don't know any of his little quirks."

Here it comes, Brianna thought. Another condemning tirade about how all that was her fault. But instead Marco stroked his son's cheek and started to speak softly to him in Italian. Brianna hadn't forgotten how gentle he could be, how tender.

She shook away the memories. There was no use for them now. Slowly stepping around Marco and Enzo, Brianna silently made her way to the stairway.

Marco heard the water come on upstairs. It would be very hot, he knew. That was how Brianna liked her showers. There would be steam rising off her silky, smooth skin. She was likely using a lavender soap, rubbing it over her curves.

Stop it.

But how? She was no less beautiful than when he'd fallen for her three years ago. It was taking everything he had not to go up to her now. He knew she would respond. No matter what had happened between them and how far they'd been apart, she was sure to respond. The way she responded to him had never been the problem.

He just wished he understood her.

The nanny's words echoed through his head. *Entertaining a gentleman.*

The woman must have witnessed something to speak as she did. Had she found Brianna "entertaining" in the past?

He clenched his fists.

He had to consider the possibility. Despite being her husband, he hardly knew Brianna. When they'd first met on that fateful business trip to oversee expansion of the family's North American operations, Brianna had still been training then, barely out of culinary school. One look at her had triggered an attraction unlike any he'd ever felt. Nothing he'd ever shared with any other woman even compared. Maybe that was why he'd behaved so foolishly that week and then had actually thought they might make it work.

Memories of that first night came back to him. Marco had made his way to the kitchen just to get away from all the noise and chaos of a rapidly growing melee. Also to perhaps find something to drink rather than the steady flow of champagne.

He'd nearly run into Brianna as he'd stepped through the door. She'd been a whirlwind of activity, in charge of catering the affair. Somehow, in a white chef's hat and stained apron, she was still breathtakingly striking.

Plus, she'd been so genuine, so real compared to some of the other attendees at that party. He'd been drawn to her immediately. And then when she'd actually ordered him to season appetizers, telling him he may as well make himself useful if he was going to dally in the kitchen.

No one had ever approached him that way.

He'd insisted on taking her out that evening, surprised and relieved when she'd agreed. They'd made arrangements to see each other at least once during his weeklong stay, despite the urgent matters he needed to tend to. Instead, they'd seen each other daily.

Uncharacteristic as it was, he couldn't seem to help himself despite the demands on his schedule. He'd found himself unable to focus on anything but a primitive need to have her.

A need that apparently still possessed him today.

But after they were married, his responsibilities had often kept him away from home. She was his wife. She may as well have been a stranger.

When did it change? When did their love affair become a cold battle? She'd told him he spent too much time working. Too much time away for his business. She didn't appreciate the pressure someone in his position faced.

A tug on his leg brought his attention back to his son.

He crouched down to Enzo's position. "Hey, little man."

Enzo lifted up his empty cup.

"More juice?"

Enzo shook his head.

"That means yes, right?"

The boy covered his face.

"Well, now I'm confused." Marco stood up with Enzo cradled in his arms. Setting him on the couch, he gave the boy a very serious look then sat next to him. "I believe that was your third nanny in six months, no?"

Enzo gave him a grin that revealed three upper front teeth. Marco started to smile despite himself. He tried to resume the serious expression on his face but gave up when Enzo grabbed a tuft of his hair. The boy had an amazingly strong grip. Pride in his son's strength overrode his pain as Enzo tugged. Hard.

Marco knew he should chastise him but found he couldn't. Too much time had passed since he'd seen his son.

Marco sighed. The sooner they worked out custody, the better. He needed to know he would see Enzo for a few days at least once a month. Anything less would be unbearable.

He and Brianna had no business being married, but their mutual business now was little Enzo. They would have to work to make sure the little boy grew up healthy and happy. It would be difficult, with a mother in New York and a father across the globe in Italy. But it was doable. As soon as Brianna came back from work tonight, he would tell her that. Then he would leave.

CHAPTER THREE

BRIANNA WISHED SHE could crawl back into bed.

In the few short hours since Marco had reentered her world, it had turned upside down. At work, she'd been flustered, clumsy and distracted.

And she'd been fired. After several warnings, Chef Ansigne had finally relieved her of her position as second line chef. Not that she was surprised. All the incidences of tardiness, then today's repeated mistakes, had sealed her fate. Apparently, lumpy mashed potatoes and droopy salads were Chef Ansigne's breaking points.

And now Brianna had to contend with her soon-to-be ex-husband. Had it only been just this morning he'd shown up at her door? She felt as though she'd lived a whole year since. She let a moment pass on the front porch before inserting her key and entering the house. There was no way she could tell him she'd lost her job.

The sounds of Marco and Enzo playing together resonated through the hallway, Marco's husky voice punctuated by childish squeals of laughter.

She hung up her coat and made her way to the kitchen. The two of them were sitting at the center table, which presently held an array of toys. When Enzo saw her he lifted his arms and yelled, "Mama!"

Brianna went over and gave her son a fierce hug, avoiding eye contact with Marco.

"I thought you weren't going to be home until very late."

She shrugged. "I asked to leave early."

"Hmmm."

Brianna looked up. "What?"

He'd rolled up his sleeves and unbuttoned his collar. His hair was already in disarray, the telltale lock falling forward over his eye. He looked devilish. And incredibly sexy. Her fingers itched to go smooth his hair back, to touch him. She clasped her hands together behind her back.

"Why did you ask to leave early?" he asked.

"Because I didn't want you to feel overwhelmed watching him all by yourself." That was one doozy of a lie. She'd never seen Marco overwhelmed by anything. This was the man who had taken over the family business and doubled it in size. He knew several languages, could seal any deal, and he was an ace boater who won trophies every year.

And somehow he'd ended up married to an orphaned nobody who couldn't keep a job.

"As you can see, we're doing fine," Marco said, then handed Enzo a toy train. "And you're a bad liar, dear wife."

"Don't call me that."

"But that's what you are—my unemployed wife."

The blood drained from her face. How could he know?

"You no longer have a job, do you?"

She swallowed. "Of course I do. There wasn't that much—"

Marco didn't let her finish. "Darling, your chef Ansigne called here. It appears you left your box of knives and tools behind. He'd like you to come get them as soon as possible as he needs the locker for your replacement."

"Fine. I was fired today. Does that make you happy?"

"Of course not. But you don't need to worry about finances."

"That's what you say."

"It's a fact. You're the mother of my child. Technically, you're still my wife."

"I won't be much longer."

"Even so, there's no need to rush. You and Enzo will always be financially secure. I'll see to it."

Of course he would see to it—it meant he could toss her aside with no guilt.

How in the world had she ended up in this predicament? Her career was on the cusp of taking off before she'd gotten pregnant. Apparently, a three-year break could be career suicide.

"Take care of your son, Marco. You have no need to take care of me. I can fend for myself. I always have."

"Ever the independent one."

"In any case, you don't really need to concern yourself," she said, just to spite him. "Seeing as our adventure is over."

"Enzo, why don't you go play with the train track we set up in the other room?" he said, his eyes never leaving hers. The child immediately obeyed. Which was very surprising, for Enzo.

Marco moved around the table and closed the distance between them. Brianna's heart pounded as he approached. Why couldn't she keep her emotions in check when it came to this man?

"As brief as our affair was to be, the fact remains that it resulted in a child." His voice was cold and tight.

"It should have never resulted in marriage."

"I apologize if my wish to legitimize my son put a cramp in your lifestyle."

She sucked in a breath at those words. "What makes you think it did?"

Her regret came too late. The falsehood broke the last of Marco's hold on his temper. In less than a second, he had moved to within inches of where she stood.

"You dare toy with me about such things?" he demanded, his breath hot against her cheek.

To Brianna's horror, her wayward body immediately reacted. A curl of deep, scorching heat erupted in her belly and traveled slowly lower. She wanted to move but seemed unable to. All she could feel was his heat.

"Marco, just stop. I can't fight with you right now," she pleaded, totally depleted of energy all of a sudden. Having him here was wreaking havoc on her senses. A part of her longed for him, had ached to see him and feel him again. But another part, a more logical one, knew better.

That was the part she needed to focus on. It took all of her will to step away. Scooting back around the table, she fought to catch her breath.

Marco stayed where he was. She suspected Enzo's presence in the next room was to thank for that. His breathing was harsh.

"Bree, I don't want to fight either. It's just—"

She held up a hand to stop him from saying any more. "I wish you hadn't shown up here unannounced."

"But I am here."

"Right, to see Enzo. Well, you have. Please leave."

He looked away and shoved his hands into his pockets. "Is that what you really want?"

"Yes," she managed to choke out.

He nodded once. "And what of all the loose ends?"

"Which are?"

His eyes fell on Enzo. "Visitation arrangements."

Of course. "I promise you I'll compromise fully," she said. "I have no interest in keeping him away from you."

He remained silent a moment, his eyes still fixed on his

son. "Thank you for that." Then he glanced back at her. "There is also the matter of finances."

"I fully intend to go back to work."

"How? You have no sitter."

"I told you, I have a backup. I've already spoken to him. He can start full-time tomorrow."

Marco's eyebrows shot up just as Brianna realized what she'd said.

"He?" Marco asked.

"Now don't start anything."

"So you have a gentleman friend who watches my son."

She really didn't want to go down this path. No good could possibly come of it. "He's hardly a gentleman friend, Marco. He's a local college student studying elementary education, and he happens to love being around children."

"Who else does he love being around?"

"He's merely a caregiver," Brianna said through gritted teeth. "A very good one. And he's very dependable. Unlike Mrs. Schelling."

Marco leaned over and gripped the table with both hands.

"Curtis only sits for me."

"I see. Exactly how well do you know him?"

Brianna didn't want to care that he was jumping to all the wrong conclusions. She didn't want to care that he didn't trust her. Why would he? He'd never bothered to know her fully, to know her true character.

One uncharacteristic night of her life, due to a recent breakup, her broken heart had driven her into the arms of a stranger. She'd met Marco only hours earlier, and was in awe of the fact that someone like him actually found her attractive. In a party full of starlets and models, one she was merely attending as the hired help, he'd somehow sought her attention. It took her only hours to fall head over heels in love. And about the same amount of time for her to fall into his bed.

It had been the most intense week of her life. In many ways, she'd been drawn to Marco more than the man she'd been seeing for close to two years before he'd unceremoniously dumped her to pursue a career in Los Angeles.

It had all been so awkward afterward. They were no more than strangers but they'd been intimate. Then, when she'd found out she was carrying their child, it hardly seemed the time to discuss ways to get to know each other better. Not when major decisions had to be made.

"How well, Brianna?" he repeated.

"I know him well enough," she said, suddenly angry. Marco had no power over her. And he had no right to repeatedly judge her so. She noticed his grip on the table tighten.

"Oh, for goodness' sake," she said loudly, then glanced at Enzo. He wasn't used to his mama raising her voice. "Curtis is a very fine young man, just barely in his twenties. There is nothing between us besides an employer-worker relationship."

"You're not out of your twenties yourself."

There was no point in defending herself. It wouldn't work. She shouldn't even need to, not if he truly loved her.

That was laughable. Love had nothing to do with their marriage, not for Marco. He'd just said it himself—it was merely an attempt to legitimize his son.

She smiled, uncaring now that it would inflame his anger. "Nevertheless, I've made my decisions," she said. "I already have some job prospects I can call about. My replacement sitter is lined up. And as soon as you and I work out visitation rights, you can leave."

She was turning to get Enzo when his next words stopped her.

"There's only one problem with all of that."

"And that would be?"

He crossed his arms in front of his chest. "I have no intention of leaving. I'll be here at least the week."

Where had that come from?

Marco watched Brianna's eyebrows rise nearly to her hairline. Well, he was surprised himself at what he'd just said. But it was quite logical really. The woman was a wreck. For goodness' sake, she'd just lost her job, she couldn't hold on to a babysitter and now she was suggesting that Enzo stay in the care of a young man. Brianna needed someone with a strong, sure hand to take care of such issues in a mature, logical manner. Someone like *him.*

The flush on her cheeks and the eyes throwing daggers at him made it clear she thought otherwise. "I didn't realize this was to be an extended stay."

Neither had he. "It just so happens, some business came up that I need to tend to in New York." That was the absolute truth. So what if the "business" he was referring to directly involved her?

"Of course you have business."

"What does that mean?"

"Nothing. Only that I should have realized you would find a way to multitask."

What he wanted was to find a way to keep his son safe. Who exactly was this Curtis to his wife and child? What if Curtis was the type who wanted to just step in and take over another man's life? He would have found an instant family with Brianna and Enzo. The thought had his blood pressure pounding.

"And where do you plan on staying?" Brianna asked.

"Your place is small but there should be enough room."

She gave him a withering look. "My place?"

"That's right. I'll stay here."

She planted her hands on her hips. "Now, why wouldn't

you stay at a hotel in Times Square near the Dirici offices?"

"Because Times Square is miles away from Enzo."

"Which would suit me just fine, seeing as he'll be very well taken care of between me and Curtis. If you have such urgent business, you can hardly be expected to spend any time with him."

"I can make time. Especially since I'm in the same city."

She remained silent a moment then lifted her chin. "No."

"No?"

"I said no."

"I beg your pardon."

"I refuse to let you stay here."

He couldn't help his smile. "Afraid to be in such close quarters?"

"I should think that was obvious."

"How about if I promise to behave?"

"You can behave in Times Square."

"Are you saying I should take Enzo with me?"

Brianna's mouth tightened. "Don't even think about it. He stays with me."

"Then I'm not quite sure what we're arguing about. All you have to do is call this male nanny and tell him the offer has been rescinded."

"Absolutely not. I can't do that."

"Why not?" he demanded.

She shook her head very slowly. "I don't want to."

He walked over and picked up the phone. "Fine. I'll do it. What's his number?"

"No, you can't. Listen, you don't understand."

"What is there to understand?"

Her chin quivered. "Curtis needs this. He really needs the position."

"What does that have to do with anything?"

"He needs the job. He just told me today that my offer couldn't have come at a better time. He's experiencing some cash problems and really needs the money."

"Why is any of that my problem?"

She moved over to him and reached for the phone. Marco held on to it. "Please. I would feel awful telling him he won't be getting the funds after all. He told me he couldn't even afford new books for next semester."

"You seem awfully concerned with Curtis's well-being."

Brianna's hand fell to her side. "You wouldn't understand."

Marco understood very well. Curtis sounded like a lovestruck adolescent. Or worse, an opportunist. The young cad was probably pursuing not only his wife but also what little money she had. No doubt he'd connected her last name to the Dirici Foods empire. He was most likely using her generosity and naivety to his utmost advantage. It merely proved Marco's point. Brianna needed his protection. She was clearly easy to manipulate.

There was only one sure way to stop the pup from sniffing around her any longer. "Tell him your husband is back."

"That's not going to help his financial situation," she said a little shakily.

Marco sighed. "How about if I pay him anyway?"

A knowing look appeared in her eyes. "Yet again, that's your solution to everything. Throwing money at it. Well, forget it. He would never accept money for work he didn't do."

Curtis had done quite a number on her. "We'll tell him it's because we're retracting the offer on such short notice."

"He's too proud."

"What a paragon. Did it ever occur to you that you might be being manipulated?"

She glared at him. “You would think that.”

He held up the phone. “Just give me his number.”

“He truly needs the money, Marco. I told him he had a full-time job.”

This was getting quite tiring. “Brianna, I’m not leaving. My son needs me.” And so did she.

Brianna nodded and looked down. “This isn’t about that.”

Oh, hell. “Fine.” He slammed the phone down. “Call him later and tell him the job description has changed.”

She looked up, searching his face. “What do you mean?”

“Essentially, he’s to be on call. I’ll ask him to come over if I need to be at the office or if there’s a business matter I’m attending to. We’ll pay him the same amount because we’re asking him to be available at all times during the week. He can either take it or leave it. It’s my final offer.”

Her shoulders dropped with clear relief and she smiled. “I’m sure he’ll take it. He told me he was really desperate for money.”

“I’m sure he is.”

“I would have felt awful, Marco. I just couldn’t tell him he was out of luck again. He said my call was like an answer to a prayer.”

A disquieting feeling settled in Marco’s chest. Somehow, he’d just agreed to help Brianna’s male nanny. This woman made him do the most foolish things. First, making him decide he’d stay, now this. “Yes, well. As long as you understand that I’ll be here for a while.”

“I understand.”

“Good. I’ll go see what Enzo’s up to.”

She stepped in front of him. “Um, I just wanted to—” She halted, looked away again.

“Yes?”

“I mean, it’s really hard to not know where your next

dollar is coming from. What you did, it was—" She hesitated and returned her gaze to his face. He pondered what she'd just said about not knowing where your next dollar was coming from. Brianna had spent her childhood moving from foster home to foster home after being abandoned by her parents. That much he knew. Though not much more. She didn't particularly like to talk about her past. He could hardly blame her. Sometimes the past was better left behind where it belonged. In that, at least he and Brianna had something in common.

No wonder the marriage had fallen apart.

"What is it, Brianna?"

"I just want to say thanks."

She smiled and he could have sworn he felt warmth in every cell of his body. How childish of him. And he'd accused *her* of being easy to manipulate.

He mumbled a brief response. Then he had to make himself turn away. Before he did something really stupid.

"Really, Marco," she said behind him.

"It's not a big deal, Brianna."

"Curtis would disagree."

"I couldn't care less what your Curtis thinks."

"I'm just trying to say that he'd appreciate it, that's all. And I appreciate it too."

He turned to tell her the truth, to just admit it. He'd relented because of her.

But something else entirely came out of his mouth. "You know exactly how to get your way, don't you?"

"What?" Brianna looked at him in bafflement. "What is that supposed to mean?"

"A flick of the lashes. A flirtatious look here and there. And I did exactly what you wanted. Your precious Curtis still has a job. And you've still got your feminine wiles. Let's just move on now, shall we?"

She slammed her hands on her hips. "Why? Why did

I think you were capable of any decency? You're still exactly the same, aren't you? Nothing's changed."

"Apparently not."

"For the briefest moment back then I thought perhaps you might have grown a little. What a fool I can be."

"Then we have something in common, after all."

"Hah," she barked. "We don't have a thing in common."

"Are you finished? I believe Enzo may be ready for bed."

Brianna threw her hands up. "Yes. I believe we're done."

She stomped toward Enzo and picked him up. "I'll be upstairs giving Enzo his bath," she said. "After that, I'm going to bed."

"I'll help you."

She whirled around.

Marco rolled his eyes. "With Enzo's bath, I meant."

She glared at him. "You'll find the spare room upstairs. I don't even want to know you're here for the next week. Do you understand?"

Now that, Marco thought, watching her go up the stairs, would be easier said than done.

CHAPTER FOUR

COFFEE. SOMEONE HAD definitely brewed coffee. There was a ray of light streaming through the small crack of the blind on her bedroom window. The bright sun outside told her it was later than her usual wake-up time. Much later. And there was something else. It was quiet. Way too quiet. She fumbled around for the digital clock. It was almost eight.

Brianna jolted upright and climbed out of bed. Something wasn't right. Enzo never slept this late.

Panic clenched at her chest as she hastened her way to his nursery. Gripping the door handle, she braced herself for all the possible horrors that might explain why Enzo hadn't woken yet. Was he ill? Had he hurt himself somehow?

Could Marco have taken—

No. He wouldn't.

When she finally found herself next to the little crib, the rush of relief brought tears to her eyes. Enzo was sleeping soundly, his chubby fingers closed around the silk trimming of his favorite blankie. She watched as his eyelids fluttered, then sealed closed again. Brianna couldn't help reaching for him. At the risk of waking him, she touched his cheek, stroked her fingers through the fine baby curls on his head. He looked so peaceful.

So vulnerable.

"He just fell asleep again."

She jumped at the quiet voice behind her. It was Marco, on the rocking chair in the corner of the room. He stood and motioned for her to follow him out into the hallway.

"He woke up at six," Marco said when they were outside. "I read to him for a while then rocked him back to sleep."

"I didn't hear him," Brianna said.

"I'm a lighter sleeper. Always have been. Besides, I know you were pretty tired."

"Well, thank you."

"There's no need to thank me for putting my own son back to sleep."

Brianna had to refrain from grunting. How many nights had Marco tucked Enzo in when he was an infant? "I just meant it allowed me to sleep in, that's all. Have you always been this hard to thank?"

He gave her that insolent stare again. The look that made Brianna feel as if he were actually touching her. "Too bad we're splitting up. I could come up with all sorts of ways you could thank me."

His words sent heat shooting through her core. At least she was better prepared this time. Unlike yesterday's thin T-shirt, last night she'd worn bulky flannel pajamas to bed. But somehow, she still felt naked to his gaze.

Marco was already dressed in casual khaki pants and a black silk shirt that brought out the hue of his eyes. He honestly had to be the most handsome man she'd ever met. All the more reason she wasn't about to touch his last comment with a ten-foot pole.

"Are you going somewhere?" she asked, changing the subject.

"I was waiting for you to wake up. I'm going to spend

the morning at Dirici's. I'll go through some paperwork then talk to the managers as they come in."

She nodded. Same old Marco. His second morning here and already he couldn't wait to rush into the Dirici offices. "I see. If you don't mind my saying, that all sounds very routine. What about the 'pressing' business matter that had you altering your travel plans yesterday?"

He frowned. "I'm tending to it."

"Well, I hope it's taken care of very soon."

A shadow passed over his face. She couldn't make out what it meant.

"Will you be here all day?" he asked.

She sighed. She certainly had nothing else to do. There was no longer a job to prep recipes for. And she'd already contacted all the possible leads she knew of about a new position. A cook's position at a decent restaurant wasn't exactly a job you scanned the want ads for. An opening such as that would be more a word-of-mouth opportunity.

"I might take Enzo down to the park for a couple of hours. I don't want to be away from the house too long though, in case any of the job possibilities pan out."

Marco's lips tightened. "You wouldn't want to miss that," he said dryly.

"Is there a reason for sarcasm this early?"

"I have to go," he said, ignoring her question and leaving the room. "I left all my numbers on the table for you. My New York assistant's name and number is there too."

Moments later Brianna heard the front door shut. Her mornings were usually hectic and stressful, with getting Enzo ready and preparing for her workday. This morning Enzo was sleeping soundly and she had nothing to do but wait for him. It was almost as if Marco's arrival had added an element of calm to her life.

Right. That was ridiculous. Calm and Marco Dirici were not words to be used in the same sentence. Ever.

The events of the last evening fluttered through her mind as she went downstairs to pour herself a cup of coffee. Her anger flared in response. The nerve of that man. She had been so surprised at the offer he'd been willing to extend to Curtis. Marco wasn't terribly flexible by nature. For a brief instant she had deluded herself that he may have a heart.

But then he'd turned on her. Which made no sense at all. She'd simply been trying to thank him. Marco had to care a little about her feelings to have made the offer he did.

Or so she'd thought. Until he had turned surly and accusatory again.

She gulped down several swigs, not even bothering to season it with her usual packet of raw sugar.

What did it matter anyhow? It wasn't as if she had to bother trying to figure out Marco or his mood swings any longer. She'd spent enough time over the last three years trying to do that. Every time he went away on an extended business trip with barely a goodbye, she had tried to determine what she might have done to upset him. Or the times he returned and retired to his own suite with barely a nod in her direction.

She slammed her mug down on the table. The few times he had spoken to her it had been to issue an ultimatum or question her about this or that. Where had she been? Who had she seen?

My attempt to legitimize my son.

His words shouted through her mind. That was how he'd referred to their marriage. And even though she'd known that was all their union had been about, the way he'd said it so casually had sliced through her heart.

The shrill ring of the kitchen phone broke into her thoughts. She hadn't even had half a cup yet, wasn't really awake enough to talk to anyone. But she had to answer it before it woke Enzo.

"Hello," she said.

"Brianna Dirici, please." Brianna gripped the phone tighter. She recognized the deep accent immediately. And it was as welcome as ice cream on a hot day.

"This is she."

"Ms. Dirici. This is Chef Ziyad of the Ruby Room on the Upper East Side. I'm calling regarding your expressed interest in a cook's position."

Of all the places she'd applied to, this one was her top choice. The Ruby Room attracted the kind of clientele every chef longed to cook for. Dare she hope?

"Yes?"

"I imagine you are still in the market for a position?"

Was she ever. "That's correct."

"Ms. Dirici, we might have an opportunity for you."

Yes! "Please, call me Brianna."

"Very well then. Brianna. Your reputation indicates a specialty with ethnic mix cuisine."

"It's what I've spent the bulk of my career working on, Chef Ziyad. Spanish tapas for the most part."

"And I understand you're quite skilled with puff pastry."

"Mainly Mediterranean appetizers."

"Well, we attract quite a number of international diners. And I'm looking to expand our mezze menu. Would you be able to come in and discuss all this?"

Brianna cleared her throat. It wasn't wise to sound too desperate. Never mind that she was actually jumping up and down in her kitchen. "Whenever you'd like, Chef Ziyad."

"Excellent. I'll give you my assistant's information. Please call him and set up a time." Brianna took down the information and hung up. A huge grin settled on her face. She'd done it! And it had taken less than a day.

"So there, Josef Ansigne," she said aloud. "Who needs you?"

Her gaze fell to the piece of paper Marco had left with his numbers on it. She walked over and picked it up. He'd indicated that his cell phone would be the best number to call first. She ran her finger over his writing, outlining his sharp, bold strokes.

If theirs was a real marriage, her husband would be the first person she'd call to celebrate the good news. She couldn't help but imagine how good it would feel to have Marco say he was happy for her. That he was proud of her.

She put the slip of paper back down.

It wasn't a real marriage. And Marco wanted nothing more from her than for her to live in Italy and care for their son while he himself went about his own life. Far from celebrating such news, Marco would be upset about the development.

She should have her head examined for having such fantasies. The time for hoping for anything meaningful with Marco was over. All she had to do where he was concerned was get through the next few days until he finished whatever he had to do. Then he could go back to Italy. Then they could get their divorce.

Somehow the utter giddiness of just a few short seconds ago had fallen away completely. She glanced at the clock above the oven. Nine o'clock. Enzo had slept in long enough. If she didn't go wake him now, his whole schedule for the day would be off. By evening she'd have a cranky, sore little tyrant on her hands.

She started up the stairs to go get him. Any further celebrating would have to wait.

Marco continued to stare at the column of numbers in front of him. The same column of numbers on the same screen he'd been staring at for the last fifteen minutes. Finally, in disgust he pushed his chair away from the desk and swiveled around to stare out his floor-to-ceiling office window at the traffic outside. Forty-Fifth Street was fully alive. Pedestrians were out in droves cutting through rows of stationary cars.

For someone who prided himself on his concentration skills, Marco certainly didn't feel focused today. He'd wasted the better part of an hour accomplishing next to nothing.

He rested his head back and stared at the sky. The sun had abandoned it hours ago. Thick rolling clouds littered the horizon. A faint haze of drizzle curtained the atmosphere.

All in all, the day had changed to match his mood completely.

What in the world was he doing here? Nothing in the paperwork or the operations needed immediate attention. If anything, his managers were going to great lengths to pretend he wasn't in the way. His unexpected visit had cut into various meetings and several executives' schedules. He was merely hampering business.

That made him angry. That reminded him of the reason he was in New York in the first place. Brianna.

The woman was a thorn in his side. The plan had been so simple. Go to New York. Check on Enzo. Come to a fair agreement regarding his son and all the other loose ends that unraveled at the end of a marriage. It all brought him back to the same question. Why was he still in New York?

Because he was a jealous, mindless fool. Over a woman who was never really his. If he witnessed one of his friends in the same situation, he knew exactly what he'd do.

The phone rang and he snatched it to his ear. "Marco Dirici."

"I know who you are. At least I think I do."

His grandmother. A smile tugged at his mouth. "Hello, Nonna."

"I'm your nonna in name only, I see so little of you."

"You usually can't wait to get rid of me."

"You know that is absolutely not true."

"There are times I wonder."

She snorted. "How is our little *bambino*, eh? I've so missed him."

At the mention of his son, warmth spread through Marco's chest. "He's wonderful, Nonna. You should see how he's grown in the months since we've seen him."

What followed was a virtual quiz. Nonna asked him about everything from Enzo's diet to his toilet habits. Then she hesitated. When she spoke again, Marco immediately sensed unease in her voice. "How are things there, Marco?" she asked.

He sighed. "You mean with Brianna."

"The house just isn't the same without her."

He picked up a pen, tapped it against the desk, then dropped it. "Our separation was for the best."

"You can be so sure?"

"Nonna, I don't have time for this."

"You don't have time for your grandmother? Of course not, Mr. Hot Shot Businessman. Why would you want to speak to a silly, feeble old woman?"

That comment was downright laughable. His grandmother was about as feeble as an army general. "Nonna, that won't work. You're not going to guilt me into talking to you about this."

"Fine." Nonna's voice was brusque. "But I won't let you hang up without giving you some hard-learned advice."

Marco sighed. Nonna had made it clear before he left that his only goal on this trip should be to bring his wife and son back. She had no idea how irreparable things had gotten between him and Brianna. This was so not the time to try and explain it to her. "Unwanted advice would be more accurate."

"I don't know what went wrong between you and that

lovely bride of yours. But you should do everything in your power to rectify it." She paused, as if considering whether to add her next comment. Marco wished she hadn't. "I saw the way you looked at each other, son. Surely there's still affection between you two."

Marco did not want to get into this. And certainly not with the woman who'd raised him. He'd rather walk through hot coals. What Nonna had interpreted as affection was nothing more than a fierce physical attraction that had struck him nearly blind with wanting when he'd first met Brianna. An attraction that had resulted in a child the very first time they'd been together.

He was trying to come up with yet another tactful way to say "none of your business" when Nonna continued. "That child, my great-grandson, I only have his best interests at heart. I care more for that boy than—"

"Nonna." He cut her off, and this time the warning was clear in his voice.

She wouldn't be intimidated. No surprise there. "You listen to me, young man." Marco had no doubt she was shaking her finger at the phone. "That child needs to feel secure, he needs to sense that he's completely protected. It's so important for the stage he's in."

Marco closed his eyes and pinched the bridge of his nose. "That's why I'm here, Nonna. To make sure he knows I'll always be there for him." And to make sure that Brianna knew that as well.

"I mean now, Marco. Presently, when all these decisions are being made."

Enough was enough. "Nonna, I love you, but you really don't need to concern yourself with this." As in, *it's really none of your business*. A concept older Italian grandmothers didn't seem to understand.

"Of course I do, I love that boy. You and Brianna are

pulling his world apart. Do everything you can to give him any sense of comfort possible. Or the consequences…"

Marco straightened in his chair. As much as he was trying to resist, he somehow couldn't help taking the bait. "What do you suggest?"

"Ay, ay, ay," Nonna said, as if he was missing something very obvious. "Bring them home. You have given up on your wife much too easily. Why will you not fight? Until the two of you figure it all out?"

"Nonna, I'm not going to beg a woman to stay when she doesn't want to. We both know the humiliation in that."

Silence. Then he heard a deep sigh on the other end of the line. "Listen," she began. "Brianna is nothing like the woman you try to compare her to."

Marco's fingers tightened around the receiver. He had to bite his tongue against the reply he wanted to blurt out. She *was* still his grandmother. "Brianna's made her decision. I will honor it."

He heard a disagreeing grunt from the other end of the line. The woman was persistent. "You're wrong about that. You need to tell her, Marco. But first you need to see it."

By the time he hung up, Marco felt as if he'd sailed an hour through a turbulent storm. His grandmother's words replayed in his head. Particularly her warnings about Enzo and his need for stability at this stage.

But Marco was truly at a loss. How much more could he do? The whole reason for this trip was to make sure he remained a steady and solid part of the boy's life. As far as his wife was concerned, that was a whole different story. Nonna was the one who was wrong. It was way too late to try and work things out with Brianna.

CHAPTER FIVE

A BRISK AUTUMN breeze rustled the trees and nipped at Marco's face as he made his way toward the gazebo in the middle of Memorial Park. According to the note she'd stuck on the door, Brianna had taken Enzo here to play.

It was late afternoon and Marco found himself enjoying the fresh air. The brief walk from Brianna's house had started to work out the kinks in his joints garnered from an unproductive, frustrating morning at the office.

Surprising as it was, he was looking forward to spending time in the kiddie park with his son and his…well, Brianna. He had to stop thinking of her in terms of being his wife.

Marco's stride faltered. She was only that in the most literal sense of the word. And wouldn't be for much longer. Just cold, hard fact. They both needed to move on.

He heard them before he spotted them. Brianna's punctuating laughter mixed in with a small boy's giggles. They were under a large oak near the gazebo. Brianna had her arms spread wide, twirling around in circles. Enzo ran madly around her. He stopped, bent to grab an armful of dry leaves, then threw them at his mother. Brianna laughed harder.

Almost everyone else in the park stared at the spectacle. A couple of women were smiling. Several other ladies looked to be snickering to each other behind cupped hands. A few merely stared as if they thought her mad.

Marco knew Brianna wouldn't care about any of that.

She looked like a gypsy. A crimson-red band wrapped around her head did a very poor job of containing her long tangle of curls. A fitted black sweater hugged her hips and stopped midthigh. Beneath it, her long, shapely legs were clad in black leggings. On her feet were trendy chunky-heeled shoes, the ones that arched the foot in that sexy way that made a man want to tear them off and run his hands up her legs.

She was so different from the women he'd dated before her. Those ladies wouldn't have been caught dead letting themselves be covered with leaves. Even a trip to the park would entail the utmost preparation and wardrobe prep. Not that many of them would venture to a park to begin with. Compared to his previous paramours, his wife was downright Bohemian. Before he'd met her, Marco would have never guessed just how attractive he found it.

None of his previous relationships had even come close to becoming serious. Which had suited him just fine, he'd liked it that way. But then he'd met Brianna. Her earthiness, her sheer zest for life called to him like no one else ever had.

And the way she treated their son. At times like this it took his breath away. Memories assaulted him. He wasn't much older than Enzo when his own mother had packed up and left the first time.

He would do anything to spare his own child that level of pain.

He made himself tear his gaze away. The only other man in the park had his eyes set firmly on Brianna; his look was clearly appreciative. Marco cleared his throat and scowled at him when the man finally managed to look his way.

Brianna noticed him as well. His eyes met hers and the laughter immediately stopped. She stopped the twirling and bent down to brush leaves off Enzo's hair.

Marco jammed his hands in his pockets. There was no reason to treat him like a killjoy ogre. The pleasant greeting he'd been ready to approach her with died on his lips.

"We didn't think we'd see you so soon," Brianna said, lowering herself onto the blanket behind them. She didn't sound very happy about it.

"Disappointed?" Marco asked as he picked Enzo up and tousled his hair.

The blush on her cheeks deepened. "Surprised."

"Why is that?"

She shrugged. "I just figured you'd be at the office all day. In Italy, you never returned home until late. Sometimes very late."

He turned to look at her as he set down his squirming son. She had her hands wrapped around an insulated cup. Her gaze was fixed on Enzo as he moved to the sandbox a few feet away.

"If you weren't expecting me," he continued, "why did you leave a note?"

She took a small sip and he had to force himself not to watch her lips. "That note was for Curtis. He said he might stop by. You know, to go over what we expect of him over the next few days."

Curtis. Marco felt a cold chill slither over his skin. She'd been expecting to meet Curtis here. This quaint scene before him. His wife. His son. It was all meant to be shared with someone else, with another man.

He stood abruptly. The note he still held seemed to burn his palm. He crumpled it up and stuck it in his pocket.

"Sorry to disappoint you."

She blinked at him. "I expected you to work late and left

a note for Curtis because he said he might come by before we left. I fail to see why that compels you to snap at me."

He gritted his teeth. "I was merely apologizing, *cara*. That I showed up rather than your so-called nanny."

Brianna drew back. Then stood as well and reached for Enzo's hand. "Let's go, baby."

"Are we leaving?"

"It's time for his nap. So yes, Enzo and I are leaving." She placed the child gently in his stroller then buckled him in. "You are more than welcome to stay. Maybe the fresh air will clear your head."

With that she brushed past him, pushing the stroller in front of her. Marco had to step out of the way to avoid having his toes run over. Taking a deep, calming breath, he turned and followed them out of the park.

The image of her laughing and playing with Enzo from just a few moments ago had completely evaporated. Why had he ever thought he could be part of such an image in the first place?

Her fingers were tingling. Brianna looked down at her knuckles and realized she couldn't possibly grip the stroller handle any tighter. By the time the three of them made it to the wooden gate in front of her house, she was as red-hot mad as an oiled skillet. The brisk walk in the strong autumn wind had done nothing to douse her ire. She was grateful for that. She needed the anger, welcomed it. Because if she let go of being mad, she knew she would have to acknowledge how deeply he could hurt her.

She pushed Enzo's stroller into the front yard and gently lifted him. The afternoon of play followed by the short stroll back had put him to sleep. Without a word to Marco, she carried Enzo up the porch steps and into the house.

She longed to slam the door behind her, right in Marco's face, but didn't dare with the sleeping child cradled in her arms.

She'd had enough. She managed to change Enzo without waking him and settled him in his crib for what she hoped would be a long nap. Then she stormed into her own room without bothering to go back downstairs where *he* was.

This was the reason she had left Italy. This was why she and Marco had to be apart. Marco had nothing but disdain for her. She was far too unrefined for him. Too impulsive.

Too common.

It was a wonder he'd ever wanted to marry her in the first place. Though that decision had nothing to do with her and everything to do with his traditional values and culture. He simply wanted to claim his child. This whole sham of a marriage was her fault. She'd known his true motivations.

Someone like Brianna Stedman should have known better. For heaven's sake, his proposal had been made over a very tense lunch one afternoon after she'd called him to tell him about the pregnancy. He'd flown back the next day. She hadn't been able to eat a thing on her plate, and it had nothing to do with morning sickness.

No, it was all because every cell within her was screaming that this was all wrong. The man across her at the quaint restaurant table was merely doing what he thought was the responsible thing. Love or emotion played no variable in the equation. Marco had even listed all the reasons their marriage would make sense, as if reading off some document in bullet form. He was approaching it as practically as another business deal.

She'd known all that and had said yes anyway. Foolish as it was.

In her blind desire to finally become part of a family, she'd rushed into a marriage for all the wrong reasons, hoping it would somehow all work out. Like some kind of Cinderella story. Well, real life went hardly the way of fairy tales.

Stomping toward the bathroom, she peeled off her clothes and stepped into the shower. It took a while but the pulsing, steamy water slowly started to ebb the edge off her emotions.

She shut the water off and wrapped a towel around herself.

Marco was waiting for her outside the bathroom door.

Brianna pulled the towel tighter. "I'm not dressed."

He turned his back and crossed his arms in front of his chest.

Exasperated, but too tired to tell him to leave, Brianna went to her closet and retrieved her long thick robe. Yanking it on and tying it around her, she let the towel drop.

Marco chose that moment to turn back and watched the towel fall to the floor. He looked at her with clouded eyes. Despite the bulky terry robe, Brianna felt naked and exposed under his gaze.

She pushed past that thought and grabbed at the anger again. "Listen, Marco. This arrangement is not going to work at all if you keep behaving the way you have been."

"How exactly would that be?"

"You have to give me room and you have to give me leeway. I'm simply trying to move the best I can."

He merely nodded. A surge of relief spiked through her that he wasn't going to argue. So she went on.

"It's something I need to do. For my son. And yes, also for myself."

"Very well, *cara*." Marco spoke with all seriousness after several moments of silence. "Your point is made."

For the next few days, Marco seemed to do his best to heed Brianna's wishes. He was polite, considerate and genteel.

She hardly recognized him. During the day, he went to his office. In the evening, he spent hours with Enzo either reading to him or playing on the floor. A foolish part of her would even be sorry to see him leave. He was due to depart in the morning.

He seemed to be a completely different man from the one she had lived with in Italy. And watching him with her son was doing near damage to her psyche. If she wasn't careful, she could easily fall for the man. Again. She had to remind herself this wasn't the real Marco. Here in New York he was in a different setting, a whole different atmosphere. Upon his return to Italy, Brianna had no doubt he would turn into the hardcore, determined businessman who spent most of his hours running a global conglomerate.

She couldn't harbor any pretense that the Marco she was currently observing was the true personality of the man.

It was the reason she had to make sure to maintain her emotional bearings and move on. She had to make her own way, find her own direction. Growing up being bounced from one foster home to the next. Making a name for herself in her chosen field would mean the world to her.

That was why it was so frustrating that she'd been unable to get hold of Chef Ziyad's assistant. After several attempts and messages, the man still hadn't returned her calls.

Brianna sighed and picked up the phone once more to give it yet another try. Again, she got voice mail. Fighting the urge to slam the receiver back in its cradle, she bit back the surge of disappointment. She had to acknowledge that perhaps Ziyad's offer had occurred on an impulsive whim. The man was notoriously spacy and temperamental.

It was quite likely that, as far as her career was concerned, she may very well be back at square one.

Here she was, no real career prospects and a marriage in shambles. Failure at every turn. As far as orphan tales went, hers was clearly not to be a success story.

CHAPTER SIX

IT WAS PAST two in the morning when Marco heard the first shriek. He felt the next one as much as he heard it. A jolt of alarm shot through him. Enzo.

Marco sprinted to the nursery. Brianna was already there, lifting the baby out of his crib.

Marco watched helplessly as she tried to soothe him, rocking him back and forth, whispering into his ear. It was all to no avail. The scene made Marco's blood run cold. Something was terribly wrong with his child.

Brianna lifted her eyes and found his. Even in the dim light afforded by the small night-light, he could see the alarm in her face. Enzo was wailing frantically now, flailing his arms. Marco noticed she was having trouble holding on to him.

"Here, let me have him."

Brianna hesitated. Then she carefully handed him over. Enzo didn't seem to notice he'd switched hands. His screams continued.

"It's okay, little man," Marco whispered in his ear. "I'm here. Just calm down. All right, son, just calm down."

Enzo wasn't having any of it. He started pumping his legs furiously, his screams becoming louder. Brianna seemed in a near panic now.

"It's all right," Marco said in his gentlest voice, not

sure if he was addressing her or his son. "Everything's fine, love."

He nuzzled Enzo's ear, whispering the same phrase repeatedly. He lost count how many times he said it.

"Son, I want you to calm down. It's all right. Papa's here."

The ticking of the cartoon character wall clock seemed to echo throughout the room between the screams. Shadows moved across the opposite wall as a car drove down the street outside. Enzo continued to yell, his tiny fists clenched tight.

He could do nothing but pace with his child in his arms. At some point, his words turned to Italian. He hadn't even realized he'd switched over. Maybe it made a difference because Enzo's wails gradually grew quieter. Eventually, they went from shriek-like screams to sad, woeful moaning.

Finally, Marco saw him open his eyes wide. He focused for a full moment on his father's face. Then suddenly, he threw his arms around Marco's neck. Marco rubbed the tiny back, still whispering in Italian. Enzo tightened his arms around his father's neck. His little legs slowed their jerky thrusts. The tiny arms around him loosened their hold but remained tight around his neck.

Marco was afraid to move, afraid any change would resume the screaming. So he just stood there, dropping the barest of kisses on the top of Enzo's head.

He finally looked up to Brianna. Some of the color had returned to her face. She still looked shell-shocked. Marco took the risk of shifting Enzo ever so slightly to reach for her. He gently ran the back of his fingers down Brianna's cheek then gave her what he hoped was a reassuring smile.

She bit her lip and felt Enzo's forehead. At her touch, Enzo's wails stopped completely.

Several moments later, once Enzo's breathing had gone

from sharp short bursts to the long sighs of a child in deep slumber, Marco slowly, gently placed him back in his crib. He stared at him a moment. Enzo looked completely peaceful, if not a little exhausted. Marco stepped aside as Brianna covered him up. She placed a plush teddy bear to his cheek, which Enzo immediately grabbed.

For a while, they both just stood and watched him. He had no idea how much time had actually gone by. When Marco was certain Enzo had settled for good, he guided Brianna by her elbow to the door.

Out in the hall, he turned the hall light on and rubbed a weary hand down his face. Brianna was trembling.

"Hey, try and get a hold of yourself, Bree. He's fine now."

She nodded. "I've never seen him like that." She looked up at him, her eyes full of fear. He wanted to go to her, to pull her into his arms. Soothe her with gentle words and soft kisses, the way he had with Enzo in there.

He crossed his arms before he could reach for her. "So he's never done that before?"

She shook her head vehemently. "No, not even close. He wakes up all the time during the middle of the night but usually acts like he just wants to play."

"He must have had nightmares before."

"Of course. But nothing to even make note of. He awakens, I rock him back to sleep and that's the extent of it. What he did just now—" She hugged her arms around herself. Marco couldn't help reaching over this time, he just couldn't. She looked so frightened, much like a child herself. He gave her shoulder a small squeeze and quickly tried to pull his hand away. But she grabbed it, held on to his fingers as if he was pulling her out of treacherous waters.

"Do you think it's us, Marco?"

He gave a weary sigh. “Perhaps. My being here may have triggered memories of his old life.”

She’d finally voiced the thought he was certain they’d both feared. Marco ran his hands through his hair. “*Cara*, I just don’t know. We don’t let him see us argue, but I daresay he’s sharp enough to sense the tension between us.”

Brianna threw her hands up. “But he’s never acted like this. We’re not doing anything all that different than the way we were in Italy.”

“Old habits die hard,” he said dryly.

“Maybe he’s just older now and it affects him more.”

Marco let out a deep breath; perhaps he’d been holding it since he’d heard the first scream. His eyes stung from tiredness and he rubbed them until they hurt. “Looks like you were right. My being here has had a negative effect on him.”

Brianna stepped to him and touched his arm. “No, please don’t think that. He’s been so happy these past few days every time he sees you. His behavior has greatly improved.”

Marco couldn’t believe she was trying to comfort him. About this of all things. He looked down where her fingers lay on his bare skin then looked back into her eyes.

“No, if anything, it was me,” she continued. “I’ve put him through too many changes. Just the turnover of our nannies has led to too many adjustments for someone so small. He must feel so helpless, while all these decisions are made around him.”

The words were almost an exact echo of Nonna’s earlier. He hated it when the old woman made sense.

Brianna searched his face. “What is it? What are you thinking?”

“We’ve both been neglectful of his needs, Brianna. We didn’t give him enough credit because he was so young.”

“I guess neither one of us saw how intuitive he is.”

He looked up at the ceiling. "The only one who did was Nonna."

"How do you mean?"

"I spoke to her that first day after I arrived. At the office. She was very concerned about the effect all of our maneuverings were having on Enzo. I didn't want to give her concerns much thought."

"What exactly did she say?"

"Something quite close to what you just did. That all sorts of decisions are being made around him and he's probably confused." He shrugged. "Frightened."

"She's right. She saw it better than we did. Did she say it was my fault?"

"Brianna, she doesn't think that."

"Do you?" she asked, her lips giving an almost imperceptible tremble.

"Of course not."

She looked far from convinced.

Marco sighed. "Listen, we both neglected to gauge his response properly to our splitting up. We just need to be more careful."

"What else did Marie say?" she asked.

"It doesn't matter."

"There's something you're not telling me, Marco. I can see it."

He shrugged. "You're not going to like it."

Brianna rolled her eyes. "I don't like any of this."

"That he needs to be in more familiar surroundings, near familiar people, during all these changes."

She narrowed her eyes. "Like the villa he was born in and great-grandmother who doted on him and the staff he's known since he was merely days old."

Marco nodded. "She thinks it would be better for Enzo if the two of you were back in Italy while we finalize what to do about the end of our marriage."

Brianna moved away from him and paced the small hallway. She didn't say a word for several moments, just moved up and down from the door to her room back to where Marco stood.

He had known she wouldn't like what Nonna suggested. It was, after all, the very thing Brianna wanted to be done with; their life together in Italy. But right now, he couldn't read her at all. All she did was pace.

Finally, he couldn't stand it any longer.

"Bree, I'm sorry. But I'm tired and will be travelling most of the day tomorrow. I should at least pretend to sleep."

She halted and turned to him. "You can't be apart from Enzo now. It would only upset him all the more after having you for only a few days."

That set him back a step. "But you said you wanted me to leave, vehemently. Several times."

She bit her lip. "I do. You can't stay here."

"Brianna, what exactly is it that you do want?"

She shook her head. "I'm not sure I know anymore."

Marco waited.

"Nonna's right," she finally said.

"What exactly do you think she's right about?"

"About all of it."

"All of it?"

She looked over to Enzo's door. "I can't risk damaging my son. I just can't risk it. I don't know what we should do in the long run. I just know I never want to see him that upset again."

Marco blinked. "Let me make sure I understand. You're willing to return to Italy."

She pulled back her hair. "I guess we have to. Between his behavior issues and what he did just now…" Her voice faltered, as if reliving it.

"For how long?"

"I don't know exactly. A week perhaps. Maybe a month. I guess we'll have to reevaluate everything as Enzo improves."

"I see," Marco said. "What about what you were trying to do here?"

The lip quiver again. But then she raised her chin. "It can all wait until I'm sure Enzo's all right. If I have to, I can give up the house. My landlord would love to let me out of the lease. The housing market has gotten tighter since I moved in, he can make much more renting to a new tenant."

"I see," Marco said. "And I suppose it's as convenient a time as any, given that you're no longer employed."

Something flooded her eyes before she quickly looked away. "Right," she said. "Can you postpone your return flight a day or two? There are things I need to wrap up here."

"Of course. And I'll let Nonna know to expect all of us. She'll be thrilled."

Brianna looked back up to study him. "Please make sure she understands. This is nothing more than an extended visit. To make sure Enzo's all right."

Marco nodded, suddenly feeling exhausted. "I'll explain it, *cara*."

"And you understand that too, don't you?"

He stared at her. "You mean I shouldn't entertain any notions that you're doing this for any other reason than for Enzo."

"Well, yes."

"Don't worry. I know you can't wait to be rid of the husband you no longer want to be with. I won't forget that."

"That's not what I said. I just feel that you and I should focus on how to move on as individuals, despite this temporary setback."

He came close to telling her to forget it, this whole situation was impossible. And now she was essentially telling him not to get his hopes up. With a firm grip on his anger, he forced himself to give her a careless smile.

"What makes you think I haven't moved on?" he asked. "And that this isn't a setback for me to suddenly have my wife back in residence."

His wife. She was that in the legal sense certainly. But something had happened to sever the initial connection they'd shared. An undeniable fact. Around the time right before Enzo's birth. Her health scares during pregnancy were more stressful than he would have cared to admit. Coupled with the frustration of not being able to touch her, the tenuous bond they'd been building had suffered an unrecoverable blow. Tenuous it must have been indeed.

Brianna seemed to mull over his statement as she chewed her lip.

"Don't worry that I'll misunderstand, Bree," he said. "You're returning to our home. I have no expectation that you'll return to our bed."

Brianna crossed the note to call Curtis off her to-do list. She'd apologized profusely and made him accept his would-be salary because of all the unexpected changes to the original offer.

She looked around at the tidy colonial house she'd called home for the past six months. Everything had been packed up hastily and the windows were all sealed. Though they'd been comfortable here, she'd be hard pressed to say she would miss it. For all she knew, it had been the mistake of her life, coming here to New York. Had she in fact caused serious damage to the psyche of her son? Had all of his behavioral issues been the result of her leaving Italy and all that he'd known?

She shuddered at the thought. If true, it would be something she'd never forgive herself for.

Going back was the right thing for little Enzo. Oh, but she knew it was the wrong thing for her. The last thing she needed was to be back in Marco's home. Marco's romantic villa had been the ultimate location for an impromptu honeymoon. Set amongst the lush, high hills outside of Positano, the Mediterranean-style house had taken Brianna's breath away when she'd first seen it.

While she'd been passed from one location to another during childhood, her husband had been born and grown up in a mansion his ancestors had built and maintained. On land his forbearers had cultivated.

And Marco was the true master of his ancestral home. He'd taken her through every room and given her a detailed history of the structure and the lands on which it had stood for close to a hundred years. He'd kissed her on the veranda overlooking the sea. That was one of the last good memories she had of living there. Before everything had gone sour.

Dear heavens, how would she cope being back there and the sure damage it would cause to her heart?

But staying here was definitely not worth the risk. Not when it came to her son. And after all, it wasn't like she really had much of a life here at this point. She'd lost one job and another one she thought had opened up turned out not to bear out. There hadn't been much time to make any new friends. All her old ones were busy with their own lives with focuses on career advancement and social activities. They no longer had much in common with the mother of a temperamental toddler.

It was time to return to Italy. She would have to reevaluate her life once she got there. All that mattered now was her little boy and his well-being.

Even in a private jet, it was not easy to travel with a small child. Marco pulled Enzo onto his lap for what seemed like the hundredth time. The boy apparently had made a game of it to crawl from his mother's lap to Marco's over and over again. Marco wasn't sure how he'd handle the hours on the flight if Enzo kept it up.

"Isn't there anything in there that might keep him occupied?" Marco asked, pointing to the canvas bag full of toys Brianna had carried onto the plane.

Brianna blew a strand of hair off her face. "He seems not to be interested in playing with toys."

He wrestled with Enzo as the child tried to settle himself just right. "Couldn't you have brought along things he enjoyed?"

Brianna's eyes widened. "Why, Marco. I hadn't thought of that. What an excellent source of child-rearing logic you are."

Her sarcasm was so cuttingly sharp he couldn't help but laugh. He tapped his forehead with mock seriousness. "I'm a very astute thinker."

She rolled her eyes playfully and smiled at him. It was nice to see her smiling. She'd been so tense since Enzo's episode. Clearly worried about the boy. So was Marco. He'd always led a pretty adventurous life. Quite a few moments out at sea on his boat had turned harrowing and challenging when an unexpected storm hit midsail.

But he could honestly say Enzo's episode had made him more scared than he'd ever felt.

Enzo twisted in his lap again and kneed him in the groin.

"I told you he wasn't easy in cramped spaces," Brianna said, in response to his grunt. She rummaged in her large bag. "Here, try this." She pulled out a picture book.

Marco opened the book and Enzo seemed mollified for the moment.

Marco glanced at the laptop bag underneath the seat

in front of him. "So much for getting some work done on this flight."

"Not unless he falls asleep."

"I'll pray for it."

She shifted in her seat to look at him. "It's quite an adjustment for you, isn't it?" she asked.

"What is?"

"You're always so structured, so in control of your life and your work. Then Enzo and I come along and disrupt it all."

He turned to her. "Is that what you think?"

"Isn't that why you were away from the house so often while we were living there?"

"My work has always taken me away for extended periods. Did you honestly think I was trying to get away from my son?"

She shrugged. "Not necessarily your son. But maybe you wanted to get away from the chaos a child can inflict. Especially one as high energy as Enzo."

"Brianna, I can in all honesty tell you that I never used business as a way to get a reprieve from my child."

"Then perhaps it was a reprieve from the wife you ended up unintentionally saddled with." Brianna bit her lip as soon as the words left her mouth. "I'm sorry, I shouldn't have said that."

He wasn't sure how to respond. She looked away out the window. Marco had to acknowledge the truth in her words. He had thrown himself full force into his work after his marriage. Things had been awkward when she'd first moved in. Neither of them had seemed to know what to say to the other.

Adding to the new dynamic was the reaction of those around them. The whole household, the whole town had seemed infatuated with the newest Dirici. Brianna had found herself the instant subject of unending attention. No doubt some of the buzz had been his own fault. Marco's reputation as a swinging bachelor had taken quite a hit when he'd suddenly gotten married. Everyone who knew him wanted to learn more about the woman who had finally "snared" Marco Dirici.

Judging from her expression right now and her words, his absence had bothered her more than he'd noticed.

"The business was in a major growth spurt," he told her. "It still is. I couldn't ignore that."

"Is that the only reason you had to be away so often? Or for so long?"

"What else?"

"I don't know. Maybe when you were at work you could pretend none of it had ever happened."

There was clear hurt in her voice. How could he have missed it? Things were just so hectic during the months after Brianna had first moved to Italy. She'd been on bed rest for a considerable amount of time. He'd wanted to make sure she got all the rest she needed. And he'd been in the middle of a major expansion with Dirici enterprises.

"I was simply trying to catch up, *cara*."

"Catch up?"

How to explain? Brianna's pregnancy had been a variable he hadn't foreseen. Hadn't planned for. It had thrown his whole life plan out of the proverbial window. He rubbed his forehead. "There were things I wanted to have in place before starting a family of my own."

"What kinds of things?"

"For one, I wanted Dirici Foods to have reached a certain standing on the global stage. I've always known I wanted to expand into North America. The more growth, the more financial security."

"What else?"

What was the point of getting into all this? Her expression told him she really needed an answer. "I guess I always thought I'd be...older when I started a family."

"More mature?"

He shrugged. "I suppose."

She sighed. "Yeah, me too."

Marco reached over to tousle his son's hair. Enzo gave him an adorable smile then started sucking his thumb.

"So you were racing against time to cover the distance you'd lost?" Brianna said. "That's why you were gone so often and for so long."

He supposed that was an interesting way to put it. Accurate, as well.

"It wasn't like you'd been left alone," he argued, though it sounded weak even to his own ears. "Nonna practically doted on you since the day you arrived. Not to mention, we have a full staff at the mansion who are practically family."

A cloud of emotion flooded her eyes. "None of that is the same as having one's husband around."

The words shocked him. He knew she spoke the truth. She was right about him grappling with his new reality when they'd arrived. He'd always had full control of his life and emotions. Then suddenly he found himself a married man with a small child. A wife he could barely contain himself around. It was easier just to stay away and focus on what he was good at. Being a businessman.

She shrugged. "I just finally decided it was fair to move on with my life since you were so consumed with your own," Brianna said, looking out the window.

Marco took a moment to let that sink in. For the past six months he'd come to all sorts of conclusions about why his wife may have left. All his theories had revolved around her. Not once had he considered how his own actions may have led to her decision. Until now.

He had not, by any means, been purposely avoiding her. Had he?

She tightened her seat belt and turned in her seat, reclining back as she did so. “Read the book to Enzo, Marco.”

CHAPTER SEVEN

IT WAS LIKE stepping back in time. After a long, exhausting flight during which Enzo grew more and more restless, Brianna found herself finally stepping into the large Mediterranean-style mansion that had been the Dirici home for close to a century. Up until six months ago, it had been her home as well. It certainly didn't feel that way now. Actually, she thought, as she followed Marco through the front door, it had never really felt like home for her. Despite all her attempts to fit in here, and despite all the kindness Marco's staff and grandmother had shown her, she'd always felt out of place. Everything from not being fluent in Italian to the unfamiliarity of the countryside served as a barrier to feeling as if she belonged.

Enzo was clearly a different story.

His baby squeals of joy echoed through the foyer as they entered the house. How could a toddler so small even know? But he seemed completely familiar as he looked over the pillars at the base of the stairs, the high ceilings and the shiny marble tiles on the floor.

A horde of people descended on them at once. The Diricis' housekeeper, doormen, even the cook who'd always treated Brianna like an imposter looking to take over the kitchen.

"Ms. Brianna, so glad to have you back."

"We've missed you both, Ms. Brianna."

So many words of welcome echoed around her, Brianna wasn't even sure who said what. A strange emotion swelled in her chest and she felt a slight sting in her eyes. Enzo was getting even more attention. And he clearly enjoyed it. In his father's arms, he pumped his legs furiously, laughing and gurgling at everyone.

"Where is he? Where is my precious, precious little boy?"

Nonna rushed toward them with her heavy waddle and trademark neck scarf. Today it was a pretty red one with a paisley pattern. She seemed every bit as matronly as Brianna remembered. It was an act. Marie Dirici was as far from a matron as a bull. She was closer to a force of nature. Made all the more effective by her demure disguise.

Nonna wasted no time in pulling Enzo out of Marco's arms and into hers. For a moment, Enzo seemed to disappear in his great-grandmother's ample bosom. When he reemerged, he appeared a little disoriented. His smile returned even wider when Nonna handed him a chocolate biscotti.

Then she turned her attention to Brianna. "Dearest Brianna, how are you, my child?" Brianna found herself in the same tight bear hug.

The greeting both surprised and warmed her. Brianna had, after all, been the reason Nonna and Enzo had been separated for all these months.

"I'm fine, Nonna. You're looking well." The woman was absolutely beaming.

"I'm more than well. Now that you and Enzo are back."

Nonna turned to Marco and placed a large hand on his cheek. "Thank you for bringing them back home."

Brianna waited for Marco to say something, to state the truth behind their return. Nonna had to know this was just a temporary arrangement.

He simply nodded. "Why don't you hold on to Enzo while I help Brianna get settled," Marco said, taking Brianna by the elbow and leading her up the stairs. Carlo, the Diricis' valet, followed behind with the rest of her luggage.

Brianna took a deep breath. She would make sure to set things straight with Nonna as soon as she could. Right now, she could use some time to freshen up a bit and be alone. All those hours in such close proximity to Marco had taken their toll on her emotions. Everything could wait while she took a breather and adjusted to the time and climate change.

She also had to adjust to the return to a life she thought she'd abandoned for good. Even if it was only temporary.

Brianna found them on the veranda. Marco, Enzo and Nonna sat on the plush wicker patio furniture with a pitcher of iced coffee. Marco's face was hidden behind a newspaper, his foot resting casually on the chair opposite him.

Nonna had Enzo perched on her knee. They were looking at a photo album. Enzo dropped it and ran to Brianna when he noticed her.

She felt a silly sense of relief, that even with all the excitement and attention, he still reacted to the sight of his mother.

"Did you get a chance to freshen up, dear?" Nonna asked with a warm smile.

"Yes, thank you."

"Come sit. Shall Violetta bring you some tea? I know how much you enjoy it in the afternoon."

She shook her head. "I'll just run down to the kitchen and get some later."

"The kitchen," Nonna said and smiled. "I'll have you know, Marisa made sure all your cooking tools remained exactly as they were. Wouldn't let anyone touch them.

Kept saying you'd want them where you'd left them when you returned."

Brianna forced a weak smile. "That was nice of her."

"We're just glad you're back to use them again."

Brianna gave Marco a sharp look, waiting for him to say something. The newspaper remained where it was.

"I must thank her," she said.

In a gesture she wasn't sure what to make of, Enzo gave her leg a hard squeeze, then ran back to Nonna. He scampered up to her lap, the photo book once more in his hands. He opened it up and pointed to one of the pages.

Nonna laughed indulgently. "I take it that's my hint to get started again."

Brianna watched the two of them as she pulled out a chair at the table and dropped herself into it. Enzo certainly did seem happy. Rarely had she seen him act quite this enthusiastic. Sure, he'd always been an energetic, loud, rambunctious little boy. But the grin between his chubby cheeks right now and the pleasure radiating from his eyes were altogether new.

Something squirmed in the bottom of Brianna's belly. She had taken Enzo away from all this. Was that separation really the true source of his issues today?

Enzo let out a squeal of laughter in response to something his great-grandmother said. It had been a while since Brianna had heard him laugh like that. He pointed to something on the page. "Mama."

Nonna nodded. "That's Mama, yes."

He moved his pudgy finger an inch. "Papa."

"Yes, that's right," Nonna answered.

Enzo looked up at Brianna. Then he switched his gaze to his father. "Wuv Mama. Wuv Papa." He started to clap.

Brianna's heart gave a thud. Marco finally lowered the newspaper. What in the world was she to do now?

* * *

Marco watched the myriad of emotions that drifted over Brianna's face. He watched her features tighten, the way she sucked in her lower lip.

She looked so wistful, so sad. So alone. Was that how she'd felt before she left six months ago?

...wasn't the same as having one's husband around.

He stood and extended a hand to her. "Here. Let's go."

"Where are we going?"

"I could use a walk. There's been several additions to the vineyards. I'll show them to you."

Brianna stared at him a moment, then finally stood without taking his hand. Marco took her gently by the elbow and led her off the veranda.

"Be right back, Nonna," he said over his shoulder.

"Those two are getting along splendidly, aren't they?" Brianna asked after they'd walked a few steps.

"Nonna's always enjoyed his company."

"He's always so well-behaved around her."

"Unlike with all his nannies?"

"All except for—" Brianna stopped.

Marco sighed. "You were going to say Curtis, weren't you?"

She gave him a sideways look and nodded.

"Don't worry," Marco replied. "I'm not going to go rabid at the sound of his name."

"Back in the States, you said he might be trying to manipulate me. What does that mean, exactly?"

"Is it so hard to understand? You're a mature woman, fairly established. He must know you have financial resources. I'd say it was fairly obvious."

"In other words, he may be a gold digger?"

"He wouldn't be the first one I've encountered in my lifetime. I was going to allow you to hire Curtis back, remember?"

"Only after I managed to convince you Curtis would never take money he hadn't earned."

"Yes, well he'd be the rare exception."

She huffed out a small laugh. "Are you saying some of the ladies you've dated were only after you for your money? I find it hard to believe. Handsome and charming as you are."

A childish surge of male pride went through him at her words. Immature as it may be, he liked it that she saw him that way. "I wasn't referring to my past dalliances."

Her eyes grew wide as fire ignited in the green depths. "Then who? You can't mean—"

"Of course not, *cara*. I've never entertained that notion."

"Nor should you." She hesitated before continuing. "Do you mean your mother?"

Marco looked off into the horizon. Thick fluffy clouds glided slowly across the sky. "Even as a child I could see my mother was only in it for the money. The lifestyle."

"She was?"

He nodded. "It was no coincidence that her frequent absences started right around the time the company started floundering." His chest tightened with anger. "The funny thing is, she's partly the reason for the company's financial woes at the time."

"How so?"

"My father was so distracted by his new bride, he sorely neglected his duties as head of Dirici Foods. Not to mention all the money he spent on her. It was a vicious cycle. The more he tried to appease her, the worse things got. Till one day she left for good."

Brianna started to reach for him. For one insane moment, he waited for her touch, yearned for it. To feel her soft skin against his. She pulled back and brought her fingers to her lips instead. "I'm sorry. For what you had to deal with. As a child."

He shrugged. "Don't feel sorry for me. I had Nonna. My dad was the one who never really recovered. Continued to pine for her. Like a lovesick fool. For years." He grunted in disgust.

"So Nonna came to care for you."

Marco leaned forward on the gate and rested his chin on his forearms. "There was no one else to do it. My father was barely functioning at that point."

"And he withdrew from his only child." She blew out a breath. "You never told me if she ever came back to even visit."

"At first she did. And for those brief moments it felt as if the world was right once more. For me, anyway. She was refreshed, joyous almost. She'd actually get down in the dirt and play with her child. As if she'd found her true nature again."

"That must have been so confusing for you as a small child."

"In any case, what happened with my mother has nothing to do with what's going on with Enzo."

"Maybe. Maybe not."

Whatever she meant by that, he was in no mood to delve into it. What use was it to wallow in the past? It was all water under the bridge. Muddy, filthy water.

"At least you had Nonna," Brianna said, with a wistful hitch in her tone.

Thank the heavens. "And Nonno, for a good while." A pressing thought suddenly occurred to him. What a selfish dolt he could be. Brianna was an orphan, abandoned at birth. She'd never even known her biological mother and father. So while he'd had loving grandparents to bear the load and lessen his pain of abandonment, Brianna had had no one that he knew of.

"It couldn't have been easy for you either, *cara*. Growing up the way you did."

She looked away. "The worst part was just moving from household to household as a foster kid. None of those places had a stable enough environment to last long. And I was hoisted away once again. A different town, a different school. It was impossible to make friends."

Marco plucked a grape and pretended to study it. He waited; she would continue if she wanted. But he was beginning to understand Brianna's fierce desire for independence, to provide stability and grounding for herself and her child.

"There was one home that actually felt safe. Loving. My foster mom was pretty young at heart, so to speak. It was like living with a loving older sister." After a while, she took a deep breath. "She was a former dancer."

"You mean she was in the ballet?"

She laughed. "No, her form of dancing was a bit more, um, exotic than the ballet."

Marco's brows lifted to his hairline. "You're kidding?"

Brianna had to laugh. "No. She'd cleaned up her act and had procured more traditional employment by the time she applied to foster children. But she still had connections to that world. Enough so that she still danced occasionally to make ends meet. Once that tidbit was discovered we were removed."

"I see." Marco still looked shocked at what she was revealing.

"Foolish really, the most loving home they'd put me in but they deemed it inappropriate." Brianna said the last word as she gestured with hand quotes. She was smiling, but Marco could see the hurt underlying her casual words. "Ironically, it was really the only place I felt like I fit in. Like I belonged."

That included this home too, Marco had no doubt. Brianna had never felt like she fitted in here with him at the

Dirici estate. He had to acknowledge that. And the pain it must have caused her.

She reached for a grape and threw it in the air, catching it in her mouth. The innocent gesture gave him a glimpse of the child she must have been. A terribly lonely and solitary one apparently. Yet that unfortunate history had done nothing to diminish her spirit.

Silly really, to be finding out so much about his wife this late in the game. He looked at her carefully; her brow was creased, a troubled frown framed her lips. She was beautiful. An enchanting princess. She brushed past him further into the fields. He wanted to stop her, to pull her toward him, to kiss that frown away until she was moaning beneath him, until she forgot everything but Marco Dirici. The buzz of his phone with an incoming text snapped him out of the senseless thought.

"Looks like Nonna might be our most preferred parenting guide," Marco said dryly, ignoring the message on his phone. "Perhaps we should formulate our own parenting scheme then. Not proceed by example."

"I've been thinking along those lines myself."

"Yeah?"

Brianna wiped her brow with the back of her hand. The afternoon had grown fairly warm for this time of year. "Well, maybe we should take Enzo to see someone. You know, a professional."

"You want to take him to a, how do you Americans say it, a shrink?"

"I think we should consider it."

"I fail to see what good that would do."

"It would help to chart any progress."

Suddenly Marco understood. "And it might let you know when it's safe to take him back to New York."

She was silent. For several moments, neither of them spoke. Finally, she looked away, out into the distance. "I can't stay here forever, Marco. There are things back in New York waiting for me."

Marco remained where he was though he wanted to go grab hold of her and shake her, demand to know exactly why. She hadn't been in his house a full day yet and she was already figuring out how and when to leave. What was he supposed to do? Beg her to stay with him?

Out of the question. There was no point in prolonging the inevitable.

"It's hot and my appointment is approaching," he said. Even as he made the statement, his phone went off with a series of texts and buzzing sounds. Someone was desperately trying to get a hold of him from the corporate office. He swore as the signal dropped. Reception out here was spotty at best. "We should probably head back," he said, begrudging the intrusion.

A cloud of disappointment washed over Brianna's features. "I'd like to stay awhile longer, if you don't mind."

He didn't feel right leaving her. But the calls and texts were coming in fast and furious now. And he hated to take her away from the serenity of the vineyard. Shame he couldn't stay longer himself.

He would have to make a point of it to come out here more often. With Brianna.

"I trust you haven't been gone so long that you can't find your way back."

She nodded. "I won't be long behind you."

An insane urge to ignore the calls tempted him. But in the end discipline won out. After all, she'd said he was free to go. One of them should be able to enjoy the day out here. And the walk back alone would give him some time to process everything he'd just learned. Not only about his wife, but about himself.

He gave Brianna a small nod and turned to go.

CHAPTER EIGHT

BRIANNA BLEW A tuft of hair off her face as she watched Marco walk away. As much as she would have preferred he stayed, she didn't want to push. Some of what he'd said on the plane about being established financially fell into place now. She'd had no idea just how insecure he was about finances. Just went to show, sometimes even a vast amount of money wasn't enough.

He'd revealed quite a bit, in fact. A lot of it rather surprising.

They'd been so guarded with each other all this time. So distant. But now their little boy's well-being was at stake. They had to make peace with each other, if not as man and wife then as co-parents. Understanding one another better would make significant strides toward that end.

She walked further into the vineyard. It was so peaceful out here, so serene. She had to enjoy it awhile longer. Enzo was in fine hands with Nonna. It was a beautiful afternoon and Brianna had nothing to do, really. She would just stay out here, walk along the property, take in all the beauty of this enchanting land.

A solitary stroll would help clear her mind. That was the most she and Marco had ever confided in each other. It was a small start, but it was something.

Marco had seemed genuinely disappointed at having to leave her.

His expression before he left reminded her of the night of Enzo's nightmare. How vulnerable Marco had looked when he'd held and rocked Enzo as he comforted him.

That was dangerous territory. Seeing Marco as vulnerable or weak in any way would be a mistake on her part.

So she wouldn't think about how boyish his eyes had appeared beyond the hardened masculinity of his face as he spoke of his childhood. And she absolutely refused to think about the way he'd made her feel in the field earlier, nor the scent of him wafting up to her, or the hardness of his thigh when it had rubbed up against her leg mistakenly during the plane ride.

She squeezed her eyes shut. As a matter of fact, she wouldn't think about anything at all. She'd just enjoy her surroundings. This area of the property was very new. She'd just stay here and see how Marco had expanded the varieties of grapes, what new vintages he was experimenting with. In a couple of years, she was certain he would be a prime supplier of Italian wines to fine restaurants all over the world. He was already one of the leading suppliers of fine Italian olive oils and specialty vinegars. And Dirici Foods was also a top company serving as middleman in acquiring and distributing fine cheeses and premade desserts. To think he'd done it all as practically an orphan, with a mother who'd left and a father too broken to care. The new knowledge added another dimension to the man she'd married but hadn't really ever known.

Brianna had no doubt he would be just as successful when the wine was ready. He would start small, providing a few bottles to local restaurants. And in no time, he'd grow that aspect of the business too. He was smart, dedicated—

She huffed out a breath.

So much for taking him off her mind. She had to figure out a way to wipe Marco out of her brain. She'd rather focus on the beautiful afternoon air, the wonderful smell of the grapes, the acres and acres of lush green grass that stretched out far into her line of vision.

Too far.

She paused and looked around. And come to think of it, the smell of the grapes was no longer nearly as pungent. She looked up to see she wasn't even in the vineyard anymore.

Brianna turned. The house was no longer visible. The time had passed quickly. She had to turn around or she'd never have enough time to get cleaned up before dinner. In this part of the world, the evening meal was a nightly event one didn't simply just show up for. Particularly not after strolling through dusty fields and working up a sweat.

She started walking toward the road. Within no time, the fashionable sandals on her feet felt like torture devices. Definitely not shoes meant for long trails through the Italian countryside. She was so busy cursing her lack of a decent sense of direction that it took a while to notice the distant whir of a car engine. Behind her. She turned around as the car drew alongside her, breathing a sigh of relief when she recognized the person in the driver's seat.

Leonardo Soldaro. Marco's business associate and childhood friend. She'd met Leo several times. He was funny and charming, one of the people who had made her feel at ease when she'd first married Marco and moved out here.

Brianna couldn't help the grin that spread across her face. The car stopped a few feet in front of her and Leo got out.

"Brianna. Is that you?" He walked toward her, the car still running.

"No other."

"You're back then." He was a foot from her now and leaned in to give her a small peck on both cheeks.

"Just a few hours ago."

"What in the world are you doing out here?"

She laughed. "Quite foolishly, I wandered too far after Marco and I parted ways back at the vineyards."

Leo's smile deepened. "I can't believe that fool of a man lets you out of his sight at all."

"Still as charming as ever, I see."

"Yes, perhaps you could persuade others, particularly those of your fine gender, of the extents of my charm."

"I certainly will. Who would you like me to start with?" she asked, just to humor him. Leo had a reputation throughout this whole side of Italy when it came to women. It rivaled only Marco's. That thought ebbed the tide of her pleasure so she pushed it aside.

"Well, come then." He guided her to the car. "I was actually headed to see that thickheaded associate of mine. He picked a most inopportune time to chase you back to the States, you know. Several things need immediate attention."

Brianna didn't bother to argue that point. The notion that Marco would jeopardize even the smallest business matter for her sake was quite laughable. His son, however, was another matter. Enzo was the real reason Marco had flown to New York. Not her.

She crawled into the stylish convertible and sucked in her breath as air fanned her face when Leo started to drive. It was too pleasant in the cool, comfortable car to utter more than a few words. Leo asked about her son but for the most part they rode in silence. She watched the beautiful scenery whiz by and thanked the heavens that Leo had come upon her when he did.

* * *

"Where have you been? I've been worried out—" Marco's words died on his lips as Brianna stepped into the foyer followed by Leo right on her heels.

"I wasn't gone that long, Marco."

She was right, it hadn't been that long. And clearly she was safe and sound. So why was his blood pounding in his veins? He had to admit it was guilt. He'd felt guilty for leaving her, even though she'd said it was all right.

The matter he'd been summoned about wasn't even anything that pressing. He'd regretted it immediately once he'd gotten back to his study. And like the bastard that he was, he was oh, so ready to take it out on her. To make matters worse, another man had come to her assistance when he had left her alone.

Quite the husband, he was. How many instances had there been in the time Brianna had lived here that he'd been as equally inconsiderate? Downright cadlike?

He pinched the bridge of his nose. "You're right. I was simply concerned as I thought you'd be fairly close behind me."

Leo wasn't even hiding his smirk at Marco's agitated state. "I found Brianna wandering by the main road. I gave her a lift on my way over here."

"How gallant of you," Marco stated, his voice dripping with such sarcasm that it earned a gasp from Brianna. Leo simply barked out a laugh.

"Well, thanks again for the ride." Brianna headed toward the stairs, clearly having had enough of the both of them. "I'm going to go get cleaned up."

Marco turned toward his study and motioned for Leo to follow. They had several items to discuss now that Marco had returned and he had to get his mind in gear.

"It's really too bad that we have so much business to go

over this afternoon." Leo made the mundane announcement as he strode into the study and sat in the chair opposite Marco's desk.

"And why is that?" Marco hoped Leo's usual penchant for small talk could somehow be cut short this day. He was in no mood for it.

"Because you look like you could use a drink."

"Thanks for that observation," Marco said dryly.

Leo's gaze sharpened. "Tell me what's going on."

"I can give you the New York updates later. I thought you were here to tell me about some critical issues. I'm guessing the pasta project has hit a snag." Marco pulled a file from the corner of his desk and opened it, then punched in the appropriate keys on his laptop to call up the information.

He looked up to see Leo staring at him intently, his fingers steepled in front of his face.

"I mean with you and Brianna," Leo said.

Marco's first urge was to tell him to mind his own business. Especially where Brianna was concerned. He still didn't like the way they'd looked when they'd walked in together. Nor the way Leo had come across Brianna so conveniently.

"She's back for Enzo's sake," Marco said. "Nothing more. Once we figure out the best way to help him adjust to our separation, she will return to New York."

"I see," was all Leo said.

Marco lifted an eyebrow. Leo's comment definitely held a certain tone to it. "Something you'd like to say?" he asked, knowing he would regret the question.

He was right. "I can't believe you'd be fool enough to let that woman go. Again."

Marco sighed. As if Nonna wasn't bad enough. He really didn't feel like taking this from Leo as well.

"Whatever the issue is, I'm sure it's your doing," Leo

boldly added as only a lifelong best friend could. Even still, his remark bordered rather close to uncalled for.

Marco didn't rise to the bait, he was simply too weary. "We have a few issues we need to address, if you must know."

"Such as?"

"Such as we don't really seem to know each other that well."

Leo nodded with satisfaction. "See, I knew it. It is all your doing. You're way too closed off, too guarded. Always have been."

"How is this any of your concern?" Marco demanded to know, barely acknowledging that the other man's comment had hit too close.

Leo shrugged. "It's not. I just try to steer you in the right direction. But you often refuse to listen."

He really was too much. "You've had your say, Leo. Now we really should get to work."

Leo hesitated before nodding slowly. The next few hours passed at a hectic pace. Leo was right. Several details needed Marco's immediate attention. He had to schedule an on-site visit to the Rome distribution center as soon as possible. The new project leader had been remiss to say the least. Marco realized he should have given Leo more authority before he'd left. By the time Violetta knocked on the door to announce supper, he was surprised just how much time had passed.

"You will join us?" he asked Leo, knowing Nonna would have his hide if he didn't.

"No. I should head back. I have a dinner meeting."

Marco stood and dropped his pen. "Knowing you, I doubt it involves much of a meeting. Or dinner for that matter."

Leo flashed him a grin. "It wasn't so long ago that you had those same 'meetings', my friend." Leo stood too.

"Speaking of which, I should like to say goodbye to that beautiful wife of yours before I leave."

Marco knew Leo well enough to realize the mischievous set of his mouth, and to take notice of the merriment dancing around the other man's eyes. But try as he might, he just couldn't resist the need to respond to his goad.

"I think you've spent enough time with my beautiful wife today. You are quite fortunate we're not outside *discussing* that issue right now."

Leo barked out a laugh. "For Enzo's sake, you said. Right."

Before Marco had a chance to comment on that, Brianna knocked and stepped into the room. "Nonna wants to make sure you invite Leo to eat with us." She was glaring at Marco, as if she had no desire to speak to him at all. But when she turned to Leo, her face was all smiles. Marco had a sudden urge to punch Leo in the nose.

"I'm afraid I can't stay, love," Leo said as he walked toward her. He kissed her cheek. "I shall see myself out."

"You do that," Marco said.

Leo laughed and shut the door behind him.

Brianna made her way downstairs and into the dining room to join the others. To her surprise, Marco was the only other person at the table. "Where's Nonna?" she asked, pulling out a chair and sitting down across from him.

"Apparently, she's not feeling very well and decided to skip dinner."

Alarm raced through her chest. Nonna wasn't exactly a young woman. "I hope it's nothing serious."

Marco gave a nonchalant shrug. "Probably her arthritis. It always acts up before rainstorms."

As if responding to his words, a big flash of lightning lit up the sky in the window behind him.

Marco didn't seem all that concerned about Nonna's health. She decided to take his cue. But then a twinge of apprehension started to take hold for an entirely different reason. The scene she and Marco found themselves was almost intimate. Just the two of them, right before a storm, the lights of the room dimmed low. She cleared her throat and tried to reach for a topic that might make for small talk. She came up blank for an immeasurable amount of time.

Marco, for his part, didn't make any attempt at conversation.

"The grapes seemed to have fared well," she ventured, grabbing a crusty focaccia from the bread bowl. "Looks like a good harvest."

He nodded. "If the weather holds all season, we should do very well."

A flicker of pride fluttered through her chest. Her husband was skilled at so many things. "You must be so proud," she began. "A successful winery would add yet another dimension to Dirici Foods. All thanks to you."

"I've been thinking about it for years, getting into the wine business." Brianna couldn't help but notice that he said it with an odd laugh.

She looked at him in question. "Why do you find that laughable?"

"You wouldn't understand."

Oh, no, not this again. She thought they'd made some strides in the vineyards earlier. Was he really going to backtrack yet again?

Marco must have sensed the direction of her thoughts. He put down his knife and fork to level her with an unflinching gaze. "It's just that I'd planned on having so much in place for Dirici Foods before a certain…age, shall we say."

He may have said "age" but she knew what he really

meant. Perhaps she shouldn't have pushed after all. "You mean before you started a family."

Marco didn't blink. "I don't regret our son, Brianna. You must not ever think that."

Of course she didn't think so. But the fact had to be acknowledged that Enzo was the result of an unplanned pregnancy. Someone like Marco who planned everything out with meticulous detail, who'd had to endure the abandonment of both parents, would have certainly hoped to have a bit more control over starting a family, raising a child.

In that regard they weren't terribly different, were they?

She swallowed down the lump of emotion that had suddenly formed at the base of her throat. "I know that, Marco. I really do. I think we both have to just admit that each of us was unprepared in a different way. That doesn't make us less loving or enamored with our child."

His shoulders seemed to drop with relief. Somehow, she'd managed to say the right thing. But it was her heartfelt truth.

He waited a beat before picking up his utensils once more. "In fact, I'm thinking about taking Enzo down to see the vines. I think he'll enjoy seeing the rows and rows of hanging fruit."

"I'm sure he'll love it, now that he's old enough to appreciate it a bit. Though he's much too young to truly fathom just how fortunate he is to have all that land at his disposal."

Marco paused in the act of piercing some gnocchi with his fork. "You were placed in mostly inner-city homes, weren't you?"

She nodded. "Not a lot of land to run around or play. You were lucky to have it as a child."

Marco swallowed. "Yes, well. I didn't always feel so lucky."

He wouldn't have. Not as his family was falling apart

around him. It was yet another lesson in looks being deceiving. A heavy silence settled between them, suddenly turning the moment awkward. Brianna cleared her throat.

"You might want to be careful while you're out there with him," she said teasingly, to lighten the mood.

He looked up at her with question. "Why's that?"

She finished a bite of bread before answering him. "To a toddler, all those grapes are simply going to look like numerous little balls that he can launch and throw. I'm guessing you'll both be quite sticky afterward." That image prompted a giggle to erupt from her throat.

"You would find that funny, would you?" Marco asked with mock offense.

"Very."

"If that's the case, there's really only one thing I'd be curious about," he said.

"What would that be?"

"How good is his throwing arm?"

Brianna smiled at the silly question. "Quite capable actually. He likes to throw slightly bigger objects, like his sippy cups usually. But tiny orbs that explode on impact would provide him immense entertainment, I'm sure."

"Good to know. As an Italian, I would have preferred a football—sorry, soccer—playing son but baseball's a respectable sport for you Americans."

That comment led to a particularly heated discussion about the merits of one sport over the other. By the time they finished eating and started clearing the dishes, Brianna was relieved to find that the awkwardness of earlier had completely dissipated.

In fact, it had been a surprisingly enjoyable dinner overall. She was discovering more about Marco since returning to Italy than she had the entire time she'd lived with him.

He was finally opening up to her. She could only hope it would last. She had to admit, after all this time, it was nice finally getting to know her husband. Even if it was much too late to save their marriage.

Bright sunshine flooded into the room from the window across the bed. It didn't seem right, Brianna thought, slowly coming awake. Not after listening to the rain and thunder for most of the night.

Someone had brought in a pot of coffee sometime during the early morning hours. She stood and poured herself a cup, drinking it quickly. It had gone completely cold but the caffeine nevertheless did its job.

Scenes from the previous day ran through her mind like a movie. Marco's look as he'd talked about his mother leaving when he was just a small child.

She remembered the way he had opened up to her earlier in the day, and the lighthearted banter during dinner.

The way she'd bared a bit of her soul so that he may offer a glimpse of his. Brianna sighed and poured herself another cup, walking to the bathroom as she drank. A long, hot shower would feel like heaven. She felt like she'd lived about a year in the last few days alone.

After that, she wanted to go find Enzo. She couldn't even remember the last time he'd woken up to anyone else besides his mama.

When she made it downstairs she found Nonna on the front veranda sipping tea and nibbling on her usual light breakfast of toast and fruit with a full pot of espresso. Brianna felt a sense of relief that she was feeling better. When she saw her, Nonna welcomed her with a large smile.

"Brianna, darling. Please do join me."

"I'd love to. Where's Enzo?"

"Marco took him out about half an hour ago, dear. They're walking to the pond. He said he wanted to show Enzo how full it gets after a storm such as the one last night."

"Oh," Brianna said with disappointment, realizing she'd dearly missed her son.

Brianna pulled out a chair and sat. Violetta immediately appeared with a full cup of coffee and a basket of the baked goods Brianna enjoyed so much. The comfort and luxury of the Dirici estate was not something she'd gotten used to even while living here.

"We missed you at dinner yesterday," Brianna said, peering at her over her cup. "Are you all right?"

The older woman gave a dismissive wave of her hand. "It was nothing. Just feeling a little weary in these old bones. I'm good as rain."

"Glad to hear it, Nonna. We can't have you not feeling well."

"And I'm glad we have a chance to speak, dear. It's been ages since I've been able to really talk to you." She set her cup down. "How have you been? Truly?"

Brianna shrugged. Despite not having known her all that long, Nonna was as dear to her as anyone. More of a maternal figure than any other lady in her life, Nonna was just one of those people who always made others comfortable. But Brianna's emotions were too close to the surface to risk a heart-to-heart chat right now.

"We've been adjusting," she answered.

"You both seem terribly worried about Enzo. He seems like a perfect little boy to me."

Brianna sighed. "For the most part he is, Nonna. He just has some…issues. Disciplinary and otherwise."

"You mean about his nannies."

Brianna nodded. "Among other things. He's only a baby really. But once he decides he doesn't like someone, he's pretty much made up his mind. It's becoming embarrassing how many sitters I've had to employ."

"Tell me, then. In the beginning, does he give these nannies a chance?"

Brianna squinted in the early morning sun. "I suppose."

"Ah," was all Nonna said.

Brianna waited for her to continue. For several moments, it didn't appear as if she would. Finally, Nonna spoke.

"Don't you understand then, dear?" she asked.

Brianna shook her head. Understand what?

"Enzo isn't overly rambunctious. He just isn't terribly forgiving after a transgression." She patted Brianna's hand. "Perhaps at some point these nannies uttered a harsh reprimand, or ignored a plea, or any number of things that a small boy wouldn't understand. It's a genetic trait, I dare say."

"You're saying it might be enough to color his impression of that person." Brianna put her pastry down and leaned back into her chair. "It's a trait he gets from Marco, isn't it?"

"I'm afraid so, dear. He also doesn't tolerate transgression very well."

Did Marco see her leaving as such a transgression? And what did that mean for her if he did?

"Well, no matter now," Nonna declared. "All that matters is that you and Enzo are back."

"I only came back because of Enzo." Nonna had to realize this wasn't meant to be a reunion between man and wife.

Nonna smiled slightly. "So you both keep telling me."

Brianna found she didn't have the stomach to try and belabor the point right now. Nor the desire to continue eating. And the third cup of coffee on a relatively empty stomach was starting to make her insides churn. She wiped her lips with her napkin and stood. "Please excuse me, Nonna. I really would like to go find my son."

"I think you should, dear. Of course you remember where the pond is."

"I do," Brianna replied, and started making her way to it.

The air felt crisp around her. Each light breeze brought with it the delicate scent of the ripe wine grapes. Marco's lands were lush and beautiful. And very vast. The vineyard hadn't even been part of the Dirici estate when Marco had inherited it. He'd expanded his lands just as he'd expanded the business. Under Marco's management, Dirici Foods had gone from a small Italy-based company to a major global supplier to fine restaurants everywhere.

He was a complex, multidimensional man. One she admired and respected. But was he one she could live with? It was obvious they cared for each other and of course there was the fierce attraction.

And given what Nonna had just told her, Brianna didn't think she'd have too many opportunities to figure it all out. If things didn't work out between them this time, Marco would close the door behind her and their previous life together without looking back. She'd already figured that, Nonna had just further clarified.

The fact was, a part of her had wished Marco had asked her not to leave six months ago—a truth she was finally allowing herself to acknowledge. But her leaving seemed to have triggered something. It was almost as if they were meeting for the first time, without the pressures of an unexpected whirlwind marriage hindering them as they got to know each other.

Brianna finally approached the small hill overlooking the large pond. As she moved closer, Enzo's bubbly chatter punctuated the air. When she made it to the top, she realized with surprise that both Enzo and his father were actually in the water. She noticed the pile of their clothes on the bank. Enzo was laughing now as he kicked water at his father's heels, Marco wore a huge smile on his face and pretended to be upset at being splashed. Brianna's heart warmed. Enzo was clearly enjoying himself. He was completely naked. And Marco wore nothing but shorts.

And sweet heaven, it took her breath away. Even from a distance, his toned muscular body made her heart pound. He was the golden tan color of beach sand. A shade earned from hard work and equally hard play outdoors.

Unlike the men back in New York who worked for their physiques in the gym, Marco achieved his by helping tend to his lands and by sailing competitively. The results were havoc-wreaking.

He's just a man, like any other man, Brianna told herself. A small voice in her head laughed. Marco would never be like any other man she'd ever known.

Marco pretended to fall in the water and Enzo let out another loud squeal of laughter. She was only a few feet away when they finally noticed her.

"What is the meaning of this?" she demanded with mock outrage.

Marco halted. His gaze traveled from her face down the length of her body. Her pulse quickened.

"Mama!" Enzo cried and ran out of the pond to hug her legs, soaking her in the process.

"Good morning, sweet one. What happened to your clothes, huh?"

Enzo just laughed and jumped back in the pond, landing on his feet with an agility that surprised her. She looked back to Marco.

"An early-morning dip," he said by way of explanation. Water streamed down his chest, highlighting the hard contours. Brianna had to fight not to lick her dry lips. Marco smiled salaciously as if he could read her mind.

"Isn't the water cold? After the storm and everything?"

Marco shook his head, still knee-deep in the pond. "The storm is what's made the water so refreshing. It's much deeper now. I thought Enzo would enjoy it."

"He most definitely seems to be."

"You should try it out for yourself." Marco made a move toward her. Brianna stepped back quickly.

"Oh, no. I am *not* going in there."

Enzo clapped. "Mama een. Mama een."

Brianna laughed. "No, Mama's not going in."

"We'll see about that," Marco said and moved toward her again.

This time Brianna jumped back. "Don't you come near me," she said, shaking her finger with warning.

Marco stood where he was and lifted an eyebrow. "Enzo, it appears your mother is the typical prissy city girl who's afraid of water."

He said it with such seriousness, Brianna was almost offended. "Hey," she replied. "Not fair. I'll have you know, I was one of the strongest swimmers in summer camp every year."

"In a nice, clean, chlorinated pool I'm sure," Marco said with a shudder.

Brianna crossed her arms in front of her chest. "No, in a large forest pond that would put this puny one to shame."

Marco shook his head as if to clear his ears. "You mock my pond?"

"I would call it a puddle."

He looked up at the sky with a hilariously wounded expression on his face. "You know you're going to have to pay for that insult."

"Awfully sensitive about the size of your water, aren't you?"

This time he smiled at her *double entendre*. "Brianna, Brianna, Brianna," he said. "We're going to have to teach you a lesson." She wasn't sure what he intended and she moved back another step just in case. But then he picked up Enzo and Brianna breathed a sigh of relief. Until he set him down on the bank. Enzo sat down right on the pile of clothes then wrapped himself in his father's once crisp clean shirt.

"Watch this, son."

Before she could make out what he was up to, Marco bolted toward her. Brianna turned and ran, laughter bubbling up in her chest. She wasn't fast enough. Marco's arms snaked around her waist when she hadn't even gone five feet. She felt herself being lifted off the ground.

Marco turned and carried her back toward the bank. Brianna struggled to get out of his arms, but his grip was so tight and by now she was laughing too hard to protest with any conviction.

She stopped laughing when he stepped in the water. "Marco, don't you dare," she said. "I'm warning you. You will regret it."

Enzo continued to sit on the pile of clothes, intermittently giggling and sucking his thumb.

"What have you got to say about my pond now, hmmm?"

Brianna couldn't resist. "You are referring to your puddle, right?"

"My dear, you are in no position to fling further insults." He lowered her an inch or so. She flung her arms around his neck to brace herself. His reaction was immediate. Brianna suddenly forgot about the threat of being immersed, she forgot about the playful banter. There was a sudden warmth in Marco's eyes, something else entirely mixed in with the amusement.

It hit her full force, how much she cared for this man. She'd fallen in love with him that first week in New York City and she'd never gone back.

He was perfect. He was flawed. He would do anything for his son. Brianna had never come across a father who cared so much. And he made her feel emotions she wouldn't have thought she was capable of. Her expression must have changed because Marco's playful mood suddenly disappeared. His eyes grew even darker.

"Brianna?" he whispered.

Glancing at Enzo to ensure he still sat safely on the grass, she reached up to touch his face, traced his lips with her fingers. She desperately wanted those lips on hers again. She'd never stopped wanting him. But now she wasn't sure at all that she could fight it. Or that she wanted to.

Marco closed his eyes on a sigh and gently kissed her fingertips. Brianna swallowed a moan. She didn't want to lose him again. Maybe there was a way they could work on their differences. Maybe there was a way they could fight for what they had. She pulled her fingers away, inching her head closer to his. Would he respond?

A squeal of delight from her son had her pulling back on a gasp.

"Mama een!"

Marco's eyes snapped open. He looked over at his child and laughed. Just like that, the moment was gone.

"Sir, I demand that you put me down this instant," Brianna said. Her attempt to sound totally authoritative must not have worked.

"If you insist."

Before Brianna could protest that he'd deliberately misread her words, she hit the water with a resounding splash. Landing on her bottom, it took all her arm strength to keep her head above the water line. It was surprisingly clear and much warmer than she'd been expecting.

She was nevertheless stung.

Enzo squealed in delight. Brianna wiped off her face with the palm of her hand.

"You will pay for that."

Marco's grin only widened. "What are you going to do? Splash me? Get me wet?"

Enzo's giggles reverberated in air from where he sat. Brianna dug her hand into the muddy bottom. She lifted her other hand to Marco. "At least help me up."

Marco hesitated, enjoying her predicament. Then he bent down and took her outstretched hand.

She waited until just the right time. One, two…

The mud caught him square on the chin. Marco appeared shocked, even staggered back a bit. Brianna's laugh tore from the depths of her belly. Marco dove in the water, practically on top of her.

"You fight dirty, don't you, dear wife?"

The literal and figurative slant of his words made her laugh even harder. She no longer cared how wet she was.

"Here, let me wipe that off." She brought her hand up to his face, making sure to grab another handful of mud. She slapped it on his cheek.

Marco had been expecting it. He didn't look the least bit surprised. Enzo was laughing so hard, Brianna turned to make sure he wasn't going to fall over and do a face plant on the grass.

It was a mistake. Marco took the opportunity to strike. In one smooth movement, he shifted onto his bottom and sat, pulling her onto his lap. Gripping her by the shoulders, he gently but firmly ducked her further into the water. Brianna sputtered about. She could no longer tell whether she or Enzo was laughing harder. She glanced over her shoulder at Marco. The thick mud still clinging to his face made her laugh even more.

His hand reached in the water and she just knew what he was going for.

She went completely still and made herself stop laughing. "Wait, wait. Hang on." She rubbed her knee. "I think I hurt my leg."

Marco let go of her so fast and he looked so concerned,

she felt somewhat guilty. But she didn't hesitate. She sprinted up and made a dash toward dry land.

Again, she wasn't fast enough. Marco pulled her back down and this time moved on top of her to pin her down. And now her shoulders were completely immersed. She couldn't possibly get any wetter.

"Okay, okay," she muttered. "I give."

"You do, huh?"

"Yes."

"Then tell me this is the most magnificent body of water you have ever laid eyes on. That it parallels the mighty oceans—"

Oh, he was too much. Brianna purposely stuck her head in and came back out spitting a stream of water in Marco's face.

This time when Enzo laughed, he did manage to lose his balance and topple himself off the pile of clothing. Brianna and Marco both bolted to his side. Marco lifted him upright. He appeared unharmed and continued to laugh. But definitely dirty. Beyond dirty.

"Perhaps we should head back and get this little one cleaned up," Marco suggested.

"I think you and I could use a hot shower, too."

Heat danced in his eyes. She hadn't meant it that way. But she couldn't help but picture it. Marco feeling her skin as hot water poured over the two of them.

The lightheartedness they'd been enjoying suddenly turned to something else. Brianna stole a glance at Marco. He looked fierce. And determined. The remaining smears of mud on his face made him look like a rugged warrior wearing tribal battle paint. A shudder bolted through her.

She had no doubt his lips would be on hers if the two of them were alone.

She picked up Enzo. "Come on, little guy."

Marco retrieved their clothes and wrapped his shirt

tighter around their son. Together, the three of them slowly made their way back to the house. For all the excitement, Enzo appeared spent. And utterly oblivious to the electricity crackling between his parents.

If only she could be equally unaware.

Marco watched Brianna as she cradled Enzo in her arms. She was cuddling him close. Enzo's eyelids started to droop and he looked more than content snuggled up to his mother.

"Looks a little worn out, doesn't he?" he asked.

Brianna smiled and rubbed her cheek against the top of her son's head. She tightened her hold on him. "He doesn't seem to be cold."

Unlike Brianna herself. Marco noticed the goose bumps along her arms. Without thinking, he put his arm around her shoulders.

Brianna looked up at him in surprise but she didn't say anything. A moment later, he could have sworn she nestled in closer to him. Probably just to keep warm, he told himself. But he felt oddly elated.

It was such a simple thing really. He was walking back to the house with his wife and son. But he'd never felt more content. Despite all his material possessions, he'd never felt wealthier than he did right now. All this time, he'd been busting his butt at the office in order to ensure that he was a good father. Look how that had worked out. Perhaps he should have been doing more of this instead, spending more time just enjoying the family he had.

But at this moment the picture of family harmony was little more than a façade, a fact he had to accept and acknowledge.

He'd had this for real but had somehow blown it. Good fortune was often fleeting.

Neither said anything as they walked slowly back to the

house. Enzo's eyelids drooped lower and lower. Finally, the mansion appeared before them.

Nonna opened the door before they'd reached it. "What in the world happened to you three?" she asked and reached for Enzo who had completely fallen asleep.

"We slipped," Marco replied and gave Brianna a conspiratorial wink. He closed the door behind them. Enzo was so deep in slumber he didn't even awaken when passed over to his grandmother.

"I'll have Violetta brew some espresso," Nonna said. Carlo appeared with three large towels. He handed one to Nonna for Enzo then gave Marco the other. Marco took the third towel from him, perhaps a little abruptly, and wrapped it around Brianna's shoulders.

"You're shaking." Did he dare hope it was due to more than just the cold?

Nonna headed toward the stairs with Enzo in her arms. "I'll try to get him dried off and changed, I hope he doesn't wake up."

"Oh, he won't," Brianna said with a smile at her son. She turned to Marco. "Your boy can sleep through anything."

"Our boy," he corrected her. For some reason he felt the need to reiterate the fact, to remind her of the connection that they would always have, no matter what happened between them in the end. "You should probably go take a shower. Before you start to smell as bad as the pond."

Brianna gave him a surprised, questioning look. Then a smile pulled at her mouth. She turned toward the bathroom and he couldn't resist giving her a playful pat on the bottom as he followed her upstairs to get cleaned up himself.

Marco made his way up to the suite and made himself wait until his pulse slowed. As much as he wanted to, he wouldn't allow himself to remember those early days when she would have invited him into the shower with her.

And he would have wholeheartedly followed. He fisted his hands by his side.

"Marco?"

He leaned closer to her adorably muddy face and gave her the gentlest, merest brush of a kiss.

"Enjoy your shower, *cara*."

CHAPTER NINE

SHE'D BEEN AWAKE for hours before the knock sounded on her door. It was Marco; even the way he knocked had a distinctive quality. Memories of the day before had been rushing through her mind all morning. The way he'd held her. The gentle kiss on her cheek as he'd bade her goodbye.

"Come in."

Marco entered, clasping on his watch as he walked in. He gave her a smile—a lazy, closed smile that didn't quite reach his whole face. A smile that appeared too strained.

His expression told her everything she needed to know. He had withdrawn.

It was all wrong. Things were being left unsaid. Again.

He moved over to her and leaning in, gave her a small peck on the cheek. A kiss which held nowhere near the affection of the one yesterday.

"Wanted to check on you. I have a few phone calls to make. Then Leo and I have a meeting."

She nodded silently.

"Is something wrong?" he asked.

Yes, everything. "No, not at all."

Reaching for the robe that lay across the bed, Brianna slipped it on and secured the belt. She made her way over to the vanity and sat down in front of the mirror. With absentminded motions, she ran a brush through her hair.

What they'd shared yesterday had been something out of a sweet, romantic movie. But this morning, they were back to acting like strangers.

This was a pattern. Based on past history, such moments of closeness and intimacy were usually followed by days and days of long hours at the office or traveling for work. Other than Marco stopping by during a lunch hour to spend some time with his son, Brianna would barely see him.

A clear withdrawal every time they seemed to get close. He was doing it again. How could she have not seen it coming? Simply because she'd left him six months ago?

"Are you certain there's nothing the matter?" he asked.

She looked up at him in the mirror. Well, she certainly wasn't going to sit around moping.

"Actually, I was going to ask you if Cook could use a day off or two. There are some new recipes I wanted to experiment with. But I don't want to take over her kitchen."

"I'm sure she'll be cooperative. You may even be able to get her to help you."

Brianna shook her head. "No help. I need to work on these all by myself."

"And why is that?"

"Because they'll be my audition dishes. It was a fluke that Chef Angelo Ziyad offered me a job last week."

Marco lifted an eyebrow just as Brianna realized what she'd let slip.

"You were offered a job before we left?"

She nodded.

"That quickly?"

She shrugged. "I told you, it was more of a fluke."

"Chef Ziyad, you said. Sounds familiar."

"He's one of the best."

Marco contemplated her for a moment.

"That's quite impressive. I mean, in the sense that you'd

just gotten started before you had to take an extended break. Then not long after your return to the business, a master chef is already aware of your talents."

He sounded genuinely impressed. Why did that send a giddy pleasure through her heart?

"So what happened? How did you leave it with Chef Ziyad?" he asked.

She shrugged. "I wasn't able to get hold of his assistant. And then it turned out we had to rush here to Italy."

"Why didn't you tell me?"

"There was no point."

"I see," Marco said. He looked up at the ceiling and sighed deeply. "It sounds like quite an opportunity."

Brianna looked down at her toes. "There will be other ones," she stated, not entirely sure who she was trying to convince. "My son comes first."

He shocked her by kissing her full on the lips.

"What was that for?"

"For being such a caring mother." Marco rubbed the back of his hand down her cheek. "I'm ashamed to admit I didn't give your career nearly enough consideration after Enzo was born."

She shook her head. "I don't blame you for that, Marco. I was only focused on one thing right after I gave birth. I was just so grateful that Enzo was born healthy and at full term after all the pregnancy complications. I wanted to concentrate on nothing but being the mother of a newborn."

He nodded. "I know, *cara*. It's why I hired the nannies. To give you a break now and then."

He didn't really understand. She could have never left her baby in the care of strangers for any extended length of time back then. Not when she herself had been abandoned at birth. And with Marco being gone all the time, most of the parenting had fallen to her.

"I wanted to be the one nurturing him when he was born," she countered. "But now that he's a bit older..." She let the sentence drag off.

"What is it?"

Brianna considered telling him what was foremost on her mind. After all, this was the perfect time given the conversation they were surprisingly having. She'd gotten an idea during the early hours of the morning when she couldn't sleep. This had to be some kind of serendipity.

"There's something else I wanted to discuss with you."

He gave her a quizzical look in the mirror. "What would that be?"

"Nonna mentioned Dirici Foods is ready to launch a new line of herb-infused oils, some rather savory combinations."

"We are. And?"

Brianna decided to just blurt it out. What did she have to lose at this point? She had to keep busy while here. And this idea would give her one more thing to do. In the past, she'd nearly been driven insane with Marco constantly gone and Enzo napping a lot of the time.

"I'd like to work on some recipes incorporating the new products." She continued before she could change her mind. "Maybe you could even print them on labels as a marketing strategy."

Marco's eyebrows lifted. High. Brianna held her breath. He hated the idea. Now he had to try and come up with a way to turn her down.

Instead, he surprised her yet again. "*Cara*, that's fantastic."

She blinked. "It is?"

He leaned over and kissed her soundly on the cheek. "Absolutely. It's actually better than anything that's come out of the advertising agency. And it would serve to get you back in the kitchen."

Brianna resisted the urge to pump her fist in the air like an excited teen.

"When can you get started?"

Brianna sucked in some air, nearly dizzy with all the possibilities. This would give her an opportunity to do what she loved most—creating and perfecting recipes in the kitchen.

"This very moment. That is, if Cook will allow it."

"I'll speak to her before starting my calls."

For some reason or another, perhaps unfairly, she'd fully expected him to turn down her offer. That he'd accepted with such enthusiasm pleased her beyond any level she would have thought. "Marco. Thank you," she said simply.

"You can thank me by starting with the rosemary blend. That would make the perfect start for a new marketing initiative."

She would. Brianna could think of numerous ideas right off the cuff for ways to use rosemary olive oil.

But what exactly did this mean for the two of them?

Of that, she had no idea whatsoever.

Marco stared into Leo's face and tried to focus on what the other man was saying. Something about a supply chain glitch that had been repaired easily enough but that Marco should be aware of. But his thoughts kept drifting back to Brianna and the developments of this morning.

He'd clearly underestimated Brianna's talent and possibilities as a chef. She'd thrown herself wholeheartedly into motherhood after having Enzo. Marco had never realized how much of her identity and self she'd sacrificed in the process.

Shame on him for that.

"And then the project leader grew another head," Leo said across the desk.

Marco nodded. "Well, make sure you tell—" *Wait a*

minute. He threw his pen down and leaned back in his chair.

Leo sat grinning. "You haven't been listening to a thing I said."

"There's a lot on my mind."

"Are you thinking about the regatta? It's still a while away."

He was referring to the sailing boat race along the Amalfi coast that both men participated in every year. In fact, Marco had almost completely forgotten about it. No wonder, between the demands of Dirici Foods and with all that was happening in his personal life.

"No, that's not it. Though I do look forward to beating you yet again."

"As if," Leo said, then looked at him expectantly. Marco really didn't want to get into all this. No better time than the present though.

"Leo, are you still interested in doing more at Dirici Italy?" Marco hadn't even realized he was ready to ask Leo such a question. But he thought about the days he'd spent in New York, away from Dirici headquarters. The time he'd been able to devote to just being with his son while there. And how gratifying it had been just to spend a few hours with him kicking around in the pond.

He thought of Brianna and all she had put aside without ever even dwelling on it or questioning it.

Leo sat gaping at him. "Of course I am. What did you have in mind?"

A rapid knock sounded on the door just before Brianna burst in. Marco knew what she was going to say, could tell by the flush on her cheeks and the excitement that shone in her eyes.

"Sorry to interrupt," Brianna gushed then shifted her gaze completely to Marco. "Marco, can you come into the kitchen when you get a chance. I'd like you to do a little taste test."

"I look forward to it."

Leo lifted an eyebrow in question after Brianna shut the door. "What's that all about?"

"Brianna's coming up with some recipe ideas for our latest product."

Leo gave an impressed nod. "Excellent. Now about what you were asking me..."

"Just stay tuned, my friend. Stay tuned."

Marco worked hard to finalize some notes after Leo had left his office. This working from home thing wasn't so bad, after all. He thought there would be many more outside interruptions. But the only interruption to his concentration right now was of his own making. He really ought to just finish up here but was too distracted by the thought of what Brianna might be cooking up in the kitchen.

Her offer this morning to work on recipes for Dirici Foods had pleased him in a way he couldn't have imagined. How in the world had he not thought of such a thing himself?

Because he'd been thoughtless when it came to her from the very beginning. In all fairness, things were so hectic after they'd eloped and moved here that finding ways to keep his new bride occupied had been the last thing on his mind. Right or wrong, it was the truth. He'd had so much on his plate, right in the middle of a big global expansion, the prep it took to get ready for a new baby. And Brianna's pregnancy hadn't been the easiest.

All the more reason he should have thought to be more considerate of her. Even if they had been barely more than strangers.

He shook off the useless thoughts that would do him no good now and clicked open a spreadsheet. If he didn't get these sales projections entered in right now, he may never get around to it. Then he would go and see what concoction Brianna had come up with. He could hardly wait. There was no good to come of wallowing in the mistakes he'd made in the past where his wife was concerned. All he could do was try and take things day by day and find ways to make up for it all. He made quick work of the entries and powered off his laptop. A good start would be to go and try this recipe she was working on.

He found her elbow-deep in pots and pans in the kitchen amidst a cloud of steam. A rich aroma of spices and herbs greeted him.

"Ah, there you are." She gave him a wide smile. "Come here and try this. I feel like it needs something else."

Dipping a large wooden spoon into a saucepan, she held it up to his mouth when he approached.

"Careful, it's really hot."

An explosion of taste erupted on his tongue when he took a bite of what she offered. Sure, she'd cooked for him before but never anything she was experimenting on. This was unlike anything he'd tasted. She'd incorporated the Dirici flavored oil and added some type of pepper. Not really spicy hot but it definitely held a zing.

"It's good."

"Well, don't look so surprised."

The truth was, he sort of was surprised. Not so much at her talent but that she'd come up with something so quickly.

"I'm simply enjoying it, *cara*."

"Well, thank you. I'm glad you like it. I'll have a detailed recipe for you at some point. It still needs some work."

"I can't wait."

"Good. In the meantime, why don't you go wash your hands?"

"What for?"

"If you're in here, you may as well make yourself useful and help me."

For a strange moment, neither one of them said anything, a baited silence hung in there. Then they both burst out laughing. Those were the very same words she'd said to him the first time they'd met, as soon as he'd wandered into the kitchen at the cocktail party he'd been attending and she was catering. It was like being catapulted back in time. And he was every bit as attracted to her now as he was then.

Finally, Brianna turned back to her pans and started to stir the contents as Marco walked over to the sink and washed his hands.

"Hand me the jar of pepper paste, would you?" she ordered as soon as he was done.

He gasped with mock outrage. "So comfortable ordering me around. Fine, at least I'll have a front row seat to witness your sorcery." He stepped closer to her and lifted her chin with his finger. "But just one thing first."

"What's that?"

"I'd like a taste of something else before we get started."

His gaze fell to her lips and she couldn't help but let out a soft moan. An eternity seemed to pass as she waited. And then his mouth found hers. Sighing with pleasure, she leaned into him, moved her hands up his shoulders. This was Marco; he tasted exotic and new yet oh, so familiar. It was like she'd known him forever and loved him just as long.

Exactly like the first time he'd kissed her.

CHAPTER TEN

BRIANNA SET ENZO down gently into his crib and pulled the soft terry cover over him. As exhausted as he was, it had still taken several bedtime stories to finally get him to fall asleep. She breathed a sigh of relief that he was finally down and stepped into the outer area of the nursery, shutting his bedroom door softly behind her.

What was Marco doing at the moment? He'd surprised her earlier by holding his meeting with Leo at the house. She'd fully expected him to run out and stay gone for at least the rest of the day. But by some miracle, he'd stayed home.

And he'd surprised her even further by helping her cook.

Maybe she'd find her husband now and ask him to join her on the veranda to share an evening drink. They could always discuss some more recipe ideas. Or other subjects for that matter.

But first she had some tidying to do. Enzo's toys and books were strewn all over the floor. As tempting as it was, Brianna couldn't leave this to deal with the next day. She got to work picking up and putting items away. Shelving the books, Brianna realized they weren't all toddler hardcovers. A few photo albums lay on the floor next to the bedtime fairy tales. Nonna must have brought them in here to look over with Enzo. She remembered the first afternoon they'd come back, Enzo had sat on Nonna's lap as they perused through photos.

She opened one of the albums and flipped through a couple of pages. The first thing that struck her was how much her little boy looked like a younger version of his father. Especially in one particular shot taken of Marco smiling on a small toddler bike. If the photo hadn't looked worn, she'd be hard pressed to say whether it was her son or husband beaming back at her in the image.

After several moments of browsing, she finally got ready to close the album and put it away. But a wayward thought nagged at her. The Dirici home had several shelves of photo albums and there were framed pictures decorating various walls of the house. Yet she'd never seen any pictures of Marco's mother. It was as if the woman had never existed.

How could she have never noticed it before?

She grabbed another photo album and flipped through the pages. Within a few short minutes, she'd gone through every book. None of them held any photos of her whatsoever. In fact, one book was dedicated completely to Marco's birth, with no sign of the woman who'd borne him.

Her eyes started to sting with tears. When exactly had Marco tried to erase the memory of the mother who had abandoned him? As a child? How vulnerable that little boy must have felt, how truly betrayed and alone. Brianna rubbed her eyes and made her way out of the room. She wouldn't say anything to Marco about any of it. Mentioning the curious lack of any images of Marco's mother would no doubt only serve to open old wounds. But how deeply she yearned that he would trust her enough one day to willingly tell her on his own.

Nonna was coming up the stairs as she stepped out into the hall. Brianna managed to summon a smile.

"Are you all right, dear?"

"Yes, I'm fine, Nonna. Thank you."

"It just took a while to get Enzo down," she added when Marie looked less than convinced. "I may have dozed off in the rocking chair myself."

"I see," the older woman replied. Her eyes studied Brianna's face. Marco's grandmother had always been way too perceptive.

"In fact, I think I'll take a quick walk around the gardens to get myself awake."

"I wish I could join you but I'm still feeling somewhat under the weather."

"That's okay." Brianna smiled and started to make her way down the stairs. Then her feet seemed to stop of their own volition before Brianna made it down the first step. She knew it was oh, so stupid what she was about to do. But she couldn't seem to help herself.

Nonna gave her an expectant look. "What is it, dear?"

"I wanted to ask you something. I hope you don't think it sounds gossipy."

The older woman gave her an indulgent smile. "This sounds serious. Ask away."

Brianna sucked in a breath of air. Why was she doing this? "It's just. I wondered if Marco had heard from his mother. I mean, recently."

"What brought this on?" Nonna asked.

At the question, Brianna felt even more foolish for pursuing the matter. "Never mind, Nonna. Please forget I said anything."

"Nevertheless, the answer is a sad one."

"It is?"

"We received an official letter about three years ago. Notifying us that she had passed. A car accident, it said. A solicitor who was tasked with letting us know."

A rock dropped into Brianna's stomach. "Three years ago?"

Nonna nodded. "That's right. Right before he was due to travel to the States, in fact."

Right before they'd met. Had Marco simply been seeking solace in her arms then? Did he just need a gentle touch? Or worse, a mere distraction?

If true, look at the fundamental changes all of it had led to. For both of them.

"Anything else?" Nonna asked at Brianna's continued silence.

Brianna gave her head a shake. "No. Thank you. I was just curious."

Nonna waited a beat before replying. "I will see you at dinner then, my dear. Enjoy your walk." With that, the older woman turned and made her way toward her own suite of rooms. "I rather feel the need for a quick nap myself."

"I hope you have a good rest, Nonna," Brianna said and managed another forced smile. It didn't come easy.

"I was hoping I would catch you before running into the office today." Marco approached the counter where Brianna stood pouring herself her first cup of coffee of the morning. She'd had a restless night, tossing and turning.

She turned to him with her mug to her lips. "You're going in today? On a Saturday?"

He fixed a cuff link on his left wrist. He looked impeccable. In a steel-gray tailored suit and sky-blue tie, Marco was every inch the successful business tycoon. "I've got some sales meetings with consultants flying in from all over Europe. This was the only date that worked."

She couldn't resist reaching up and straightening his tie clip, though it was nowhere near askew enough that anyone else would probably have even noticed. Standing next to him, in her rumpled flannel robe with her hair all tangled, she must have looked like the lowly peasant standing next to the regal prince.

Why couldn't she be one of those women who went to bed in silk flimsy nighties with matching covers?

Brianna blinked away the thought. "What did you want to see me about?"

Marco reached behind her for a cup but he turned to the silver carafe which held fresh brewed espresso. How he and Nonna could drink such harsh brew first thing was a mystery to her. He started to drink it straight.

"Leo reminded me of the regatta happening next week."

"The one you had to miss last year?" He'd had to miss it because Enzo had come down with an ear infection and the resulting temperature readings had alarmed them both. Marco hadn't attended the year before either, that time due to Enzo's recent arrival.

"Yes, that's the one."

"What about it?"

He set his cup down on the counter. "Why don't you come with me? We can make a trip of it."

She hadn't seen that offer coming. "Won't you be racing?"

"Yes. But it's so much more than just a race. There'll be festival activities. Not to mention some of the best Italian cuisine this side of the country."

"It sounds amazing."

"It is. Every port along the fifteen-mile coast of the race has something special to partake in. I think you'd enjoy it."

"What about Enzo?"

He tapped her nose playfully. "I have a full staff here. Not to mention, he has a very capable Nonna at his very disposal."

Brianna mulled it over. She'd never been on so much as a harbor cruise let alone on an actual sailing expedition.

And this was a big part of Marco's life. He'd always been an avid boater. Here he was, asking her to share that part of him. She'd be hard pressed to turn it down.

"He has been sleeping through the night since we got here." She glanced toward the ceiling in the direction of her son's bedroom. In fact, he was still asleep at the moment. "I would hate to do anything to set him back though."

"Why don't you think about it?" he told her, clearly dismissing the subject. "I take it you'll be working on some more recipes today?" A small spark of disappointment settled in her chest. He obviously wasn't terribly invested in the idea of her accompanying him given the way he was ready to change the topic.

She nodded. "Yes, I have some more ideas about what other ingredients I might add to that last dish."

"Excellent. I'll be very late tonight." He grabbed his case off the ground and walked out of the kitchen. Moments later, Brianna heard the roar of his engine. There was no question she wouldn't be seeing him again today. Not with the workday he'd just described.

She wanted to kick herself. Why had she even hesitated rather than simply accepting his invitation?

What if he didn't ask again?

Marco gripped the steering wheel of his late-model Lamborghini and slowly pulled down the mansion's long, winding driveway.

She needed to think about it. About whether she wanted to accompany him to the regatta. The notion was somewhat demoralizing. His own wife needed to consider before agreeing to a week spent sailing along the coast with him.

They'd never done such a thing before. In fact, they hadn't even gone on a proper honeymoon. There hadn't been time or opportunity given the pregnancy and complications. The regatta would give them an opportunity to finally spend some time together. Alone. Maybe even get to know each other a bit better.

But Brianna hadn't jumped at the prospect. She had a solid reason, her concern about being away from Enzo. Marco knew he was being silly. Downright immature. What was it about his own wife that brought out that unflattering side of him? He just couldn't help but feel somewhat slighted that she hadn't seemed more…well, excited about the whole prospect.

He turned onto the road and tried to focus on the day that was ahead. The meetings before him were way too important to let his focus scatter in any way.

She hadn't said no. He supposed he should be happy for that much at least.

CHAPTER ELEVEN

MARCO WASN'T USED to waiting. Particularly not having to wait for Brianna. The woman had always been prompt and timely since he'd met her. For some reason, she was taking an annoyingly long time this morning.

But then she stepped out into the sunshine and he couldn't think at all. He could barely breathe. In a light, flowy sundress that hung on her curves with precision, she looked like a Roman princess.

And her hair. She'd done something differently; her curls were tamer, secured at the base of her neck with a few soft tendrils framing her face.

Correction, she looked like a Roman goddess.

All in all, what she wore appeared to be a very reasonable, even sensible uniform for a day of intense sailing. But for some reason it looked far from that. In fact, it was knocking the sense right out of him.

"Is something wrong?" Her voice shook as she asked the question. He'd been blatantly staring at her.

He could only manage to clear his throat.

"I could go change if this isn't appropriate," she added, again with hesitation in her tone and rubbing her hands down her sides.

"Don't you dare."

She blinked at him, confusion etched in her features.

"I mean, that's perfect. What you have on will work great."

Relief flooded her face. "Thanks. Nonna helped me pick it out."

He made a mental note to thank Nonna profusely as soon as they got back home from this trip.

"I've never done anything like this before. I wasn't quite sure what to pick out," she added.

Marco felt guilty at that comment. "I must apologize for that. I should have found a way to get you on the boat."

She stepped up to him, placed her palm against his chest. "Oh, no. Don't apologize. I was in no mood to go sailing when we first arrived in Italy. And once Enzo was born, there was hardly time to eat or sleep, let alone do anything leisurely."

Her words served to lighten his guilt somewhat. But he couldn't shake the feeling that if he'd really wanted to, he would have figured out a way to take her. He would have found a way to share that part of his life with her. Among other things.

He guided her to the passenger seat of the sports car. Then he threw their bags in the back.

"We'll be at the marina in just a few minutes," he told her as they headed off. In no time, they were driving along the coast and traffic increased exponentially. The race always drew a great amount of people to the area. Observers as well as other sailors.

They reached the entrance to the marina and seemingly had to wait an exorbitant amount of time before being able to park. Once they did, it was a small walk to the Dirici slip.

Marco guided Brianna onboard while a porter carried and deposited their bags. Despite the strange circumstances surrounding this trip—an attempt to get to know better a woman he was already married to—he finally, slowly felt himself begin to relax. Being on deck with the sunshine, the refreshing breeze, and anticipatory hum in the air before a big race had the usual effect of settling his soul.

Brianna for her part appeared in awe. "This is what you called your small sailing boat?"

"Do you like it?"

Brianna ran a hand along the rail. "It's gorgeous. And it's hardly a sailboat. It's more like a yacht!"

Marco felt an almost giddy satisfaction that his craft had impressed her so. How childish and silly was that?

"Not really. Just a fifty-foot sailboat with an inboard engine. Serves me fine. I've had it for several years." He hadn't had time to do much on it for the past couple of years though. He found he was very much looking forward to the competition tomorrow.

He'd never actually stopped to think about exactly how much had changed in his life during such a short span.

Marco motioned for Brianna to follow him below deck. "Here, I'll show you the living quarters."

When they got below, Brianna's jaw seemed to drop even lower. "This is almost a mini apartment."

He laughed. "Well, the tour won't take long." He pointed straight in front of him. "Kitchen, bed, and the bathroom is to your left."

Was it his imagination, or had Brianna's eyes lingered on the bed for just an instant before looking away? He found himself focused on it as well, his mind wandering to what the night would entail as they shared it.

He turned before his body could react any further. Taking Brianna by the elbow, he led her to the mini fridge. "Can I get you something to drink? There's chilled wine, soda. Or water if you prefer."

"I don't dare have wine on an empty stomach." She clapped her hands. "Oh, that reminds me. I made some sandwiches for us. They're in an insulated bag in my luggage. Would you care for one now?"

As thoughtful as that was, this regatta was just as much about the food as it was the actual race. He should have been clearer. "You didn't need to trouble yourself. There'll be food and drinks at every stop."

Her smile deflated before he spoke the last word and Marco wanted to kick himself. He should have just eaten whatever she'd prepared. But they had plans at the very next stop for a meal. Again, something he should have shared with her much sooner.

"I just thought we might get hungry before..."

"No, as I said it was a very kind and thoughtful gesture. But I didn't get a chance to mention that we have plans to eat at the next stop."

"We do?"

He nodded. "Some friends are meeting us. We'll be getting there just in time for an early evening dinner. I apologize for not telling you sooner."

She waved her hand in dismissal. "Don't be silly. I'm a chef, eating at new establishments is a thrill for me."

Her words didn't seem to match her tone. He detected a subtle yet clear hint of disappointment.

"You know, I think I am kind of hungry," he lied. "I'll have a quick bite after all. It will be close to an hour before we eat, now that I think about it."

He moved to go retrieve her bag with the sandwiches when she stopped him. "Uh-uh. No way. As a professional, I will not let you spoil your appetite before a five-star restaurant meal."

"No, really—" he began to protest.

"It's okay, Marco. We'll just save the sandwiches for another time. I'm just going to freshen up." She turned without another word and stepped into bathroom.

Such a silly misunderstanding, Marco thought, watching her retreat.

He would make it up to her somehow. He refused to let something as trivial as uneaten sandwiches mar this trip before it had even started.

She was so clueless.

Brianna rummaged in her bag for her lip gloss in the small stately bathroom of Marco's boat. What a simpleton. She'd made sandwiches. Like they were going off on some picnic. A true fish out of water, Brianna Stedman was. Her last name might be Dirici now but in her bones she was still southern New Jersey. Girls like her didn't realize that sailboats could be this large or have living quarters this luxurious. She wasn't sure what she'd been expecting but it certainly hadn't been anything this elaborate.

The earth moved under her feet. Brianna grabbed the edge of the sink to steady herself. They must be departing.

She'd spent so much time picking out exactly what to wear, so much time on getting her hair just right. At least all that effort seemed to have paid off. Marco looked appreciative when he'd first laid eyes on her earlier today. In fact, the look he'd given her had sent heat curling through her stomach.

She just wished she was a bit more worldly. Heavens, she'd never even been on a boat before. Unless you counted paddleboarding on the Jersey shore. This was a large part of Marco's life. She wanted to understand it more. She wanted to be part of it. But it was completely alien to her.

She would have to shape up. And she would have to do it quickly. They were to meet people in a few short moments. And she didn't want to give the impression that she didn't know what she was doing or how to behave.

Marco's friends would be cut from the same elite cloth that he was. European upper class.

She studied her face in the mirror and almost had to laugh. How had she ended up here? She was in Italy on the Amalfi coast with her billionaire husband on his yacht before a race.

No, not a race. A *regatta*.

If someone had suggested such a thing to the young adult she was a few short years ago she would have laughed in their face. Actually, she would have been too tired to laugh, between long hours at culinary school and putting herself through it by working odd, low-paying jobs.

Her present predicament was certainly a far cry from where that young lady had been. She'd ended up in a completely different universe without even really knowing how it had happened. At first she'd simply been too focused on her new baby boy to really acknowledge all the changes that were happening to her life. But there was no denying, Brianna Stedman was a totally different person in a totally different world.

The few short years in between felt like they could have been an entire lifetime.

So how come the reflection staring back at her now from the mirror taunted that nothing about her had really changed at all?

CHAPTER TWELVE

SHE COULDN'T ALLOW herself to be sick.

Brianna leaned over the rail and stared at the water below. They were about half a mile from the coast from what she could tell, traveling at a steady speed. The blue-green of the sea was broken by white-capped foam where the boat's hull met the water.

Every once in a while she caught Marco's eye as he stood steering at the helm. She gave him a tentative smile and gripped the railing tighter. Her legs felt wobbly but she didn't dare sit. She didn't dare move. Her stomach insisted on doing queasy flips. Her throat burned with acidic bile. This was so much worse than any bout of morning sickness she could remember. And this wasn't even the race yet, they were simply cruising to their first destination.

So this was what seasickness felt like. As if Brianna needed any more proof that she was utterly out of her element.

Marco appeared oblivious to her discomfort. Hopefully, she'd be able to keep it that way. With any luck, it would all go away once she got something solid in her stomach. Though the thought of food immediately made her stomach go from a minor flip to an all-out heave.

She gripped the steel rail so tight her knuckles turned white. What had she been thinking? She could be back at the mansion right now, rocking her little boy to sleep with her feet on solid ground.

What seemed like an eternity later, Marco seemed to pull in toward land and maneuver around several other crafts. Brianna closed her eyes and willed her body to behave. She heard the engine shut off finally and then Marco's footsteps approaching behind her.

That had to have been the longest hour of her life.

"We're here."

She turned to face him and was struck momentarily by his wide grin. His cheeks glowed a healthy red, a bright twinkle in his eyes. Unlike her, he'd apparently enjoyed every minute of their ride.

"The coastline looked beautiful," she managed to mutter.

His brow suddenly furrowed and the grin disappeared into a tight frown. "Are you all right?" he asked with concern. "You're looking a little pale."

She forced her mouth into a smile. "I'm fine. Must have been the wind blowing in my face."

Marco hesitated and studied her some more. Brianna bit the inside of her cheek to keep from gagging. Hard.

"Are you sure? You're not seasick, are you?"

She made herself shake her head, the effort resulting in a nasty pounding in her temple. At least morning sickness had never involved headaches.

"No, not at all." What a talent she had that she'd never known about! Being able to lie so blatantly even while feeling this miserable. "Shall we go then? Meet these friends of yours?" Holding on to Marco's arm, she made her feet move. If he noticed how tight her grip was, he didn't let on.

Stepping on dry land only offered minimal comfort. The marina was crowded and noisy. Someone was playing Italian opera at a high decibel from a nearby speaker. A group of teen girls jostled her as they rushed by. Brianna found herself shoved close to Marco's side and for a horrifying moment she thought she might lose her control and be sick over his arm.

Taking a deep breath, she tried to steady herself.

"There they are," Marco said above her ear.

Brianna looked up to see a group of well-heeled people about twenty feet away, right by the water. They sat around a metal table at some sort of outdoor café; two opened bottles of wine seemed to have been casualties already. Three women and two men. A laughing Leo sat right at the center, sipping from a long-stemmed glass. Brianna felt a small hint of relief. At least there was one familiar face amongst them.

"Let's go," Marco said and gently fought their way through the crowd toward the group. Brianna forced back yet another surge of bile at the base of her throat.

One of the ladies looked up just as they approached. She was stunning, so much so that Brianna missed a step. She regained her footing and just barely avoided crashing face-first into the chest of a passing stranger.

Brianna shut her eyes tight and said a small prayer. Maybe when she opened them again she would realize she'd overestimated the woman's beauty.

The prayer went unanswered. The vision before her had to be some type of model or actress. The other females at the table also held their own in the looks department.

Brianna ran her hand through her unruly curls. No amount of primping would put her on par with the likes of the ladies before her right now.

Leo stood as soon as he spotted them and pulled two nearby chairs to their table. "There they are," his voice boomed through the air. "The lovely Brianna and her boor of a husband."

Marco replied with some type of hand gesture Brianna

didn't understand. Definitely not anything she'd seen in New York. Leo only laughed louder.

Any other time and she would have laughed at the men's humorous banter. Right now, it was taking all she had to simply stand straight. Between shock and nausea, it was proving to be quite a battle. So not the first impression she was shooting for with Marco's friends.

Marco guided her to the table as laughter and mock cheers greeted them. Brianna managed a weak wave but didn't dare try to speak. Opening her mouth would be too risky. The brunette stood and gave Marco a kiss. Only on the cheek but it was definitely a lingering one. She said something to him in Italian and Marco barked out in laughter. Brianna slammed a hand against her belly. Her stomach had gone from flips to all-out gymnastic level cartwheels.

Finally, the brunette turned and directed the focus of her shapely, dark eyes right on her. High cheekbones, dark eyes, a pert nose. The woman could have been an image straight out of a painting, the descendant of a Renaissance portrait subject.

She addressed her in English with a heavy accent and a warm smile. "I'm Natalia, but I'm called Talia."

The woman continued speaking but Brianna could hear nothing through the roaring suddenly echoing in her ears. The world started to shift around her and then it began to spin.

There was nothing for it. She couldn't even pretend anymore. She was going to be sick.

"Excuse me," she managed to blurt out and turned on her heel. Covering her mouth with the back of her hand, she tried to put as much distance between herself and the group as possible.

She barely made it to the edge of the water in time.

* * *

What kind of man didn't know his wife had never been on a boat before?

Marco could simply stare as Brianna shoved past him and hurled herself through the crowd. He lost sight of her for a split second in the bustling sea of people. When he spotted her again he bit out a sharp curse in Italian. She stood bent over by the edge of the water. Violently ill.

"Scusa," he said to his shocked friends and made his way over to where his wife stood.

"Brianna?"

She lifted a hand but didn't turn to look at him. "Please, Marco. Just leave me alone."

How was he supposed to do that? What did she expect? For him to just walk away and hope she didn't pass out or anything? "Uh, can I get you some water? Or ice?"

Her response was another heave. He reached for her tentatively before dropping his hand back down by his side.

"Is there any chance you'll walk away?" she asked between what sounded like several violent hiccups.

"Probably not."

This time the response was an elongated groan. So much for showing Brianna a fun time today. He'd failed miserably. It hadn't even occurred to him that she might have an issue on the water. He'd grown up on the water, had been sailing since his teens. He and his grandfather had spent hours cruising along the coast every weekend before the man had passed away several years back.

"I wish there was something I could do for you, *cara*."

She shook her head and wiped her mouth. Marco signaled to a passing vendor selling various ice smoothies. Fortunately, the man also had bottled water. Marco paid the man quickly then held the plastic bottle in Brianna's direction. It took her a minute to notice he was holding something to her. She took it with a shaky hand then brought it to her forehead.

"I'll be all right in a few minutes. Luckily, I hadn't eaten much of anything."

"Yes, you appear quite lucky at the moment," he quipped in an attempt at comic relief.

She didn't appear to be in the mood. All he got was a grimace in response. "I'm so sorry about this, *cara*," he told her.

"Why in the world are you apologizing to me?"

"This trip was my idea. You are my responsibility."

She gave him an incredulous look. "I was the one who got ill in the middle of meeting your friends for the first time ever."

"You can't blame yourself for not being accustomed to the water. I should have thought to take precautions."

She turned to face him fully then. Marco tried not to react to the way she looked. Her pallor had gone completely ashen, dark smudges framed the area beneath her eyes. Her hair had escaped its noose and fell haphazardly around her face and neck.

Somehow, she still looked stunningly beautiful.

He shook his head to clear it. What a fanciful thought. They had more pressing matters than how Brianna looked after an episode of seasickness.

"I'm your wife, Marco. Please don't call me your responsibility."

Where had that come from?

He hadn't meant it the way she seemed to be interpreting the statement. For the first time since he'd met her, Marco entertained the possibility that they might have some kind of a language issue between them. They did after all have different first tongues. "I simply meant—"

She held up a hand to stop him. "Please, not now. I just need another minute."

Marco shut his mouth before he could say anything more to upset her. Not only was she not feeling well, she was angry. At him. But she didn't want to hear him apologizing for her predicament. So what was she upset with him about? Brianna turned back and stared at the horizon. He stood silently as she did her best to collect herself. Glancing back to where his friends stood watching them with concern, he gave a reassuring wave.

This trip was turning out nothing like the way he'd imagined.

The scene at the marina still tugged at her mind though they'd gotten back three days ago. Brianna had toughed it out through the rest of the trip, refusing to return home or letting Marco pull out of the competition.

But she hadn't enjoyed a moment of it. And something had definitely shifted between them afterward. Their brief interlude of a makeshift truce had faded to one of tension and underlying strife. Now, she was moving forward with the decision she'd come to even before their return from the regatta.

Correction, it was the same decision she had made over six months ago when she'd left Italy in the first place. She and Marco belonged to two different worlds. And they definitely didn't belong together.

Marco had been in emotional pain when they'd met. Grieving for his lost mother, whether he'd known it or not. It was only that pain and confusion that had led him into her arms. His anguished state of mind had played the only role in the way he'd behaved that week when they'd first met. What were the chances someone like him would have otherwise even glanced in her direction?

She glanced down at the list of names she'd researched. Names of renowned child psychologists in the Amalfi area. A couple were located as far away as Rome. If she had to, she would make the trip. It was time to get Enzo evaluated, not only to make sure he was thriving, but also to ensure he adjusted properly to the inevitable. His parents weren't going to be a couple that stayed together.

The next step after that would be to try and contact Chef Ziyad again. She had to pursue that possible avenue of employment harder than she'd been able to back in New York.

She didn't know how long any of that would take. But she wasn't going to put it any of it off any longer.

She'd tried, she really had.

Brianna bit back a sob as she reached for the phone to call the first professional on her list. This was so much worse than when she and Marco had failed the first time.

Marco chose that moment to walk in through the front door. His expression was guarded, his demeanor stiff. Things had been that way between them since they'd gotten back. Even now, as she took in his tailored suit, his coal-dark hair, she had to resist the urge to run into his arms and ask him to kiss her.

How foolish she could be when it came to this man.

"Where's Enzo?" he asked without so much as a hello.

"Nonna took him out by the pond."

He nodded, seemed to look her over. "I'll be in the study for most of the evening. I'll take my dinner in there when it's ready."

"I wanted to talk to you for a moment first."

"Can it wait? I've got a lot to get through before a staff meeting tomorrow."

"I'm afraid I'd rather not delay." She stood before he could get far. Better to just get this over with. "Before you hole up, there are some things we need to go over."

"Hole up? That's how you're going to describe me trying to get some work done?"

Really? That was the battle he wanted to pursue at the

moment? Wait till she told him what she'd spent the afternoon doing. "It's just a figure of speech, Marco."

He dropped his briefcase to the ground and rubbed his forehead. "Very well. What is it that you'd like to discuss?"

For an insane moment, Brianna had an urge to voice the questions she really wanted to ask him. If he'd ever thought he might have genuine feelings for the woman he'd inadvertently ended up married to. Despite the unconventional way they'd met, despite the inner turmoil that had led him into her arms.

She cleared her throat. "I've been doing some research since we returned."

"What kind of research?"

"Experts in child rearing."

"I see." He crossed his arms in front of his chest.

"I'd like to get Enzo analyzed. By a child psychologist."

"Has something happened?" A flash of concern flickered in his eyes.

"No. He's actually been a happy, well-adjusted toddler since we returned."

He lifted an eyebrow. "Then I don't see the point."

Brianna let out a deep breath. Yes, he did. Of course he saw the point. He was just going to insist on making her say it, to make her admit her motives out loud.

"I'm trying to think of the long term."

"You're looking for reassurance that it will be okay to take him away again. I thought we'd already had this conversation."

"But we never resolved it. You and I both know this isn't going to work, Marco. We gave it another go. It's not like we didn't."

"Perhaps you're right."

"I am?"

"If you're going to be this temperamental about living here then maybe it will be easier to just make a clean break once and for all." He stepped forward and lifted a finger accusingly. "But I will not have my son adversely affected. We'll see what your experts have to say about any of that."

His words and his whole attitude stoked her temper. She'd wanted so badly to discuss all this with him in a calm and mature manner. She should have known better. "I know what they're going to say. That children are never better off in the long term if the parents aren't happy in their marriage."

"Is this about the race?" Marco sighed and pinched the bridge of his nose. "Look, I'm sorry you had a miserable time. I'm sorry I made you go."

Did he honestly think that was what her decision was about? The events of that day had simply been the trigger that made their incompatibility glaringly obvious. Yet again.

"It's about so much more than the race."

"Right. It's about being stuck in an unhappy marriage and incompatibility."

He may as well have added *blah, blah, blah* to the end of his statement.

Brianna fought the urge to stomp her foot like a child. "No, more so about how we're from completely different worlds and backgrounds. And you have no interest in trying to address any of that."

"I was the one who asked you to go to the regatta, remember?"

"Yes, and I appreciate the attempt." She inhaled a deep breath as her voice shook. "But how could you have thought it would be enough? I need more than a day boating with you, Marco. I need you to talk to me."

She'd known this wasn't going to be easy. Trying to get through to Marco about her concerns never was.

"What exactly is it that you want me to say, Brianna?"

She wanted him to tell her that it would all right. That

he was ready to share his life with her. She wanted to hear that he would never doubt their future together. For the sake of her child and her heart, she wanted that guarantee.

But she knew that would all be asking too much. Sooner or later, it would all turn for the worse.

Maybe not tomorrow, maybe not next week. But it was a certainty. Why had she ever thought she could fit in with the likes of Marco Dirici?

He was yachting and vineyards and international corporate offices.

He'd only turned to her during a time of torment and confusion after finding out his estranged mother had died after abandoning him years before. If not for his shock and certain anger, he probably wouldn't have given someone like Brianna Stedman the time of day.

After all, she was nothing more than a cook from New Jersey.

CHAPTER THIRTEEN

MARCO LOOSENED HIS tie and shrugged off his jacket. With all the frustration and agitation he was feeling, he threw them onto the sofa. Then he wished he had something else to throw, something that would break and shatter. His wife stood in front of him like a small waif facing a royal guard. Under any other circumstances, he might actually admire her determination.

Everything had gone so wrong. He wished he'd never entered that godforsaken regatta. Then maybe Brianna wouldn't be looking at him right now like a wasp she wanted to swat away. He'd expected too much, put too much faith in one little trip. A foolish part of him thought he and Brianna would be returning from the coast with a renewed sense of solidarity and family. The exact opposite had occurred.

Instead, she was telling him she wanted to leave again.

Served him right for having such ridiculous thoughts in the first place. Did he think one sailing trip was going to make any kind of difference? If he hadn't been able to make his wife care for him after all this time, what did that say about the kind of man he was? To think, he'd ridiculed his own father for so many years for essentially the same thing.

"I again have to ask, what exactly would you like me to say, *cara*?"

A brief flash of emotion flickered in her eyes. He didn't have it in him to try and analyze it. Not now.

She clasped her hands in front of her belly and for an insane moment he wanted to reach out to her. He wanted to take those hands into his and bring them to his mouth. To tell her that things would be all right. That they would figure it all out. That they had to try for the sake of their son. He almost took a step forward in her direction before he caught himself.

"You have nothing you would like to say?"

"Not a thing I can think of."

She seemed to deflate like a balloon before his very eyes. "I have no choice then. I'd like to move forward with my plans to have Enzo seen by a professional. Would you like to provide any input?"

"As far as?"

She wrung her hands tighter. "About the doctor we take Enzo to. About how to prep him for the return to New York. I'm sure we should go over some of this together."

We?

She was serious. Did she honestly expect him to help further the process along under these circumstances? Did she not see that he felt totally cut off at the knees? "I really have no interest in any of that. Like you said, *cara*. These are all *your* plans."

"But don't you—?"

Marco was done listening. He dismissed her by turning away and then picked his briefcase off the floor. "Update me as necessary. I have work to do."

Brianna let him go without further argument. He didn't know whether to be relieved or disappointed.

Marco closed the door to his study and walked over to the large window overlooking the south lawn. This scene always soothed him. The pathway that led to Nonna's precious gardens, the rolling hills in the distance. It was one of the reasons he had chosen this room as his at-home office. For the sense of calm this view provided him.

But not today.

He'd let her down. He'd placed Brianna in a predicament and environment she was utterly unprepared for. And then he'd been unable to help in any way.

Biting out a curse, he grabbed the glass paperweight off his desk and got ready to throw it against the wall. A rapid knock on the door stopped him midthrow.

"Come in."

Brianna had followed him. Her gaze fell to the paperweight Marco still gripped viselike in his hands. But she didn't comment on it. "I'd like to continue discussing this."

Marco set the paperweight down as Brianna stepped into the room and shut the door behind her.

"I already apologized for taking you sailing, Brianna."

She gave an exasperated huff. "You think that's what this is about?"

"What else? You must blame me for not realizing you would get sick."

"That's a ridiculous notion, Marco. It's not your fault I got sick."

"Maybe not directly." The truth was, he should have at least asked her about her past experiences on the water.

"Or indirectly," she countered. "I got sick because I've never really been on a boat before. But my husband's an avid sailor."

He blinked. "Is there supposed to be some kind of logic behind that statement? A metaphor perhaps?"

She slammed her hands against her hips. "The fact is I'm completely out of my element here at times. I don't really know what I'm doing."

She was clearly referring to more than just being on a boat. "You're saying we're not a good match."

"Can you deny it?" she demanded to know. "We never would have even gotten married if it wasn't for Enzo."

He studied her. She seemed absolutely certain of what she'd just said. "You can be so sure?"

His question shocked her, as if she'd never really entertained an alternate possibility.

"If that's wrong. Then why?"

"Why what?"

"Why are you so distant? So guarded? You refuse to open up to me about anything. Not even what you were dealing with that week we met."

So she'd found out about his mother and the news he'd gotten right before traveling to the States that first time.

But before Marco could come up with a response, they were interrupted by a sharp knock on the door.

It was Carlo; he'd gone deathly pale. "Signore Marco, come quick. It's your grandmother."

"What happened?" Marco demanded to know as she chased behind him to Marie's suite. Brianna's heart thudded in her chest at the thought of what they might find.

"I don't know exactly," Carlo answered then followed up with something else in Italian.

Marco barked something in response to the other man who quickly turned and dashed the other way down the hallway. Presumably to call medical attention, Brianna figured.

When they got to her suite, Nonna didn't appear at all well. She was breathing heavily, her skin the color of ash. Marco immediately ran to her side and crouched down next to her.

"Nonna? Can you speak?"

Marie made a futile attempt to brush away his concern

with a wave of her hand. "I'm fine. Just trying to catch my breath. I must have overdone it in the gardens earlier."

Brianna's mouth had gone dry. Whatever was happening to Marco's grandmother appeared to be much more than simple overexertion.

"I'm sure it is." Marco was trying to reassure her. "But we're going to have you checked out just in case, okay?"

Nonna made an attempt to sit up, then gave up and settled back into the cushion. "That's just silly. I wish you hadn't called them."

Brianna uttered a silent prayer of thanks that Enzo was asleep and not around to see his great-grandmother in such a state. She was having enough trouble taking in the scene herself. Nonna had never been anything less than formidable since Brianna had first laid eyes on her.

Marco took his grandmother's hand, whispered softly to her in Italian. Brianna's eyes began to sting. He looked so tender, so concerned. Nonna had been the one to bring him up, more a mother to him than his actual parent. Brianna didn't want to imagine what it would do to Marco if he lost her.

Finally, after what seemed to be an eternity, they heard the sirens outside.

The next few minutes went by in a blur. A team of medics fitted Nonna with an oxygen mask, started checking various vitals, and then carried her down the stairs. Brianna didn't even realize it, but at some point she'd reached for Marco's arm with both hands and was holding on to it tight.

"I'm going to go with her," he told her as they watched Nonna being carried away.

He started to pull free but Brianna didn't loosen her grasp. "If you don't mind, I'd like to come with you."

He nodded once then turned and looked at her for the first time since she'd summoned him earlier. His eyes held such apprehension, such downright fear. For one surreal moment, she imagined she might be looking at Enzo after a particularly nasty nightmare. Her strong, formidable husband looked anything but. Right now, he looked like a scared little boy.

Brianna thought her heart might break at the thought.

"I'd like that," he told her.

CHAPTER FOURTEEN

MARCO WATCHED BRIANNA just outside the emergency clinic entrance as she spoke into her cell phone. She was calling to check on Enzo. A glance at his own device told him it was almost 10:00 p.m. They had pulled Nonna out once more about twenty minutes ago to run yet more tests. He'd never been a terribly patient man, and waiting for such long durations under these circumstances was just about driving him *pazza*.

Brianna stepped through the doors and made her way back to the seat next to him. "Violetta says Enzo is still asleep. The sirens and all the activity didn't even stir him."

"Good. That's good."

"Everyone back at the mansion is terribly concerned. Violetta bombarded me with questions. I tried to tell her we just don't know much yet."

Marco rubbed a hand down his face and tried to focus on her words. He hated this clinic. Though it had gone through several renovations over the past few years, the overall setting and the pungent smell of antiseptic hadn't changed.

"I told them Nonna's personal doctor was here," Brianna was saying. "That he was nice enough to come in to oversee her procedures. That seemed to reassure everyone somewhat."

"Yes. Dr. Gia is also a dear friend."

"Did he mention Nonna having issues recently?"

Marco shook his head. "No, in fact he appeared as shocked as the rest of us. Nonna had just recently been in for a routine physical and he declared her fit as an ox."

"Let's hope that means this isn't anything terribly serious."

Marco rested his elbows on his knees. He suddenly felt beyond tired, utterly weary. Brianna edged closer to him. Hesitantly, she reached for his hand. He let her take it then squeezed his fingers around her small palm. He allowed himself to just breathe for a moment and enjoy the warmth of her touch. They were the only two people in the waiting area. A family of four with a crying baby had left within the hour. For several moments, neither of them bothered to speak.

"I'm glad you're here, *cara*," he finally admitted. She had no idea how much he meant it. Being here a little over a decade ago was one of the worst experiences of his existence.

"I wasn't going to make you wait for word here alone, Marco."

"The last time I was alone."

She turned to him. He felt her studying his profile. "The last time?"

"My father was rushed here several years ago before being lifted to the main hospital in the city. Nonna and Nonno were away in Greece for a family wedding. I was the only one to accompany Papa when he fell ill. He never made it back home."

"Oh, Marco." She sighed his name and he felt her soft breath against his cheek. "How old were you?"

"Barely nineteen. I hadn't started university yet."

"That's an awfully young age to not have either parent."

He shrugged. "Maybe. But in truth I'd lost the better

part of him long before that. Twelve years before to be exact."

"When your mother left."

"They may as well both have left that day. I never got my real father back after that. If he was ever really there to begin with. He just couldn't seem to recover from her loss."

"A broken heart can be impossible to recover from for some people."

Marco studied the tile between his feet. It had been scrubbed to a high shine. Was that the same tile he'd stared at ten years ago? Or had it been one of the things that had been changed? He'd tried hard not to think about those hours he'd spent worried and scared. He'd wondered if he should try to find his mother. To tell her what was happening to the husband she'd deserted. But he hadn't had a clue where to start to try and locate her.

"A broken heart coupled with the sting of betrayal." He rubbed his eyes. "I think it's actually what killed him. Slowly. He ignored his responsibilities at Dirici Foods. The company suffered terrible losses for months until Nonno took over the reins again. And Nonna was sharp enough to realize the same neglect was probably being suffered by his child."

He'd never spoken of these things. Not even to Nonna. Definitely not to any other woman. Had no idea why he was doing so now.

But it felt good to have her next to him, to feel her soft skin against his. And to know that whatever the doctors came out to tell him, she would be there with him when they did. So he let himself continue.

"I blamed myself that night," he told her. "Felt consumed with guilt."

"I don't understand. Why would you feel that way?"

"Because maybe the demands of a child had been too

much for her to deal with. Maybe she would have stayed if it wasn't for me and he would have remained the vibrant, happy man he'd once been."

"But you were just a child."

"I know. It made no sense. And then I blamed myself for not trying harder to find her when I was older. Maybe if I had just convinced her to at least see him again before he'd gotten sick." He sighed.

She leaned into him; he could smell the lavender scent of her shampoo. It had a soothing effect on his frazzled nerves. Whether it was the scent or her closeness he didn't even know. Nor did he care. He was just grateful.

"You asked me earlier this evening about being guarded."

He heard her suck in a breath. "Yes?"

"You're right. I was so afraid of becoming like my father—losing control of his whole grip on life—all because of an ill-fated relationship. I did everything in my power to avoid it at all costs."

Brianna didn't respond. Just nuzzled closer into his shoulder. He found himself leaning into her as well.

That's how Dr. Gia found them an hour and a half later.

She'd somehow dozed off. Brianna jolted awake when Marco suddenly gripped her shoulders then stood. The doctor was approaching from the patient area down the corridor. Marco strode to meet him halfway with Brianna fast on his heels.

"Sorry to keep you waiting, Marco," Dr. Gia said as they reached him. A short thin man with kind eyes and silver-gray hair, he had a soft soothing voice that must have served him well given his profession. "You can breathe easy. She's stabilized now and breathing without the aid of an oxygen mask."

Marco blew out a loud sigh. His shoulders visibly dropped.

"The better news is that there appear to be no signs of a cardiac event."

"Oh, thank God," Brianna said, and a surge of relief nearly had her knees wobbling beneath her.

"Then what caused all this?" Marco demanded.

The doctor pulled off his glasses and started wiping them with his lab coat. "Her blood pressure when she came in has me quite concerned. She responded to the medication given to lower it. But it's still not anywhere near within normal parameters."

"What could have possibly caused that?" Marco wanted to know.

"That's what we'll need to figure out. But it certainly could have caused the shortness of breath and the heart palpitations."

"I see. May we take her home?"

"Yes. She's free to go. But I want to see her tomorrow. There are some lifestyle changes we need to discuss. And that blood pressure needs to be monitored going forward."

"Lifestyle changes?" Brianna asked.

"I'm afraid Signora Dirici's days of Gusto espresso are over," Dr. Gia declared with finality.

"You'll have to be the one to tell her," Marco told him with a smile that didn't quite reach his eyes.

By the time they got Nonna home and tucked into her bed, Brianna felt like she'd run a half marathon. Between holding herself so tense as they'd awaited news and the hard plastic chairs in the waiting room, her body actually ached. She and Marco had parted ways at Nonna's suite when he'd gone to reassure the staff who had stayed awake to hear about her condition. Brianna had sworn she could hear their sighs of relief all the way up on the second floor as she'd been checking on Enzo.

As tired as she was, she knew she wasn't going to get any sleep. The adrenaline surge of the past few hours wouldn't abate any time soon. She made her way to the kitchen. Her throat felt dry and scratchy and Violetta always kept fresh lemonade on hand.

She found Marco standing in front of the fridge with the door open. The kitchen was dark save for the small lightbulb in the door of the appliance. For a moment she could do nothing but stare. He still wore his suit pants and work shirt. His sleeves were rolled up and his hands were jammed into his pockets. Brianna's heart lurched in her chest. He'd been so worried about his grandmother. And when she thought about the things he had confided in her, she wanted to weep for the young man who'd had to grow up way too soon.

What would he do if she gave in to the urge to go wrap her arms around him? Would he turn around and reciprocate? So much had happened between them in such a short amount of time. She honestly didn't know how he would react to any kind of gesture right now. Yes, he'd been very open at the clinic. But that was an entirely different circumstance. They were back home now.

She couldn't bring herself to risk it.

"You must be hungry," she said instead. "I'd forgotten we missed dinner."

He turned slightly over his shoulder. "Actually, I was going to make sure to remove the pitcher of iced coffee Nonna keeps in here and drinks throughout the day. Based on what the doctor said, it's now off limits."

He was still worried. For all his strength and hardness, she'd never seen the vulnerability he'd shown while at the clinic.

"Then I want to go check on Enzo," he continued. "Unless you're concerned I may disturb him."

"No. But I've just left his room now. He's sleeping soundly."

"Good. Maybe I'll wait till morning then." He still

hadn't shut the fridge door, still stood staring into its depths. She would bet he wasn't actually looking at anything.

"Are you sure you're not hungry? Can I prepare something for you? I can make a mean omelet."

"Your expert chef skills?"

She shrugged. "More that I just load it full of bacon and gooey, fatty cheese."

He let out a small laugh. "Maybe some other time."

Finally, he turned to face her. Against the backdrop of the light, shadows fell across his face. Even with such little light, she could see the tenseness of his features. He was barely holding on.

"Brianna?"

The timbre and longing in his voice sent a shiver down to her toes. "Yes?"

"You don't know how much it means that you were by my side tonight."

"Your grandmother is one of a kind, Marco. I was as scared as you were."

"Everything I know about love and acceptance I learned from that woman."

"I know."

"That is, until you and Enzo came along."

Brianna couldn't help her gasp. It was the closest Marco had ever come to admitting any kind of affection toward her. She had to wonder how much it had taken him to do so.

"Brianna?"

"Yes?"

"Would you please come here?"

Her feet seemed to move on their own. When she reached him, she knew she'd stopped breathing. Her pulse pounded in her veins. He lifted her chin gently with his finger and leaned in close. She didn't know what to expect, but it wasn't the soft, featherlight touch of his lips against hers. His kiss was gentle yet somehow full of passion at the same time.

Her hands moved up to his upper arms.

She knew what he was asking for. A respite from the world and all it had thrown on his shoulders when he was still too young and years before he was ready. He was asking for solace, for comfort.

She wanted that too, with him. With the only man she'd ever really cared for. He'd just admitted how much he cared for her too.

Warning bells rang in her head. After all, this was how it had all started, hadn't it? The first time they'd become intimate, Marco had turned to her for soothing and comfort. History was about to repeat itself, no denying it. Her heart might not be able to handle the fallout this time around. But she shoved those thoughts aside. Maybe she was being foolish, naive even. So be it. She loved him, she always had. She couldn't deny that fact any longer either.

Her husband needed her now. She wouldn't turn him down.

Her legs left the ground as he picked her up and cradled her in his arms. All the while, he maintained the soul-shattering kisses she knew she might never recover from. Then he carried her upstairs.

"Good morning." Brianna opened her eyes to see Marco already showered and dressed. How did the man manage to summon so much energy? Particularly after the night they'd had? She herself could use a whole other night's sleep.

"You let me sleep late."

"I figured you needed it."

"But Enzo."

"Enzo is fine. I fed him his breakfast as soon as he

awoke. And now he's playing quietly in his pen." He indicated the baby monitor across the room. Blessedly, all she could detect were the sounds of toddler play.

"See, there was no need to wake you. Enzo is fine. And Nonna is still resting comfortably. Plus, her appointment isn't for another few hours."

Brianna stretched and the silky sheet covering her slipped lower. She pulled it back up but not before Marco's eyes flickered over her bare skin. The heat in his eyes triggered a fluttering in her chest. Images from the night before assaulted her mind and her breath caught in her throat. "Then why are you dressed already?"

"That's a really good question. Now that I look at you, I feel I might have rushed a bit."

She resisted the urge to purr as he started to unbutton his shirt. There were times she hardly recognized herself around this man. This was one of those times.

She'd never been quite so brazen, so downright wanton with anyone else. But with Marco, that uncharacteristic streak had started the moment she'd laid eyes on him.

A nagging thought slithered into the back of her brain about all the questions that still plagued their relationship. All the times they'd fallen into each other's arms before only to turn around and have fate tamper or mar it in some way. She shook her head to eradicate the thought.

And she didn't even want to think about the regatta and what had happened there. The harsh truth was that none of the matters they'd been grappling with had altered in any way. Did that mean she had to focus on those issues entirely? Could she let herself, just for a while, focus instead on the current moment? Surely, the heavens wouldn't open up and the world wouldn't sink if she was just simply selfish for a bit.

Nonna had given them both quite a scare last night. Though her health scare seemed to be something that could be addressed, the episode had served to remind Brianna how temperamental life was. How fleeting any good fortune could be. It had also prompted Marco to finally confide in her in a way he never had before. So right now, she was only going to let herself focus on the here and now.

And right now, her husband had just crawled back into bed with her. It would serve her well to focus on that for as long as she could.

Before reality reared its head once more.

"That man is a quack. I don't think he even went to a decent medical school," Nonna declared as Marco assisted her into the back of the town car. He'd wanted to drive her to the appointment himself but she'd insisted being hauled around in that contraption he called a vehicle would trigger her heart palpitations again. As a result, he'd accompanied her in the back as Carlo drove them the twenty minutes to Dr. Gia's medical office.

She was not very happy with her long-term physician at the moment. Though the appointment had gone well, Nonna didn't like Dr. Gia's recommendations in the least. The one about the coffee and espresso elimination had been particularly ill met.

He would have to warn the household that Nonna's mood would border on unbearable as she adjusted. Marco sat down in the seat next to her and motioned for Carlo to start driving.

"He's been your physician for close to two decades, Nonna. You've never had a complaint before."

"Well, this is the first time he's lost his mind, that's why." Marco pinched the bridge of his nose. All that mattered was that it appeared she would be okay. With some medication and lifestyle changes, Nonna would be as good as new.

He didn't dare tell her that. Better to let her just vent.

Not that he really blamed her. A lady her age would be set in her ways.

"Well, it appears the only pleasure or joy in my life will have to be provided by that great-grandson of mine," Nonna declared as Carlo shifted into gear. "Thank goodness for him at least."

At the mention of his son, an uneasiness settled into Marco's chest. Things between him and Brianna were confusing to say the least.

Her decision to move away again had been somewhat interrupted by Nonna's scare. But he didn't dare conclude that she'd changed her mind. The simple truth was he'd been too anxious to ask her, for fear that her answer would be that she still planned to leave.

He didn't want Nonna to have to find out the hard way if that was the case. He took a deep breath. "Enzo adores you too," he began. "And he's lucky to have you. But you know, you can have other interests and pursuits. Your garden for instance. And all your friends at church."

His grandmother turned in the seat to give him a steely glare. "Is there something you're trying to say, son?"

Perceptive as always, Marco thought, and tried to stifle a groan of frustration. This was really not the time or the place that he wanted to have this conversation. "I simply mean that there are other aspects of your life that can be sources of joy and comfort."

"Not like that little angel, there aren't. Now what are you getting at exactly?"

Better to just come out and say it. His grandmother wasn't one to let a matter drop when she had a strong opinion. Which was most of the time. "We can't assume that Enzo's permanent home will be here, Nonna."

"And why can't we? Are you trying to tell me you two are still having differences? That young lady didn't leave your side last night as you were waiting at the clinic."

"That doesn't necessarily mean anything."

"I believe it means a great deal."

"She was worried about you, Nonna. We can't read more into it than that."

"I believe she must have been concerned about you as well."

"Perhaps. We just have to be careful about making any assumptions."

She flung her hands up in the air in true Italian grandmother style. "I have a novel thought. You could just ask her. You know, tell her how you feel about her. See what she says in return. It's called having a conversation."

"Is one of the side effects of your new medications a penchant for sarcasm?"

"It's a serious question."

Marco sighed and looked out the window. "I'm not going to push her, Nonna. We both know there's no good to come of pursuing a woman who doesn't want to be pursued."

"Are we still on that, then?" She sounded disappointed, which in turn made him feel like the time when he'd been seven and had been caught stealing his cousin's gelato.

"Still on what?"

"Brianna is nothing like your mother. Not in the least."

Marco merely sighed. Any other time, he would have found a way to cut this conversation off. He was being indulgent because of what Nonna had gone through last night. But he had his limits, even under these circumstances.

"It happens to be the truth. And here's something else you haven't considered."

"What's that?"

"You are nothing like your father either. He was my son, and I loved him with all my heart. But he expected to win at everything. And for most of his life, he did." Her voice shook as she continued. "Perhaps that was our fault. Perhaps we made life too easy for him at first. Being the only child, with your Nonno and me unable to have any more, he was the center of our universe. I admit we spoiled him. He was used to getting everything he wanted."

She huffed. "That was probably why he didn't know how to handle it the one time he didn't."

Marco considered her words for a moment. It was an angle he hadn't really considered. His papa's reaction had been just as important a factor as the way his mother had behaved.

"Have you heard of a *profezia auto-avverante*, son?" Nonna asked.

Of course he had. Loosely translated, it meant self-fulfilling prophecy.

CHAPTER FIFTEEN

"MISS BRIANNA, THERE'S a call for you. Overseas. From the States."

Brianna took the house phone Violetta handed her with mild curiosity. Who would have possibly tracked her here?

"Mrs. Dirici? This is Anton Seville, I'm Chef Ziyad's personal assistant." So she hadn't imagined that call back in New York before they'd left for Italy after all.

"Yes?"

"My deepest apologies. I know you were trying to get a hold of me a few weeks back and were unable to."

"This is quite a surprise, Mr. Seville."

"Please, call me Anton. Again, I'm sorry that we were unable to touch base. I was having some personal issues which made me somewhat inaccessible."

"How did you find me?"

"It took some sleuthing. Luckily, your surname is quite well known in the industry. But we searched New York first, your number was disconnected."

"I had to make an unexpected move," she explained, trying to control the excitement in her voice. One of the top chefs in New York had not only called her to begin with, but he'd instructed his assistant to search for her.

"So I've learned. I understand you're out of the country. Do you plan on returning to the States anytime soon? We'd like you to come into the restaurant."

Brianna cursed the air. Why was the timing in her life so often this misaligned? "I'm afraid I don't have any immediate plans at the time. Things are very…uncertain."

"I see. Perhaps you can send us some audition recipes then. And we can decide afterward where to go from there."

"I would love to."

Brianna's heart hammered. This was an opportunity she would be foolish to pass up. But it was truly a *Sliding Doors* moment. Her life had taken a drastic turn after Ziyad's initial phone call back in New York. She was here now, half a world away. With Marco and her son. Her circumstances had completely changed.

She'd been working her whole life for such a moment, but it was far from a cut-and-dried decision.

Still, what could it hurt to develop some audition recipes and send them over? At the very least, she'd learn if she had what it took to be hired by one of the best chefs on the East Coast.

With a myriad of conflicting emotions, she made her way to the kitchen and started pulling together ingredients, then took several pots out of the cabinets. An idea had taken hold already and a heady excitement took over as she started to work. Eventually, she was fully engrossed in the process.

She was still there three hours later when she heard the sound of the front door opening. Marco was home. His footsteps grew louder until he eventually appeared in the kitchen doorway.

"What is that delicious aroma? I swear I could smell it as soon as I turned past the gate into the property."

"Come, have a taste."

She dipped a spoon into the thick creamy sauce and reached it to his mouth.

"Mmm." True delight was clear in his voice and Brianna felt a pang of professional pride.

"That is really good, Brianna. Very creamy, though. Which one of Dirici's oils could you possibly incorporate into that?"

Brianna bit down on her cheek. He thought she was working on the marketing recipes they'd discussed several days ago.

"None, actually. This won't work with anything less than ghee."

He lifted an eyebrow in question. "Are you not working on a label addition then?"

Brianna's mouth had suddenly gone dry. The steam from the pots rose and swirled around them, adding a further ominousness to the air. "No, in fact this is for someone else."

"Someone?"

"I got a phone call today," she admitted. "From New York."

Understanding dawned in his eyes. Along with disappointment. Marco Dirici was a very smart man. "I think I can guess," he said and pushed his hair off his forehead with clear frustration.

"Chef Ziyad's assistant finally found me," Brianna blurted out, just to get it over with. "He wants me to send him some recipes."

"Because he'd still like to hire you."

"Yes."

A flurry of emotions flashed across Marco's face. Confusion, frustration, anger. Then she watched as he completely shut down. Again.

She had to try and clarify. "I'm just going to send him a couple of ideas. Simply to—"

"I leave you to it then." He turned to go but she rushed to catch him.

"Wait. I haven't made any kind of decision, Marco."

"Seems to me that you have." He tried to pull free but she gripped his arm tighter. He had to at least hear her out.

"No, that's not what this is."

"Is it not?" He pointed to the range and the saucepan that was now on the verge of boiling over. "Careful, you don't want to burn your sauce. That's going to look like Mount Etna any moment."

"Oh!" Brianna rushed to the stove and turned the dial to the off position. But she hadn't reached it in time. Sauce flooded over the side of the pan and poured onto the surface of the range like an erupting volcano. Gripping the handle with a holder, she managed to spill a few drops onto her wrist and gasped at the painful burn. "Ow!"

Great, her husband was livid. The kitchen looked like a scene out of a disaster movie. And the top of her hand was stinging with burns.

Yep, everything was a complete mess.

She brought her hand up and blew gently on the tender skin.

Marco stepped over to the counter beside her. "Is it bad, *cara*?"

"Nothing I haven't experienced before."

He took her hand gently and led her to the sink, held it under cold water where the hot liquid had splashed. Angry red welts had already formed above her knuckles.

"This is quite the mess, isn't it?" she said softly against his ear.

Marco looked up and their eyes locked. She could be referring to the kitchen or the whole sorry state of affairs.

"Quite."

But they had to tackle it. And they had no hope of cleaning anything up if they didn't approach it together. Why couldn't he see that?

"Sometimes that's just what life hands you, Marco. Life itself is often messy and unruly with unexpected turns and sometimes events just spill over and someone gets burned."

She blew out a breath and leaned over to turn the tap off. Then added, "You can't control everything all the time."

"Is that what you think I try to do?"

"Most definitely."

He handed her a kitchen towel. "Well, it appears I'm failing miserably at it all then."

Marco leaned his forearms against the wooden rail of the veranda overlooking the gardens and the hills in the distance. Brianna was upstairs securing ointment to further protect her damaged skin. Thank heavens the burns were minor.

He'd been so excited when he'd walked in and the delicious aroma of her cooking had greeted him. He'd known right away that it was her doing rather than the cook's. Her style had a distinctive characteristic all its own. Just like her. Only to find out she was working to apply for a job back in the States.

Marco slammed his fist against the railing and bit out a curse. He'd known it. This was exactly what he'd been trying to explain to Nonna during the car ride.

Every time he harbored any kind of illusion that Brianna might be a steady fixture in his life, she threw him some kind of curve. Since he'd met her his life had been like a fairy tale shattered by harsh bursts of reality in between scenes.

It would drive him crazy. The same kind of madness that had driven his father to ruin all those years ago. Well, he wouldn't let it. His reaction would be very different. Unlike his father, he could be strong and determined. And he could move on.

He heard her tentative footsteps behind him and tried to control his temper.

"Marco?"

"Do you need another taste tester, *cara*? If so, I'm afraid you'll have to find someone else."

"That's not why I'm here."

"Then what is it?"

She came to stand next to him. For endless seconds they both just stood side by side and stared at the scenery. At the beauty of Nonna's luscious, colorful flowers and bushes set against the backdrop of the dimming sunshine brought on by early evening.

"I simply wanted to send him some ideas, Marco. Just to see what he said. How could I have passed that up?"

"So you were merely looking for validation?"

He felt her shrug. "I suppose I was. Is that so wrong?"

"That's not something you want me to answer."

"That might be an answer in itself."

Marco pinched the bridge of his nose. Even now, he wanted to turn to face her. To take her in his arms and make her forget about that blasted phone call she'd received. A phone call that had sent their lives into yet another tailspin. "Then I have a question for you."

She let out a long, weary sigh. "What would that be?"

"What would you have done afterward? Once Ziyad gave you his answer?"

"Well, that would have depended on his answer."

Suddenly the frustration bubbling up within his chest threatened to overflow. Like her saucepan. "Don't be coy with me, Brianna. You know what I'm asking. I think I have a right to ask it."

"Fair enough."

"You're not answering."

"I don't know, Marco. I don't want to deal with hypotheticals."

He almost wanted to laugh at that. "The man located you half a world away. Chances are he was going to ask you to come work for him. The recipe was probably just a formality."

"Maybe you're right." She hesitated and he knew what she was going to say next, though he desperately hoped to be wrong. "I guess I would have wanted to see about accepting."

Marco felt something in his heart give way. He wasn't surprised. But the disappointment cut sharper than it should have. He should have known better than to let her get under his skin again. A family was just not in the cards for him. Not as a child. And not as an adult.

"But I wouldn't have just made the decision and then hoisted my choices onto your shoulders," she implored.

"What exactly does that mean?"

"It means we could have talked it over. Together. We could have discussed the pros and cons. Tried to come to some sort of mutual understanding."

"We would have fought."

She blew out a puff of frustration, turned to him. "This is what I mean about hypotheticals. All of this is moot until and if I actually get any kind of offer."

Did she even realize she was practicing clear avoidance?

He'd had enough. They could keep going around like this in circles. With Brianna there would always be the next potential opportunity, the next pursuit.

The next chance to escape. Just like his mother.

His temper spiked further. "You want to tell me that we can discuss things as a couple, come to a mutual decision. Is that right?"

"That's exactly what I'm saying."

"Then why didn't you tell me you were going to send in your recipes? Why was *that* not a matter of discussion?"

She actually stomped her foot. "You weren't even home! I had an idea and I just wanted to get started."

"Right." He stood upright and pivoted on his heel. Another useless conversation that was getting them nowhere. Marco felt tired. And angry. He hadn't even had a chance to change out of his work clothes. Whether she wanted to admit it or not—even to herself—Brianna had already made all sorts of decisions without consulting her husband.

"Don't walk away, Marco. It's what you always do."

She didn't understand. He had to walk away or things between them would take one of two turns. They'd either say things there would be no coming back from. Or they would fall into each other's arms. Neither scenario produced any kind of a lasting happy ending.

"It's been a long day, *cara*. And I believe you should tend to that burn some more."

"That can wait. It's not so bad anymore. I just want you to understand."

"Understand what exactly?"

"What it would mean to someone like me to be able to say I made it as a master chef one day. In one of the most competitive markets of the world, no less."

"Oh, but I do understand. You've told me countless times."

Her cheeks grew red with anger. "If you really did understand, you wouldn't have just said that. Why can't we ever just have a civil conversation? Just to hammer some things out?"

Why was she doing this? Why was she taunting him? Didn't she realize how close he was to the edge?

"You are not the kind of woman who wants her man to be civil, *cara*." He had no logical reason to say such a thing. He'd done it just to throw her off balance. He ignored the shame that came with admitting that to himself. But not the satisfaction that the comment seemed to hit the mark.

That seemed to take her back a step. "Stop that."

"Stop what?"

"Stop turning what I say into something seductive. I'm trying to have a conversation with you here."

"Is that what you're trying to do?"

"Yes. I'm trying to see if we can maturely, like adults, come to a solution about what was obviously a too hasty decision."

"Right. Your moving here. You appear to regret it now."

Her lower lip dropped. "Me? *I* appear to regret it? You've been a miserable troll just because you saw me working on some recipes. Don't even pretend differently."

He didn't know whether he was supposed to deny that. Was she looking for reassurance? If anything, that was too weak a word. He was beyond miserable. And he was beyond angry. More so at himself than anyone else. "So let's just decide what we want and work to rectify things."

What he wanted was to somehow go back to that day at the pond. When she'd been laughing and joking with him as they both played with their son. He wanted to somehow hold that moment in time and suspend it forever.

Marco bit his lip. This was ridiculous. He had to get away from her now. "Fine. Then work it out."

"What? Work what out?"

"You heard me. Ask the experts when it's safe for you and Enzo to return to the States."

"What?"

"That's what you want."

"I didn't say that's what I wanted."

"Because you don't really know. You never did. But I'm tired of arguing. Just figure out how quickly you're able to get back to New York." He bit out a curse. "You're right. Having two confused and warring parents is not in Enzo's best interest. We might be doing him a favor in the long term."

She raised her hands, palms up. "So that's it. I should just see about leaving with Enzo?"

Marco nodded, not even certain of what he was saying any more. He just wanted to get out of this conversation, get out of this house.

"Find your child psychologist. I'll put all the resources Dirici Foods has to ensure he gets the best professional money can buy. And I'll make sure he knows his papa will be a constant presence in his life. Just do what you have to do, Brianna. And then leave me alone."

She was shocked enough to let him pass this time. Marco raced upstairs for his car keys. He didn't want to think about what he'd just said. Or what he would do if Brianna took him at his word. Right now, he just wanted some fresh air. A long drive along the curvy stone cliff roads leading to town. Then perhaps he could drown his confusion in one of the bars there. It seemed like a good night to spend in a hotel.

He reached his suite and threw open the closet door to change into some fresher clothes. Something tugged at his attention and he glanced at the dresser drawer beneath the television. It always tugged at his attention but he never actually took it out. He should get rid of it, tear it up. Had meant to years ago. All the others had been disposed of.

Today. Right now. He pulled open the bottom drawer and pulled out the piece of paper, wilting and discolored due to constant handling by a small child years ago.

There was no need to hold on to it. No sentimental reasons, none due to happy memories.

He tore it into more than a dozen pieces. A mysterious letter he'd received from his mother about eighteen months after she'd left, telling him about her travels and her plans to visit again. A visit that never happened. The previous one had been the final time he'd seen her.

Then had come word decades later that she had passed.

It was about time he destroyed the letter. The last remaining reminder of Antonia Dirici. He should have destroyed it years ago, along with her photos.

Brianna chose that moment to step quietly into the room. "What was that?"

Marco bristled at the question. But he would answer it. "A letter. From *mi madre*. Right after she left for the last time."

He pointed to the shredded pieces of paper on the floor. "That's what broke my father finally and for good. Her sending me that letter left no doubt that she wouldn't be coming back. Not that time."

"Yet you kept it all these years."

"To remind myself. Of exactly what she did to him. So that I would never forget."

Brianna's words when she spoke were soft but firm.

"I didn't know him at all, but I have no doubt whatsoever that you're a much stronger man than your father."

"Then why did you leave?" He wasn't sure which one of them was more shocked at the question. He had no idea he'd intended to ask it. Let alone that he'd been thinking it.

He turned to study her. Brianna did indeed look as if at a loss for words. Finally, she found her voice. "We had a lot working against us, Marco. We were both unprepared."

"I wouldn't argue with any of that."

"Nor can you deny that you were not in a good place when you first met me. You were dealing with the news of your mother having just died."

He simply nodded.

"One of the many things you never told me, that you never shared."

"There was no point."

She sucked in a deep breath. "The point was that I was your wife. But you weren't really looking for one. You were looking simply for solace. Maybe even just a distraction."

"And what of you, *cara*? If I recall, you were nursing some wounds yourself. Your relationship had just abruptly ended. Would you have found yourself in my arms otherwise?"

"Maybe not. We clearly didn't give any of it enough thought. But the difference was, I was willing to try."

He quirked an eyebrow at her. "And you don't think I was?"

Her eyes started to glisten with tears and he wanted to kick himself. But all of this needed to be said. Here and now. Though her next words seemed to be causing her physical pain as she said them. "You clearly weren't ready to share your life with someone, Marco. Certainly not someone like me."

CHAPTER SIXTEEN

BRIANNA HEARD MARCO'S sports car roar to life and drive away from the garage toward the main gate. He hadn't told her where he was going, or how long he'd be gone. Nonna was resting. The staff were all busy. And Enzo was winding down before dinner.

She felt utterly alone. Unable to bear the solitude after her argument with Marco, she made her way to the door to head for the vineyards. She had to get out of this house the same way Marco had.

She didn't know how much time had passed when she heard a cheery masculine voice behind her. "We have got to stop meeting like this."

"Leo!" She turned and gave him a tight hug. Leo was one of those few people who could lighten the darkest mood. That was exactly what she needed right now.

"What are you doing here?" she asked him.

"I brought over some papers for Marco to sign. But it turns out he's not home."

"No, and I don't know when he'll be back."

Leo's smile faltered almost imperceptibly but he didn't ask any questions. "Then as I was driving past the vines, I saw you strolling along. Thought I'd stop by and say hello."

"I'm so glad you did."

"Need me to drive you back home again?"

She was nowhere near ready to return to the house, still needed the fresh air. "Actually, I'd like it much more if you walked with me a bit."

Leo held out his arm for her to take. "It would be an honor."

Slipping her hand into the crook of his elbow, she took the lead and resumed walking. "I never got a chance to apologize to you," she told him.

He squinted at her. "Whatever do you need to apologize for?"

"That day at the harbor. Before the regatta. I was horribly ill. I know it dampened the mood and probably ruined everyone's time." It had certainly ruined Marco's.

"Of course you don't have to apologize for that, dear. You can't help getting sick."

She wanted to kiss him on the cheek for his kindness. He'd never been anything less since she'd met him. Why couldn't she have fallen for someone like Leo? He was sweet-natured, lighthearted, with a good sense of humor. So unlike her husband.

And so not in any way enticing to her. Again, also very unlike her husband. She had to face it, she'd been drawn to that man without any hope of being able to resist.

"Still, it wasn't how I wanted to meet Marco's sailing friends for the first time."

"Those are more than just sailing friends. We've all known each other since childhood. They will most certainly understand."

"That Marco is married to someone who clearly doesn't belong?"

Leo stopped in his tracks, forcing her to halt midstride as well. "Brianna? Is there something specific on your mind?"

Brianna felt the sting of tears and bit the inside of her cheek from crying on Leo's shoulder right then and there.

"Isn't it obvious? I was like a complete fish out of water that day. If you'll pardon the pun."

Leo gave her a gentle smile.

"You just have to get used to the sea. It takes some people longer than others. We all grew up on it, including Marco. Sometimes we forget others are more landlocked."

"You're a kind soul, Leo. But none of that erases that fact that Marco has much more in common with people such as yourself and—" She made herself stop. This was so useless.

"And?"

She should stop this right now. At the least she was going to sound like a jealous insecure besotted fool, something she'd swore she would never be.

"And say for instance the ladies who were there that day. Like Talia for example."

Suddenly, understanding dawned on Leo's face. "Ah, I see," he said and looked away. Then he shocked her by laughing out loud.

"Shouldn't you be having this conversation with your husband?" he asked mid-laugh.

Ouch. He was right. She'd been too cowardly to do so. "You're right. Of course."

Leo's expression suddenly turned serious. More serious than she'd ever seen him. "I hope I'm not overreaching here, *mi tesoro*. But I've known Marco since we were both babes and...let's just say he can be complicated."

That was certainly putting it mildly. Brianna had to try hard not to roll her eyes. "Oh, I've definitely discovered that little fact on my own."

"He's also one of the most loyal men I've ever met. It's a rare quality these days."

Brianna inhaled deeply, taking in the sweet scent of the flowers and vines. "I just want to understand him, Leo. He doesn't make it easy."

Leo rubbed his chin. "No, I'm sure he doesn't. But maybe it will be enough to understand this—he's never been as happy as he has since little Enzo arrived. He truly loves that boy and relishes his role as a father."

He wasn't telling her anything she didn't know. Marco had done everything he could to make sure their son knew he was a cherished and loved child. She couldn't have hoped for more in that regard.

Leo went on before she could respond. "I've also never seen him so taken by a woman."

That statement did in fact surprise her. Leo was simply just trying to charm her, as was his nature. "Come on, Leo. I'm sure a man like Marco has had multiple liaisons. I'm not naïve."

Leo gave her a mischievous wink. "I didn't say he was a saint. But he's never acted so…affected, let's say."

She affected Marco?

Leo rubbed a gentle hand on her shoulder, the way an older sibling might to reassure a younger one. "Don't sell yourself short as far as your husband is concerned, love. I know my friend well and have no doubt that he cares deeply for you. You shouldn't either."

The sun had yet to set when Marco returned home. The drive had done him worlds of good. But unsettled feelings still churned in his gut. He made a beeline to his son's suite. He hadn't seen the boy all day and was dearly missing him. It was one thing to have him far away when he was a baby, but now that the boy was older he was such a sight to observe. Marco would be doing a lot of business in his New York offices if Brianna ended up back there.

At this point, that seemed very likely. Eventually, Brianna was going to make her way back to America. All signs pointed in that direction. Unless he did something about it. Unless he told her that it was the last thing he wanted.

He found Enzo in the tub. Brianna sat next to him as he played with an armada of plastic boats. He was up to his little armpits in foamy bubbles.

Brianna gave him a tentative smile when he walked in. Too weary to engage with her yet again, he simply motioned to his son. “Do you mind if I take over?”

Brianna stood. “Uh. Sure. He just got in though. He’ll be a while, the ships have a lot of maneuvers to complete.”

“That’s fine. I’d like some time with him.” Maybe the soothing presence of his son would help him pull some of his thoughts together, give him some kind of action plan.

She appeared on the verge of saying something else. Then seemed to think better of it.

“Certainly.” Handing him a baby towel, she walked out the bathroom door.

Marco crouched down on his knees by the side of the tub. Enzo gave his father a wide smile then shoved a boat under the water.

“That’s not a submarine, little man.” The innocuous comment earned him a loud giggle.

“This one is,” he said and plucked one of the toys out of the water.

“Toot. Toot.”

It was Marco’s turn to laugh. “Submarines don’t—” He stopped himself from making the correction. To a boy Enzo’s age, submarines could absolutely make train noises. The world was endless, the possibilities limitless. He would try to instill that belief system in his son.

He picked up another boat and held it in front of Enzo. “What sound does this one make?”

The boy actually roared.

Marco gave his hair a tousle. "There's something I want you to know," he told him even though he knew Enzo was too young to understand what he was about to say. "I want you to know Papa loves you. And he always will."

"Papa!" Enzo repeated with gusto.

"That's right. No matter how big you get, I'll always be your papa. Do you understand?"

Enzo nodded so enthusiastically his chin hit the water.

"Good. Remember that always."

Enzo would never be lacking a father. Marco had learned firsthand how important that was.

A soft knock at the door pulled him out of his thoughts. "I thought you might need some help getting him out and dry," Brianna said, sticking her head through the door.

"That'd be great, thanks."

As she stepped in with the towel, Marco lifted the boy up and placed him in his mother's arms. For one brief moment, their eyes locked. Marco had a strange urge to tell her all the things he'd just spoken to his son. Brianna needed to hear them too.

He should have said them long ago, when little Enzo was first born. He wanted her to understand that there were some things he was just barely coming to terms with himself. In his efforts to avoid falling into the trap his father had, Marco had subconsciously chosen avoidance. Rather than confront his fears of being a bad father himself, he had chosen to stay away. He'd learned as a child that it was easier and better for everyone involved if you kept your emotions in check.

Except that approach hadn't exactly worked out for him where Brianna was concerned. So he had to make the effort. He had to find a way to tell her that he would try. He would do everything he could to not only become a better husband and father but also a better man. And he would do it for her.

Brianna clutched Enzo to her chest and turned away as she nuzzled his cheek.

And the words escaped him. Yet another moment to say anything was gone.

CHAPTER SEVENTEEN

SHE'D NEVER BEEN this nervous preparing a meal before. Brianna glanced at the kitchen clock hanging on the wall above the sink. Marco would be home soon and it looked like she had pretty much timed everything perfectly.

The birds were ready to come out of the oven, the wine had been suitably aired, the salad adequately chilled. She had just enough time to shower and dress while the main course cooled. Thank the heavens.

He would be pleased. He had to be.

Though if she were being honest with herself, she had to admit this was as much for her as it was for her husband. Meal preparation had become almost a chore for her, part of her career aspirations. She had let her professional ambitions color the entire reason she'd wanted to become a chef in the first place. For the sense of home and family inherent in sharing a meal with loved ones.

Sighing, she took off the stained apron and undid her hair as she made her way up the stairs.

Yes, this evening was about more than simply preparing a meal. Hopefully, Marco would see that too. This was about Brianna Stedman proving her skills, her determination, and the sheer number of obstacles she'd overcome in her life.

So while Marco might not share much in common with

her in terms of background or privilege, maybe that wasn't so bad. Maybe that was what had drawn them together in the first place.

Maybe it was what would keep them together.

Brianna was waiting for him when Marco walked through the door after returning from the office. Whatever she had in mind, Marco wasn't sure he was up for it.

It had been a hell of a day. A simple deal had hit all sorts of snags and one of his vendors had threatened not to renew a very lucrative contract. The type of contract that would immediately affect his profit margin if Dirici Foods lost it. He couldn't allow that to happen. Marco would now have to fly out to Paris as soon as he could to meet with the man personally. So he wasn't quite ready with a response when his estranged wife greeted him as he entered.

But then he noticed she was dressed up. Very dressed up. In a sleek, shimmery little black dress that fit her form like a glove. A pink pearl choker adorned her neck. Her hair was piled atop her head with just enough wisps escaping to soften the effect.

She took his breath away. Marco had to tighten his hands into fists to keep from reaching for her. A better man would have figured out how to keep a lady like her by his side. A better man would have moved heaven and earth to make the marriage to her work out. He'd failed.

"Are you going somewhere?" he asked her.

Her smile was subtle, her lips curved in a sensual way. "Yes, as a matter of fact. But it's not far."

He'd never be able to figure this woman out. "And do you need something from me before you go?"

She walked over and took him by the arm. "You're coming with me."

What was she playing at? He really was in no mood for

any shenanigans after the day he'd had. If she knew him even a little, she would have sensed that.

"Brianna, I've had a rather long day. I just want to eat some dinner—"

She cut him off by actually touching a finger to his lips. The unexpected contact sent a shock wave through his cells. She hadn't so much as touched him in days.

"That's exactly what we're going to do," she told him. But instead of the main dining room, she led him over to the veranda.

What greeted him there looked like something out of a foodie magazine spread. A table covered in white linen sat where normally the patio lounge furniture would be. A warm, comfortable fire had been started in the fire pit. The table had been set with full place settings.

For two.

Brianna reached for a bottle of Cabernet sitting on a side table and began pouring it.

Well, this was all unexpected. "What is this?"

"Dinner."

Okay... "Where is everyone?"

"Nonna took Enzo with her to visit some of the ladies from church. And I gave everyone the day off."

Marco couldn't guess what she was up to. Nor could he quite figure out what to make of it. Deciding the easiest course would be to just let her explain, he shrugged off his jacket and tossed it on one of the chairs.

"I know it's a little earlier than our regular dining time, but I don't know how long Nonna and Enzo will be gone." She handed him a full glass of wine then held hers up. "Cheers."

The explanation wasn't forthcoming any time soon, it appeared. Marco took a large swig of his drink.

Setting his glass down he met her eyes. "Brianna, what is this?" he repeated.

"I told you. We are having dinner." She motioned for him to sit. He did so and she took the seat across from him. Several covered platters and bowls sat in the center of the table.

She cleared her throat. "It occurred to me that the only meals I've ever made for you were entrees like lasagna or *piccatta*. Or something along those lines."

"And?"

"My specialty is Spanish tapas. With some Mediterranean fusion incorporated, I've trained extensively to perfect such meals. Or I was before we…met."

Marco steepled his hands in front of his face as she started serving. "Is this some kind of attempt to convince me of your talent? Because I assure you it's hardly necessary. I don't even see the point—"

She cut him off. "This is arugula and basil salad with candied pecans and aged feta cheese. It's our first course. This won't be the traditional Italian menu. Like I said, as luck would have it, that's not my specialty."

"Am I to just accept that you woke up this morning and decided that what you wanted to do most today was cook for the two of us?"

"I've actually been thinking about it since we argued."

She had? "You're serious. You just up and decided that the thing we needed right now was to have you prepare a meal so that we could eat together?"

She nodded, swallowed her bite of salad and took another sip of her wine. "Partly. Our main course is to be young game hen with a raspberry coulis sauce and a side of truffle creamed paella. As for dessert, that's also not in my area of expertise. Therefore I just ran out for some chocolate gelato earlier this afternoon."

Yet another evasion. Was she trying to make him crazy? Here she was talking about gelato and game hens when he had no idea what was happening between them at the moment. "What do you mean 'partly'?"

She slowly set her fork down on the side of her plate. "We never really had romantic dinners, or date nights, or even went to the movies for that matter. Did we, Marco?"

"No, I guess we didn't." He was starting to see her point. What little he and Brianna knew about one another, even after all this time, had been learned on the fly. After they were already husband and wife. Almost like a modern-day arranged marriage.

A spark ignited in his chest. She was making an effort. It surprised him how touched he was.

"Do you want to know why I became a chef, Marco."

He swallowed. "Very much so."

"Remember that foster mother I was telling you about?"

"The ex-dancer?"

She smiled at him, clearly pleased that he remembered. "Yes, that's the one. See, she had this routine. Despite all her faults, she was good to me and the other children. Her lifestyle wasn't the best but she did a lot of things right."

"Such as?"

"Such as always making sure we had a warm meal. Every evening, no matter what was happening, she ensured something hot was on the table."

"She sounds like a remarkable woman."

"She was. I lost touch with her over the years. After a while, it was too painful to keep in contact." She gave a small shrug of her shoulders. "And she didn't try very hard either. Who knows, maybe my days in her home meant more to me than they did to her." Her eyes glistened with tears. "The day they pulled me out of that house, the most secure, stable one I'd ever been in, I swore I would never forget the importance of having that meal on the table."

"I'm glad you've finally told me."

"I should have told you before." She wiped away the

moisture from her eyes with the back of her hand. "I realize now that I put too much in your hands. You weren't exactly ready for marriage and a child either." She chewed the inside of her cheek. "It's just that you've always seemed so strong to me, so capable. I figured I'd lay most of the burden on your shoulders. But now I've come to realize that I'm both those things as well."

She picked up her fork again, but didn't continue eating. Just sort of twirled it around her fingers. When she spoke again her voice was stronger, more firm. "You were right that I wasn't very open myself. See, I thought I had an excuse. I was ashamed. Embarrassed about who I was and how I'd grown up. But that doesn't matter. I'm me. I may not know much about Italian cooking. I'd like to work on that."

"Bree, you don't need to—"

She cut him off with a wave of her hand. "I want to. But in the meantime, I'd like you to discover and enjoy what I do have to offer."

Marco's mouth went dry. His wife was one brave and remarkable woman. How could he have ever doubted that about her? How could he have doubted her strength or resilience?

He owed it to her to be brave in return.

The parallels in their respective pasts were striking if one thought about it. Why she was so determined to make her own way, to be successful in her own right. Also the reason she was so afraid that their marriage might not be successful long-term.

Whatever it took, he would prove to her that it could.

She took a large gulp of her wine and looked into his eyes. "So you see, Marco. We're much more alike than you would have ever guessed. It appears we both need to draw on some patience until we figure all this out. Are you willing to do that? With me?"

His mind went numb, he had to scramble for the right words. "Yes, *cara*. More than anything. And there's no one else I'd rather share my life or a child with."

A wealth of emotion cascaded over her face. "We're so lucky to have our boy, aren't we? And he's growing up so fast."

He couldn't help his grin of pride. "Like an active vine during harvest. Bree, I don't want either of us to miss a moment of it. I want both of us to be there for him when he attends his first day of nursery school, when he makes his first best friend." He gave a mock shudder. "When he throws his first pitch of a baseball."

"I want all that too," she said with a rasp. "It's all I've ever wanted. To truly live as a family. With our son."

Marco itched to go to her, to lift her in his arms. He forced himself to remain seated instead. There was so much more he owed it to her to say. "But Enzo deserves a mother who feels fulfilled."

Her eyes grew wide. "What are you saying?"

"I don't want you to give up your dreams, Bree." He took a deep breath, steadying himself to say his next words. "If you still want to make a name for yourself in New York, we'll find a way. We'll make it happen."

Her eyes filled with tears once more. "You don't know how much that means to me, Marco. But I've been thinking. And I've had a change of heart."

He could only blink at her. After all her training, all her drive, she couldn't mean she was ready to give up her career. "You have?"

She nodded. "Working on those marketing recipes gave me a taste of what it would be like to be independently employed."

"I don't understand."

"I'd like to keep coming up with recipes for your product line. If you could still use them."

She had no idea. "Of course. But will that be enough for you, Bree? That was meant to be just a temporary plan."

"I've also got some ideas for another project."

"What kind of project?"

Her face lit up like a child on Christmas morning as she began to speak. "I'd like to work on a cookbook. To be published under my maiden name." She searched his face. "So there isn't any influence based on the Dirici brand. You do understand that, don't you?"

Rather than answer, he stood and walked around the table. Gently taking her hand, he pulled her up to stand next to him.

"*Si.* And there's something I'd like you to understand."

"What's that?" she asked as he took her by the waist and pulled her to him.

"That about three years ago, when I inadvertently walked into that kitchen, I met the woman I was supposed to spend the rest of my life with. The woman I was meant to fall in love with."

Brianna sucked in a breath and leaned against him. "And I met the man of my dreams. The man I've been in love with ever since."

As if on cue, the fire behind them sparked, sending bright golden embers shooting into the air. He watched over Brianna's head as they drifted and fluttered on the breeze.

"There's one more thing," he added, rubbing her cheek. "I just decided I really rather like poultry served cold." Then he took her lips with his own.

"You do, huh?" she whispered, breathless from his kiss.

"*Si.* And another thing, I don't want dessert either." He took her by the hand and headed inside. "Not until much, much later," he added, as he led her upstairs.

EPILOGUE

HOW IN THE world had she been talked into this? Brianna took Marco's hand and allowed him to help her up the steps and onto the boat. Immediately, she felt a small tickle at the bottom of her stomach. They hadn't even left the slip yet.

"I don't know about this," she declared and gripped his fingers tighter.

"It will be all right, *cara.* Trust me."

"If you say so."

He pulled her up against him, his back to her chest. Then he tilted her chin up to look out at the ocean. "There are lots of ways to avoid the seasickness. I'll show you."

Brianna bit back the apprehension that only served to make her nausea worse. "Fine. What do you suggest?"

"Okay, first of all, keep looking at the distance. It's like being up high. Do not look down."

"All right. What else."

"Keep your knees slightly bent."

He couldn't be serious with this, could he? "My knees?"

He nodded against her cheek. "*Si, cara.* It helps to maintain your center of balance."

She did as she was told. "What else?"

"As soon as you feel an inkling of dizziness, pinch the inside of your palm." He took her hand and demonstrated. "Do that as often as necessary. All that will certainly help."

"That's it?" she asked, incredulous. "That's all I need to know to keep the seasickness under control?"

He seemed to think for a moment. "Wait. There is one more thing." He reached into his pocket and pulled out a small plastic bottle. The label had Italian lettering and pictures of a plane and a ship. "You should also just take one of these. Then you won't have to do all that other stuff I just told you. It's all actually pretty useless."

Motion sickness medicine.

Brianna gave him a playful slap on the hand. "Ha-ha. Very funny."

He kissed her then, and she felt the heat clear through her core. The man's effect on her would be her undoing. And she would love every minute of it.

"I'm serious," Marco told her. "You need to have a good supply of these on hand. A good portion of our honeymoon will involve quite a bit of sailing."

Had she heard him correctly? This morning, he'd surprised her with an invitation to the marina, so she could get accustomed slowly to being on the water. Was it possible this was more than that?

"Honeymoon?"

"It occurs to me we never really took an official one. I'd like to rectify that."

Words failed her. The act was so thoughtful, so heartfelt she felt tears spring to her eyes. She didn't realize Marco had actually cared about the informal and rather rushed way they'd begun their marriage. "I'd like that very much."

"There's also something else I'd like to rectify."

"What's that?"

"I never actually offered you a proper proposal," he said, then shocked her by getting down on one knee.

Reaching once more into his pocket, he pulled out a small velvet box. Then opened it to reveal a shimmering emerald surrounded by diamonds on a delicate gold chain.

Enzo's birthstone.

Marco cleared his throat, his voice hoarse when he spoke. "You already have a ring. So I thought this might be more appropriate."

Brianna's fingers trembled as she reached for it. "Oh, Marco. It's lovely." So beyond merely appropriate, this delicate piece of jewelry was the perfect symbol of the renewed bond of their marriage as well as their devotion to their child. He had put so much thought into the gesture.

"Brianna Dirici, would you please do me the honor of marrying me? Again?"

"Yes!" She kissed him with all the love and all the elation that was currently bursting through her heart. "I would be honored to marry you! Again and again and—"

She didn't get a chance to say any more.

* * * * *

A BRIDE FOR LIAM BRAND

JOANNA SIMS

Dedicated to my sister, Beth Elaine…
Thank you for being one of my first editors
and shaping the writer I have become.
I love you.

Chapter One

"Mommy!"

Callie's scream caused Kate King to drop the heavy Western saddle she was carrying and run toward the sound of her daughter's voice.

"Mommy!"

"Callie!" Kate ran down the wide, center aisle of her fifty-stall barn. "Callie!"

The mother and daughter nearly collided when Kate rounded a corner at the end of the long, concrete aisle.

"What's wrong?" Kate put her hands on her daughter's shoulders, giving her face and body a cursory check with her concerned eyes.

Callie's round face was flushed bright red and drenched with tears and sweat. Her daughter was eighteen-years-old, an adult by any standard, but Callie had been born with Down syndrome. Negative emotions, in particular, were difficult for Callie to process.

"Take a minute." Her daughter was gasping for air, struggling to speak. "Catch your breath."

Callie leaned forward a bit, closed her eyes, coughed several times and followed her mother's instructions.

"Visa..." Callie finally got the words out. "He's hurt, Mommy!"

Kate was, at first, relieved that her daughter wasn't the one injured, but the last thing a horse owner wanted to hear was that one of the herd was injured. So, the relief she had originally felt was fleeting.

"It's okay, Callie." Kate gave her daughter a steady look. "Let's go see what's going on with him."

It was just a fact of life that her daughter didn't have many friends in their community; Bozeman, Montana, was a small town surrounded by ranches and uninhabited swaths of land. There simply weren't any other young adults with a similar disability living close by—so every animal on their ranch was Callie's friend. And she took it hard if any of her friends were injured or sick.

Visa, whose registered name was Expense Account, was a rare member of their horse-breeding ranch. The majority of the horses on the Triple K Ranch were Quarter horses with excellent pedigrees. Visa, on the other hand, was a Dutch Warmblood and Hanoverian mix, and he was Callie's favorite.

Together, they walked quickly out to the pasture closest to the barn; each horse had its designated pasture and turnout time. Visa, who wasn't the most assertive horse in the herd, was always turned out with the older, more experienced geldings.

Kate spotted typically social and "in everyone's business" Visa, standing alone and away from the herd. The owner of the Triple K, her brow furrowed with concern, unlatched the gate to the pasture.

"Wait for me here, please, Callie."

"I—I want to help." Her daughter said.

"Callie." Her tone brooked no argument. "This I need you to wait here, please."

Callie, in her own right, was a talented horsewoman; she had been raised working with these elegant creatures and had been riding before she could walk. But, in this moment, Kate didn't want the distraction of watching out for Callie while she tried to figure out what was going on with Visa.

"Hi, good-looking boy," Kate said as she approached Visa. She spoke in a calm soothing voice that she used with all of the horses.

Visa was a beautiful russet-red with black legs and a black mane and tail. The horse, which typically greeted her with a friendly head bump, pinned back its ears at her, gnashed his teeth, and tossed his head aggressively. Visa loved to scratch his face by rubbing his head on her shoulder and arm; his unusual behavior served to underscore the fact that something was wrong.

"Okay. Okay," Kate said in a low, gentle voice, ignoring the pinned ears and his attempts to bite her while she began to take inventory of his physical state. The biggest red flag for her was the fact that he wasn't putting weight on his right hind leg.

"Why are you standing way out here all by yourself?" Kate ran her hand along the young horse's muscular body. "That's not like you."

Careful not to move in a way that would spook Visa,

Kate kept her right hand on his haunch while she bent forward to get a closer look at the hind leg. There was a distinctive gash above Visa's hoof it looked like a crescent, and she immediately suspected that the young gelding had got too nosey with one of the older horses and been kicked for his trouble.

"Easy, Visa. Let me just take a quick look. Did you get kicked?" She ran her hand down the leg; the moment she got near the gash with her fingers, Visa lifted his leg to pull it away from her.

Kate straightened her body, acid beginning to roil in her stomach. A leg injury in a horse was never good news.

"Okay," she said softly to Visa. "Let's see you walk."

The horse trainer hooked her finger into the horse's halter and clucked her tongue to get Visa to walk a step forward. The horse jerked his head, resisting at first, before he agreed to take a couple of steps forward. The second he tried to put weight on that right hind leg, Kate's suspicions were confirmed: Visa was lame. She couldn't know, without an X-ray, how bad the injury was. But there was an undisputable truth of horse ownership—no legs, no horse.

Kate called out to her daughter to fetch her a lead rope. Red-faced and sweaty, Callie handed her the rope.

"I-is he hurt b-bad?"

"I'm not sure, kiddo. Let's get him back to the barn and we'll call Dr. McGee. Do me a favor. Go check Visa's stall and make sure it's been cleaned."

While her daughter rushed back into the barn, lead rope in hand, Kate headed back to Visa.

"This is going to be hard, Visa. But we'll do it together." She clipped the lead rope to the horse's halter and began the painstaking walk back to the barn.

Along the way, the rest of the herd, curious creatures, tried to join them in their journey, but Kate shooed them away. One of Visa's pasture mates had seriously injured him, that much she knew, but she couldn't pinpoint which horse had done the damage.

Callie hurriedly opened the gate so Visa could limp through.

"I-is he going to b-be okay? He looks like he's hurt b-bad." Tears had returned to Callie's brown eyes.

"It might be a broken leg, Callie. I'm not sure." Kate had always told her daughter the truth. "But I do know that we have to be strong for Visa. We have to be calm so he can stay calm. You have to try, okay?"

"Okay," Callie said as she shut the gate behind them. "I—I'll try."

It took a long time to get the lame horse back to his stall; once he was settled, Kate asked Callie to get Visa a pad of hay to keep him occupied while she called her regular vet.

"Oh, Kate," Dr. McGee's receptionist, Dawn, said, "I'm so sorry, but Dr. McGee is out with the flu—sick as a dog, poor man."

Kate shook her head in frustration. Dr. McGee had been her vet for years, and she simply didn't trust anyone else with her horses.

"It sounds like you need someone right away." The receptionist filled in the silence. "I can refer you to Dr. Brand. I have his number right here if you'd like to have it."

Kate had gone to school with Liam Brand, starting in kindergarten. Yes, she grew up with him, and yes, she ran into him every now and again in town. But she had no idea what kind of veterinarian skills Liam Brand had. Unfortunately, she wasn't in a position to question her own vet's referral. Kate took the number, thanked the receptionist for her time and then immediately called Dr. Brand.

"He-*llo*." Liam Brand tapped the green telephone symbol to answer the phone quickly so he could still keep his eyes on the road.

"May I speak with Dr. Brand, please?"

"You got 'im."

"Hi, Dr. Brand. This is Kate King." The woman on the other end of the line paused for a second. "Triple K Ranch?"

Large-animal veterinarian Liam Brand didn't want to let on, but he didn't need any additional qualifiers beyond Kate's name to identify who she was. He was a little old to have a crush, he supposed, but she certainly had caught his interest when their paths had crossed from time to time in the small Montana town of Bozeman. They had known each other all their lives, but Kate wasn't much on small talk with old acquaintances, so he typically admired her from afar.

"How can I help you, Ms. King?"

"Kate," she corrected. "One of my horses turned up lame this morning. Dr. McGee is out sick today, as I'm sure you know by now. I really need someone to come out to the ranch and x-ray Visa's leg. Would you be able to fit me into your schedule? I know it's short notice, but I'd really appreciate it."

Liam already knew that he had back-to-back appointments—it was foaling season, so he was typically booked dawn until dusk.

"I do know about Dr. McGee—I've been getting calls all day from his clients. I'm double booked."

"Dr. Brand." Liam could hear the stress in her voice. "I know you're swamped, but any help you can give me would really be appreciated. It doesn't matter how late you get here." She paused before she added, "Visa is Callie's favorite horse."

The minute Kate mentioned her daughter, Callie, Liam felt that familiar tug on his heartstrings. He'd watched Callie grow over the years; for a while there, before the divorce, his son had attended the same school. She was a special little girl—always smiling, always laughing. If Kate was trying to sway him by mentioning her daughter, it had worked.

After taking a couple of moments to make a decision, Dr. Brand finally said, "Here—let me pull over so I can figure this out."

"Okay. Thank you."

Liam pulled his mobile-vet truck onto the side of the road so he could take a closer look at his schedule. All of his clients were so far apart that driving time made his logjammed schedule even more complicated.

"Let's do this," he finally offered. "I'll come to the Triple K after my last appointment. I'll warn you now—it's gonna be late. After dark, for sure."

"That's not a problem! Whenever you can get here!" Kate exclaimed in a way that made him smile a bit. "I can't thank you enough, Dr. Brand. Truly. Thank you."

As he had predicted, Dr. Liam Brand arrived at the Triple K Ranch after dark. For Kate and Callie, it had been a long day of waiting. When they heard Dr. Brand's truck wheels making a crunching noise on their gravel driveway, both Kate and her daughter abandoned their mucking and jogged to the entrance of the barn to greet Dr. Brand.

"I'm sorry I couldn't get here any sooner," the large-animal vet told her.

"We're just so grateful that you could come." Kate offered her hand. "I know you've already had a long day."

Liam Brand was over six feet tall with a slender physique of a man who took care of his health. His hair, cut short, had turned a dark honey color over the years, which offset, in a very appealing way, the sky blue of his eyes and the golden color of his skin. He was wearing jeans, stained from a day on the job, with the logo of his vet clinic embroidered on the left chest of a light-blue cotton top.

"Hello, Calico." Dr. Brand took the time to acknowledge her daughter.

Liam knew that her daughter's nickname was Callie, but he had always used her formal, given name "Calico" whenever he spoke to her.

Callie smiled shyly at Liam; Kate knew that look in her daughter's large, brown eyes. The young woman developed crushes in the blink of an eye and Liam Brand, Kate observed, was Callie's official new crush.

"Hi," Callie said, ducking her head to the side and gave an embarrassed laugh.

"Let's go see what's going on with Visa," Dr. Brand said after he lifted his rolling mobile-vet kit out of the back of his truck, which had been outfitted with everything a traveling large-animal vet would need to do his or her job.

Dr. Brand wanted to see Visa walk on the concrete; the horse had taken only a few steps before the vet nodded. He asked that they put Visa in cross ties, and then, silently, methodically, with the seriousness Kate appreciated, the vet began his physical exam of the Hanoverian mix. After a thorough exam, Dr. Brand offered some possible diagnoses. The possible culprits for Visa's lameness had all occurred to Kate as well—it could be laminitis, it could be a soft tissue injury, there was a possibility of an abscess in the hoof. But the last possibility that Dr. Brand mentioned, a fracture of the short pastern bone, the bone right above the hoof, was the diagnosis Kate feared the most. Most equine ailments could be healed with the right care and the right perseverance. A fracture? That was a whole different ball of wax. Kate didn't hesitate to agree to get Visa x-rayed.

Kate and Callie stood by Visa's head, offering him encouraging words as the vet set up the portable X-ray machine. If she had wondered about Liam's ability as a veterinarian, watching him now dispelled all of those notions. No, he wasn't as experienced as Dr. McGee, but he was thorough, deliberate and spoke as if he had memorized every textbook he read. While he worked, Liam discussed the recent literature and findings from current research. There wasn't a question she asked him that he didn't answer with the breadth and depth of a man who knew his business. When Liam had as many years of practice under his belt as Dr. McGee, he was going to be a top-notch veterinarian.

Dr. Brand released Visa back to his stall, and by the time Kate returned, the vet was ready to discuss the results of the X-ray. With her arm around Callie's shoulders, as much for her own support as to comfort her daughter, Kate stood close to Dr. Brand so she could see the X-ray of Visa's hind leg projected on the screen. The news wasn't good—she could see that before he even began to point to the hairline fracture in the short pastern bone.

"I-is he going to b-be okay?" Callie already had tears in her eyes; yes, her daughter had a serious intellectual disability, but she understood much more about life than most people would give her credit for.

Kate tightened her arm to hold her daughter to comfort her.

"Well." Dr. Brand's words were measured as he addressed them both. "If Visa was going to have a fracture on his leg, this is the best place to do it."

She had been holding her breath again; Kate told herself to keep on breathing. She was fully expecting Liam to tell her that Visa, only five and so young, would have to be put down.

"If you keep him on stall rest for two months, I can come back and take another X-ray to see if he's done some healing," Dr. Brand said. "Of course, Dr. McGee would be able to help you with that, as well."

Kate took a second to process the information before she replied, "You've started with him. I'd feel better if you just stayed with this case."

"I'd be happy to do it."

All three of them turned to walk in the direction of the vet's truck; Kate already had her checkbook in her back pocket to pay.

"How much do we owe you?"

"I don't really handle that part of the deal. Go ahead

and call the office tomorrow. Ask for Irene—she handles all the billing." He pulled a card out of the console of his truck and handed it to her. "She'll take care of you."

"Okay," Kate said, surprised that Liam didn't take payment on the spot. "Are you sure?"

"Yep." Liam opened one of the storage lockers built onto the back of his truck.

"Do you like chili?" Callie asked the vet.

"Sure do." Dr. Brand loaded his mobile kit into the locker.

Kate liked that Liam didn't disregard her daughter—he included her, he looked at her directly and spoke to her like she had value.

"Do you want to have chili with us? That's what we're having for dinner."

Kate hadn't expected her daughter to extend a dinner invitation to Liam; even more unexpected was her own follow-up to Callie's invitation.

"We have plenty," she told Liam. "It's the least we could do. I'm sure you skipped dinner so you could come out here."

Liam didn't say yes or no as he loaded his equipment into his truck.

"Do you like orange or grape soda?" Callie asked Liam. "Which do you want?"

Kate put her hand on her daughter's shoulder. "He hasn't accepted your invitation yet."

Liam locked the back of his truck. "I like grape."

For the briefest of seconds, Liam caught Kate's eye, and she saw something so strong and kind in those blue eyes that she had to remind herself to look away.

"I—I like grape, too!" Callie told the vet excitedly,

as if she had just discovered that they had something very special in common.

Her daughter spun around and headed off in the direction of their modest ranch-style house with the new steel roof and fresh coat of moss green paint.

"I'm sorry," Kate told him when her daughter was out of earshot. "I hope she didn't put you on the spot."

"I'm hungry, and all I've got in my icebox is a piece of suspicious cheese and condiments." Liam adjusted his long legs so he could keep pace with her.

Kate cracked a smile. "Well, then, I'm glad she invited you."

She caught Liam staring at her profile. "I don't usually say yes. But we're talking about chili and grape soda. An offer like that doesn't come up every day."

It had been a long day for Liam Brand; he was grateful and honored that a man like Dr. McGee—a man he admired—would send his clients to him when he was out sick. But the 50 percent increase in appointments, which entailed juggling his already booked days with Dr. McGee's overflow, had put him under the gun and way behind. He was exhausted—and he usually wasn't exhausted. If it had been anyone other than Kate King and Callie who invited him in for dinner, he would have gracefully declined and headed home.

"We weren't expecting anyone," Kate told him as she picked up random items on the way to the kitchen.

The King home was cozy and lived-in. The outside of the house had some updating recently, but the inside was like stepping back in time to the 1970s. Kate was known in the greater Bozeman area as one of the best horse trainers and breeders in the state of Montana. Her techniques for training horses and riders in a humane manner was the stuff of legends; on the other hand, homemaking did not seem to be much of a priority. The furniture hadn't been updated since Kate was a kid. In fact, Liam remembered sitting on that same forest green and navy blue plaid couch back when he was in elementary school one summer when his father came out to the Triple K to buy some new horses from Kate's father. It was obvious that every bit of her heart, her soul, her time and her money went to taking care of her daughter and her horses. That was her love, and he could appreciate that about her because that was exactly how he felt about life: family and horses mattered more than stainless-steel appliances and granite countertops.

"Something smells mighty good in here." Liam sat at the small kitchen island with the sunshine-yellow laminate countertop.

What the King house lacked in decor, it more than made up for it in the homey feel and a tantalizing aroma permeating the kitchen.

"Grandpa taught me." Callie lifted the lid off the large pot on the stove.

"I didn't know you were the chef of the family," Liam said to Kate's daughter.

"Callie is the only chef in this house," Kate gave her daughter a quick hug from behind. "Thank goodness she loves to cook, or we'd both starve. Isn't that true, kiddo?"

Callie nodded seriously. "That is true. I-I have saved us from starving."

Liam sat at Kate King's counter, watching the horse trainer interact with her daughter, while he gulped down grape soda, which he hadn't had since he was a kid.

This visit to the Triple K Ranch was an unexpected blast into his past.

Every time he emptied a can of soda, Callie would put another cold can of it in front of him. He didn't even have to ask. It had been a long time since Liam felt like he was part of a family; he'd been separated for several years, and the divorce had finally been settled the year before. The judge had granted full, physical custody of their two children to his ex-wife and liberal visitation to him; now he was a long-distance father to two teenagers. His son and daughter lived in Seattle, Washington, with his ex-wife and her new husband. Although he had known that his ex-wife, Cynthia, had been dating during their separation, it had still been a shock when she remarried so quickly after the divorce had been finalized. He hated being a video-chat father and a "see you on your next school break" dad. But, that fight was over and he had lost—big time.

He'd always been the kind of man who wanted to be married, to have kids, to make a home with a woman. But it hadn't worked out that way. Liam had his work—his salvation—and a big family with lots of siblings, yet he always went home to an empty house. He liked being in Kate King's house, chitchatting and laughing about nothing in particular while Calico stirred the chili and put an extra place setting on the table.

Once Callie announced that she was ready to serve, Liam joined them at their little square table, wobbly on its legs, and hungrily dived into the large bowl of chili. Perhaps he shouldn't have been so shocked at how good the chili was—perhaps he underestimated Callie because of her disability—but Callie's chili was incredible.

Two bowls later, Liam was completely stuffed and wishing he hadn't been so greedy. He felt more like curling up on Kate's old plaid couch than driving forty-five minutes back to his family's ranch, Sugar Creek.

"That was the best chili I've ever had," he told Kate's daughter. "Hand's down. The best."

Callie smiled shyly with pleasure, sometimes finding it difficult to look him in the eye.

As she picked up his bowl to take it to the sink, Callie said, "I-I'm making steak and garlic mashed potatoes tomorrow night."

Liam smiled at her. "I'm sure that's going to be another masterpiece of a meal, Calico."

She stood by his chair, his bowl in hand. "Do you want to come for dinner tomorrow?"

Liam saw Kate's expression, fleeting as it was; she had no idea Callie would invite him for a second dinner, and she wasn't on board with the idea. Kate sanitized her expression quickly as she said, "Callie, I'm sure Dr. Brand can't come out all this way just for dinner."

"Actually—" he didn't plan it; the words just popped out of his mouth "—I think that steak and garlic mashed potatoes are *definitely* worth the drive. What time's dinner?"

Chapter Two

"I still don't know *what* possessed you to invite Dr. Brand for dinner tonight, Callie!" Kate said as she was attempting to stuff a family pack of paper towels onto the top shelf of her pantry.

"He likes my cooking."

Kate had been irritated all day about their dinner guest. She was annoyed with her daughter for extending the invitation, and she was even more annoyed with Liam for accepting.

"Everyone loves your cooking." She shoved the paper towels hard with both hands.

Callie put her hand over her mouth and giggled. "True."

No matter how hard she shoved that stupid pack of paper towels, it refused to fit into the space. Kate stared at the offending paper towels before she sighed, grabbed ahold of the plastic encasing the paper towels and yanked on it until she pulled it free and dropped it onto the floor.

"We don't have company during the week." She picked up the paper towels and put them on top of the refrigerator.

"I—I know." Her daughter was busy gathering the ingredients she would need to make dinner. Callie always needed help with measuring, but she could follow her list of ingredients and then double-check after she was done. "B-but," her daughter said as if she were the parent, "you're gonna need someone to eat dinner with when I—I'm living in New York."

This had been a conversation that had been going on for years. In spite of her disability, Callie was a very goal-oriented young woman. She wanted to live in New York City on her own, go to culinary school and then open a restaurant. Kate had always supported Callie's dreams, but there had to be limits.

"You know that New York isn't an option, Callie. Our life is here at the Triple K."

"That's why I—I'm going without you." Her daughter put her armful of ingredients on the counter. "You stay here, and I—I go to New York."

This was said with another giggle.

Kate walked up behind her daughter, wrapped her arms around her shoulders and kissed her on the cheek. "I love you, sweet girl."

Always affectionate ever since she was a baby, Callie turned in her arms and hugged her tightly. "Don't be afraid, Mommy. I—I'll be okay."

"If you want to move out, Callie, you know I support that. But you've got to take baby steps. Get a place in town."

"I-I'll live in New York first."

This wasn't the first, or last, discussion about New York. Down syndrome hadn't quelled Callie's ability to dream big for herself; she was goal-oriented and ambitious, dreaming of attending culinary school in New York City. For someone born with Down syndrome, Callie was on the higher end of the spectrum as far as her IQ was concerned, but there would never be a time when she could live independently in a small town like Bozeman, much less in the largest city in the country. Her daughter was so full of life, so full of dreams, but simple, daily tasks, like taking money out of an ATM machine, stumped Callie.

It was important to Kate that her daughter gain as much independence as possible; they had often spoken about Callie finding an apartment in town. Kate had even been in touch with a local, non-profit organization that supported individuals with disabilities to review options for transitional living in Bozeman. But every time they discussed moving, Callie inevitably circled back to her goal of moving to the Big Apple.

"You may move out and hate it," Kate teased her daughter.

"No." Callie said, emphatically. "I-I know what I want."

She waited for Callie to slowly go over the ingredient list, check each item off as she doubled-checked to make certain she had everything she needed. Her daughter leaned her elbows on the counter, her face very close to the enlarged print on the recipe card, talking aloud to herself as she went along. It had taken years to develop this routine, this step toward independent life, and Kate was proud to watch Callie make continued progress. Her daughter had gotten the King stubbornness and determination quite honestly.

"I—I'm ready," Callie told her.

Kate stayed with Callie, making sure all of her measurements were accurate, before she headed back to the barn. The barn, the ranch, was both her albatross and her solace. When she was angry or upset, there was nothing better for it than mucking out stalls. But the work was never ending and there was always something that needed to be fixed.

"Well, Visa." She had ended hours of work back at the injured horse's stall. Now that he was stall bound, she spent more time with him. He was a young horse and to be stuck in a twelve by twelve space for months was going to be tough for him.

Kate rubbed the space between Visa's eyes, then twirled his long, black forelock around her finger.

"Guess who's coming for dinner?" The horse trainer frowned at the thought.

Halfway through her work, she had thought to call Liam and give him a chance to get off the hook. But in the end, she thought better of it. Liam was a smart man; he'd figure out that she was trying to revoke her daughter's invitation. No, if he wanted out, he'd let her know. She knew that she had a reputation in Bozeman for being private and a bit standoffish, but no one could legitimately pin rudeness on her and she'd like to keep it that way. All she could really do was hope that Liam's schedule would prevent him from coming all the way out to the Triple K. The rest of the afternoon, while she paid bills in the office above the barn, Kate hoped that her phone would ring. But often times, hoping wasn't enough to make something happen.

"Howdy!" Liam Brand had been looking forward to heading out to the Triple K all day.

In fact, the day didn't seem to go by fast enough.

"Hi, Dr. Brand." Kate was kneeling at the front of the barn, surrounded by a pride of ragtag barn cats who had seen better days.

Liam sensed that the horse trainer was still in the process of warming up to the idea of him having dinner at her ranch for the second night in a row; even when she wasn't smiling, with the light of a smile reaching her eyes, Liam still thought she was mighty pretty.

"I'd appreciate you callin' me Liam." He stopped a few feet away from her. "We go back an awful long way."

Instead of responding, Kate finished feeding her barn cats. "I have to have the oldest barn cats ever. I've got to feed them now—they're too old to catch mice anymore."

Liam laughed. Kate's cats were bony from old age, with noticeable cataracts, scraggly fur and weak meows. One brown tabby cat with narrow shoulders, curled white whiskers and a barrel belly broke away from the group to greet him. Her scratchy meow touched his heart as he knelt to pet her.

"Sissy." Kate glanced up from her chore. "She's the flirt of the barn."

The old feline rubbed her face and body against Liam's knee, purring hard and loud, before falling onto her side at his feet. Sissy gave him a slow blink, a sign of love from a cat, while her paws curled under happily.

"Love has always been more important to her than food."

Liam petted the retired mouser until the feline decided it was, indeed, time to fill her belly. Kate stood and he joined her. They watched the ex-mousers make short work of the food she had put down for them.

"I can't seem to get her eyes cleared up," Kate said after a minute or two. "They're always so swollen. Allergies, I suppose."

"I'll give you one of the ointments I like to use with cats before I leave."

"Thanks." She seemed surprised when she said, "I'd really appreciate that."

Liam wanted to check on his patient, swinging by Visa's stall before he strode beside Kate back to the house. It occurred to him, as he walked next to the horse trainer, that he didn't have to measure his stride. She had some long legs of her own, and it was nice to walk beside her.

"Look who I found!" Kate said to her daughter when they entered the small ranch house.

"Hi, Dr. Brand!" Callie immediately met them just inside the door and hugged him in that friendly way of hers.

"It smells mighty good in here again, Calico," Liam told the young lady.

"She's been cooking all day." Kate shut the door.

"I've been thinking about your cookin' all day," he said.

"I hope you brought your appetite," the pretty rancher said. "I think my daughter cooked for ten."

"Trust me." He took his place at the kitchen island. "I brought my appetite."

For the second night in a row, Liam sat in the King home and felt right at home. He liked watching the mother and daughter, so close in their relationship, work together to get ready for dinner. Now that it was his second time sitting at their dinner table, Kate handed him a stack of plates with the silverware so he could help set the table. That gesture alone made him feel even more "a part of it."

They sat down together, held hands for a prayer, and then Liam dug into the incredible fare Callie had prepared. He didn't stop eating even when he began to feel stuffed. The only time he got this kind of cooking was any Sunday he made it out to the family ranch for breakfast. Home-cooked dinners were far and few between for him. So was the conversation they had during dinner. It had been a long time since he had someone to share his day with, talk about his passion of caring for animals. Kate got it. They weren't exactly in the same business, but the animals on her ranch were more than just part of her business—they were part of her family.

"I'll have Callie fix you some leftovers," Kate said with a laugh. She must have noticed him still eyeing the food on the table after had already filled his plate twice.

"Are you sure?"

The horse trainer smiled at him again, and this time the smile reached her eyes. "I'm sure. It'll give the chef an excuse to cook something new tomorrow. Isn't that right, Callie?"

The young woman nodded, but her attention was distracted by the sound of a video call coming in on a tablet on the counter. Kate's daughter jumped up, ran to the counter looked at the screen and then squealed with excitement.

"I-it's Tony!" Callie snatched the tablet off the counter, accepted the call and hurried down the narrow hallway leading to the three small bedrooms at the back of the house.

Kate sighed, staring after her daughter.

"Tony?"

She stared down the hallway a moment longer before she responded. Kate's shoulders lifted ever so slightly. Was it a sign of frustration or resignation? He couldn't be sure.

"Callie's boyfriend. They met in an online support group for young adults with Down syndrome. If I had known this was going to happen, I'm not sure I would have been so excited to sign her up."

That shocked him. Just like Callie's amazing talent in the kitchen, it hadn't crossed his mind that she would have a boyfriend.

They began to clear the table with the sound of Callie's laughter and excited talking drifting down the hall.

"Serious?" He put the last dish on the counter.

Kate breathed in deeply and sighed again. She tucked a couple of wayward hairs behind her ear, a gesture he'd seen her do many times that night. "I think she's taking it way too seriously. She thinks she's in love."

Liam stood at the sink, turned on the water and waited for it to get hot.

"You don't have to do that." She frowned at the running water.

"I've got this." He wasn't ready to get kicked out just yet.

While he rinsed the dishes and loaded the dishwasher, Kate fixed him containers of leftovers, giving him the lion's share of the rest of the food.

"So, you think being in love is a bad thing?" He asked his hostess.

"No." Kate frowned at the question. "I don't. But Callie doesn't always see the big picture. She thinks that what she sees in the movies is what love is all about. That's not real life."

"No. It's not. Marriage is hard work."

And he was living proof that hard work wasn't enough to sustain a marriage.

Kate sent him what he assumed was a sympathetic look, dispelling any notion that news of his divorce hadn't spread all over the small town.

"Relationships, in general, are hard," she said.

"Well, Calico is mighty lucky to have you to help her navigate through life."

Kate laughed as she snapped the Tupperware lid into place. "Trust me. My daughter has grown weary of my advice."

"That's about as typical as it gets, isn't it?"

"Yes." That made Kate smile. "I suppose it is."

They didn't talk much after that, and that was okay with him. Kate wasn't chatty—she was quiet, inward in her thoughts, and even though he'd like for her to open up to him, he wasn't in any hurry. He had a feeling that if he wanted to get to know Kate better, he was going to have to work the long game.

"Coffee?" she asked him. "For the road?"

He knew that was her not-so-subtle way of letting him know that it was time for him to begin to be on his way.

"I could sure use a cup. I'm fighting the desire to take a nap on your couch."

He'd gotten her to smile more than once tonight—

he was making some progress. Kate had always been focused, determined and serious, even when they were in high school, but she seemed to have lost some of her joy. Had he even heard her laugh?

"Mommy!" Callie came bounding into the kitchen clutching the tablet to her chest. The young lady, her brown eyes shining, her round cheeks flushed, spun around in a circle, giggling happily.

"Do I even need to ask how the phone call went?" Kate brushed back her daughter's hair and then put her hands on her Callie's shoulders.

"He asked me to be his date for the dance!" Callie told her mom excitedly, giving a little jump. "I can't wait!"

"Callie," Kate said gently, but seriously, "you know we can't go this year. We talked about this."

The young woman's face fell. "*You* can't go. Why can't I—I go? I—I'm old enough. I—I can go *b-by myself*."

Callie started to cry; Kate brushed her daughter's tears away with her thumbs, her eyes soft with understanding and something else—sadness.

"Callie, we have company," she said. "We'll talk about this later. Okay?"

"Okay." Callie frowned. "B-but I-I'm old enough to go b-by myself!"

The young woman stomped out of the living room, down the narrow hallway, and slammed the door to her bedroom.

Liam and Kate took a cup of coffee out to the porch and sat on the porch swing, with the warm summer air filled with the sound of crickets and a night owl howling in the distance.

"I appreciate you indulging me." He held up the coffee cup. He was actually too tired to think about driving the nearly hour home.

Kate nodded as she took a sip of her own coffee.

After a moment of staring after her daughter, Kate said with a sigh, "Sorry about earlier. It's the annual Down syndrome conference. I try to take her every year. Now that Tony is going, missing it is going to be tough for her."

"No need to apologize." Liam tried to reassure his hostess. "Love is serious business."

"That's true. But Callie's disability makes all of this so much harder to navigate." Kate tucked her hair behind her ear. "I never even thought about a boyfriend when she was growing up. Now she wants to get married. Have babies."

"I suppose that's natural," Liam said after a second of thinking it over. The fact that Kate was talking to him so openly about her daughter was a welcome surprise. He didn't want to screw it up by saying something stupid or unintentionally insensitive. He wanted to find a way to be a part of Kate's and Callie's lives.

"Yes," she agreed, holding her warm cup with both hands. "But Callie is never going to be able to live on her own."

"She seems really independent."

Kate sent him the smallest of smiles. "She is. Everyone with Down syndrome is different, just like the rest of us. We were lucky—Callie's intelligence is higher on the range. But…" Kate frowned into her coffee cup. "She'll never be able to live without support, and no matter how many times we talk about it, I just can't get her to understand. She wants to move to New York

City and go to culinary school and open a restaurant. She also wants to move to California, marry Tony and start having babies. In her mind, it's possible to do both, at the same time."

"I wish my daughter were that ambitious," he interjected, and he meant it.

"Callie is ambitious." Kate nodded. "She has so many dreams and goals—none of them here in Montana.

They finished their coffee, and when they went back into the house, Callie, seemingly recovered from her outburst, gave him a big hug when he came into the kitchen to put his coffee cup in the sink and pick up his leftovers. This time when Callie asked him to dinner for the next night, he declined. He couldn't keep on accepting the daughter's invitation to be able to spend time with the mother.

"I appreciate you letting me come on out tonight." Liam put the containers in the front seat of his truck.

"Callie invited you."

He shut the door to his truck and then stood in front of the trainer; her arms were crossed in front of her body.

Liam chuckled. "I was waiting all day for you to uninvite me."

The half-moon was putting off enough light for him to see a fleeting expression of guilt flash across her face.

"I wouldn't do that."

Liam ducked his head, putting it just a little closer to hers. "Admit it, though. You thought about it."

Kate turned her face away from him, her lips pressed together as if she wanted to stop herself from admitting it. Then, unexpectedly, she laughed.

"I'm sorry." She looked into his face then. "I'm not much on company."

He didn't say anything, because he sensed she had more to say.

"Callie wants me to start dating again..."

Their eyes met and Liam felt a spark. He felt it, and he was pretty sure that Kate felt it too.

"Are you saying I'm part of some evil plan to get you back into the dating game?"

A nod.

"Calico doesn't know, then, that you've already turned me down once before?" he asked in a lowered, private voice.

Kate took a small step back, but he wasn't going to let her get off the hook that easily. He took a small step forward.

"It's not that I don't like you, Liam." Kate, usually so sure of herself, sounded off balance with a shake in her voice.

"That's good to know."

In that moment, in the soft moonlight, Liam acted on instinct instead of listening to his head. He reached out, took Kate's face in his hands and kissed her on the lips.

It was a short kiss—sweet, gentle, instead of romantic or sensual. But that kiss was a kiss full of promise. It was a kiss that could be his future.

Surprised, Kate stepped backward again. His hands fell away from her face and they stood there, quietly, staring at each other.

"That's good to know," he said again, "because I like you, Kate. A whole heck of a lot."

Chapter Three

"He actually *kissed* me," Kate whispered into the phone. She was in bed, but she wasn't ready for sleep. She had brushed her teeth and then stood in the bathroom staring at the lips that Liam Brand had just *kissed* without any warning or invitation.

"Good for him," her friend Lorrie told her.

Lorrie also had a child with Down syndrome, a little girl much younger than Callie. Lorrie had started an organization to connect parents in Gallatin County and ever since they had worked together to establish an annual, one-mile Buddy Walk in Bozeman to raise awareness and inclusion for people with DS.

"Good?"

"Yes," Lorrie reiterated. "Good. He listened to my advice."

Now Kate sat upright in bed. “What advice was that?”

Lorrie stopped to say something to one of her kids before answering. “He was here to give Dude and Max their shots. He might have mentioned that he was interested in you.”

“And?”

“*And* I told him that he’d have to be unconventional. That’s all.”

Kate couldn’t think of a response right away. Her mouth popped open, and she shook her head before she said, “So, you encouraged him to assault me?”

“Okay—now that’s way dramatic. All he did was give you a kiss. Tell me you didn’t enjoy it. Liam is handsome, smart, *nice* and he’s one of the most eligible bachelors in Montana.”

“That’s not the point.” Kate flopped back into the pillows. “I have Callie and the ranch.”

“I do know.” Lorrie said kindly. “I do. But, just because we have children with special needs doesn’t mean we can just put our lives on a shelf. Callie is an adult now, Kate. She needs your help—she’ll always need your help—but you’re going to have to find something else to do with your life other than focusing all of your attention on Callie. Why not shift some of that focus onto someone like Dr. Brand?”

Quiet for a moment of thought, Kate couldn’t deny her friend’s logic. Had she been holding Callie back, in part, because her daughter had always been the center of her world? Was she holding Callie back for her own sake? Part of her, deep down, knew that it was, at least, possible.

They talked for another twenty minutes before

they hung up. Lorrie was one of the few people who genuinely understood her struggles with Callie, from fighting for services in the school system, accessing appropriate health care, and the feeling of isolation that could creep in with so many miles between families in a similar situation. She trusted Lorrie; they told each other the unvarnished truth. Her friend had a point. It was time for her to begin to find a new center of her life. Callie was growing up.

"Good morning, Kate." Dawn from Dr. McGee's office had called her out of the blue. "How are you today?"

"I'm good. Just doing barn work, as usual."

"Well, I won't be keepin' you too long." There was something in Dawn's voice that signaled that this wasn't going to be a positive call. "But I do have to share with you that Dr. McGee is going to be retiring."

Up until that point, Kate had been holding the phone between her shoulder and cheek while she continued to muck the stall she was working on. The news made Kate put her pitchfork down; she stood upright and held the phone to her ear with her hand as the receptionist continued.

"He's given me permission to tell all of his longtime clients that he's having some serious health problems and he has to retire."

Kate felt her chest tighten—she loved Dr. McGee. She'd known him since she was a kid and had always assumed that he would keep on working until he took his last breath.

"I'm so sorry to hear that."

"So are we." The receptionist sounded as if she was choking back tears. "It's a…shock."

After she hung up the phone, the weight of the phone call began to hit Kate. Beyond the sadness she was feeling in her heart, and the fact that she was going to have to break the news to Callie, who was crazy about Dr. McGee, what was she going to do about her horses? She had a huge barn to run and having a vet was essential to the health of the horses in her care.

Kate finished mucking out the stall, pushed the cart away from the stall, dropped the pitchfork into the cart and then walked outside to think. It was a blue sky day, not one cloud, and it was warm, just how she liked it. Hands on her hips, Kate ran several ideas through her head before she finally landed on her first move.

"I'll be upstairs in the office if you need me," Kate told two of her regular stable hands. Whenever she conducted business, she liked to sit at her desk in the office above the barn. Sitting at her desk now, with the view of the flat expanse of the pastures abutting the mountains in the background, Kate was always reminded that she was blessed to be living in paradise. But even paradise came with a price.

"He-*llo*."

The way Liam answered his phone always made her smile.

"Hi, Dr. Brand. It's Kate."

"Hi, Kate King," Liam greeted her enthusiastically. "So, we're back to Dr. Brand, are we?"

Kate touched her fingers to her lips, the lips this man had kissed several nights before. It was a kiss, so fleeting, that hadn't been far from her mind.

"This is a business call."

"And here I thought you had finally come to your senses and were calling to ask me out on a date."

He was teasing her—at least in part, he was—and it took her a moment to catch up with him. He had a way of catching her off guard with his humor and his kisses. He spoke before she had a chance to regroup.

"I'm thinkin' that this call is about Dr. McGee retiring?"

"Yes." The words came out of the blue, but the minute Liam echoed the news, Kate felt tears, unbidden, fill her eyes and fall onto her cheeks.

Not wanting Liam to hear her crying, Kate quickly wiped off her cheeks, steeled herself against the sadness she was feeling and focused on the business at hand.

"I've obviously been beaten to the punch," she added.

"Look, Kate." Liam said, his voice reassuringly strong and steady. "If you need me, I'm gonna be there for you. So you can take that worry right off your shoulders."

Relieved, she dropped her head into her hand. "Thank you. You know how important it is to have a support system in place."

"I do," Liam said. "That's what I'm here for."

Their phone call was cut short, making Kate wish that they had more time—he had arrived at his next client and she was hosting a clinic for a group of owners and horses. But just from that brief phone call, Liam had made her feel better. She felt that it was going to be easier to face her day without the worry about who she was going to call if one of the horses in her charge took ill or got injured. Now she knew that she could call Dr. Brand. Liam.

* * *

When word got out that Dr. McGee, a most beloved fixture in the Bozeman area horse scene, was retiring, it wasn't long before a retirement party was organized. Kate, who didn't typically take the time out of her business life to go to parties, carved time out of her schedule to attend. Callie and Kate washed up, put on some clean jeans and boots, and then loaded into one of the King Ranch trucks to head into town.

"I should drive." Callie always said the same thing when they headed off King property. Callie drove, under supervision, on the ranch and, since they owned thousands of acres, she had plenty of dirt roads to drive. But she hadn't been able to pass the driver's license test that would allow her to drive off property and her daughter couldn't seem to accept it.

"You know what I love about you, Calico?" Kate pulled onto the road that would take them into Bozeman.

"Everything?" Callie laughed with a broad smile.

"That's right." Kate reached over and squeezed her daughter's arm. "Everything."

They arrived at The Baxter Downtown, a venue often used in Bozeman for weddings, special events and, in this case, a retirement party. Dr. McGee's wife and staff had reserved the Wilson Suite, a smaller, cozier room accented with dark wood fit for a dignified man.

"Dr. McGee isn't going to like all of this fuss," Kate whispered to her daughter. "At least on the surface."

So many people gathered in the small space while Dr. McGee sat at the head table with his wife and closest staff members; she knew the man well enough to know that he was touched by the turnout, even though she had heard him blustering about all of his friends acting like he was about to be pushing-up daisies when he wasn't ready to go quietly into that good night just yet.

"Is this seat taken?"

The minute Kate heard the sound of Liam's voice, her body responded in the most unusual way. Her heart started to beat a little faster, and the hair on the back of her neck stood up.

"No." Kate found herself smiling at the handsome vet. "Be our guest."

Callie jumped out of her chair and threw her arms around Liam. "Hi, Dr. B-Brand!"

Kate watched Liam closely—he treated her daughter with so much respect and dignity, every time, that she couldn't deny that this was a part of this new feeling she was experiencing for the man.

"Hi, Calico." Liam started to take the seat on the other side of her daughter, but Callie shook her head and sat down in the chair instead.

"You should sit next to Mommy."

"Callie." Kate glanced around quickly, knowing that people were paying attention. "Let Dr. Brand sit where he wants."

"Okay," Callie said sullenly.

Liam took a moment, waited for the mother and daughter to negotiate the situation before he took the seat between them.

He leaned over to say, in that low, baritone voice of his, "This is where I wanted to sit."

Kate wasn't someone who embarrassed easily; she was a woman in a world still dominated by men. But she felt her cheeks grow hot, and she knew that if anyone was watching her face closely, the pleasure she felt by that simple comment was right there in her eyes and the small smile on her lips.

Two of the biggest gossips in Bozeman were sitting directly across from them at the banquet table. The Mendelsohn widows, Beatrice and Emma, were very interested in the new "dynamic" of the handsome eligible veterinarian and the relationship-skittish horse trainer.

"How long have the two of you been courting?" Beatrice got straight to the point.

"We aren't." Kate crinkled her brow a bit. Was it that obvious that she felt "something" akin to happy nerves sitting next to Liam?

"Not yet," Liam added after he took a large sip of his water without ice.

"They make a very handsome couple," Emma told her sister.

"They do," Beatrice agreed. "Very handsome."

"Everyone always said that about John and I," Emma continued. "That we were a handsome couple. Of course, Beatrice was always the prettier one of the two of us. But even my sister has had to admit that my John was the most handsome man—so tall and straight."

Beatrice put down her teacup with a small smile. "Don't pay a bit of attention to Emma. I've never admitted to such a thing."

Emma raised her eyebrows at her sister, puckered her lips a bit and then turned her attention back to them. "You make a very handsome couple. I approve of this match."

"As do I." Her sister agreed loudly enough for the people seated at the table behind them to hear.

Kate and Liam exchanged a quick look, both of them understanding that to make any more denials that they weren't an "item" would only give the sisters more fodder for their gossip. So they both just nodded and smiled, and let the conversation naturally drift in a different direction.

The speeches given by the staff at Dr. McGee's clinic were emotional; even though Kate didn't show it on the outside, she felt such sadness that this amazing man was leaving the profession before his time. Mrs. McGee spoke and then by unanimous applause, Dr. McGee agreed to say a word or two.

"I don't know what's wrong with all of you," Dr. McGee said in a gruff voice laced with an unusual undertone of emotion. "I'm not dead yet. But since y'all are probably the same folks who might make it to my funeral one day, this gets you off the hook for that shindig."

That was the entire speech. That was Dr. McGee. After that brief speech, everyone started to leave. Liam stood, pulled out Callie's chair first, and just as she was pushing back her own chair, she saw the vet reach out his hand to her.

Kate looked at that hand for a split second; it was such a small thing, taking an offered hand, but it seemed like a big deal to her.

Her hand slipped so easily into his—his hand, strong, rough from clinical work in the field, was a perfect fit for hers. She had big hands for a woman, and whenever she held hands with a man, as rare as that was, she always felt like the "dude." With Liam, she felt like a woman holding the hand of a man.

They walked out together, the three of them, and Kate hated the feel of curious eyes on them. It was such a small town that no doubt word had gotten out that

Liam had sat at her table two nights in a row and now they were sitting together at Dr. McGee's retirement party. Gossip was a pastime for some in their town.

"You like Mommy, don't you?" Callie asked Liam when they reached their truck.

Liam, as he always did, took Callie's questions seriously, answered them directly. "Yes, Calico. I do."

Kate sighed at her daughter's question. Callie was Callie, and no matter how many discussions they had about "polite questions," there were just some things that her daughter wasn't going to be able to change.

Callie giggled at Liam's response, turning her head and covering her mouth with her hand.

"Do you want to come over for dinner tonight?" Her daughter threw out of invitation before she got into the truck.

Liam looked directly into Kate's eyes before he said to Callie, "I really appreciate the invite, I really do. I'd love to eat some more of your good cookin,' but the next time I come over for dinner, it's gonna have to be your mom who invites me."

That could have been a moment for her to invite him, but she just wasn't ready. She was feeling things for Liam—she was—and he hadn't been subtle about his attraction to her. But this was territory that hadn't been explored in over a decade! Kate wasn't the type of woman to make drastic changes in her life; she was a tugboat, not a speedboat.

"It was nice spending lunch with you," Kate said, after she climbed behind the wheel.

"Likewise." Liam had a way of looking at her in a way that no other man had in a very long time. Maybe not ever. It was as if he liked everything he saw when he looked at her face.

"I'm sad about Dr. McGee," she admitted to him.

"So am I." Liam had one hand tucked into a front pocket and the other holding her open door. "I could work a lifetime and not feel like half the vet that man is."

"I don't know about that," Kate objected. "I was really impressed with how you handled Visa."

Liam nodded and then shut the door for her. "I appreciate that. I hope to see you again real soon. You too Calico!"

They said their goodbyes then, and she drove away. In the rearview mirror, she saw Liam still standing in the parking lot watching them as they left.

"Mommy! Why didn't you tell him he could come over for dinner?"

"I don't know." Kate told her daughter. But that wasn't entirely true. There was something there between them—she felt it and she could tell that Liam could feel it too. It was something real, something tangible. And it genuinely scared the crap out of her.

A couple of days after Liam had seen Kate and Callie at Dr. McGee's party, he had really struggled with his next move. He could tell that Kate felt the same attraction to him that he did with her. But he could also see that she wasn't ready to jump into a relationship. If he wanted to explore his feelings for Kate, he was going to have to be strategic. Instead of calling, which he wanted to do, he decided to just give her some time to mull over the lunch, and the *kiss*, they had shared.

"He-*llo*!"

It was Kate King on the line.

"I can't believe I forgot about this," the trainer told him. "But I have a prepurchase vet check scheduled for tomorrow. The woman's coming in from Helena, and she's already called several vets..."

"I think she may have called me already," Liam told her.

"She did. I know this is a big ask—but I'm really in a bind. The prospective buyer has no flexibility in her schedule."

When he first got the call from the woman out of Helena, she had mentioned the King Ranch, but his scheduled was still overflowing because of Dr. McGee's sudden retirement. Thankfully there were a couple of other vets in the area who were able to step up their game.

"I just can't get out there today, Kate. I would if I could," he said, and then added in the silence that followed, "I hope you know that."

"No. I know," Kate told him, her disappointment obvious to him. "I appreciate it."

After another moment of odd silence, she asked, "Could you come out tonight? I know it's a lot to ask, but the indoor riding ring has lights. We ride at night here all the time."

She continued in a lowered voice. "Please, Liam. She's a really big connection for me. If I get this deal done, there could be so much business for the Triple K." After another pause, she added, "I really need this."

The worry he heard in her voice convinced him that he had to find a way to help her. "Okay."

"Okay?"

"I'll be there. As soon as I can. It won't be until six or seven. I already know that for sure."

"Whenever you can get here. I'll let the buyer know," Kate said. "And, Dr. Brand… Liam…I can't thank you enough."

He was already exhausted when he parked his truck in front of Kate's barn. The prospective buyer, a rather fancy-looking woman with platinum hair who was originally from Oklahoma, greeted him with Kate at her side. He was lucky that the exam was uncomplicated—the horse was sound, had good hooves, and had negative flexion tests and X-rays. Although a prepurchase vet check could take up to four hours, this exam went smoothly and he was wrapping up with the potential owner after two hours.

"You shouldn't have any difficulty using this horse for the purposes you've stated," he said to the client. "I should have a report to you by tomorrow afternoon. I won't be able to get it out tonight."

"Tomorrow will be just fine." The woman with the heavy Oklahoma accent smiled at him.

Liam packed up his equipment, while Kate showed the woman to her car. They met back at his truck just as he was finished loading.

With a sigh, Kate, in cutoff shorts that showed off her long, slender legs, muscular from years of riding, leaned against the truck.

"Long day," she said, her loose hair blowing in the gentle night breeze.

He nodded.

"Are you hungry?"

Liam slipped his keys into his pocket with a nod.

"Callie made chili again. You seemed to really like it the last time."

"As a matter of fact, I loved it."

Kate tucked her hair behind her ear. "Join us for dinner?"

Liam sent her a tired smile. "That's the best offer I've had all week."

Chapter Four

"Man oh man." Liam sank onto one of the rocking chairs on the porch. "Your daughter is an amazing cook. I swear I haven't tasted any better."

Kate took the seat next to him, liking the feel of the hot mug of coffee in her hand, enjoying the night view of the land she loved. And, yes, having this new person in her life to talk about the events of the day. A person who seemed to appreciate her daughter in a way that she didn't often see. It didn't feel *normal* or *certain*, but it was a change. Perhaps a genuinely good one.

"She puts a lot of love into her food." She took that wonderful first sip from the hot, black coffee.

She caught Liam looking at her profile out of the corner of her eye as he said, "I believe that. You can taste when someone has put their heart into their cookin'."

It wasn't awkward, the frequent silences. Both of

them were exhausted from their busy days, and speaking seemed like a chore. After Liam finished his coffee, he sighed heavily, and she understood exactly what that meant. He still had a long drive and reports to write.

"Well…" he finally said, "I suppose it's time for me to hit the road."

Kate stood as well and held out her hand for his empty cup. She put the cups on a small table just outside the front door before walking with the veterinarian to his truck.

"I feel like I've had an awful lot to thank you for these last couple of weeks," she said, her eyes looking off into the distance.

They were standing closer than usual, Liam by his open driver's door and she facing him.

"I feel the same way." He reached out and tucked her hair behind her ear.

She looked at him then, drawn in by the kindness she saw in his bright blue eyes. "All we did was feed you a couple of times."

"No." Liam was slow to withdraw his hand as if he enjoyed touching her as much as she realized she liked being touched by him. "You've given me much more than just a couple of meals. I feel like I belong somewhere again."

He added with a laugh, "But don't give me wrong—the food matters too."

Kate felt a knot form in the pit of her stomach—was she ready to encourage Liam to feel like a part of the Triple K? It seemed too fast.

"Hey." Liam drew her back to the conversation, back to the present. "Go out with me."

Kate crossed her arms in front of her body, hunched

her shoulders forward protectively. "Won't that be a conflict of interest? You being my vet, me being your client?"

Liam, who usually laughed off things like that, didn't crack a smile. "Did you hire me just so you could keep me an arm's length away?"

"No." She laughed in a way that made it sound like a lie. "I hired you because you are a damn good vet, and I need a damn good vet."

For a second time, Liam seemed to want to jump several spaces on a game board. He put his hands on her face and kissed her. This time, it wasn't a peck. He took his time, explored her lips with his. And she let him. And she liked it.

Slowly, the most eligible bachelor in the greater Bozeman area lifted his lips from hers. But he didn't step away from her. His hands resting on either side of her neck, Liam waited until she was looking at him once again.

"I'll promise not to overcharge you, you promise to pay me on time. How's about that?"

"I always pay my bills on time," Kate said.

"And I never overcharge."

Any retort she was formulating in this oddly flirtatious banter was cut off by another kiss. Kate felt this kiss all over her body—little lightning bolts fired in her stomach, on her spine and between her legs. By the time Liam moved his head away, her head naturally followed.

When she opened her eyes, he was smiling at her, so fondly, and with a little humor.

"Where do you want to take me?" she asked him, knowing now that what they were feeling between them—this pull, this chemistry—wasn't something that she wanted to deny or ignore.

"Let me think on it." Liam gave her a final kiss on the lips. "I want it to be something real special for you."

"I think that's awesome." Lorrie had trailered one of her horses to the ranch for training. "You realized you've just bagged a man who has a high bounty on his head."

"I didn't *bag* him." Kate laughed. "He came willingly."

"That's the best way." Lorrie swung a Western saddle on her Appaloosa's back. "If I weren't already married, I'd have been all over that a long time ago."

That seemed to be the general consensus on Liam Brand. She knew that he was smart and handsome and successful, but she didn't know just *how* sought after he was. There were going to be a lot of sad bachelorettes if this "thing" with Liam worked out. Kate knew that the town was talking about them, and she didn't like it. What was there to be done about it?

"Hey, he likes you." Lorrie slipped a bitless bridle onto her horse's head. "They lost, you won. That's how the cookie crumbles."

Kate walked with her friend out to the nearby round pen where they would work for the next hour. Once Lorrie mounted and walked her horse into the pen, Kate followed and shut the gate behind them.

"It's not like this is a done deal," she told her friend. "We haven't even had one date."

"I've got a feeling about this." Lorrie told her. The woman was always having "feelings" about things—truth was, she was more often right than wrong.

Kate tightened the horse's girth before she patted the Appaloosa on the haunch. "Okay. Let's focus on training for now. We can start planning my wedding later."

It was an afternoon date, and Liam insisted that he pick her up at the ranch like a *real date*. They had talked on the phone every day since she had agreed to go out with him; they both agreed that going into town, the hotbed of gossip, wasn't the way they wanted to do it for their first date. Instead, Liam took her to his family's ranch, Sugar Creek, where there was enough room for them to ride up to the mountains on the property and have a private picnic.

It had always been difficult for Kate to be separated from Callie, but Fred, who had been the barn manager at Triple K for nearly twenty years, was the one person Kate trusted to watch Callie whenever she was away from the ranch. This was, however, the first time she had ever left Callie in Fred's care so she could steal away for an afternoon date with a hot veterinarian.

"I could have driven myself." Kate was still objecting to the fact that Liam had come to pick her up. It wasn't logical. "This is going to add hours of travel to your day."

Liam pulled onto Sugar Creek land: the Brands were a large family, wealthy, powerful and well-known. Liam had seven siblings total, and many of them had their own homesteads within the larger Sugar Creek holdings.

"This is my little corner of the world." Liam pulled up to a small log cabin.

"It's a really nice corner."

Once they were out of the truck, Liam gave her a

quick tour of his small homestead. There was a workshop with a shed, a four-stall barn and a chicken coop.

"I thought we'd ride up to the peak over there. I know a spot that's got great views."

Her hands tucked in to the back pocket of her jeans, Kate nodded with a smile. "Sounds perfect."

"I hope so," Liam told her. "I'm gonna grab our food if you want to start tacking up. You'll be riding Doc Holliday. You can't miss him. He's the big buckskin."

Kate found her ride and began to groom the beefy golden quarter horse with hooves that looked like soup plates and a beautiful black mane and tail.

"You're a good boy, aren't you?"

"He's one of the best horses I've ever had." Liam walked into the barn with a soft-sided cooler.

"I appreciate you letting me ride him." Kate picked up Doc's front leg to pick out his hoof before she made the rounds to all of his hooves.

They finished tacking the horses, mounted and started out on a trail that would lead them up to the peak of the mountain off in the distance. It was a beautiful afternoon, sunny, blue skies, perfect for a horseback ride and a mountain picnic.

"Thank you!" Kate called to Liam, who had taken the lead up as they entered the woods at the base of the mountain.

Liam spun around in his saddle so he could smile at her. "Having a good time?"

"Yes!"

Why had she fought this idea for so long? Why had she deprived herself of the simple pleasure of spending a day with a man? It seemed reasonable at the time, focusing all of her energy on the ranch and on raising Callie. But, now, it was beginning to be *her* time too.

They both loved to ride in quiet when they were in the woods; they had spoken about it more than once, and now that this was their first ride together, they honored that desire. It wasn't until Liam halted his horse at the end of the trail that they begin to talk to each other again.

"Sugar Creek is incredible, Liam." Kate dismounted and took the reins over Doc's head. "Your family is so blessed."

"God's country, for sure," he agreed. "But then again, so is the Triple K."

Yes, the Triple K was a beautiful swath of land—and she loved it and intended to live out her life there—but there was something magical about Sugar Creek. It was Montana beauty on steroids.

"We can leave the horses here. That way we can keep an eye on them while still taking in the view."

They tied off the horses, giving them their heads so they could nibble on some of the nearby foliage. Together, they climbed up the side of the expansive, gray, smooth granite that covered the top of the mountain.

"Oh, Liam!" Kate exclaimed as she got the full view the mountain provided. "I love it here!"

"I'm glad." Liam set the cooler down. "It's one of my favorite spots."

They sat down together on the sheer face of the mountain, side by side on a padded blanket Liam had packed for them. Her date had already interviewed her about her favorite foods, what she liked to drink and her favorite desserts. Yes, it was a private, quiet first date, but it was perfect for her. The effort he had taken to make sure he packed all of her favorites made her feel cared-for special.

"For you." Liam handed her a single, pink tea rose, her favorite flower.

Kate favored him with a small, pleased smile, as she took the rose, brought it to her nose and took in the sweet scent of the little flower.

He then handed her a wineglass.

"I can only have one of these." Kate watched her date pour her favorite white wine into the glass. "Drunk riding."

Liam laughed. "We'll be fine. I want you to stop worrying so much and start enjoying the day."

She raised her eyebrows at him in surprise. "Do I not seem like I'm enjoying myself?"

Liam rested one arm on a bent knee while he held out his glass to her so they could touch rims. "There's part of you that's not here with me. I'd like to have all of you here. Just for an hour or two."

After a sip of the wine, Kate tilted her head to the side and looked directly at Liam. "I'm sorry. I didn't know it was so obvious." She gestured to the side of her head. "My brain is always splitting duty."

"Hey..." Liam leaned on his side next to her. "I get it. It's hard to take a break. But just look at this, Kate. We're in paradise. Not everyone gets this gift. Wouldn't it be a crime not to give this 100 percent of our attention?"

"Actually. Yes. It would."

That was the turning point for Kate and her first date with Liam. She forced herself to put her stresses with the Triple K out of her mind, as well as putting aside her worries with Callie's future dreams and goals; instead, Kate focused her attention on the mind-blowing views that stretched for miles in the distance, and the handsome man who was bent on making her laugh and making her feel like a desirable woman again. The years had etched lines on her forehead, around her mouth and around her eyes. Those pesky nasolabial folds had deepened, and there was an annoying pad of fat gathering beneath her chin. It wasn't often that she dwelled over her aging appearance—she had a business to run and a daughter to support. But every once in a while, she would stare at her reflection and wonder where Kate King had gone. Liam wasn't the cure for all of that, yet his interest in her—the way he admired her face with his eyes—made her believe that she could still be a desirable woman. It wasn't too late for her.

Liam couldn't believe that he finally had Kate King on a date, on his mountain, after years of wanting to get to know her better. All of the pieces had just fallen into place for them, and at least physically, the horse trainer was sending off signals that she was enjoying his company as much as he was enjoying hers. They laughed together, they savored the silences together, and yes, they had a lot in common, starting with their passion for horses.

"Did you get enough?" Liam had already begun to pack up their trash and any food that hadn't been eaten.

"I did. Thank you."

He set the cooler aside, glad now to just look out over the land of Sugar Creek Ranch and beyond. Liam hooked his arms over his bent knees, turned his attention to Kate who was sitting cross-legged beside him on the blanket.

"I'm having a really good time with you," he told her.

"Me too." She tucked a few loose hairs behind her ear.

"You want to do it again?"

Kate turned her face toward him then; there was a softer look in her eyes now when she looked at him. Wordlessly, with the smallest of sweet smiles, she nodded.

"Good." He was satisfied. Getting Kate lined up for a second date before they had finished their first had been a part of his plan.

Liam lay flat on his back, sighed happily while he tried to figure out what shape the only cloud in the sky was forming.

"A sheep."

"What?"

"The cloud."

Kate tilted her head back, examined the cloud thoughtfully for a moment, then shook her head. "No. That's an alpaca."

"You're crazy."

She laughed and joined him. Kate leaned back, lay flat on her back beside him, her hands on her stomach.

"This is the most relaxed I have been in years, I think."

Liam admired her profile—he found that there were so many things for him to like about her. From her pixie ears to her strong chin and nose with the smallest of humps in the center. She was tanned from years of training horses outside, and there were sunspots on her shoulders and her chest. Kate was a salt-of-the-earth kind of woman—pretty in an unembellished outdoorsy kind of way.

"I'm glad." He decided to take a risk and reach for her hand. "You deserve to take some time for yourself, Kate."

When Kate King let him hold her hand, up there on top of his favorite mountain peak, Liam felt as if he had conquered the world. He didn't want to make too much of the date, but for him at least, this felt like the beginning of something rare, something unusual—something that had the potential to last for the rest of their lives.

They spent another hour up on that mountain, eyes closed, letting the cool air brush over their bodies, holding hands the entire time. The sun was slipping in the sky, and the temperature on the mountain had begun to drop. Kate hated to leave, she genuinely did, but it was time. As they reached Liam's small homestead, the sun was a bright orange ball disappearing behind the horizon.

"Thank you for the ride, Doc." Kate gave the large buckskin one last pat on the neck before she put him back in his stall with several pats of hay.

Liam gave her a quick tour of his modest bachelor cabin before she loaded into his truck. After she clicked her seat belt, Kate breathed in deeply and let out a long, slow, sigh.

"You okay?" Liam cranked the engine.

She nodded. "I feel happy."

After Liam pulled out onto the highway, he took her hand once again in his. When had she last held someone's hand like this? Holding hands had never really been her thing, but with Liam, it felt natural. It felt right.

"Callie was so excited that I was *finally* going out on a date."

"Is that right?" Liam smiled.

"Yes," Kate replied. "She thinks if I'm busy, she'll be able to do whatever she wants. Little does she know I can multitask."

She continued. "I never really hear you talk about your kids. How are they?"

Kate didn't have to be a psychologist to read the tension in the veterinarian's jaw and mouth—his children seemed to be a sore spot.

"They're great, as far as I can tell. We spend a lot of time video-chatting, but I sure as heck haven't felt like a parent for years."

She nodded, wanting to give him a chance to vent if he needed to.

"I don't feel like their dad, and that's the bottom line. Once my ex moved them out of the state, and remarried, I feel more like an afterthought than their father. This isn't how I imagined things."

"I'm sorry."

Liam's jaw jumped when he clenched his teeth. "No, I'm sorry. I don't need to end our first date by griping about my ex. My kids are great—I just miss them. And…it hurts to think about how much of their lives I'm missing."

Kate let the conversation about his children fade into talking about the new horse on his property. It was a nice neutral subject that they both could get excited about, and it immediately changed the mood in the truck from somber and tense to free-flowing with ideas.

"I'd actually love to bring Chief out here and have you work with us," Liam said, excited by the prospect.

"I'd love to work with you." Kate nodded. "I think he'd be a great prospect for a bitless bridle."

Liam pulled into her driveway, and Kate immediately began to think of all the things she had *not* gotten done by wiling the afternoon away with the handsome veterinarian. This was why she had such a hard time giving herself permission to have some downtime—all of her work backed up.

Liam hopped out of the truck and jogged around to her side so he could open the door for her.

"Thank you. Again," she said to him. "I had such a great time."

Liam was leaning back against the truck; he reached out, gently pulled her into his arms and kissed her. It was a sweet kiss, not too demanding.

"I have to go now." Kate took a small step back to break the contact. "There's always so much to do around here."

Liam walked with her up to her doorstep; he stayed at the bottom of the steps while she opened her front door.

"I'll be callin' you," he said with a tip of his cowboy hat.

Kate could hear that Callie was video-chatting in her room, which was the reason why she hadn't barreled outside the moment they pulled in.

"I'll look forward to it."

Chapter Five

As good as his word, Liam called every day. Sometimes she was too busy to talk; sometimes he was too busy to say more than "Hi, how ya doin'." But it was the fact that she had begun to count on that call that was the biggest surprise to her. She had to be self-sufficient, self-reliant, so it was really hard for her to relinquish any of the independence. Letting someone into her life felt as if she were giving up some of her independence, allowing herself to rely on another person, and that scared her.

"I-is Dr. B-Brand coming for dinner tonight?" Callie asked her as they, along with the other stable hands, finished dispensing the morning hay for the horses.

"As far as I know." Kate brushed loose pieces of hay off of her arms and shirt. "I asked and he said yes."

Callie had hay all over the front of her T-shirt; she

always hugged the hay to her body, no matter how many times Kate had showed her how to carry the hay in a manner that wouldn't result in covering her in loose hay.

"I-is he your b-boyfriend?"

Kate had been avoiding this daily posed question—Callie loved love, and wanted her mother to be in a relationship. Yet she still hesitated to label Liam.

The horse trainer handed her daughter a pitchfork. "I suppose so."

Callie took the pitchfork in one hand, but ducked her head and giggled behind her other. "Are you going to get married?"

Kate laughed at the thought. "No! We just started dating, Callie. That's too fast."

"Are you going to have a b-baby?"

Another laugh. "No, honey. I'm not going to have a baby. You're my baby."

"I—I'm not a b-baby." Callie shook her head, her face serious. "I-It's time for me to have my own b-baby."

Her daughter had been fixated on being a mother for years. Now that she had a boyfriend, that topic seemed to move to front and center all the time now. In addition to the obvious reasons why Callie shouldn't have children, there was the practical matter of basic knowledge about sex. Even after several sex education classes designed for individuals with intellectual disabilities, Callie still had a very naïve understanding about sex. For Callie, kissing was having sex.

Kate put her hand around her daughter's shoulders. It always hurt her to feel like she needed to regulate Callie's expectations for her future.

"We'll talk it about later, Callie. We've got a lot of work to get done today."

"There's always a lot of work to get done."

Callie was right about that. There was always something that needed to be fixed around the ranch. There was always someone getting sick or quitting or moving on—horses came and went, clients came and went—but she was always here at the Triple K.

"That's true." Kate nodded. "So, let's get to it."

Dissatisfied, Callie's smile dissolved into a frown. "When I—I marry Tony, I—I won't have to muck any more stalls."

"Let's cross that bridge when we get there, Callie."

The problem was, what was waiting for them on the other side of that bridge? It was easier for Kate to bury herself in the work, to focus on the business, in order to avoid this looming confrontation with her daughter. Callie wasn't letting go of the idea of moving to New York City and she certainly wasn't letting go of the idea of marrying Tony—this was a problem that needed to be addressed. Question was, what could she do to temper Callie's dreams with a shot of reality without crushing her spirit?

Liam headed to the Triple K after his last appointment. He'd been looking forward to spending the evening with Kate and Callie all day; the plan was to watch movies, pop popcorn and just hang out together. Having Kate in his life—a companion—was reviving all kinds of things in his life that were missing. Some he had known were missing, but other things, subtle things, were a surprise. It had been years since he'd made a night of popping popcorn and watching movies on TV, and it made him really feel like he had a family again. That was the type of thing a person did with a family.

"Hi." Kate, with her pretty, tanned face and pretty hazel eyes greeted him at the door.

He wanted to kiss her on the lips, but Callie was heading their way, and he wasn't sure if Kate would appreciate that. Instead, he kissed her cheek, lingering for an extra second to breath in the honeysuckle scent of her hair.

"Dr. B-Brand!" Callie greeted him enthusiastically, as she always did. "Are you hungry?"

He gave Kate's daughter a hug. "You better know it."

"I—I made franks and beans."

Kate shut the door while he followed Callie to the kitchen.

"That's one of my favorites."

Callie laughed behind her hand. "You say that about everything."

Kate hugged her daughter—Liam loved how affectionate they were—before she pulled a Mountain Dew out of the refrigerator, popped the top and then poured it into a glass without ice. Just how he liked it.

Liam guzzled the entire glass in several big gulps. He put the glass down with a smile. "I love Mountain Dew. It's not the best thing in the world to drink, but man, do I love it!"

Kate smiled at him, opened a second can, poured it into his glass and then pushed the refill toward him. The first couple of nights he had eaten dinner with them, she hadn't had Mountain Dew in the house. Now she kept it stocked for him.

After dinner, they all sat on the couch, with Kate sandwiched in the middle; on her lap was a giant bowl of popcorn, a little burned, and heavy on the butter.

"What's on?" Liam asked before he put a handful of popcorn into his mouth.

Simultaneously, Kate and Callie, leaning their heads together, said, "Hallmark Movies!"

Liam stopped chewing for a second, then finished chewing, swallowed and asked, "Are those action movies? Thrillers?"

Callie, her legs tucked up to her chest, rolled sideways toward her mother, laughing. "No! They're *romantic*."

Kate smiled at him. "Chick flicks, back to back, all night long. Can you handle it?"

Liam made a face. "What do you take me for? An old-fashioned guy? I'm modern. I'm sensitive."

The veterinarian couldn't really care less about the movie—he cared about the company. He stretched out his legs, letting his thigh press up against Kate's thigh, and kept a steady stream of popcorn heading into his mouth.

In between bites, he pointed to the screen. "This is a Christmas movie."

"I know," Kate said in a dreamy voice. "It's Christmas in June!"

Callie leaned forward so she could see him. "Do you love Christmas?"

"Yes," he said truthfully. "I do. I like it in December, though."

"Shh." Kate hushed him. "You don't want to miss the beginning."

"Absolutely not," Liam said with a dead-pan expression.

Perhaps it was his full belly, or perhaps it was because he was just really comfortable in Kate's home, sitting on Kate's couch, next to Kate, but one minute he was watching a Christmas romance about a woman who unwittingly begins to date Santa's only son, and the next he was being awakened by Callie squealing in excitement.

"It's my b-boyfriend!" she announced loudly.

Kate's daughter jumped up and ran with her phone to her bedroom.

Liam sat up a little, rubbing his hand over his eyes. "Did I fall asleep?"

Kate was looking over her shoulder down the hall toward her daughter's bedroom.

"Yes," she said when she turned her attention back to him.

"Did I snore?"

"Yes!" She laughed. "I had to turn up the volume, it was so loud. You really need to get that checked."

"Man." Liam shook his head, embarrassed. "I'm sorry I fell asleep on you."

He put his arm around her shoulders and pulled her closer to him. He'd been wanting to sneak a kiss all night, and now that Callie was occupied with her own love life, it was his turn to focus on Kate's love life.

Liam hooked his finger beneath her chin and gently turned her face toward him. He kissed her, slowly, lightly, taking his cues from her. Kate didn't deepen the kiss; instead, she gave him one last quick kiss, and then moved her head away from him. He understood—she didn't want Callie to catch them kissing. Not just yet, anyway.

"I missed you today," he told her.

She didn't want to make out with her daughter down the hall, but Kate slipped her hand into his and threaded her fingers into his.

"Isn't that funny." She rested her head on his shoulder. "I missed you too."

They sat like that, in the silence, with the next Christmas movie in the lineup playing with the volume on mute, and the sound of Callie laughing and giggling drifting up the hall.

"Did she end up marrying the heir to the Santa Claus throne?"

Kate squeezed his hand with a little laugh. "Yes. As a matter of fact, she did."

He had begun to become part of the fabric of their lives. They expected him for dinner more nights than not, and Kate was beginning to count on his counsel. Liam was a levelheaded, thoughtful man. She tended to be black and white in her decision making—Kate also knew enough about herself to realize that she could make snap decisions that she would regret later.

"I know you have some valid disagreements with Callie's father," Liam said.

Kate raised her eyebrows and frowned. That was a serious understatement. Callie's father, Lloyd, had turned out to be a disappointment on every possible level, beginning with his outright rejection of Callie when she was born with Down syndrome. Yes, he had come around over time. But he was always letting Callie down, even as recently as last month, and he was behind in his child support by years. She had always been able to support herself, and her child, so Kate had decided long ago not to complicate her life by pursuing Lloyd for back child support.

"But he is Callie's father. And she wants to visit him."

They were sitting on garden swing beneath one of the old oak trees on the other side of the circle drive. It was a balmy night, humid and a little windy, with a promise of rain in the air.

Kate could hear in Liam's voice an echo of a man who felt as if he had been geographically cut out of his children's lives. But Lloyd was no Liam Brand. Liam was a dedicated provider who paid his child support; Liam was a man of honor and decency who treated Callie like a worthy and worthwhile person. Callie's father had turned out to be a major disappointment on just about every level a man could disappoint a woman.

"I know she does," Kate conceded. "She wants a lot of things. Not all of them are good for her."

Liam was quiet on that comment.

She breathed in deeply and let out a long, tired sigh. "She's never traveled without me. I have always been there, in the background, just in case. Callie has seizures."

"That I didn't know."

She nodded. "And the thought of her flying by herself, to New York..."

"Why don't you fly with her? You could catch a flight back the same day."

"I thought of that too," she answered. "But that's a lot of money. And time."

She sighed again with a shake of her head. "I love Callie more than anything. But she exhausts me."

"Hey..." Liam reached for her hand. "Let's just table

this for right now. You don't have to make a decision tonight."

Kate rested her head on Liam's shoulder. "I'm glad that I have you to hash this stuff out with. You know… I've never really had anyone to discuss Callie with before."

Liam pressed his lips to the top of her head, then rested his chin lightly on her hair. "I love being with you, Kate. I love being here with Callie and you."

She moved her head back, tilted her head upward, so he could kiss her lips. It didn't take any more than that silent invitation to bring Liam's lips to hers. He brought his hand to her cheek, deepened the kiss. That simple kiss lasted for several minutes, until Liam shifted uncomfortably and made a frustrated noise in the back of his throat.

He rested his forehead against hers. "Come to see me tomorrow, Kate."

She knew that there was more to that invitation than an afternoon of horseback riding. They had been in a kissing stage of their relationship for a while now—and it was sweet and lovely and tender—but their bodies were beginning to demand more. Much more.

In the low dusk light, Kate stared into Liam's deep blue eyes.

"Will you?" Liam rubbed his thumb over her lower lip.

She knew what she was saying yes to, and after another second of thought, Kate gave the slightest affirmative nod.

The horse trainer was rewarded for her response with another, deep, slow, passionate kiss from a man she was beginning to fall for, head right over heels.

* * *

The next day, Liam was waiting for her on his porch. When she shifted into Park, she noticed that he was pacing back and forth, his brow furrowed.

"What's wrong?" she asked him when he opened the door to her truck. "Are you okay?"

"I don't even know how to say this to you."

Kate had that sinking feeling that a person got when bad news was imminent. "Just say it."

Liam had almost a pained expression in his eyes; he looked around as if they weren't completely secluded. Instead of saying anything, he grabbed her hand and began to lead her into the house.

Off-kilter, and not expecting this greeting, Kate didn't resist being led into Liam's cabin, but pulled her hand from his.

"Tell me what's going on, Liam!"

He shut the door, his head bent for a moment, before he gestured to his groin. "I can't ride a horse like this."

Kate glanced down at his jeans and saw, quite plainly, that Liam was obviously aroused. As all women did wonder, she had wondered about Liam's endowment in that area. There was no need to wonder any longer.

Liam took a step toward her, his eyes so serious. "I've been thinking about making love to you, Kate. I *want* to make love to you. It's driving me just a little bit nuts."

She was temporarily stunned and didn't respond.

"I'm sorry," he added. "I know I was supposed to take you riding."

Kate finally laughed and threw her arms around him. "I thought you were going to break up with me!"

Liam took her shoulders in his hands so he could

look in her face. "Kate—don't you know that I'm crazy about you?"

Her heart gave a little jump of excitement as Liam wrapped her in his arms and pressed his lips to hers.

"Hmm." She loved the way this man kissed her.

A tingling began in that most private spot at the apex of her thighs; it had been such a long, long time since she had allowed herself to even entertain the idea of her own sexuality. She had been Callie's mom—her protector, her advocate—for so long, that she had abandoned her own needs as a woman. Liam was bringing all of those needs flooding back into her body with a vengeance.

Her hips naturally pressed into his and she wrapped her arms tightly around his body.

"Kate." He broke the kiss, his voice tense with desire. "Kate…?"

"I shaved my legs."

That broke the sexual tension, and Liam threw his head back and laughed. His eyes returned to hers as he brushed her hair over her shoulder.

"Oh, Kate. You make me laugh."

She was laughing too. She had no idea why in the world those words had come flying out of her mouth.

"Was that your way of saying 'yes' to making love?"

"Yes." Still laughing, she nodded. "Shaving my legs is a big deal. It doesn't happen all the time."

He took her to his bedroom and peeled back the clean sheets of his neatly made bed; then he peeled off her clothing before he removed his own. His body, long and lean, was a thing of beauty. Kate stared at him shyly from beneath the soft, cool cotton sheets. Was making love like riding a bike? Would her body remember what to do?

"You're beautiful, Kate." Liam joined her under the covers.

"You're handsome." Kate pressed the palm of her hand to his chest, taking comfort in the steady beating of his heart.

To the touch, Liam's skin was warm and surprisingly soft. Kate lightly scratched her fingernails through the brownish-blond hair on Liam's muscular chest. She hadn't ever considered herself to be a chest-hair fan, but on Liam, everything looked good to her.

Smiling at her with his eyes, Liam captured her hand, kissed her wrist. "We'll go slow."

"Not too slow." She moved closer to Liam.

With a satisfied groan, Liam pressed his body against her, his strong fingers roaming her back downward to the curve of her derriere. Their bodies pressed tightly together, Liam pulled the covers over their shoulders, cocooning them in their own private, sensual world. Kate dropped kisses down his neck and along his collarbone, her hesitant fingers exploring the contour of his back and shoulders.

"I am going to make you feel so good, my sweet Kate," Liam whispered into her ear.

His breath on her neck, the feel of his teeth gently nibbling on her earlobe, sent a shiver a pleasure down her spine. The center of her body ached for his touch.

Eyes closed, her head rolling back onto the pillow, Kate threaded her fingers through Liam's hair as he pulled her nipple into his mouth. Every touch, every kiss, felt like an awakening of something that had been dormant inside of her for years. Skin to skin, their legs intertwined, Kate sighed happily. Liam had been kissing her sweetly on the lips; at the sound of her sigh, he pulled away so he could smile down at her.

"It feels incredible to finally have you in my arms." He told her quietly.

"You feel good."

Liam's roaming hand slipped between her thighs; his warm hand cupped her, sending little shockwaves down her legs. Perhaps it was years of deprivation; or perhaps it was the fact that Liam was the sexiest man she'd ever known. But, when Liam began to play with her, rubbing her most sensitive nub with his finger, an orgasm, so unexpected and raw, crashed over her body. Her back arched, her arms wrapped tightly around her man, she pushed herself into Liam's hand. He stayed with her, pushing her to feel more, to keep riding the wave, until she was panting and languid in his arms. Liam kissed her eyelids, and her cheeks, and her neck, all the while murmuring sweet words in her ear.

Kate ducked her head into Liam's chest, embarrassed. It was so unusual to have a man want to give her pleasure without any expectation of receiving pleasure for himself. Liam held her close, gave her a moment to collect herself. When she was ready, Kate reached between their bodies and took him in her hand; quickly, the harness and the urgency returned to Liam's body.

"Do you have something?" Kate asked.

Liam leaned back, opened the nightstand drawer and grabbed a condom. He rolled away from her for a moment to put it on and then rolled back to her. The moment he covered her body with his, the moment he pressed himself between her thighs, Kate knew that this union was right for her. He filled her so completely, holding her hands above her head, while he rocked into her.

"Does that feel good?" Liam asked gruffly.

Kate wrapped her legs around his hips and held on for the beautiful ride he was giving her.

"Yes," she gasped. "Oh, yes."

He must have felt her tightening around him, must have known that she was building to another peak, because Liam quickened his pace, going deeper, pushing harder.

"Come on, baby," he urged. "I feel you."

Somehow, Liam knew all the right notes to play; somehow he knew all the right buttons to push. Twisting beneath him, Kate cried out again. This time, her orgasm was so intense, so strong, that Liam couldn't seem to hold back a second longer. Liam buried his face in her neck as he buried himself as deeply inside of her as he could. She felt him shudder and heard him groan; it was the most satisfying sound for her to hear.

"Are you okay?" Liam lifted up so he wasn't crushing her beneath his weight.

She nodded, afraid that she was feeling too emotional to speak. Making love to Liam…was unlike anything she had known before.

Liam left her for a moment to go to the bathroom; while he was gone, she curled onto her side, snuggled beneath his covers, and looked out the window at the mountains in the distance. She felt Liam climb into bed beside her; his arm went around waist and he pulled her backward into his body.

He kissed her shoulder. "I needed to do that. With you."

They hugged each other, quietly, until Kate heard

Liam begin to snore. She couldn't remember the last time she'd tried to take a nap in the afternoon and she wasn't so sure that she could. Instead, she lay beside her man, her mind trying to make sense of this new reality. They had taken a monumental step today; neither of them made love casually. This was, as much as anything, a commitment to each other and a commitment to their growing relationship.

Unable to sleep, and growing restless, Kate turned in Liam's arms so that she was facing him once again. Fast asleep, Liam didn't budge. Kate tapped her finger to the end of his nose.

"Liam."

"Hmm?"

"Are you awake?"

"Now I am."

She smiled. "I'm bored."

Liam stretched his arm in the air and opened his eyes; he looked at her groggily. "We can't have that."

He ran his hand down her arm. "What do you want to do? Go riding?"

"Yes."

"Okay. Let's go do that." Liam started to roll away from her, but she stopped him by putting her hand on his thigh. His eyebrow raised when her hand moved from his thigh to a more private spot.

"I didn't really mean that kind of riding," she said, knowing that her newfound brazenness was making her blush.

Willing, Liam lay back and let his woman have her way with him. Once Kate was ready to enjoy her creation, Liam rolled on another condom. Kate took him inside of her, sinking down until their bodies were joined.

"Hmm." Kate curled her body down onto Liam's chest, rocking her hips back and forth, her face breathing in the sexy scent of his skin.

Nothing—nothing—had felt this good to her. She wanted to savor all of the sensations she was feeling; the friction of their skin, the sensitivity of her nipples against the hair on his chest, the feel of his tongue in her mouth.

Liam held onto her bottom, pulling her downward so he could push more deeply inside of her. And, then, just like that, there is was again—that building, and pressure and sparks at the core of her body.

"There you go, baby," Liam murmured as she began to moan. "There you go."

Kate bit his shoulder, holding on to his body so tightly as she writhed on his rock hard erection. Her cry was stifled against his hot skin and Kate closed her eyes until the last shudders of the climax danced over her body.

After a moment to catch her breath, Kate sat upright with a surprised laugh.

With a tender smile, Liam said, "You're so beautiful, Kate."

Liam rolled her onto her back, rejoined their bodies so he could find his own release. And then the dance began again. He moved inside of her, hard, fast, demanding; skin to skin, legs intertwined, Liam thrust several times and then threw his head back with a growl of satisfaction.

"Lord, woman." Liam laughed, his forehead wet with perspiration. "I think you damn near wore me out."

Pinned down by his weight, their bodies slippery with sweat, Kate took his handsome face into her hands.

"You're the best thing that's happen to me in a long time, Liam."

Her lover kissed her sweetly on the lips. "My sweet Kate. I am yours for as long as you want me."

Chapter Six

"Thank you, Mommy!" Callie screamed while she simultaneously hugged her around the neck and jumped up and down. "Oh my gosh! Oh my gosh! I have to call Daddy right now!"

Was it the afternoon she had spent in Liam's arms, making love, talking, and then dozing off for a well-needed nap? Or was it just the fact that she realized that she was fighting a losing battle? Maybe it was a combination of both, but when she returned home later that afternoon, she gave Callie the greenlight to go visit her father and her sister in New York. It required her to block out two days when normally she would be training horses or clients, and it required her to spend the extra money, money that wasn't abundant, to fly to New York and back.

"I hope I don't regret this." Kate stared after her

daughter for a moment before she headed back into the barn to check on the progress of the evening chores.

As she always did, she swung by Visa's stall first. The poor boy, normally such an easygoing fellow, was beginning to develop some food aggression from being stuck in his stall for so long, pinning his ears and nipping at her when she brought him his hay. Liam was scheduled to x-ray the hind leg in a week; she was so hopeful that Visa would get the green light to go back to work.

"Fred!" Kate stood in the middle of the aisle, her hands on her hips, furious. "Where are you?"

Her barn manager came around the corner, a concerned look on his face.

"Yes, Ms. King?"

"None of these stalls have been cleaned." Kate pointed to several of the stalls. "This entire aisle is filthy. The water buckets haven't been washed today, and if I'm not mistaken, it's on the list for today, is it not? What's going on around here?"

"I don't know." Fred seemed as surprised as she was. "I'll get the crew on this right away."

"You do that," Kate said, annoyed. "These horses have a right to have clean stalls. They can't do it themselves."

Everyone who worked for her knew that she had zero tolerance for letting any of the housekeeping chores slide in the barn. She didn't have much of a temper, except when it came to slacking in the barn.

"I'm sorry, Visa." Kate rubbed the gelding's forehead. "We'll get your stall fixed up right away."

Now that she was taking some time for herself, all of the cracks that she normally filled when she was on-site were starting to show. She was going to have to rethink the business if she was going to continue to spend extra time away from the ranch. The thought of *not* spending alone time with Liam didn't seem like a good option. She had begun to count on that time for a little stress release.

Her phone began to ring; she pulled it out of her pocket, satisfied to see two stable hands enter the aisle with pitchforks and carts to begin mucking the stalls.

"Lloyd." That was the name that came up on the caller ID. It was a name she rarely saw, and she liked it that way.

"Hi, Lloyd."

"Katie."

Silence. That was how most of her conversations went with Callie's father.

"How have you been?"

Kate winced. Small talk with Lloyd was a less desirable task than getting her gums deep cleaned at the periodontist.

"Great," she said quickly. "I take it Callie told you the good news."

"Yeah. She just called."

Another odd silence. A sick feeling in her stomach, often associated with Lloyd, bubbled up in her gut. She moved down the aisle away from prying ears.

"Lloyd. What's wrong now?"

"Nothing." He sounded, as he typically did, like a worm trying to squirm off a hook. "Nothing at all really. It's just I didn't know about this trip, is all."

That information stopped her in her tracks.

"What do you mean, *you didn't know*?"

"I didn't know."

Kate took the phone away from her ear, closed her eyes, cursed under her breath several times.

What had possessed Callie to lie to her about something as big as this? Yes, her daughter was known to tell white lies, but this was a whopper.

"She told me that you invited her. That Bethany invited her."

"No." The sound of Lloyd scratching the stubble on his face, something he had done when they were together, made her cringe.

After another uncomfortable silence, she asked, "How did you leave it with Callie?"

"I told her that we'd work something out." Lloyd surprised her with that response, but with her ex, it was always "I'll believe it when I see it."

"You'd work something out? What does that mean? Is she coming to see you or not?"

"Well, now, Katie…"

"Kate."

"…this is all getting sprung on me out of the blue. I need to check my calendar, shuffle some things around—I'm in between jobs right now. You how my business is—feast or famine. Let's just see how it goes."

"Sure." Same old wait-and-see Lloyd. "Let's do that."

Without giving him the courtesy of a goodbye, Kate stabbed her finger on the red "hang up" button more times than needed to actually end the call.

"Damn him." She shoved her phone into her back pocket. "Damn him all to hell."

Kate went to find her daughter; she stood in the doorway of Callie's bedroom and watched her daughter balling up clothing and pushing it down into the open suitcase on her bed.

"Watcha doin', kiddo?" Kate walked over to the bed and sat down.

Callie had that smile on her face that she reserved for moments when she was super excited about something.

"I—I'm packing," Callie said happily.

Kate had to force down tears—tears of frustration and sadness for her daughter. Callie wanted to have a relationship with her father, and Lloyd had always let her down. No matter how gently or how often she had tried to explain the situation to her daughter, Callie simply couldn't grasp the complexity of the situation. In her mind, she had a father and he didn't love her. Maybe there was some truth to that simplistic assessment.

"Come here and sit down with me for a minute, okay?" Kate pushed the suitcase back a little and patted the mattress next to her.

Callie joined her and immediately leaned her body into hers and put her head on her shoulder. Kate put her arm around Callie's shoulders and hugged her.

"Sweetheart, I spoke to your father."

"Did he tell you that I—I was going to see him?"

"Here." Kate moved away from her daughter so she could look into her eyes. "Look at me."

Callie sat back, her brown eyes so full of hope.

Kate moved her daughter's long, brown hair over her shoulder before she took her hand and held on to it.

"Callie, your father told me that he didn't know about the trip."

Kate watched her daughter's face carefully. Callie didn't always know right from wrong, but she did know that it was wrong to lie.

Callie looked away, her cheeks and neck turning red and blotchy.

"Did you lie to me?"

Still keeping her eyes averted, Callie nodded.

"What have we said about lying, Calico?"

Her daughter slipped her gaze back to her for the briefest of moments. "I—I can't do it."

"Not that you can't do it—that you *shouldn't* do it."

Callie nodded again. "B-because it's wrong."

"That's right."

Her daughter's sweet face crumpled, then the tears began to fall.

"Come here." Kate took her daughter in her arms, just as she had when she was a little girl. She couldn't force Lloyd to be an engaged father; she could only be there, time and again, to pick up the pieces of Callie's broken heart.

"I—I wanted to go see my dad." Callie sniffled.

She wiped away the tears on her daughter's cheeks with her thumbs. "I know you did, sweet girl. But that's not an excuse to lie, Callie."

"I—I know. I—I'm sorry."

She stood, hands on hips, and assessed the mess in Callie's room. "How 'bout I help you clean all this up, and then we can go in to town and pick up some ingredients for whatever you want to cook today."

Yes, it was a temporary bandage for a wound that was never going to truly heal, but it was worth it to see a new smile on her daughter's face. This wouldn't be the last time that she had to deal with the fallout from Lloyd's absence in their daughter's life. That was just the harsh truth of the reality she had been living since the day Calico was born.

* * *

"It breaks my heart every time," Kate told Liam the next day. "Why does he have to be such a jerk? Yes, Callie did the wrong thing by lying, but she lied because she can't make sense of the fact that her father doesn't want to see her!"

"I don't know." Liam was sitting next to her in their favorite spot at the top of the mountain.

She glanced at his profile—they had agreed to keep talk about their exes at a minimum in order to focus on the present and their relationship. It wasn't difficult to read his unsmiling expression—her ex wasn't a top-priority topic for Liam.

"Sorry."

He reached for her hand. "You don't have to apologize. You need to be able to vent to me, and I need to be able to vent to you. We both have children with other people—no matter how hard we try, our past relationships will always resurface. I accept that."

She squeezed his hand gratefully.

"Are you sufficiently vented?"

With a laugh, she said, "Yes."

Liam had a real smile on his handsome face. "Good. Because I'd hate to think I schlepped this blanket up here for no reason at all."

She knew what he was driving at—one of her bucket list items was to make love outdoors, and today was the day they had slated to make love on their mountain. With all of her moaning and bellyaching, they were wasting time.

Kate stood quickly, stood in front of the man who had become more than just a lover—he had become her best friend—and pulled her T-shirt over her head and dropped it on the ground. Now she was standing on top of the mountain in her bra, the balmy breeze brushing over her naked shoulders and stomach.

Liam leaned back on his arm and took off his sunglasses so she could see his eyes admire her.

"You're a beautiful woman, Kate."

She smiled in response and unsnapped the button on her faded jeans. "Are you gonna keep talking? Or are we going to do this?"

Liam grinned at her, stood and pulled his T-shirt over his head. "Oh, we're definitely doing this, lady."

She had grown to love Liam's chest hair. She reached out and ran her fingers, tigress-like, through his light brown chest hair. Liam captured her hand and pulled her closer to him. He kissed her on the lips, on the neck, holding her tightly.

"Are we doing the full monty?" he asked against her neck.

She reached down between them, happy to discover that he was already aroused and ready for her.

With a laugh, Kate pushed away from him so she could finish undressing. "Yes. I want to be like Adam and Eve. Minus the fig leaves."

"You don't have to ask me twice." Liam winked at her as he stripped off his jeans and underwear.

He was naked, with the exception of his socks, before she could unzip her jeans.

"Something tells me that this isn't the first time you've been naked up here."

Kate unzipped her jeans, but she couldn't take her eyes off Liam. He was so well-built, slender, with lean muscle all over his body, tanned on his arms and neck.

The fact that he had a beautiful hard-on, just for her, only added to his appeal.

"Come here." Liam patted the spot next to him on the blanket.

Still in her underwear, bra and socks, Kate sat next to him on the blanket. He took her hand and kissed her shoulder.

"I like the way you smell," he said as he unhooked her bra.

"Manure and hay."

He laughed, gently slipping the strap of her bra down her shoulder. The moment the air hit her breasts, she knew that this feeling, this feeling of freedom, was exactly what she was looking to experience. She let him slip her bra completely off her body. Now sitting on top of their mountain, naked save her underwear and socks, Kate felt more free, and more adventurous, than she had in years.

As he always did, Liam began to fondle her breasts, massaging them just how he knew she liked it.

She dropped her head back. "Hmm. That feels so good."

"You feel good," Liam murmured before he kissed her nipple.

Kate thread her fingers through his hair, pressing his mouth harder to her breast. His mouth felt so good, so right. Her body was revving up, anticipating what was to come next. There was a tingling, an ache, between her thighs, building so quickly that she knew she would soon be pulling him on top of her, begging him to fill her.

"Lay back," Liam said, his eyes hooded with desire.

She followed his direction, lifting her hips a bit as he

slipped her underwear off her hips, along her thighs and past her ankles. Now she was naked, on a mountaintop, with the sun kissing her skin as the man she was growing to love kissed the inside of her thighs. She let her thighs fall open when Liam knelt between her legs. She knew what he wanted—he thought she tasted so sweet.

The moment his lips touched her, the moment his tongue slipped inside her, Kate forgot where she was and cried out with pleasure. With his hands beneath her bottom, Liam brought her closer to his mouth, loving her, tasting her, enjoying her. Kate moaned and writhed, pressing her head hard into her body; it was easy for her to ignore the sharp edge of the boulder pressing into her back. It was easy for her to lose herself and just enjoy the feel of Liam's mouth kissing her.

"You liked that," Liam said in a lover's voice as he kissed his way up her stomach and her breasts, until he was holding himself above her, the tip of his erection teasing her, asking for entry.

She reached for him with a pleased smile, wanting him so badly, needing him so badly. And then he was inside her, so deep, so thick. It felt like nothing else could. She opened her eyes and saw a look of sheer pleasure on Liam's face as he seated himself deep inside her.

"Oh, God, you feel good, baby."

The moment, which would have been perfect—which should have been perfect—wasn't perfect. The more Liam moved, the more the jagged edge of the boulder cut into her spine, and it hurt.

"Ow, ow! Wait! I have to shift," she told her lover.

Liam stopped moving, opened his eyes and smiled down at her. He braced his arms, lifted his hips off hers and gave her room to shift beneath him.

"Better?" he asked when she was done.

"I think so." She leaned back and lifted her hips to signal she wanted to continue.

They started the dance again, a rhythm they had developed over time. Their breath deepened, their eyes closed, and they both made noises of pleasure as they loved each other.

"Ow!" Kate's eyes flew open. "Wait!" She stopped moving. "Stupid rock. That really hurts!"

Making love on the mountain in her fantasy hadn't included sharp rocks poking into her butt and her back.

Liam laughed. "Hold on."

"Oh." Kate frowned as he disconnected their bodies. "It's not over, is it?"

"Hell, no." Liam lay down next to her. "You get on top. I'll handle the rocks."

With a smile, Kate put her hand on his stomach. "Are you sure?"

Liam checked the condom to make sure it was still secure. "Climb on."

She did climb aboard—happily. But then, her knees were rubbing against the boulder, ruining the pleasure of the moment. Frustrated and disappointed, her hands splayed across Liam's chest, Kate frowned. "This isn't working out as I imagined it."

"Don't worry. We'll make it work." She could tell, unlike her, he wasn't willing to call it quits.

Liam sat up a little, his arms braced behind him. "Here. Wrap your legs around me."

He positioned her so that she was sitting in his lap; it was the perfect solution. Now all she felt was his warm skin, his erection so deep inside her and the hard muscles of his thighs on her buttocks.

"How's that?"

She wrapped her arms around his shoulders, sunk her body down and began to move her hips. "Perfect."

She rode him, setting the pace, reveling in the feel of him suckling her nipple, reveling in the feel of his thick erection inside her. All she could hear was the wind rustling the leaves of the trees surrounding them and the sound of her moans of pleasure—and a laugh.

"Wait!" Kate whispered harshly, yanked back into reality. "Did you hear that?"

"No," he said against her breast. "Don't stop, Kate."

Another laugh.

They both froze their bodies, and looked around. "Is someone coming?"

"No." Liam tried to get back to business. "It's just an echo. They could be on the next mountain."

He tried to get her back in the mood, but all she could think about was getting caught, naked, doing the dirty. Liam was holding on to her, moving inside her. And, it felt so good, what he was doing, that he almost convinced her. Until she heard a male voice join that female laugh.

"Someone's coming!" she said urgently, separating her body from his. "Someone is *coming*!"

"Not me." Liam sighed in frustration. "Not anymore."

Chapter Seven

Kate was hiding behind a small clump of trees nearby, and Liam could hear her cursing under her breath as she yanked on her jeans and top. The moment, a moment he was *really* enjoying, was ruined. He had already pulled on his jeans and was bending over to retrieve his shirt when he saw his older brother, Bruce, the oldest of his six siblings, and Savannah, his sister-in-law, appear at the top of the mountain.

"Hey, brother!" Bruce, tall, broad shouldered, growing a beard, gave him a wave as he reached behind to make sure Savannah was safe.

Liam gave him a nod before he pulled on his shirt.

"Liam!" Savannah, as always, was happy to see him. She was a pretty, petite woman with auburn hair and moss green eyes.

"Who is it?" Kate asked harshly from behind the bush.

"My brother and his wife."

"Great," he heard his woman mutter. *Exactly. Great.*

Bruce and Savannah walked over to where he was standing, oblivious, at least in the beginning, about what they had just interrupted. Bruce clasped his hand and gave him a slap on the shoulder, and Savannah, now pregnant enough to begin showing, gave him a strong hug.

"We didn't expect to find anyone up here," Bruce said, looking around at the view.

Liam caught Savannah staring at the bra at his feet; for a brief moment, his sister-in-law met him eye-to-eye, her fair cheeks reddening.

"I think we should go." Savannah tugged on her husband's sleeve.

"Are you feeling okay?" His brother's immediate thought was about his wife's pregnancy. They had lost a son to a tragedy, and Bruce was hyperprotective of Savannah during this pregnancy.

Savannah, known for her sweetness, tried to smile through her embarrassment. "I just think that Liam wants to be alone..."

Bruce, who hadn't looked down and hadn't seen the bra, looked at his wife curiously, finding no particular reason why his brother would want them to leave.

"Oh, screw it," Liam heard Kate say from her hiding place.

Kate marched out from behind the shrubs, gave his brother and sister-in-law a little wave, scooped up her bra and tucked it into the front pocket of her jeans.

"Hi," Kate said with a little wave.

Understanding dawned on Bruce's face, but instead

of turning red like Savannah, he laughed a loud, hearty laugh and held out his hand to Kate.

"Nice to see you again, Kate."

"You remember my brother Bruce," Liam said causally.

Kate nodded.

"I'm not sure if you've ever met Savannah."

"Hi, Kate." Savannah shook Kate's hand. "We went to school together, but you were older, so…"

"I remember you. It's easy to remember the smartest student in school. Nice to see you again."

Savannah's face turned even redder at the compliment, one hand resting on her rounded belly, the other hand tucking a wayward hair behind her ear.

"I'm actually glad that we ran into you. I mean—I'm *not* glad that we interrupted what we…interrupted. Even though, it is kind of ironic because I was just talking to Bruce on the way up here that I needed him to text Liam so I could get your number. The whole family wants you to come to Sunday brunch."

Kate glanced at him—she knew that his family was aware that they were dating, but he'd deliberately shielded her from the craziness of his family's traditional Sunday brunch at Sugar Creek Ranch. His family was large and nosy and could overwhelm a person. He did not want Kate to feel overwhelmed while he was busy working his magic on her. Things were good between them, but by no means solidified.

"I think it may be a little soon for that." Liam blocked the invitation.

Savannah's expectant face turned crestfallen.

"Kate seems like she can handle herself," Bruce interjected. "Why don't you let her decide?"

Savannah reached over hand touched Kate's arm. "It's kind of like a rite of passage, but the food is amazing and everyone will love you. I promise."

"I can't leave my daughter alone and the person who watches her has Sundays off," Kate explained.

"She's welcome to come, of course!" Savannah assured.

Liam was surprised that Kate didn't seem completely opposed to breaking bread with his family. He'd eaten at her house dozens of times. Maybe it was the right time for her to run the gauntlet that was his family.

Liam ignored his brother and sister-in-law and turned to Kate. "I'd like you to be there. But only if you're ready."

Kate stared into his eyes as if she were trying to read his very soul before she said, "I think Callie would enjoy meeting new people."

His brother and Savannah left them to be alone on the top of the mountain after Kate agreed to join them for Sunday brunch. After their visitors were well out of earshot, Kate punched him in the arm.

"Ow!" He pulled his arm away jokingly as if she had really hurt him with that weak punch.

Kate held out her hand. "Underwear."

She knew that he had to have them because they weren't on the blanket where she had left them.

He shook his head with a smile. "No."

Hands on her hips, she frowned at him. "I'm not kidding, Liam! I can't believe that *this* is how I get introduced as your girlfriend to your brother and his wife! It's humiliating."

"No, it's not." Liam refused to give up her underwear and refused to give up on their mission to make love on top of this mountain. He'd never brought a woman to his special place; when Kate told him that she wanted to make love outside as a part of her bucket list, he knew that this was the right woman and the right place.

He pulled her into his arms even though she resisted half-heartedly. He kissed her on the neck, breathing in her familiar, sexy scent. God, he had actually fallen in love with this woman.

"They're gone," he said between kisses on her lips. "They won't come back."

"I'm not getting naked again if that's what you're thinking." Kate had her arms locked in front of her body, her forearms pressed against his chest.

"That's exactly what I'm thinking." He grabbed her bottom with both hands and pulled her groin into his. "Are you going to just leave me like this?"

"You're a big boy." She twisted out of his arms. "You can handle it."

He walked up behind her, wrapped her in his arms. He knew exactly what he needed to do to get her out of a "no" mentality and into a "yes" frame of mind. He began to kiss her ear, nibbling, licking, blowing and she immediately began to squirm in his arms, but not to get away.

She reached behind her body and put her hands over his erection. "You aren't playing fair."

"Make love to me, Kate," Liam whispered into her ear. "Right here. Right now."

She spun in her arms and kissed him, saying yes with her body, and her lips. Laughing, they stripped off their bottoms, but decided to at least leave their T-shirts on just in case.

"Crap!" he said when he realized he didn't have another condom with him.

"What?" Kate looked around expecting to see more people cresting over the mountain peak.

"I don't have another condom."

Her face went from relieved to thoughtful. "Oh."

They stared at each other for a moment, thinking. Then, Kate said, "I had my tubes tied."

That was news—they'd never really discussed it. They'd always used condoms.

He nodded, not upset. It was hard to think of either of them wanting to start all over again with a baby.

"We're…exclusive…" There was a question at the end of that statement.

"Yes," he said seriously. Definitively. "We are."

"I had myself tested after Callie's father. It's been a bit of dry spell since." she added with a raised eyebrow. "You?"

"I had myself tested last year," he told her. "So…are you okay with making love…without one?"

Her eyes drifted down to his softening hard-on, then back up to his face. "I am if you are."

Liam didn't bother to respond—he trusted Kate and if she trusted him, there were exclusive, and he wanted to make love to her in the worst way.

He lay on the blanket and she straddled him. They kissed and fondled and rubbed up against each other until he was good and hard and she was good and wet. Then, she sank on top of him, taking him inside her until he was buried so deep that it felt as if he were going to lose himself within her. She was so warm and tight and slick that he had to fight not to come right away. Without the condom, the sensations were so much more intense for him.

"God, baby." He gripped her hips with his hands, his eyes closed, fighting the feeling of wanting to explode.

"Is this okay?" she asked, her hands on his chest, her hips moving slow and steady.

"You feel so good, baby."

"I'm sorry." Kate stopped moving. "My knees. Can you sit up again like before?"

With one arm holding her close to his body, Liam leveraged himself into the sitting position. Kate wrapped her legs around his hips, and they were body to body, so close, holding each other so tightly.

Kate began to rock against him, taking her pleasure; this was a much better position because he could watch her beautiful face. He took her face in his hands and kissed her lips.

"Kate..." He said her name softly. "Open your eyes, Kate."

Her breath was shallow, her lips wet from his kissed. She opened her eyes. "I love you, Kate."

Her eyes widened in surprise at his words and, even though she didn't say the words in return, he could see the love in her eyes just before she closed them again; with a sigh, she wrapped her arms around his waist and rested her head on his shoulders. She came then, held so tightly in his arms, their groins pressed to together. She whimpered so sweetly, shuddering with the orgasm, Liam joined her. He had held off for so long that there was a sense of pain mingled with the pleasure.

"I love you too, Liam," Kate whispered.

Still connected, they held each other, their brows sweaty, their breathing rapid and shallow. For Liam, he couldn't remember ever feeling this way when he made love to a woman. This time was different—it was special. *Kate* was special. And it occurred to him, right then, that he wanted to make this woman his wife. He wanted to marry Kate King.

Kate was running late for Sunday brunch; he could tell by her harried voice on the phone that she was having "one of those mornings" when everything seemed to go wrong. Yes, things had gone wonky with her morning—a couple of hands called in sick and that put her behind. But he also knew that meeting anyone's family was stressful, and Kate had to be feeling that stress too. He knew he was, and to make matters worse, his father was on the warpath because one of his brother's daughters, a brother he hadn't spoken to in over twenty years, had been in contact with Savannah about her nonprofit. He'd almost told Kate to just scrap the brunch, but then again, she might as well see what kind of dysfunction she would be getting if she agreed to marry him.

"I don't give a good goddamn who contacted who and who did what first. I don't want any of Hank's kin on Sugar Creek Ranch! What in the hell were you thinkin', Bruce?" Jock Brand bellowed, slamming his hand on the table.

Savannah, whom Jock had always favored and had never had a harsh word for, spoke up. "I'm the one who answered Jordan on Facebook. Not Bruce. She wanted to donate to Sammy Smiles, and I wasn't going to turn her down. It's for Sammy's memory."

The table went temporarily quiet when Savannah mentioned her son, who had accidentally drowned when he was just a toddler. Savannah had started a nonprofit to spread the word about household hazards that could lead to accidental drownings, and everyone in the family knew that this was a "hands off" subject.

Jock frowned, his long, tanned, deeply lined face sullen. Savannah was pregnant on top of everything, and even Jock, who wasn't known for his sensitive nature, would be mindful of that. Instead of yelling at Savannah as he would any of his own natural born children, Jock balled up his fist, wrapped the table with his knuckles, pushed back his chair and left.

"I'm so sorry," Savannah apologized to the table. "We met Jordan's friend on our second honeymoon trip and one thing led to another..."

Bruce, ever protective of his wife, put his arm around his wife's shoulders and told her not to worry about it, as they all did.

After a moment, Lilly, his stepmother, a quiet, calm woman who had managed to last longer in marriage with Jock than any of them had bet, pushed back from the table.

"I will speak with my husband. Then we will have breakfast," Lilly said in a soft, but firm, voice.

"God—Dad is so uptight all the time." Jessie, the youngest, rather spoiled child and Jock's only blood daughter, was half paying attention to the discussion and half paying attention to her phone. "He really needs to seriously take a pill and get over it. Why can't I see my cousins? They didn't do anything to me, after all."

"Pop ain't gettin' over nothin'." Colten laughed between bites. "Pass those biscuits if no one's gonna eat 'em."

Liam looked at his phone to check the time—Kate and Callie were set to arrive in a few minutes, and he could hear Jock complaining loudly to Lilly about the breach of his long-standing rule—Hank and his kids were dead to them. Now, if any of them were communicating with their cousins on Facebook or any other social network, it would be mighty difficult to pretend that they were dead.

The doorbell rang and Liam got up quickly. He pointed his finger at all of his siblings. "Act normal. All of you."

"Ha!" Jessie laughed. "Fat chance of that!"

Liam beat Rosario, the house manager, to the door. "Thank you, Rosario. I've got it."

The woman gave him a curious look, then went about her business.

Liam swung open the heavy, carved door and greeted his love and her daughter.

"You have a b-beautiful house, Dr. B-Brand." Calico smiled at him.

"Thank you, Callie. Come on in."

He hugged Kate and gave her a quick peck on the lips. "Hi."

"Hi." She gave him a nervous smile. "Sorry we're late. Rough morning."

He shut the door. "Don't worry about it. It's been a rough one around here too. Let me apologize in advance for my family. They can be…challenging."

"Don't forget, I've already met everyone at least once." She was kind to try to reassure him.

"That's true," he agreed, leading to the dining room. "But you've never encountered them as a group. They can be a bit like a pack of wolves."

Kate, her hand holding on to her daughter's hand

tightly, continued to smile nervously. "We can handle them, can't we, Callie?"

"Of course," Callie said, confidently. "They aren't really wolves, Dr. B-Brand. They're just people."

Kate and Liam looked at Callie and then looked at each other. They both started to laugh; Callie had managed, in her own special way, to break the tension.

"I don't know, Callie," Liam said as he showed them to the dining room. "The jury is still out on that one."

Liam was damn proud of his family. They were on their "better" behavior for Kate and Callie, and they treated the young woman with kindness and acceptance and love. Lilly, who everyone called the "Jock Whisperer," had managed to get their hothead father back to the table. His face was still red and he looked as mad as a hornet, but his father had managed to be remotely cordial to Kate and Callie. That was more than he had expected.

"I can't remember the last time I ate so much food," Kate groaned as they walked the property surrounding his cabin. Callie had never met his horses or seen where he lived—it was time. While Callie visited with the horses for a bit longer, Liam took Kate to see one of his projects.

"Jock does everything to the extreme. He always has."

"That's not always a bad thing." Kate slipped her hand into his.

"No. Not always."

They walked in silence for a moment or two, heading to a large eight-bay garage. He pushed one of the bay doors open to show Kate what was housed inside.

"What's this?"

Liam smiled at the antique truck affectionately. "It's a Ford truck from the 1930s. It belonged to my great-great uncle."

"You're restoring it?" Kate, he could tell, appreciated the old truck.

He rested his hand on the rounded hood of the truck. This had been a project he'd been working on for years after he rescued it from the weeds.

"Little by little. It's a labor of love, really. One day, I'll take you for a ride in it."

On the other side of the hood, Kate smiled at him. "I'd really like that."

"So would I."

He was about to bring up the topic of a longer term commitment between them but was interrupted by Callie.

"Dr. B-Brand! I—I love your horses."

Callie, as she always did, greeted him with a hug.

"I—I want to b-bring my b-boyfriend here to meet them."

"That's fine," he told her. "Isn't it time you call me Liam?"

Callie ducked her head, blushed and then shook her head again.

"I told her she could call you Liam. She's just not ready."

Kate's daughter went to her side and hugged her. Then, she asked a surprising question to them both.

"I-if you guys get married, are we going to live here?"

His woman seemed caught off guard by the question—it made him wonder if she had even considered marriage between them. Yes, it was still early on in their relationship, but they weren't teenagers. They were old enough to know what they wanted and if something had a chance to work. Did Kate want more from their relationship? Or was he the only one swimming in that lake?

Kate brushed her daughter's hair over her shoulder. "We haven't talked about getting married yet, Callie."

Liam met Kate's eye. "Not yet."

That look held for a second longer, and then Kate added, "If and when that conversation does happen, you'll be the first to know."

Callie's giggled behind her hand. "B-but I—I saw Dr. B-Brand kiss you."

Kate wrinkled her brow at him over the hood of his antique truck—he had stolen a kiss, quite naturally, at the door earlier. It hadn't occurred to him that Callie had never seen them kiss, even if it was just a quick peck. He still had a lot to learn about Kate's daughter and how she saw the world through a slightly different lens.

"Yes." The horse trainer put her arm around her daughter's shoulder as they left the garage. "Liam did kiss me because we are really close friends. But just because you kiss someone doesn't mean that you are going to marry him."

"I—I am going to kiss Tony and I—I'm going to marry him," Callie said with certainty. "And I—I'm going to have a b-baby."

A pained expression flitted across Kate's pretty face. "Let's just take it one step at a time, okay, kiddo?"

Her mom's lack of enthusiasm, Liam noted, did not dampen Callie's excitement for the subject. "I-it could be a d-double wedding!"

Chapter Eight

Liam came over for dinner whenever he could—he was such a regular guest at their table that it was strange on the nights that he couldn't make it. And whenever she could, Kate took a couple of hours on his day off to meet him at Sugar Creek for a romantic rendezvous. There were plenty of bodies at the ranch to watch over Callie in the afternoon, so she had the freedom during the day to take a couple of hours just for herself.

"I hope you don't think that I'm just using you for your body." Kate had her body curled next to Liam's, her leg thrown over his, her fingers making circular patterns in his chest hair.

"I'm not sure I'd complain too much if you were," he admitted groggily, half-asleep after they had just made love. "But I'm glad you're not."

"Liam?"

"Hmm?"

"You're my best friend."

That was when he opened his eyes half-mast and looked down at her. He kissed her on the forehead and pulled her tighter into his body.

"You're my best friend too," he told her.

He dozed off, but she could never sleep in the afternoon. There was so much to do, all day, every day, that it was hard for her to shut her mind off even when she tried to sleep at night. The fact that she was willing to take an afternoon for herself was a huge change. After she untangled herself from Liam's body, she sat on the edge of the bed and stared at the man who had become her lover and her friend. He had kicked off the covers, and he lay on his back, completely naked, so handsome and strong.

Usually she would get dressed and kiss him goodbye. Today, she just couldn't resist taking control of the love-making for once. He was usually the one who initiated; he had mentioned, on occasion, that he wouldn't mind if she initiated every now and again. Perhaps it was time.

Quietly, slowly, Kate crawled over to where Liam was sleeping, glancing at his face to make sure he was still asleep. Gently, she took his penis in her hand, and, glad that he hadn't stirred yet, took him into her mouth.

She smiled when his body began to stir and his penis began to harden. Liam moaned, shifted his legs, and she felt his hand on her thigh.

Kate loved him with her mouth until he was as hard as a rock and ready to go, then she slid down on his thick shaft until their groins were pressed tightly together.

"Hello." Liam's eyes were open now, staring up her with a languid, sexy smile on his face.

"Hi, there," she said before she kissed him on the lips. "You don't mind do you?"

"Hell, no." He grabbed her hips and pushed her down hard as he was lifting up inside of her. "I love it."

At first the lovemaking was unhurried—she took her time building up to her first orgasm, and then she sighed as the sweet waves of pleasure pulsed through her body. Liam held her tight, letting her recover, before he rolled her onto her back and took charge. That's when the lovemaking became more intense, demanding; Liam grabbed the headboard behind her head so he could drive into her harder and deeper until she was sweaty and moaning and begging him to go faster. Liam exploded inside her when she started to cry out with a release so intense that it rocked her to her core. Nothing had ever felt like that before. No one had ever made her feel that *loved* before.

"What are you guys doing?" Kate had offered to wash the dishes while Callie and Liam spent some bonding time together.

"We're getting ready to video chat with Tony."

Kate sat on the couch armrest with her cup of coffee. "Is that so?"

Callie pushed the button on her tablet to call her boyfriend, Tony, and after a few rings, the young man who had captured her daughter's heart was on the screen.

"Hi, Tony!" Callie said with a giggle and a blush.

"Hi, Callie."

Tony was a little bit older than Callie, wore thick

glasses and had a crew cut. Callie thought he was the most handsome man she'd ever seen.

"Tony, this is Dr. B-Brand. My mom's b-boyfriend."

"Hi, Dr. Bwand." Tony waved.

"And you remember my mom, right?"

"Hi, Ms. King."

"Hi, Tony."

They gave Callie and her boyfriend some privacy while they went out to the swing under the old oak tree in the front yard.

"Are you okay?"

Kate didn't respond right away—her mind was racing, as it always did, whenever Callie spoke with Tony. Marriage was hard enough between two adults who didn't have a disability. You add Down syndrome, and marriage became nearly an impossible task.

"I just..." she started, and then stopped, not sure even where to begin. "Sometimes, I just don't know what to do with Callie. It would be different if there were other parents to talk to here, but there aren't."

"What about online support groups?"

"They're great. Don't get me wrong. But there's something different about face-to-face."

Liam didn't push her—he didn't rush her—he just waited for her to formulate her thoughts. This was one of the many things she truly loved about him.

"I know Callie hates it here."

"I don't think that's true."

"She does," Kate said with a shake of her head. "She wants to live in a city, where there are other people she can be friends with who have Down syndrome. When she goes to the yearly conference for Down syndrome, she's so happy. You should see her. She lights up. Here, it's as if the bloom has gone off the flower."

She breathed in and sighed heavily. She hadn't really opened up to anyone about her concerns regarding Callie.

"This is where my life is. I can't imagine living anywhere else, certainly not in a city back East."

"I didn't even know you were considering something like that."

She put her hand on his leg to reassure him. "I'm not. Not really. But what do I do about Callie? She doesn't have any friends here—she doesn't really have a life here. And she can't live alone. She'll never be able to live alone. She could live in a group home, but that would make me nuts. I would worry about her all of the time. *I've* been the one who's taken care of her since before she was even born. How can I just turn that responsibility over to strangers, no matter how competent and caring they appear to be?"

"I can't imagine you doing that."

"No. Neither can I. And now she wants to marry Tony and have babies. That's all she can talk about."

"And you don't want her to."

"It's not that I don't want her to get married and be happy, but it's so much more complicated with two people with Down syndrome. There's more than just Tony and Callie in this situation. Tony lives with his parents. Where would they live? Who would look after them? I haven't even really spent any time with Tony's parents. We actually have to get along and agree on logistics. Can you imagine that? There's more than just Tony and Callie in the marriage. Tony's parents are in the marriage too! Do you know what a mess that could turn out to be? Five people in a marriage instead of two."

"Is this...marriage even a possibility in the near future?"

Another sigh. She threw up her hands. "For Callie, it's a next week kind of thing. I don't know where Tony and his parents stand."

"Maybe it's time to talk to them."

She had been thinking the exact same thing, and then finding reasons every day not to call.

"I know. You're right. I've just been finding ways to avoid it. I don't know why."

"Because who wants to have that conversation? I'd find ways to avoid it too."

That made her laugh. She put her head on his shoulder, and they swung gently together in the night.

"You know what I'd like to do?" he asked her.

She shook her head.

"Take you out on a real, honest to goodness date. I always come over here, you come over to my place. When have we actually gone out?"

"I don't want to ask Fred to work an evening. He really needs his nights off."

Liam looked down at her, caught her eye. "Bring her along."

She lifted her head so she could get a good look at his face. "Are you serious?"

"She's a part of you," he told her. "Yes. Of course I'm serious. We'll all get dressed up and paint the town red. What do you say?"

"Yes." She kissed him on the cheek. "Of course, I say, yes."

* * *

She hadn't seen Baily, her master hairstylist and colorist for nearly a year. To sit in that chair, under those harsh lights, noticing every new wrinkle and facing sagging at the jowls, was rather painful. But if Liam wanted to take Callie and her out on the town, she needed to get her hair styled and get a new outfit. She spent her life in jeans and muck boots, smelling like manure and hay. Tonight, she was going to smell like perfume, with new hair and maybe even a dress.

"Are you going out on a hot date with Dr. Brand?" Baily asked while she combed out her wet hair.

It didn't surprise Kate that Baily knew about her relationship with Liam. It was a small town and the person who had managed to land a catch like Liam Brand was juicy gossip. But it still made her uncomfortable. She had been a private person all of her life, and even in a small town she wanted to have her business remain *her* business.

"He's taking Callie and me out to dinner, yes."

"Aww! That's so sweet!" the hairstylist exclaimed. "Handsome and nice to your kid? You need to get him to put a ring on it, quick."

Kate shifted in her chair, uncomfortable more with the topic of marriage than with her position in the seat. Liam had been bringing up the subject more frequently, and she just couldn't bring herself to get on board. Not that he was suggesting that they rush to marriage—he wasn't—but he did want to know if she had any intention of ever fully committing to him. For Liam, marriage and family had always been the goal. For her, marriage was never much of a priority. She had gone against her upbringing, her faith and her family when she decided not to marry Callie's father. His reaction to her diagnosis while their daughter was still in utero convinced her that Lloyd wasn't the type of man she wanted to marry. She was a businesswoman, independent and a single mother. Now she had an amazing man in her life as a companion and, in her mind, an incredible lover. Why rock the boat? Marriage could, ultimately, destabilize a really good thing that they had going.

"Look, Mommy!"

Callie had been in the front of the salon getting treated to a manicure and pedicure in preparation for their big night out with Liam.

She extended both of her arms and wiggled her bright pink fingernails for her mother to see.

"Pretty in pink!" Callie told her.

Kate leaned over and kissed her daughter's happily flushed cheeks. "You are pretty in pink, kiddo."

"Thank you." Her daughter ducked her head. "I—I need to take a selfie for Tony so he can see how pretty my nails are."

"I'll take a picture of you," Baily offered.

Baily took a break from her duties with Kate's hair to take a picture of Callie with her hot pink nails. Then, Callie sat in the empty chair next to Baily's station and focused on her phone.

"She's so grown up," Baily commented as she picked up her scissors. "I can't hardly believe it."

"I know." Kate nodded. "It's seems like yesterday I brought her in for her first haircut."

"Time flies, don't it?"

"Yes, it does."

Baily stood behind Kate and met her eyes in the mirror. "So. How much are we taking off?"

Kate stared at her own reflection, finding it difficult to focus on anything other than how haggard and old she was looking to her own eyes. After a moment of thought, she shrugged. “It’s time for a change. As long as I can get it into a ponytail, I’m good.”

Baily held a chunk of hair between her fingers and held it up for Kate to see. “Three inches would make a world of difference.”

It had been years since her hair had been that short. And, yet, things were changing all around her and it felt like that should be reflected in her hair.

“Go for it,” she said. “If I don’t like it, I can always grow it back.”

“Wow.” Liam stared at her as if he were seeing her for the very first time.

“It’s a lot shorter than I thought it would be.” Kate self-consciously touched her bobbed hair.

“You look…” Liam’s eyes continued to admire her. “You look so beautiful tonight, Kate.”

She hadn’t worn a dress since Callie’s high-school graduation the year before. Tonight, she wore a simple green wrap dress and a simple pair of strappy heels. Green was Liam’s favorite color; she had wanted to look especially nice for him tonight.

“Thank you. You look handsome.”

Liam was wearing a sport coat, a crisp white shirt and dark denim jeans. So handsome, this man of hers.

“Hi, Dr. Brand!”

“Calico! Look at you.”

The young woman held out her hands and wiggled her fingers. “Pretty in pink.”

Liam took one of her hands, kissed it and then spun her around. "You look beautiful."

Callie covered her face with her hand and giggled with pleasure. Liam offered each one of them his arm.

"Shall we?"

As they drove into town in Liam's freshly cleaned truck, listening to strains of Trace Adkins, all Kate could think about was how kind Liam was to her daughter. Why hadn't Callie's own father been able to be even half as kind?

"You okay?"

Kate pulled herself away from her thoughts of Callie's father and gave her companion a quick nod meant to reassure.

"I've been looking forward to this all day," she said, because it was the truth.

He took his hand off the steering wheel for a moment to squeeze her hand. "So have I."

From the back seat, Callie chimed in. "I—I have too!"

Liam took them to Emerson Grill, known for its fine Northern Italian cuisine. Callie had a very limited palate, so she stuck with spaghetti marinara and meatballs. To drink, a Shirley Temple from the bar. Yes, Kate loved spending the evening with Liam and her daughter. More than that, she loved to see how happy her daughter was to be dressed up, with her nails polished, "out on a date." It made Kate wonder—was she being selfish keeping Callie in Montana with her? Was it time to let her go?

After dinner, they caught a PG movie, and then Liam drove them home. The first thing Callie did was get on her tablet to video chat with Tony. Kate slipped off her shoes, dropped them on the floor and then joined Liam on the couch. She leaned into his body, her back resting against his chest, her head tilted to the side so it was tucked into the crook of his neck. She loved the way this man felt; she loved the smell of his skin and the feel of his hands on her body.

"Hmm," she murmured, her eyes closed. "This is nice."

"You feel nice."

His voice was groggy, and she knew him well enough to know that if she just stopped talking to him, he'd be asleep in no time. Liam had never spent the night at her house, not even on the couch. The man was so tired, it just didn't make sense for him to drive the hour it would take him to get back home.

Kate slowly extracted herself from Liam's arms, helped him out of his boots and then covered him with the blanket that she kept draped over the back of the couch. She kissed him on the cheek.

"Thank you for tonight, Liam."

He mumbled, eyes still closed, "I love you."

It was so easy for him to say to her, and yet, those words always seemed to get stuck in her mouth right before she got them out. She did love Liam—and she had managed to tell him once before. Honestly, loving him was a no-brainer. He was kind, and smart, and successful, and funny. He was so good with Callie. Why couldn't she commit herself completely to this man? Was she permanently broken? Or just too set in her ways to imagine her life as a plus one.

After she gave Liam another kiss good-night and checked on Callie, Kate went to her bedroom, got ready for bed and turned off the light. Normally, she was so tired that pretty much the second her head hit the pillow she was asleep. Tonight, she stared up at the ceiling, her mind whirling. She tossed, turned and then finally snapped on the light and threw back the covers. Sitting on the edge of the bed, beyond irritated to still be awake when she was tired as heck, Kate finally got up.

Long after Liam and Callie had gone to sleep, Kate sat up paying bills and answering emails. She just couldn't seem to get her brain to shut off, so she figured she may as well get some work done. Several hours later, she stood, stretched, her neck stiff and back aching.

"Okay," Kate said aloud to herself. "Let's try this again."

Once again in bed, Kate lay on her back, her arms under the covers, eyes wide open. And the truth was, she knew what was keeping her awake. This was the first time a man had spent the night in her home, and it was freaking her out. All he was doing was sleeping on her couch. He hadn't asked her to marry him, even though he had hinted at it, and he hadn't moved his stuff into her drawers. And, yet, this felt like a giant step further into relationship-land.

"Kate Marie." She blew out her breath. "It's not the end of the world, it's just the next natural step. What's *wrong* with you?"

Chapter Nine

"I'm exhausted." Her friend Lorrie hoisted her saddle onto the rack and slumped down onto her tack trunk.

Kate continued to clean the bridle she had just used on the trail ride she had taken with her friend.

"Everyone in the house has been sick except me." Her friend leaned back and closed her eyes. "I think this may be the first time I've closed my eyes in days."

The horse trainer finished her chore, hung up the bridle and then said, "Let's go get something to drink before you head out. I feel like it's been forever since we've had a chance to catch up."

"It's been a while." Her friend sighed before she opened her eyes. "You've been busy, I've been busy."

Lorrie dropped her hands on her thighs with another sigh, groaned a bit from the sore leg muscles when she stood. “I’ve been feeling so guilty about not coming out here and riding.”

Side by side, they walked out of the barn, stopping to give some love to the old cats gathered at the entrance of the barn. They took the stairs up to Kate’s office above the barn, where a pot of coffee was ready to brew.

Her friend sat on the small love seat. “That coffee smells so good.”

“It’ll be done in a second.” Kate sat, kicked her boots off and put her feet up on the desk.

“So…” Lorrie eyed her with interest. “How’s it been going with the hot veterinarian?”

“It’s going fine.” She shrugged noncommittally. “So far.”

A disappointed expression passed over her friend’s face. “Oh.”

The bubbling, popping sound of the coffee at the tail end of brewing got Kate out of her seat. “What?”

Lorrie wrinkled her nose a bit. “Is the sex bad?”

Kate kept on pouring coffee into a cup as she gave a surprised laugh. “Why would you think that?”

She handed her friend a cup and sat back down one of her own.

“Because…” Lorrie blew on the coffee. “If it was good, you wouldn’t use such a horrible word like *fine* to describe your relationship.”

Lorrie took her first sip of coffee. “Ah. Thank you. This is exactly what I need to help me make the drive home.”

“Fine just means fine. As in, everything’s fine between us.”

“Fine,” Lorrie said with a teasing laugh.

That made Kate smile into the rim of her cup. The

coffee did taste good, and it would give her the pick-me-up she needed to help her get the rest of the work on her daily to-do list done.

"No..." She put her cup on the desk. "Liam is more than fine. He's so kind. Considerate. A real adult, which can be really hard to find in a man..."

"Amen."

"...and he is so amazing with Callie. He treats her like she matters. He always has. I only wish I could have gotten Lloyd to treat her with half as much love and care. All he's done is disappoint her. Remember I told you about the phone call and Callie packing?"

Lorrie nodded.

"Well, I called yesterday, no answer. I called the day before. No answer. I've texted, emailed."

"No answer." Her friend filled in the obvious response.

"He's such a jerk," Kate said with a frown. "Callie deserves so much better."

"She has better now."

Kate looked up.

"Liam," Lorrie told her. "She has Liam."

"That's true," she agreed. "But nothing is set in stone there. And I'm still not sure where it's going yet."

"Do you want it to go somewhere?"

Lorrie knew her like no other, and her friend had managed to ask *the* question. Where did she want things with Liam to go?

Her friend got up to refill her cup; she held up the coffeepot. "More?"

Kate put her hand over the top of her cup with a shake of her head.

With a refreshed cup of coffee, Lorrie took one of the armchairs on the other side of Kate's desk.

"Do you think that you would ever get married?" her friend asked. "If the right man—like Liam—came along?"

She crossed her arms in front of her body.

Lorrie filled in the silence. "It's hard to give up control, I would think. You've been the head of your own life for years."

"I try to imagine what it would be like to have to answer to someone else. I'm not sure I'm really cut from that cloth."

"Liam seems like he's cut from that cloth."

Yes. Liam was definitely the marrying kind.

"We haven't talked about it, really. Not in so many words. He's hinted and I've avoided."

With a sigh, the horse trainer stood. Break time had to be over. "Why does every relationship have to end in marriage? I *like* how things are between us. He has his space, I have mine. We see each other when our schedules allow. What's wrong with that?"

"Nothing at all. It's not written anywhere that you have to get married, Kate." Lorrie stood up as well, rinsed her mug out in the sink. "Liam and you can go on like this forever, if that's what you both want. Is that what you both want?"

"Well?" Kate asked, a hint of anxiety in her voice. "Can he go back to work?"

Liam had his computer set up on a small folding table, examining the X-rays he had just taken of Visa's hairline fracture.

Visa had been a worry in the back of Kate's mind;

Liam had already been out once before, and the fracture hadn't healed enough for him to "okay" a return to work.

Liam looked up from the radiographs. "He can go back to work."

Kate's face lit up in a way that pleased him. He'd grown to love the planes of her face, the sweetness in her eyes, and the taste of her lips. He missed her when they were apart, and he couldn't wait to get her back in his arms the moment he saw her.

"Did you hear that, Visa?" Kate unhooked the straps for the cross ties and led the horse out of the bay. "You just got released from jail."

Liam walked beside Kate and Visa as she led him past the stall that had been his cell for the last several months. He had something to talk about with Kate, and he hoped that she would be as excited as he was about the news.

Kate took off Visa's halter and released him to a small fenced pasture where he could get the "silly" out, running and bucking and rolling on the ground without any interference from other horses.

The minute Visa realized that he was free, he began to run from one end of the small pasture to the other, kicking and bucking happily along the way.

One of his interests as a large-animal veterinarian was helping to heal and return to full function horses that would otherwise be put down because of an injury.

Kate, surprising him, wrapped her arms around his waist and squeezed him tightly. She didn't say anything, but she didn't need to. Her animals, all of them, were second only to Callie. Saving Visa, such a young, beautiful horse with so much life left to live, was a gift to her. And she appreciated him for it.

Liam held on to the woman he loved, his chin resting lightly on the top of her head, loving the smell of the honeysuckle shampoo that she used.

"I really thought I was going to lose him," she said after a moment.

"I was going to do everything in my power to make sure you didn't."

She unwound her arms from his waist, and he reluctantly let her go. Kate was affectionate only to a point, and rarely in public. And he understood. Here at the Triple K she had to maintain a strong leadership image for the men under her charge. Even in the new millennium, there was a lot of sexism in the industry. It couldn't always be easy to be the boss of men.

"You are one hell of a good vet, Liam." She leaned forward, resting her arms on the top of the fence. "I'm grateful to have you."

"Thank you." Liam joined her at the fence. "I'm glad to be here for you."

He wanted to be there for Kate in all aspects of her life—not just as her vet, not just as her part-time lover and boyfriend. He wanted more. But he also knew, just from her body language and facial expressions and avoidance, that trying to move their relationship further along would only be met with resistance. It was early enough in the relationship that he could afford to be patient. Yet if Kate wanted the status quo to go on indefinitely, that wasn't what would work for him. He craved companionship; he craved family. He wanted Kate and Callie to be his family.

They left Visa to graze happily in the pasture. Liam

had seen him trot and gallop without any sign of lameness. Visa was one of his best success stories, and particularly because he was one of Kate's horses, he was gratified that his plan for the young gelding had worked. There had been no guarantee that it would.

"Can you stay for dinner?" she asked as they walked through the barn back to his equipment.

"Not tonight." Liam began to pack up his gear.

It satisfied his ego to see a flash of disappointment in her eyes. It felt good to know that she wanted him to be with her, even if he couldn't be there as much as he wanted to.

Liam lifted his gear, and they walked out to his truck together. After he loaded his equipment, Liam stood next to the open driver's door.

"Callie's going to be disappointed you can't make dinner." Kate squinted against the sun.

"How about her mom?"

"She'll be disappointed too."

"Good," he said with a smile. "That's exactly how I want it."

He snuck a quick kiss before he said, "Today is a good news day all around."

She waited for him to continue.

"My kids are coming for a visit next week."

Kate's face lit up. "Liam! That's great news. I'm so happy for you."

He climbed behind the wheel. "I want them to meet you."

"Of course."

"And Callie."

Kate nodded without any hesitation in her eyes.

Liam shut the door, cranked the engine, then hung his arm out of the window. "I'll talk to you tonight."

She nodded again with a wave. They had begun a ritual of speaking on the phone every night before they went to bed.

"Hey." He started to pull away, then stopped. "I love you."

He was rewarded with a fleeting, sweet smile. "Me, too."

"Good," he said again. "That's exactly how I want it."

His kids looked different in real life—he'd been communicating with them via phone, video chat, email and text, everything but face-to-face for so long that it seemed strange to have them in the truck with him again. They were taller, older, different.

"You guys hungry?" Liam had just picked up the two teens from the airport.

"I'm gluten-free." Sarah didn't look up from her phone.

"Since when?" he asked his younger child, who had begun to mature into something resembling a woman now. She was wearing lip gloss.

"Since forever," his daughter said rather sullenly. He was well aware of the fact that Sarah hated her new school, hated her stepfather, hated Seattle, and, in general, currently hated her mother.

"Well, don't worry. I'm sure we can find some gluten-free food for you. I won't let you starve."

"Sure you won't." When had Sarah become so sarcastic.

"What about you?" he asked his son, also engrossed in his cell phone.

Both of his kids, like so many other kids nowadays, were total phone junkies.

"I could eat," Cole mumbled.

"Mom wanted me to tell you that Cole has to watch what he eats because of he just got his braces."

"Mind your own business," Cole snapped at his sister.

Sarah kicked under the passenger seat in response.

"Your daughter can be a real asshole."

Yes, he'd expected them to be different, but these were completely changed kids.

"Watch your language, Cole."

"Ooh. You're in trouble now, jerk."

Liam caught his daughter's eye in the rearview mirror. "What the heck is wrong with the two of you? You guys actually used to like each other."

It was a tense, quiet lunch, with Sarah complaining mostly about the lack of gluten-free selection. They stopped at the grocery store to pick up gluten-free food for his daughter and stock up on some snacks for his son. Cole spent most of the trip laughing at something his friends put on Snapchat while Sarah took charge of the shopping cart. He had his kids back with him for not even a half a day, and already he wanted to send them back. And he felt like a horrible person because of it.

"Everything in your rooms is the same," Liam told them when they got back to the cabin he had built as a wedding gift for their mother.

When they arrived at the ranch, a place they had called home for the first part of their lives, that was the first time he actually saw some lightness, some happiness, come into his daughter's blue eyes. It had been fleeting, but it had been there. That was a start.

Cole went straight into his room and shut the door.

"Great." Sarah paused in the doorway. "My Little Pony."

Liam stood in the great room staring at the two closed bedroom doors. This was not how he had imagined his first day with his kids. He'd look forward to this for such a long time, and it was off to a dubious start at best.

"So? How's it going?" Kate picked up her cell after the first ring.

He had stepped outside and walked over to his workshop, away from the house so his kids couldn't hear his conversation.

"Honestly." He shut the door to his workshop behind him. "They act like I'm punishing them by even having them here."

"Oh," Kate said sympathetically. "They're teenagers. It's their job to act like everything is a pain in their neck. Just give them a couple of days to shake off the grumpiness, and I'll bet they'll warm up."

He hoped she was right. One week of sullen and sarcastic would be a long week indeed.

"I think we should postpone our dinner with them."

"Sure," she said easily. "Let's just keep it flexible. There's always next time."

"No," Liam said quickly. "I want them to meet you and Callie this time. I'll talk to you tonight."

The week had passed quickly for her, but it was strange not to have Liam around. His children's visit was keeping him occupied, and the only time they really had a chance to talk was at night. She missed him. She missed making love too. Her body was actually letting her know that it missed having private time with Liam.

He met her and Callie at the door of his cabin.

"Hey!" He didn't kiss her as he usually did, but the smile on his face and the smile in his eyes let her know that he was as glad to see her as she was to see him.

"Hi, Dr. B-Brand. I—I made a gluten-free chocolate cake for you."

"Thank you, Callie." Liam gave her a hug and accepted the cake. "This looks so good I may have to have dessert first."

That made Callie duck her head with pleasure and giggle.

Liam introduced him to his teenagers. Both of his kids strongly favored Liam and the Brand side of the family; both were tall, lanky, with sandy-brown hair and bright, blue eyes. Sarah, in particular, was the spitting image of her father.

"Have you been enjoying your visit with your dad?" Kate tried to make a connection with Liam's daughter.

Sarah shrugged a little. "I used to live here."

"I remember," the horse trainer told her. "I used to see you in town with your mom."

"Yeah."

"Do you miss it?"

Sarah shrugged again.

"Do you like horses?"

That got the smallest of smiles out of the teen.

"I used to ride all the time when I lived here," Sarah told her. "I never get to ride in Seattle."

"You can come out to see my horses if you want," Kate offered.

"We have horses here." The teen pulled a face.

Sarah stood, looked as if she was going to leave without say anything in response, but she stopped and said, "Dad didn't tell me he was dating anyone."

Every second his kids were with Kate and Callie, Liam felt like he was on edge. He didn't relax from the time Kate had arrived until the time he was walking them out to their truck. They both waited for Callie to get inside the vehicle before they took a moment to talk privately.

"I'm sorry." Liam apologized right off the bat, even though she didn't expect it or think it was warranted. "They're going through a weird phase. God help me if they get stuck in it."

Kate touched his arm sympathetically. "A week is such a short time. Couldn't they stay a little while longer?"

"Perish the thought," Liam blurted out before he added. "No. Their mother and stepfather are taking them to the Bahamas."

"Well, I'm glad I got to meet them, anyway." She had seen Liam's children at school functions in passing, but that had been years ago. They had both grown so much since then.

Liam looked pained; none of this was easy for him. He wanted his kids to love their time with him, and he wanted them to love her too.

"It's going to be okay, Liam. It always is."

Chapter Ten

"Lord have mercy, I needed that." Kate rolled onto her back, naked.

Liam chuckled, his hand on her thigh. "I second that."

After taking a week off to spend with his kids, Liam had to work late nights without taking a day off to catch up with his caseload. No day off meant no time for afternoon lovemaking.

Kate pulled the covers over her body and curled into Liam's warm body, loving the scent of the man. She kissed his chest, before resting her head in the crook of his arm.

"I can't believe how much my body missed you."

Liam lifted his head a little to look down at her. "Just your body?"

She hugged him. "No."

"I missed you," he told her, rubbing her arm lightly. "I miss you all the time."

"Hmm…that's nice."

Liam sat up so he could look down at her; he brushed her hair away from her face.

"Every night that we talk on the phone, I say sweet dreams before we say goodbye and then I wonder why I'm not with you, in person, to kiss you good-night."

She reached up and put her hand on his face. "We live complicated lives."

"Not really," he disagreed gently. "It doesn't have to be complicated. Why can't we live together? I love you, I love Callie. As far as I can see, there's nothing holding us back."

Kate tried to scoot away from him, but Liam rolled between her thighs and pinned her down.

"Every time I try to talk to you about our future, you find a reason to end the call or change the subject or find something, anything, else to do."

He kissed her before she could formulate words; she'd rather kiss him than talk about taking the next step in their relationship when she wasn't all that sure that they *needed to* take a next step. This was lovely.

Kate let her legs fall open wider, wrapped her arms around Liam's waist; she felt his body begin to rouse and she welcomed the diversion. Liam reached between their bodies and guided his hardening shaft into her body.

"Ah…" Kate sighed at the wonderful feeling. Slowly, deliberately, Liam pushed into her deep, then stopped moving. They were connected, body to body, chest to chest.

"Look at me, Kate."

Liam had lifted himself up over her.

She opened her eyes; he had grown so hard so quickly that she wanted to stop talking and start moving. It was so easy to orgasm with Liam.

"This is incredible." Liam's voice was gruff with feeling, desire. "But there has to be more."

Kate nodded and shifted beneath him to get him to move within her. It took only two long, hard strokes to get her to climax. She shuddered in his arms, clinging to him, wrapping her legs so tightly around him as he picked up the rhythm, driving into her until he found his own release.

Instead of lingering in bed with her as was his habit, Liam gave her a quick peck on the lips, got out of bed and hopped into the shower. She wasn't stupid—her resistance to any type of discussion about their future plans had grated on him. No, she wasn't sure how to move forward with Liam, but she was very clear on one thing—she didn't want to lose him.

He emerged from the bedroom, his hair wet and slicked back from his face, still unshaven with a thick layer of stubble on his face. He was barefoot, shirtless, his chest hair still wet. The man *was* just sexy.

"Coffee?"

"That's exactly what I need, thank you." He walked past her—no kiss—and opened one of the kitchen cabinets and rifled through the bottles until he found the one he was looking for.

"Here you go." She put the coffee cup on the counter next to him.

Liam took out a bottle of ibuprofen, shook a couple of tablets into his palm, then popped them into his mouth.

"Aren't you supposed to get a headache before sex?"

He took a swig of coffee, wincing as the hot liquid hit the back of his throat. She could read him well enough now to know that he was irritated.

She put her cup on the kitchen butcher block island. "Look… I can tell that you're annoyed with me."

He put his cup down as well. "Not annoyed. Frustrated."

Same difference as far as she was concerned.

"Okay. Frustrated. And now I'm starting to feel frustrated with you and that's not how I want to feel."

Liam grabbed a T-shirt off the back of one of the bar stools and slipped it on over his head. Then he crossed his arms protectively in front of him as if he were gearing up for a fight. "What are you feeling frustrated about?"

"This obsession you seem to have about us moving forward." She used air quotations when she said *moving forward.* "We haven't even been together all that long. What's the matter with how things are now? I *like* how things are now. What's the big rush?"

"I already know what I want," Liam said. "I want you. I want to be with you. I want to wake up with you in the morning, I want to go to bed with you every night. And the fact that you don't want the same thing makes me question what the hell I'm doing in this relationship."

"You question why you're with me?" Kate asked, stung. "Just because I'm not jumping up and down at the thought of getting married?"

"You don't have to say it like it's a dirty word."

"I didn't."

"Yes. You did. That's the problem. You and I don't have the same vision for the outcome of what we've started here. I've never made it a secret that I want to be a part of a family. My *own* family. We could have that, you and me and Callie."

She gestured around her, to his cabin, to his homestead on Sugar Creek Ranch. "And what? Callie and I move here? You move to the Triple K? Change everything about our lives?"

Kate started to scratch at her neck, feeling hot and itchy all over her body.

"Just because things change doesn't mean it's for the worse. And to answer your question—I would leave Sugar Creek. For you."

Liam stared at her; watched her clawing at her neck. "Jesus," he said. "Just look at you. One conversation about marriage and you break out in hives."

"Don't be ridiculous," Kate snapped. "I don't have hives. And just so we're clear, you don't understand. I've got a lot on my plate right now. I've been looking into apartments for Callie in town. She wants to be independent and I want that for her. But Callie thinks that she wants to leave the ranch, but she has a really hard time with change."

"I do understand that. Either way, we can make things right for Callie." Liam pinned her with a pointed look. "Let's be honest. You have just as much difficulty with change as Callie. Maybe even more."

A tingle of fear raced up her spine—this wasn't at all how she expected their long-awaited afternoon of lovemaking to go. The silence stretched between them until it felt awkward that neither of them was saying anything.

Finally, she spoke what they both were thinking. "What if I don't want things to change? What if I like how things are?"

Liam pushed away from the island to put some distance between them, leaned back against the kitchen sink and crossed his arms in front of his body again.

"If we don't want the same thing, Kate, then we've got to end it now. That's not what I want. But we're not teenagers. We're old enough to know what we want."

Her fingers gripped the edge of the counter as she swallowed hard several times.

"Do you—" she started and then stopped "—want to call it quits right now?"

Liam stared at her hard, his eyes filled with disappointment. "Like I just said, that's not what I want. I want us to make a plan to be together for the rest of our lives. *That*'s what I want. But if what you're saying is that all you want is this—" he gestured between them "—casual arrangement where we get together on my days off to make love and I come over for dinner once or twice a week."

He paused and she waited.

"If that's what you're telling me, then, yes. We need to cut our losses and move on."

Two weeks went by without a phone call from Liam. Kate was so busy with the ranch and the horse training and looking at assisted-living apartments for Callie in town that she was able to put Liam out of her mind most of the day. But at night, especially during that block of time when she would crawl under the covers and call his number to talk about their days, that's when life without Liam really hurt. She missed him like he was a missing limb—he was gone, but she could still feel him.

So many times, she picked up her phone, stared at it, debating whether she should call him and break the silence. Yet she knew in her heart that she wasn't ready to commit *forever* to him. Not because he wasn't wonderful and worthy—he was. And it wasn't that she didn't love him, because she did. What it came down to, for her, was that she had built a life for nearly two decades. It wasn't a perfect life, but it was *hers*. She wasn't beholden to anyone, she didn't have to account for another person other than her daughter, and she was in complete control of her money and her future. Liam wanted a marriage, he wanted a wife. If she gave in to that future, how much of her own autonomy would she lose? How much of her life would remain her own?

For her, it was a big question. It was, in fact, *the* question.

"Fred." Kate found her most trusted employee overseeing the installation of new automatic waterers for the stalls.

"Yes, ma'am?"

"I need to leave the ranch for a while. Can you stay a little late today so Callie isn't here alone?"

Fred tipped his head. "Yes, ma'am."

Kate found Callie and let her know she was leaving before she headed out. She thought she should change her clothes—it'd been raining for days, so her jeans and boots were caked with mud. But it felt as if she didn't have the moment to spare; she didn't want to wait to get to Liam. Two weeks without him had been long enough. If he had been trying to show her what life would be like without him, his plan had worked. She discovered that, no matter what change was coming down the pike, she did not like her life without Liam Brand.

At Sugar Creek Ranch, Kate parked her truck next to his truck, rushed up the porch stairs of Liam's cabin and knocked on the door. This was his usual day off, but it'd been a risk driving all the way to his ranch without calling ahead, as she knew his schedule changed with the wind, it seemed. But she was in luck—Liam was home because all of his vehicles were accounted for.

After several minutes on his doorstep without any answer, Kate knocked again, a little harder this time. When there was still no answer, she tried the front door. Not surprising, it was unlocked.

"Liam?"

Kate left her boots on the front porch, not wanting to drag mud onto his clean floors. Then she stepped inside the quiet cabin and shut the door behind her.

"Liam?"

She didn't think to check the barn or the pasture to see if one of the horses was missing—he could very well be out riding or fishing. Her plan was to check the master bedroom, because Liam was known to nap during the day, and then investigate the barn, the pasture and the workshop.

"What the hell?" Liam walked out of his bedroom, naked.

Kate jumped, startled, and put her hand on her chest. "God! You scared me!"

"*I* scared you! I'm supposed to be here."

The horse trainer couldn't stop herself from looking at Liam's naked body, from his muscular arms, to his flat stomach, to his groin. She felt a tingling sensation between her thighs; she couldn't be around this man without thinking about making love with him. She'd never felt such a strong attraction to a man. Maybe that should've been a clue.

Liam stared at her for a moment, silently, before he

turned on his heel and went into his bedroom. He emerged a few minutes later dressed in jeans and a T-shirt, but he was still barefoot.

"I knocked," she explained, feeling out of place in his cabin now.

"I just woke up." Liam pulled the refrigerator door open and grabbed a beer. "You want something?"

Yes. You.

"No. I'm good. Thank you, though."

He twisted the top off his beer, tossed it in the sink and then took a long swig from the bottle.

"So—you're good, then?" he said after he swallowed.

That seemed to be a loaded question. He was asking her about much more beyond her level of thirst.

"Can we sit down?" she asked. Why was she feeling so nervous around him? What was there to be afraid of? This was Liam, after all. He loved her. But the man was such a highly sought after bachelor in their part of the world, it wasn't inconceivable that he could have moved on to greener, more commitment-friendly pastures.

He joined her on the couch, his expression sullen and guarded. Kate knew this man well enough to know that he had not fared well during their short separation.

"What's on your mind, Kate?" Liam hadn't smiled at her once since he discovered her standing in his living room.

"I..." She had to stop to gather her thoughts before she started over. "I've missed you."

He said nothing in return.

"I'm sorry," she added.

"No need to be sorry." There was a coldness, a distance in his deep voice that she hadn't heard before. "You can't change who you are or what you want."

"I think I can," she told him quietly. "I think I have."

Even those words didn't soften his expression; his mouth was drawn down, the expression in his eyes wary.

"I find that difficult to believe." Liam gave one shake of his head. "It occurred to me the other night—maybe I'm no different than one of your horses. You come over, you take me for a ride, and then you put me back in my stall until the next ride. Just because I'm a man doesn't mean I like feeling used."

Kate realized, right then and there, that she had pushed Liam to the limit. If she were going to turn this boat around, she was going to have to take charge and get it done. She stood, moved to the cushion next to Liam, took his beer bottle out of his hand, put it on the table and then took his hands in hers. She took it as a positive sign, a bright spot in an otherwise dark moment, that he hadn't pulled his hand away.

"I love you, Liam."

He didn't return the endearment.

"I know that I haven't always said it as much as you've wanted me to. But I do. Love you. And I've missed you more than I can express. If you wanted to show me what life was like without you—" she shrugged a shoulder "—it worked. I don't like my life without you now. *You* have become essential to me."

Liam's eyes roamed her face, lingering for the briefest of moments on her lips before his gaze returned to her eyes. It seemed like a really long time before he answered, and when he did, he, of course, had to throw her off balance.

"Are you saying this just because you want to get laid?"

Kate was stunned for a split second and then recovered, hit him on the shoulder and frowned at him. "Are you being serious right now? Because I'm being serious. I'm trying to say yes to you."

"You're saying yes to me?" Liam sat up straighter, bringing his body closer to her for the first time.

"Yes."

Liam took her face in his hands and kissed her lightly on the lips.

"You're saying yes to tomorrow?"

"Yes."

Another kiss.

"You're saying yes to forever?"

"Yes." Her voice was breathier now, her heart beginning to beat faster.

He kissed her neck.

"Are you saying yes to marriage?"

She hesitated for only a second before she nodded. "Yes."

Liam gathered her into his arms, her breasts pressed tightly against his chest, his tongue intertwined with hers.

"Are you saying yes to taking me for a ride?"

Kate laughed against his firm lips. "God, yes!"

Liam lifted her into his arms and carried her to his bedroom. They stripped out of their clothes and met each other, naked, in the middle of his bed. There wasn't much foreplay—he was hard and she was wet. They wrapped their arms and legs around each other's bodies, and he slipped deep inside her, and they found that rhythm that only they knew.

After the lovemaking, Kate curled her body next to the man she loved and felt like she had finally come home. Wherever Liam Brand was, as it turned out, *that* was home.

"Kate?"

"Hmm?"

"Did you just agree to be my wife?"

She tightened her hold on his body and nodded. "Yes."

"I'll have to get you a ring."

"Okay."

There was a span of silence and then he added, "And I'll have to actually propose."

"Whatever you want."

"I have what I want." He kissed her on the top of her head.

"So do I."

They lingered in bed for an hour and then Kate checked the time on her phone and realized that the day was slipping away, and she needed to get back to Callie. Liam watched her through sleepy eyes as she dressed.

"You're beautiful," he told her, his eyes drinking her in.

"You always say that."

"Because it's always true."

Dressed and ready to go, Kate walked around to his side of the bed and leaned down to kiss him. He accepted the kiss, but reached for her hand to stop her from leaving.

"Sit down for a minute. There's something I want to talk to you about."

There was a seriousness in his tone; this wasn't going to be a light conversation.

"I've been thinking a lot about us—and by *us* I mean, you, me and Callie. I know how much you worry about what would happen to Callie if something happened to you."

That was true. Her biggest worry had always been about her daughter. Who would take care of her? Who would watch out for her? If she had gotten a different father other than Lloyd in the father lottery, her worries wouldn't be so great. But that wasn't the case.

"I want to adopt Calico."

Kate was rendered temporarily speechless. Yes, Lloyd was an absent father, but he was listed on the birth certificate. She'd been a single parent for so long that it seemed more normal than not.

"Did you hear me?" Liam prompted her out of silence.

"I did." She gave a quick nod. "I just don't know what to say."

"You don't have to say anything right now. Just think on it. I know she's an adult now, but she's always going to need someone to watch out for her. That way, she'll have a full-time father and you'll have peace of mind that if something happens to you, Callie will have the entire Brand family looking after her."

Chapter Eleven

Kate did think about Liam's offer, and the more she thought about it, the more she came to believe that the idea made sense. Callie could have a large, powerful, wealthy family on her side for the rest of her life. And the truth was, if the laws of nature unfolded in a typical fashion, that Callie would outlive both of them. Liam had a pack of siblings—someone would be there to watch out for Callie. The Bozeman Brands stuck together like glue, and once Callie was a Brand, they would take her into the fold as one of their own.

The only roadblock to the entire plan was, of course, Lloyd. It had taken him weeks to return her phone call about Callie coming to see him, and she wasn't the least bit surprised when he came up with an excuse for why his daughter couldn't come for a visit. She really dreaded discussing adoption with him, because Lloyd, from what she could gather over the phone, hadn't matured a whole heck of a lot over the last several decades. He could still be jealous, petty and downright unreasonable.

"Katie Did!"

Kate cringed at the nickname and the sound of Lloyd's voice. This time, though, she didn't correct him as she usually would.

"Two weeks in a row. This's got to be some sort of record," he added.

"How are you, Lloyd?"

"Can't complain," her ex said. "Who'd listen anyway, right?"

"Right."

"Hey, Katie Did, I'm real sorry Callie can't come see me this year. What, with the economy just really starting to come back and construction picking up, I just can't...but next year, for sure."

"Sure," she agreed, but didn't put any stock in the idea. "Look, there's something I need to discuss with you."

A tense silence on the other end of the line.

After a moment, Lloyd cleared his throat. "Now, Katy Did, I know I owe you a couple of clams..."

Kate cut him off. "I'm getting married."

Another strained silence.

"Did you hear me?"

"Do I need to get my ears checked? Did you say you were getting married?" He sounded so surprised that it irritated her. Why was the idea of her getting married so shocking to him? Should she pine for him until death?

"Your ears work just fine." Kate struggled to maintain a civil tone with the man.

"Well, isn't that something? A big surprise," he continued. "I suppose congratulations are in order. Who'd you manage to slap that ole ball and chain on?"

"Liam Brand. You actually played ball with him in high school, I think."

"Yeah." Lloyd didn't sound impressed. "I know the guy."

More silence.

"Is that all?" he pressed her, seeming a little more impatient to end the call.

"No," she replied as evenly and calm as she could. "There's no real easy way to say this, so I'm just going to say it. Liam wants to adopt Calico, and I want him to adopt Calico, which means that you need to forfeit your parental rights."

"So, how'd he take it?" Liam had arrived at the Triple K for dinner and now, as was their habit, they had taken their coffee to the swing beneath the old oak tree in the front yard.

"The phone call went downhill fast after that."

Liam wasn't surprised; he hadn't liked Lloyd back when they played ball together. Kate's ex had always been a fast-talker who'd had an even faster fastball. Everyone thought he'd make the pros one day, but it seemed like Lloyd had fallen short of fulfilling all of his potential. Particularly when it came to his daughter, Callie.

"I hate the fact that Callie's father is such a jerk. But he *is*, in fact, a *jerk*! This isn't about him wanting Callie to be his daughter, because I think we're all pretty clear on his position on fathering her. And it's not like he has any feelings for me, other than some lingering, misguided, misplaced, sense of *ownership.* As if because he was the *first* one to gain access to my vagina that he has a lifetime guarantee or something!"

"He was your first?" Why did that even bother him in the slightest? And yet, irrationally, it did. Kate sent him a withering look, and he immediately regretted asking.

"God." She rolled her eyes in frustration. "Are all men a slave to your stupid egos? Who was your first, if we're asking questions?"

Liam opened his mouth, but before he could respond, she cut him off.

"Never mind. I don't care. And neither should you."

"I don't." He finally got a word in. "Just forget what I asked. I'm a man, and as such, I tend to say really stupid things. Friends?"

Kate rewarded him with a smile. "Friends."

They talked about a strategy to get Lloyd to sign over his parental rights. Their best bet was the thousands of dollars of back child support Lloyd owed; there was interest attached and the debt was only growing over time. If Lloyd agreed to sign over his rights so Liam could adopt Callie, they would find a way to settle that debt so Lloyd was free and clear.

"We won't talk to Callie until after we have the document in our hands," Kate insisted.

"Agreed."

"How do you think your kids will react? To you adopting Callie, I mean."

Liam had thought about his kids and Callie quite a bit. Even though things had eased between him and his kids by the end of their week together, their relationship had been damaged by the distance.

"I don't think Cole will care one way or the other, really. But Sarah… She's going to be upset about the marriage and the adoption."

"But she was so good with Callie," Kate said. "Why would she mind?"

"She was good with Callie and I was proud of her for that," he said. "She wants to come back to Montana."

"To live with you?"

Liam nodded. Sarah had nearly begged him to let her stay before they headed out to the airport. They had moved to a different part of Seattle to be closer to her stepfather's work, and she hated the school, she hated the new house, and she hated her mother for moving her away from friends and her home for a second time.

"I spoke with her mom last week. She's totally against the idea."

"Could we fight her?"

Liam had been looking out at the landscape, but now he wanted to look at Kate's face. The fact that she used the word *we* was very meaningful to him. For the first time, in a long time, he felt what it was like to have a woman standing by his side.

"It's not out of the question. But we've got to get ourselves straightened around first. We need to get things settled with Callie's father before we start dealing with my ex."

"One ex at a time."

"That's right," he agreed. "One ex at a time."

"Daddy!"

Kate was in the middle of treating an infection in one of her horse's hooves, bent over with her back aching, when she heard Callie scream in excitement. This, in itself, was not unusual. Callie could get over-the-moon excited about the smallest of things. *What* she screamed, however, was an entirely different thing.

Kate put the cap on the syringe she was using to treat the hooves, patted the horse on the neck and walked, quickly, toward the front of the barn. There, she found something she had never expected to find: Lloyd standing in front of her barn hugging Callie.

"Hello, Katie Did."

"Kate," she corrected for the umpteenth time in the last decade and a half.

"Mommy!" Callie had tears in her eyes. "Daddy's here!"

Lloyd, tall, slender, with more gray in his hair than black, was still a handsome man. When they met, he was in college and she was still in high school. Oh, how she had thought the sun rose and set because of Lloyd Harrison. Not to mention that he had the hottest muscle car in Bozeman. And, out of all the girls in town, Lloyd wanted her.

"You're lookin' good, Katie." Lloyd slipped off his glasses so she could see his green eyes. He knew how women loved his unusual cat eyes because he'd been told so often.

"Callie," Kate said in an even tone, "why don't you go on in the house and fix your father something to drink. You still like sweet tea, Lloyd?"

"The sweeter, the better." He winked at her.

God, she hated him.

"Go on, kitten," Lloyd said to Callie. "Mind your mother."

"I don't need your help in that department," Kate snapped at him. That was just like Lloyd. Show up, unannounced, out of the blue, after years of avoiding the Triple K like the plague, and try to take up the role as a parent. He hadn't *earned* that right.

Kate waited until her daughter was out of earshot before she narrowed her eyes at the wayward father of her child. "*What* are you doing here?"

"Is there something wrong with a father coming to see his daughter?"

"Yes," she barked at him. "If the father happens to be you. Tell me why you're here."

"Now, Katie Did...there's no need to get all riled up." Lloyd tried to use his charm on her. He added with a condescending laugh, "Woo-we darlin'. You still have one hell of temper on you, don't you?"

The man actually tried to put his arm around her shoulders. She spun out from underneath his arm, wishing that she had a reason to shoot him. She might be able to make a case for trespassing.

"You're *not* staying here, Lloyd. Get that straight right now. Callie is going to ask, and you are going to say 'no, thank you.'" Kate began to march toward the house, her fists balled up next to her body. "God! I can't stand the fact that you're here."

Lloyd just laughed at her frustration. She was convinced, after years of dealing with him, that the man had zero ability to feel sympathy or empathy.

"Why are you so fired up, Katie Did?" Lloyd sauntered behind her, his long legs matching her stride one for two.

Kate stopped in her tracks, spun on her heel and confronted him. "I swear to God in heaven, Lloyd. If you ever call me Katie Did again, I am going to shoot you and bury your body in the compost pile!"

Lloyd, still smiling at her, held up his hands in surrender. "You've still got it, Katie. That spark that makes a man want to plug in. Lightning in a bottle."

Disgusted, Kate let her ex into her home, her private space. But only because he was Callie's father. Somehow, that gave him a pass.

Kate had to tolerate Lloyd sitting at her table, eating her food and breathing her air. She stared at him, arms crossed, while he ate like a man who didn't have one care in the world.

"Doggone, kitten." Her ex had polished off a huge plate of Callie's famous Polish sausage and sauerkraut. "You have turned out to be one heck of a cook, and that ain't no joke."

"Do you want more?" Callie asked.

Lloyd pat his stomach. "No, ma'am. I'm filled to the gills. But I thank you kindly."

"I—I'm glad you liked it."

When Callie took his plate to the kitchen, Lloyd leaned over and in a not-so-quiet whisper, he said, "I thought you were gonna do something about that stutter."

"Shut up." Kate stood, leaned toward him, put her hands flat on the table. "Shut. *Up!*"

Callie and Lloyd spent the rest of the day together while Kate buried herself in work. She knew exactly what this was about—her engagement to Liam. What else would bring Lloyd back to Montana after all of these years? He'd enjoyed her self-imposed spinsterhood. He took some pride in the fact that he had managed to spoil her for all other men.

She was hot and sweaty and smelled, as usual, like horse urine and manure. She found Callie and Lloyd sitting on the couch together, and her daughter was showing her father photo albums of when she was a baby and a toddler. It made Kate realize the days of photo albums were over. There were no photo albums of Callie when she was a teenager. All of the photos were cataloged on her computer, but she never looked at them. Not like Lloyd was looking at memories she created—memories he could have been a part of creating.

"How's it going in here?"

Callie was happy. No matter how much Lloyd made her skin crawl, her daughter was so happy to finally have her father visiting. She did not know, *could not* comprehend, why he had finally shown up now.

"We're having such a good time." Callie smiled at her broadly.

"That's right." Lloyd seconded the motion.

"I'm going to take a shower."

She locked her bedroom door before she stripped out of her dirty clothing. In the bathroom, she shut the door and locked that as well. Paranoid. But better safe than worrying that Lloyd might "accidentally" find himself in her bedroom.

Kate sat on the toilet, towel wrapped around her body, and dialed Liam's number for the third time. Frustrated that he still didn't answer, she hung up without leaving a message. She sent him a text: Unexpected visitor. Please call as soon as you can.

In the shower, the horse trainer let the hot water beat down on her muscles, wishing that the water could wash Lloyd down the drain as easily as it was washing the dirt and grime from her skin.

But, alas, when she emerged from the bedroom, Lloyd was still sitting on her couch.

"Well—" he stood "—I suppose I should get going. I don't have a place picked out for the night."

"You can sleep here!" Callie, predictably, exclaimed. "On the couch."

"No, kitten. That just wouldn't be right."

His words said *no*, but his sad puppy dog expression said, *yes, I'd love to, thank you.*

"He can't stay here, Callie," Kate said firmly. "He's got things to do in town."

Disappointed, Callie said, "Well, at least stay for dinner."

Lloyd and Callie both looked at her expectantly. After a minute, she threw up her hands. "Fine. That's fine."

That's when Liam finally returned her call. She stepped outside, away from prying ears, and said, "Lloyd showed up this afternoon."

"He's there now?"

"Yes. How soon can you get here?"

Liam blew out a frustrated breath. "I've got a few more hours out in the field. Dammit."

"Will you come out after you're done? I don't care how late it is. I need to see you."

"I'll be there as soon as I can," Liam assured her. "And Kate."

"What?"

"Keep your cool."

Callie hugged her father good-night for the third time before Kate could get her to go on to bed. Her daughter was, understandably, afraid that she wouldn't see Lloyd for a long time.

"Good night, kitten." Lloyd leaned over a bit, that smooth smile in place, and blew his daughter an air kiss.

Kate heard Callie giggling happily as she shut the door to her bedroom. With a sigh, Kate went in to the kitchen to run the water over the dirty dishes to soak them before she rinsed them off.

She felt Lloyd come up behind her, so she shut off the water. Before she could turn around, Lloyd wrapped his arms around her from behind.

"I've missed us."

The feel of Lloyd's hands on her body, the feel of his breath on her neck, made her cringe. She didn't know why, couldn't explain it later, but instead of elbowing him in the gut, her body froze. She couldn't move. And that, of course, was the moment Liam opened her front door.

"Hello." The sound of Liam's voice spurred Kate into action. She wrenched herself away from Lloyd, who nonchalantly leaned back against the kitchen counter like he owned the place and had always belonged there.

"Lloyd was just about to leave." Kate made a beeline for her fiancé. "I'm so glad to see you."

She kissed Liam in greeting, wanting Lloyd to see her kiss her man, as if that would convince him that he didn't have a shot with her. Not that he really wanted a shot. What he wanted was to screw things up for her with Liam and then bail on her for a second time.

Thankfully, Liam hadn't misinterpreted the situation in the kitchen.

"Sorry I'm late." He actually apologized, and she knew that he was apologizing for the fact that he couldn't get there sooner.

"Liam, you remember Lloyd?"

After giving her another reassuring hug, Liam crossed the room to Callie's father. He offered Lloyd his hand. "Lloyd."

"Liam."

The handshake was brief, but the eye contact between the men lingered, as if they were sizing each other up.

"I'm surprised to see you here." Liam's eyes were narrowed.

"Likewise," Lloyd retorted.

"I'm here every week."

"Is that right?" Lloyd tucked his hands into his pockets.

"That's right." Liam wasn't smiling. "I know Kate told you about our engagement."

"She mentioned something like that."

"Are you hungry?" Kate wanted to change the conversation.

"Always." Liam smiled at her briefly before he turned his attention back to Lloyd.

"What brings you to town?" he asked her ex while she fixed Liam a plate.

"Just checking on my girls."

Kate glanced over to see Liam's features harden. "That's an interesting take on this situation."

"You don't say?"

"I do," Liam said in a sharp tone.

"Katie Did." Lloyd finally, thankfully, pushed away from the counter, set to leave. "Tell our daughter that I'll see her tomorrow."

Liam caught Lloyd's arm when he tried to pass by him. "You'd better plan on moving along, Lloyd."

The man laughed, but Kate heard a new nervousness

in that laugh. Liam had gotten to him and she was glad. Lloyd may have started this game, but she had no doubt that Liam Brand was willing to end it.

"Thanks for dinner." Lloyd gave her a little salute before he walked out the door.

Kate stopped what she was doing, walked over to Liam and hugged him tightly.

"Are you okay?" He kissed the top of her head.

"No." She shook her head. "Yes. I don't know."

Liam took her face in his hands. "We're going to handle him together."

She fed him, and they both agreed that he would spend the night on the couch. But after she made up the couch with a sheet, blanket and pillow, Kate realized that, tonight, this situation wouldn't do at all.

Liam moved past her to lay down on the couch, but she stopped him.

"I want you to stay with me. In my bed."

"Are you sure?" he whispered, not wanting to awaken Callie.

She nodded. "I'm sure."

Together, they walked down the hallway to her bedroom. Lloyd had tried to ruin her relationship with Liam, she was sure of that. But he had failed. Instead, he had pushed them closer together. And for the first time since high school, Kate felt as if she were finally free of Lloyd Harrison.

Chapter Twelve

The first night after Lloyd had arrived was the first night Liam stayed over at Kate's place, in her bed. They had made love in a slow, sweet, poignant way, different from any other time. And then he had held her until she got too hot and turned onto her side and away from him. For hours, he listened to Kate breathing in her sleep. He, on the other hand, hadn't been able to fall asleep at all that night. Lloyd's sudden appearance in their lives had thrown him into crisis mode—he didn't think Kate's ex had any power over their future relationship, but he did hold the key to a future adoption of Calico.

While Kate slept, Liam thought. He tried to think strategically, trying to anticipate Lloyd's next step. But it wasn't just the ex that had kept him awake—it was Kate's mattress, which had to have been manufactured around the time of the floods. It was lumpy, hard and there was a wayward spring poking him in the back. He hoped that she wasn't seriously attached to the monstrosity because after they were married, it was going to be the very first thing to go.

At the crack of dawn, and before Callie awakened, Liam snuck out of Kate's bedroom and made a pot of coffee. Kate and Callie, both ranch women, got up just as the sun was rising.

"Hi, Dr. B-Brand!" Callie greeted him with a smile and a hug.

"Good morning, Callie." Liam was standing at the stove, overseeing some scrambled eggs. "How am I doing so far?"

Callie looked concerned. "Not good at all."

Liam laughed, handed her the fork in his hand and stepped aside. Callie naturally took over in the kitchen while Liam and Kate went out to the barn. It was summertime and the Triple K Ranch was a huge spread, so most of the horses stayed out all day and all night. The horses still in the barn were boarded horses whose owners wanted them in at night.

Kate fed her barn cats, saying, as she always did, that she needed to get a kitten who would grow up to actually mouse the barn. After his fiancée checked to make sure that the stable hands had all arrived and were on track with her protocol for taking care of the animals, she had a minute to speak to him before he left to get started with his full day.

Kate wiped her hands off on her cutoff shorts. "Do you have a busy day?"

They were standing at his truck now.

He smiled down at her—she was so pretty, with that sun-kissed skin and sun-streaked hair that was escaping from her ponytail holder more than usual because of her recent haircut. Liam brushed some strands hair away from her forehead.

"Packed."

She reached for his hand; slowly, Kate was showing him more affection. And that incremental improvement in her ability to show her feelings for him bolstered his confidence in the future success of their marriage. He was a man who wanted the touch of his spouse. In fact, one of the biggest hallmarks of the failure of his last marriage was the fact that he chose a woman who wasn't physically affectionate.

"Did you sleep okay?"

"Baby—that mattress." He shook his head with a grimace. "I hope you're not attached."

She laughed. "No. There's just always something else around here that needs fixing. We can get a new one."

"All right. First potential marital crisis averted."

Another laugh. "I didn't snore, did I?"

Liam gave her a kiss on the lips. "Not much."

It was a rough day, the day after he spent the night at the Triple K Ranch. He lost steam around noon and had to gulp down several super-caffeinated drinks just to get through the day. Kate texted him to let him know that, despite their best hopes, Lloyd had returned to the Triple K to visit with his daughter. It took every ounce of his professionalism not to cancel his afternoon appointments and head straight back to the Triple K. What kept him on the job was the fact that Kate was a strong, savvy, capable woman who was smarter than Lloyd by a long shot; Liam had a lot of faith in his woman's ability to handle her ex. Between clients, he had asked his brother Bruce to get one of the Sugar Creek Ranch hands to take care of his horses for the next couple of weeks. He also called the family attorney to discuss the process of Lloyd relinquishing his parental rights and adoption of a special-needs adult. At the end of his day, he stopped by his cabin, threw some changes of clothing into a duffel bag and then hightailed it to the Triple K. If Lloyd was going to show up every day, then he was going to make sure he was on-site every day too. Was that naked, blatant male posturing? Sure. With a guy like Lloyd, if he didn't do it, it would signal to Kate's ex that things weren't so set in stone between them. Liam had every intention of "marking his territory."

That evening, when he arrived at the Triple K, Lloyd had already taken off. Liam was relieved because he was exhausted. He wasn't even really all that hungry, but he ate anyway just to spare Callie's feelings. While he ate, Callie talked ceaselessly about her day with Lloyd. It seemed that her father, for the first time, was trying to take an active role in his daughter's life. He took her out to lunch in town and then took her shopping for cooking utensils, the quickest way to Callie's heart. Liam had to admit he was impressed with Lloyd's game, but he wasn't impressed with the motives. Lloyd coming in at the eleventh hour to assert his rights had absolutely nothing to do with love for his daughter and everything to do with his overinflated ego.

After Callie went to sleep, Kate sat next to Liam on the couch and leaned her head on his shoulder with a heavy sigh.

"He exhausts me."

"I think that's the point."

"But Callie loves him. She loves him being here."

"I know." He took her hand into his. "But how is she going to feel if he pulls another decade-long disappearing act?"

"It will crush her," Kate admitted easily. "Again."

Liam lifted his head so he could look down into Kate's face. "We can't stop her from getting hurt. I wish we could. But we can make sure she had a really soft place to land."

Kate tilted up her chin so he could kiss her. They sat together, kissing, nuzzling each other, taking comfort in the other.

"I'm so tired," he told her. "I want to make love but…"

His woman shook her head. "Don't worry about it. I'm exhausted too. I just want to take a shower and crawl into bed."

Kate stood. "You can sleep with me again if you want. It worked out that you got up ahead of Callie."

Liam was willing to do time on that lumpy, spring-loaded mattress in order to be with Kate. If it made her feel better to have him next to her, then next to her was exactly where Liam was going to be. That was true love in his book.

Much to his and Kate's surprise, Lloyd stuck around for the entire week. What they had first initially dismissed as some sort of ego-driven gain, if it had begun that way, ended much differently for all of them.

"Are you okay?" Liam asked Kate, who was sitting across from him at the Nova Café where they could get all-day breakfast.

The papers for Lloyd to relinquish his parental rights to Callie were signed and a copy was in the glove box of his truck. Ever since they left his lawyer's office, ever since they had watched Lloyd drive his rental car away, Kate had been quiet and pensive. Not at all the reaction he had expected. Not at all the reaction he had *hoped* for.

She nodded, her face pale, her eyes worried and distant.

Liam leaned his forearms on the edge of the table, leaned forward so he could speak in a lowered, private voice.

"I can see that something's wrong, Kate," he told her. "Are you having buyer's remorse?"

Another shake of her head. It occurred to Liam that she hadn't hardly said more than two words beyond ordering her food.

"Tell me what's on your mind. I can't help if I don't know what's going on."

Suddenly, there were tears in Kate's eyes. He watched her stiffen her resolve and stop the tears from falling on to her cheeks.

"Do you want to go home?" he asked, confused. "I can take you home."

"No." She finally seemed to find her voice. "No. I don't want to go home."

Now that she was talking again, he wasn't going to interrupt. He waited for her to continue.

"I think I'm…shocked that it's finally over. I finally have what I want, and yet." She paused, seeming to search for the right words. "I don't feel happy about it. Why did I think it would be so easy? The father of my child just signed over his parental rights. It feels like the ground just shifted beneath my feet."

She had been looking at the window; now she was meeting his eyes again.

"But, there's a part of me that still can't believe that he agreed to give Callie away." Tears were swimming in Kate's wide eyes. "It hurts, Liam. I hurt so much for Callie."

Liam reached for her hand across the table.

"It's just a really big deal. That's all."

He nodded. It was a big deal. But he didn't necessarily understand her shock. Lloyd had been absent before Callie had even been born. He hadn't paid one cent of court mandated child support. No, that bill had been paid by Liam, and he was glad to have done it in order to secure Callie's future.

"Even after all you've been through with him, you're still shocked that he agreed? Is that it?"

Kate rearranged her silverware. "I don't know. I guess. A little. I mean, I know that he hasn't been in Callie's life, but to sign away his rights. That's *forever.* He can't take that back."

"Would you want him to?" he asked quietly, his stomach feeling unsettled by her reaction.

It took her longer than he would have liked to answer that question. "No. That's not it. I'm glad that we can move forward with our plan. I just can't understand anyone wanting to give Callie away. She's an angel on Earth."

Liam squeezed her fingers reasurringly. "I'm sorry he hurt you. I'm sorry he hurt Callie. But in the end, we've got to give him credit for finally doing the right thing for the both of you."

Liam had spent a week with Lloyd Harrison, and even though he had every reason to dislike the guy, he'd ended the week actually liking him. Lloyd was funny, laid-back in a devil-may-care way that was appealing for the rest of the world beholden to adult responsibility. Lloyd was the guy at the bar that everyone liked, but never expected him to show up on time or keep his word or pay back the money he owed. They guy was likable, that was just the truth. And by the end of the week, Liam had begun to appreciate the fact that Lloyd wanted to see for himself that Callie would be truly taken care of by him. Humans were complicated, and it didn't make sense that Lloyd would spend years avoiding his parental responsibilities, only to show up in the eleventh hour and actually act like a dad. Liam didn't understand it, but he had found a way to respect it.

"I can't begin to explain this to Callie," Kate said after a long pause. "This is something that has happened to her, and I can't explain it in a way she would understand."

"I know, baby." Liam kept on holding her hand. "But Lloyd will always be welcome in her life, that hasn't changed. Callie hasn't lost a father—she's gained one."

Several weeks following Lloyd's departure, Liam's relationship with Kate felt strained. He had decided to return to his cabin, under the guise of wanting to get the horses back into a routine, in order to give her some space. No matter how many times he asked if she was okay and she answered yes, the feeling between them was distant. He just couldn't seem to break through with her, and the only thing he could think to do was give her some space and let her come back to him. It made him feel powerless and unsettled, but what other choice did he have? Kate wasn't the type of woman to be pushed.

He went through his routine, did his work and was always available on the other end of the line when Kate needed him. Liam kept on being a steady, calm force in his woman's life, and finally, *finally*, his strategy paid off.

"Hi, there!" Kate was working with a new horse in the round pen. "I'll be done in a minute."

"Take your time." Liam hung his arms over the top rail of the round pen.

Kate was amazing to watch with a horse. She was an incredible, confident rider, but where she really shined was on the ground with these magnificent, powerful creatures. She was an expert in natural horsemanship, and he managed to learn something new from her every time he watched her work.

"She's a beauty," he said as Kate clipped the lead rope onto the mare's halter to lead her to a nearby pasture.

"She is," Kate agreed. "This is North Star. Just arrived yesterday."

"Is she one of yours?"

Kate let the mare go into a small pasture where she could acclimate to her new environment alone.

"I wish," the horse trainer said. "She's only here for training. But I'll love her while she's here."

Kate turned to him and kissed him on the lips. "Hi."

"Hi." He smiled at her, wondering why she had invited him to the ranch in the middle of the afternoon.

"There's something I want to show you."

"All right."

Kate climbed behind the wheel of one of her ranch trucks, and he climbed into the passenger side. Today, she was steering their relationship, and from the happiness he saw in her eyes when she saw him, he was looking forward to where she was taking them, literally and figuratively.

Using one of the many dirt road veins that crisscrossed the massive ranch, Kate drove them to a hill that overlooked the barn and the homestead. She parked and they got out of the truck. Hand in hand, she led him over to a peak of the hill. Liam was surprised to see how flat the top of the hill was—it appeared to have been graded sometime in the past.

"What do you think of this view of the ranch?" she asked him.

Honestly, Liam didn't think any piece of land could rival Sugar Creek land, but this view was mighty close. Even though it wasn't the highest hill on the property, it gave a person a bird's-eye view of the pastures and barn, and in the distance, those beautiful, craggy Montana mountains.

"It's hard to beat," he admitted.

Kate gave a slight nod. "It's going to be tough, you leaving Sugar Creek. Have you given much thought to that?"

He turned his body toward her. "That's all I've been thinking about since the day I fell in love with you, Kate."

He'd thought to live out his days on Sugar Creek. It had never occurred to him that he might fall in love with a woman with her own spread, a spread that was her bread, her butter, and her heart and soul. The Triple K *was* Kate King, and he knew that if he wanted to be with her, he would have to be the one to leave his home.

"It'll be an adjustment," he added. "But I wouldn't want it any other way. I love you, Kate. I love Callie.

Whatever is best for the two of you is going to be best for me."

She squeezed his hand at his words.

"Ten years ago, I was going to build a new home on this site."

"I thought it looked like it had been graded and leveled."

She nodded.

"I had an architect draw up plans for my dream home. I had the financing and permits in place. Then one thing after another happened with the barn—I ended up replacing the entire roof—and all of my dreams for building a new home got derailed."

She turned to face him. "What do you think about *us* building a new home up here together. We could either add on to my plans or scrap 'em and design our perfect home together. Either way, we'll have enough space for your children."

Liam looked around, imagining a home on this hill. Imagining a home with Kate as his wife, Callie as his daughter and enough room for his children to visit or to live permanently.

"What do you think?" she prodded him impatiently.

Liam looked down into her expectant face. "I think this feels like home."

They embraced on that hilltop, their future as a family sealed with a kiss. Then, they stood side by side, arm in arm, both quietly imaging the house that would be built on the land where they stood.

"I'm sorry I've been so…" Kate paused, seemingly to find the right word. "Distant."

He didn't dispute her claim. She had been distant.

"I had some stuff to work through I guess."

"I'm just glad you're back."

Once again she turned to face him. "I am back, Liam. I'm back for good. I'm back forever, if you'll have me."

Was he mistaken, or did this sound like a proposal coming from his independent, commitment-phobic lady?

"What are you driving at, Kate?"

"I'm sorry that I didn't get here as fast as you did. You've always been so certain about me—about us. I just had to take a slightly longer route, that's all. But I know what I want, Liam. I'm not fuzzy about it. I'm not confused about it. I just know what I want for me and for Callie."

He waited for her to continue.

"Will you marry me, Liam? I don't want a big ceremony. I don't want a dress or even an engagement ring. I just want to start our lives together."

He kissed her, long and deep. "I want that too."

"Then let's go to the courthouse and just do it."

This was something he hadn't thought about. He had a big family, and even though he hadn't shared the news of the engagement with them yet, they would be mighty hurt if they couldn't be there for the ceremony.

"That's not going to sit well with my family."

Kate frowned. "I know. I thought about that. But shouldn't *our* family come first? The sooner we get married, the sooner we can start with the adoption."

She had him there. When push came to shove, the family he was building with Kate had to come first. And he couldn't disagree with her logic—once they were married, they could go full steam ahead with the adoption.

"When?" he asked her.

"We could get the license this week. We'll have to tell Callie, of course, but I think she'll be happy. She's always been such a romantic."

"I can meet you in Bozeman tomorrow around noon."

A light touched his love's eyes, and it warmed his heart to see it.

"We're getting married." Kate flung her arms around him with an enthusiasm that he had never experienced with her before.

"I love you, Kate King." Liam hugged her tightly, kissing her cheek. "It seems like I've waited a lifetime for you."

"I love you." She rested her head over his heart, holding on to him as tightly as he was holding on to her. "God only knows how much."

Chapter Thirteen

They were married on a rainy Wednesday morning by Judge Harlow at the Bozeman city hall. They did it quietly and alone, without any fanfare or fuss. They had debated bringing Callie with them, but ultimately decided that they would celebrate the union at Sugar Creek Ranch with both of their families, and a handful of close friends, sometime over the following several weeks. The ceremony, as it were, would be just quick, painless and just for them.

And since this was for them, they wanted to dress how they lived—casual and ready for the barn. They did put on clean, new jeans, with shined-up boots. But they weren't fancy people, so their outfits for the wedding weren't fancy either. Holding hands, the newly married couple burst out of city hall and into the rain.

A fat drop of rain splatted on Kate's nose before she had a chance to put her cowgirl hat back on.

Liam swung her around and into his arms. Right there, on the city hall sidewalk, in the rain, Liam Brand kissed her for the second time as her husband.

"It's raining!" Kate laughed, not really caring that she was getting wet.

Liam picked her up and spun around. "Frankly, Mrs. Brand, I don't give a damn!"

They kissed again before racing to Liam's truck. Inside the cab, they were dripping on the seats, their shirts and the thighs of their jeans soaked to the skin. But they were laughing. Kate couldn't have known—how could she have known?—just how happy she was going to be to say that she was Mrs. Liam Brand.

"Happy?" Liam asked her, rainwater dripping down his neck.

"Yes," she said with a happy, relieved sigh. "You?"

"This is, hands down, one of the happiest days of my life."

It was the nature of their lives that they had to part ways after the ceremony. She had a horsemanship clinic scheduled at the Triple K later on that afternoon, and Liam's schedule only allowed him to take a half day off.

"I'll see you tonight," he promised her with a kiss.

"It's our wedding night," she mused. She'd never made love to a husband before.

"Trust me." His eyes lingered on her lips. "I'm not going to miss it."

"You'd better not." She hopped out of the truck and said right before she shut the door, "I'll hunt you down if you do!"

* * *

All day, Kate's mind would drift back to the moment that she said "I do" to Liam Brand. She was *married*. It was unconventional, perhaps, and a little bit secretive. But she liked it that way. The only regret she had was for their children—Callie, Sarah and Cole still needed to be informed of the marriage, and she suspected that it was going to be a bumpy ride on Liam's end. And, yes, they still needed to tell their friends and Liam's large, extended family. Those were adults, and they could handle the disappointment. Or not.

Normally, she loved her horsemanship clinics. Today, she just wanted to get to the wedding night with Liam.

"Nice work everyone!" Kate was standing in the center of the covered round pen. "I'll see you next time!"

One by one, her clients bade her farewell. Some boarded on her property and didn't have far to go. Others had trailered their horses in, and she would make herself available in case of any loading issues. Kate was overseeing the last horse loading into the last trailer when Callie joined her.

"Hi, Mommy."

"Hi, kiddo." Kate gave her daughter a quick side-hug before she refocused her attention on the large, bay gelding loading on the trailer. "Give me just a minute, okay, Callie?"

"Okay, Mommy."

Callie knew to stand out of the way while she worked with the skittish horse. It took some doing, but they finally coaxed the gelding into the trailer with some sweet feed; the owner closed the doors of the trailer and shook her hand.

"We'll see you next month."

Once the last client was heading down the drive, Kate turned her attention back to daughter.

"What's up, kiddo?" Kate put her arm around her daughter's shoulders as they walked together.

"Tony asked me to come for a visit."

"In California?"

"Yes." Callie nodded. "He lives in San Diego with his mom and his dad."

Kate's stomach clenched. Whenever she thought of entrusting Callie to someone else, it made her feel tense and sick in the stomach. She recognized that this wasn't a sustainable position, not for someone like Callie who had a dream of her life that extended beyond the Triple K. Understanding this didn't make it any easier.

"When?"

"I—I don't know. Whenever I—I can make i-it, I—I think."

"I'll need to talk to Tony's parents," Kate warned.

"Okay."

"And we need to think about you visiting when I can fly out there with you. You can't fly alone."

"I—I know."

"I'm not saying yes." Kate tried to moderate Callie's expectations.

"B-but, you aren't saying no."

Damn, but she did have a point. "I'm not saying no."

That sent Callie running off toward the house shouting that she had to call Tony right away. Liam had changed her—he really had. Would she have so easily entertained the idea of Callie visiting Tony before her time with Liam? It was hard to imagine. Things had changed for her; she didn't feel like she had to have such a death grip on all things in her life in order to keep things from unraveling. It seemed that God had sent her the exact right man, at the right time in her life, to help her through a time of transition with her daughter. Thankfully, God had sent her Liam.

That night, they went through the motions—they sat down for dinner with Callie, cleared the table, washed the dishes and then watched TV together until Callie finally went off to bed. Like two teenagers, they rushed down the hall, careful to be quiet as they sneaked past Callie's door, until they reached the master bedroom. Kate closed the door behind them and locked it.

"It's about damn time." Liam pulled her into his arms to kiss her the moment they were safe behind a locked door.

Kate returned his kiss with the same force, the same passion, her arms around his lean waist, her fingers massaging the long muscles of his back.

"Hello, Mrs. Brand."

"Hmm." Kate leaned back against his arms and smiled up at him. "That sounds right."

"Yes, it does."

They opened the blinds so the light from the nearly full moon would shine into the room after they turned off the bedside lamp. Not wanting to wait a minute longer to consummate their marriage, they both stripped out of their clothing without any fanfare. Liam was hard and ready to go. He grabbed her hand and led her to the bed; she resisted.

"I've been working all day. I'm dirty."

Liam nuzzled her neck. "I like dirty."

She laughed louder than she intended to. "Shh."

"Let's get into bed." He started to walk forward, walking her backward toward the bed.

"No." Kate put the brakes on. "You're going to want to kiss me down there, and I've been working all day. I've got to get into the shower."

"Want company?"

"Uh-huh."

He kept right on kissing her on the neck, on the breasts, his hands roaming her body, the feel of his erection, so hard and ready for her.

"Come on." Kate spun out of his arms. "Shower first."

She got the shower running, turning the hot water on full blast, and they both climbed into the tub and pulled the shower curtain closed.

"You'll have to whisper. There's an echo in here," Kate said quietly.

He was back to kissing her neck, licking the water off her skin as the water ran over their bodies. Unable to resist, she wrapped her hand around his hard shaft, loving the sound of Liam groaning with pleasure. It made her feel powerful.

Liam spun her around, his back to the water, wrapped her up in his arms, one hand covering a breast, the other hand between her thighs. His finger found that most sensitive part of her body and worried the little nub until her knees began to buckle and she had to bite her lip to stop herself from making too much noise.

"I need to get cleaned up," Kate said in a breathy voice. "I can't wait any longer, Liam."

Liam took charge, as he often did, and she let him. He soaped up his hands and cleaned her body, his slippery hands touching her everywhere. Her husband saved washing between her thighs for last.

"Oh, God." Kate had to hold on to him it felt so good.

"That was loud." He chuckled under his breath.

"Well, what do you expect with what you're doing to me?" she whispered and then gasped when she felt his finger inside her.

"I'm clean enough," she said urgently.

"Are you sure?"

"Take me to bed, Liam!" Kate whispered the demand.

With a quiet laugh, Liam let the water rinse the rest of the soap from her body, shut off the water, stepped out of the tub and grabbed a towel. When he tried to dry her off, she pulled the towel out of his hands and ran into the bedroom.

Along the way, she dried herself off as best she could, but parts of her body were still damp when she yanked back the covers and climbed on top of the cool, cotton sheet.

"Hurry up!" she whispered harshly.

In the soft light of the moon, Liam walked into the bedroom, tall, lean, muscular. This was her man. This was her husband. And she was so in love with him.

Liam's body was still damp as he climbed into bed beside her.

"I'm glad to be here with you, baby." Her husband leaned over her and kissed her nipple.

"I'm so glad you're here."

"Are you cold?" he asked.

"No," she said urgently. "Horny."

"I can help you with that, Mrs. Brand." Liam ran his hand down over her breast, along her stomach and across her thigh. “You know where I want to start, right?”

“Yes.” She nodded, letting her thighs fall farther apart.

His hands cupping her bottom, Liam knelt between her thighs and covered her with his mouth. He always treated her like the best dessert a man could have—licking her, kissing her, until she was squirming and writhing and digging her fingernails into his skin.

“Baby? Can you come like this?”

“I don’t know,” she gasped, wishing he hadn’t stopped. “I don’t think so. I just… I just get too tense. I worry about you… I worry…”

“Don’t worry about me. I’m loving this. You’re mine. You were made with me in mind. Just relax, baby, and enjoy it.”

“Stop talking!”

Liam loved her with his mouth until all she could feel was the sensation of his tongue and his lips at the center of her being. That’s when she let herself go. This was her husband loving her. She trusted him. Kate felt herself starting to orgasm; she held on to Liam, biting her lip to stop herself from crying out. She was panting and sweaty and so sensitive between her legs that she could hardly stand it.

“Yes, baby,” Liam murmured.

“Please.” Kate reached for him. “Please.”

Her husband kissed his way up her body until they were chest to chest; then he reached between their bodies and guided himself inside. He caught her moan of pleasure in his mouth as he kissed her.

“I love you,” she gasped. “God, I love you.”

“I love you, baby.” Liam used his body to tease her,

stroking long and slow, making her wiggle beneath him and beg him for more. Beg him to go deeper, go faster, love her harder. But her husband had other plans for her. He set the rhythm, took his time, driving her mad until he felt her tensing around him.

"There it is," Liam said in a silky, sexy voice. "I feel you coming for me."

All Kate could do was cling to her husband, bite down on his shoulder to keep silent as an intense second orgasm sent sparks firing from the center of her body outward.

He held her, was there for her, until she relaxed into his embrace. That's when he gave it to her deeper, faster, and loved her harder. It was wild and intense the way Liam loved her that night. It was a first for them, and certainly a first for her. It was if he wanted to consume her, heart, mind, body and soul.

Forgetting to be quiet in his release, Liam drove into her one last time, his arms locked and tense, and found his release.

Kate pulled him down on top of her and pulled the covers over their bodies. "Shh! That wasn't quiet at all."

Under the covers, their bodies still intertwined, they held each other tightly, kissing and laughing as quietly as they could.

"How was that for you, Mrs. Brand?"

Their bodies naturally fell away from each other and he lay on his back, while she used his arm as a pillow.

"I think I had three orgasms. *Three*. That's a record."

"That's great for my ego."

"Good." Kate hugged him. "There's something about making love as a married woman that just does it for me."

"Married sex is the best," Liam agreed.

They fell asleep in each other's arms; somewhere along the way, Liam had slipped out of the room and bedded down on the couch. Before they fell drifted off to sleep, they both agreed that they would have to sit down with Callie soon. And as far as the Brand family was concerned, Sunday brunch was as good a time as any to let them know that they had gotten married.

The first person they told about their marriage was Callie. Understandably, she was upset that she hadn't been able to be a part of the ceremony. Mainly, she had wanted to get a new dress, new shoes and maybe catch the bouquet as a sign that she would marry Tony. Liam planned on telling his father, stepmother and siblings first, and then right after brunch, call his kids. That wasn't a phone call he was looking forward to making. When they were in Montana, neither of them really warmed to the idea of Kate. Which didn't make a bit of sense, in light of the fact that their mother had left him and had remarried over a year ago.

Sunday brunch was a loud affair, as per usual. His family was boisterous, opinionated and often talked over each other. He waited until most of the food was gone—his father often handled things better on a full stomach.

"Ready?" Liam asked Kate.

She nodded.

"Ready?" he asked Callie, who had been very good at keeping their secret.

Callie's eyes lit up and she nodded definitively. "Yes!"

"All right, then." Liam stood.

"Can I have your attention everyone?" He had to shout over his siblings.

"Will you guys shut it?" Jessie, Liam's sister, shouted. "Liam's got something to tell us!"

"Jessie—" Lilly's steady voice cut through the noise, as it always did "—that's not the way I raised you to act."

Jessie backed off, because Lilly did rule the roost, but she pointed to her siblings. "It's their fault! They're rude, so I have to be rude."

"What's got you out of your chair, Liam?" Jock bellowed. His father spoke only in a shout.

"Let Liam speak," Lilly commanded in her calm way.

There was one person to whom all of Jock's children deferred and that was Lilly. The table went silent and suddenly everyone's attention was on him.

"Many of you know how I feel about Kate and Callie." Liam reached for his wife's hand. "I haven't been this happy in a long, long time. I asked Kate to marry me."

His family wasn't quiet after that announcement. A flurry of congratulations flew around the table.

"Actually, I asked you," Kate reminded him.

"Well, technically, I asked you first and then you asked me."

"Have you set a date?" Lilly's voice cut through the noise again.

"Yes." Liam nodded. "We have. Yesterday."

That stumped his family for a solid second or two before they all started to talk at the same time again.

Liam tugged on her hand to get her to stand up. "I'd like to introduce you to my wife, Kate!"

Then he took Callie's hand and encouraged her to stand up with them. "And my daughter, Calico."

Standing there, a proud husband and father, with two of his best girls on either side, Liam couldn't remember a time when he felt more content with his life. The only piece missing was moving forward with the adoption so Calico was officially his daughter. Then their picture would truly be complete.

"You're married?" Jessie, loud like their father, slammed her palms on the table. "How could you go and get all married without us!"

"It was the right thing for *us*." Liam eyed his siblings, sending them a silent signal to just deal with the news.

"Welcome to the family." Lilly came to the other side of the table to hug Kate and Callie.

"You know we're going to have to have a party, right?" Savannah made the rounds hugging each of them. "Call me later today, and we can start putting something together."

Jessie threw herself at Kate, almost knocking her down. "You must be certifiable to marry into this crazy family. Welcome to the fam."

"Don't strangle her, Jess," Liam joked with his sister.

"Sorry." Jessie gave his wife a sheepish look. "That's just how I hug."

All in all, the announcement had gone better than he'd anticipated. His family liked Kate and Callie, and liked them with him, so it wasn't such a big shock after all. Everyone agreed that they would have one heck of a reception and that way the entire family would have a chance to celebrate the union.

The dining room cleared, and as it happened, Liam was left alone with his stepmother, whom he had called mom since he was a youngster. His own mother had died when he was just a boy. Lilly, so kind and caring, was the only mother he had ever really known.

Liam kissed his mother on the cheek. "Do you like her?"

Lilly sent him a gentle smile. "Yes, I do."

"But," she continued. "Do you know what I like even more?"

He shook his head.

"I like how happy she makes you." Lilly touched his arm. "I have prayed for this, Liam. I am so grateful that my prayers have been answered and you have been blessed with such a lovely wife and daughter."

Chapter Fourteen

"What do you think?" Kate had been putting off the question of California until after they had shared the news of the marriage with all of their family members.

Perhaps she was just avoiding the topic, but now it was front and center once again. At dinner, Callie brought it up. Tony had called, and really, the topic of this trip was the only thing the two of them talked about. This wasn't going away.

"Have you talked to Tony's parents?"

"Not yet." Kate took a sip of her coffee. "I suppose I'll have to."

"It's not going away."

"That's exactly what I thought tonight. It's not going away."

Liam reached for his hand, which was his way.

"Our daughter will not be contained," he said. "She's

got bigger plans for herself than anyone, even you, imagined for her."

It warmed her heart to hear Liam refer to Callie as "our" daughter. He loved Callie as his own, and Kate had a feeling that she was going to have to lean on Liam pretty heavily during this next phase of Callie's life.

"I know." Kate sighed. "Why couldn't she have been content here on the ranch?"

"Then she wouldn't be Callie."

He was right. She knew he was. But it still hurt. Her daughter wanted to leave the ranch; her daughter wanted to leave her. She wasn't ready for it, but Callie was ready to flap her wings and fly out of the nest.

"Just do it and get it over with," Liam added. "The quicker you get it done, the better you'll feel."

He was on a roll with that being right thing.

"I'll set up a video chat with them," she said after a moment. "You'll do it with me, won't you?"

"Of course. All the parents have to get along, isn't that what you said?"

"That's the way it works."

"All right, then. We'd better start getting along with these folks. I've seen the way Tony and Callie look at each other, Kate. It looks like the real deal to me. They love each other."

"Hello, Mr. and Mrs. Salviano." Kate sat stiffly next to Liam.

"Please—call us Tottie and Tony Sr."

"I'm Kate and this is my husband, Liam."

"It's so nice to finally meet you." Tottie smiled at her with a toothy, super-white smile. She had a tanning-bed tan, salon-blond hair and she was draped in very expensive jewelry paired with casual designer clothing.

"Hi, Mrs. S! Hi, Mr. S!" Callie was wiggling next to her, hands clasped, so excited that her mom was finally talking to Tony's parents about the trip to California.

"There's Callie! Hi, sweetheart."

Kate watched Tony's parents closely. Both of them, as much as she hated to admit it, were very kind and accepting of Callie. They approved, at some level, to the match between Tony and Callie.

"Where's Tony?" Callie leaned forward as if getting closer to the screen would make Tony appear.

"He had to go to work, sweetheart. He wanted us to make sure that we tell you hello."

"Hello!" Callie bounced a little in her chair.

"Kiddo, why don't you groom Visa. He's caked with mud."

Her daughter waved goodbye to the Salvianos, tilting her head sideways. "Mommy wants privacy."

Kate waited until Callie had shut the front door behind her before she said to Tony's parents, "I had no idea when I signed her up for that online support group that she would..."

"Fall in love?" Tottie completed the sentence.

Kate nodded.

"I know it," Tottie agreed with a relieved expression on her face. "It was a shock for us too."

"We thought it might fade with time," Tony Sr. added.

Kate put her hand on her chest. "So did I."

The four of them spoke for almost an hour; even though they came from very different lifestyles and parts of the country, they all agreed that Callie and Tony needed to slow things way down between them. Tony's parents confirmed that he was, indeed, talking about proposing to Callie. And, on her end, she knew that Callie wanted to say yes. By the end of the conversation, Kate felt much more comfortable with the idea of Callie visiting the Salvianos in California for a week or two.

"When am I—I going to California?" Callie asked for the third time while they were cleaning up the dishes from dinner.

"Callie," Kate said evenly. "What did we talk about earlier?"

"That I—I have to wait."

"And…?"

"And you liked Mr. and Mrs. S."

Kate dried her hands on a dish towel and hugged her daughter. "I did like them. Very much. And I like Tony."

"I-I'm going to California."

Kate kissed the top of her daughter's head. "Yes, kiddo. You're going to California."

"B-by myself."

"Well, you won't be flying by yourself. I'll have to fly with you."

Her daughter frowned. "Why can't I—I go b-by myself?"

"Because you'll have difficulty getting around the airport once you land," Kate reminded her. Callie got very confused when it came to following directions, especially when there were crowds and lots of noise.

"B-but you aren't staying?" This was a question as much as a statement.

It hurt a little, this desire that her daughter had to separate from her. But, on the other hand, typically developing kids would have gone through this in their tweens and their teens. She at least got a couple extra years with Callie close by her side.

"Did you finally get to talk to Sarah and Cole?"

They had both been too worn out to make love; they lay in bed together, the lights off, the curtains open, talking. Liam had been having a difficult time getting his kids on the phone at the appropriate moment. They were with their mom or with their friends.

Liam wiped his hand over his face with a sigh. "I did."

"Oh." Kate sat up in a cross-legged position and faced her husband. "That doesn't sound good."

"No." He shook his head. "It didn't go well at all."

"Tell me what happened."

"Cole's not upset. He likes Seattle—he doesn't mind his new school. Of course, he has a lot more freedom than Sarah. He's older. But he's also a lot easier going about things than Sarah. She takes things to heart and Cole doesn't."

"What did Sarah say about the marriage and the adoption?"

"Once I saw the way she reacted about the marriage, I didn't say anything about the adoption."

"That bad, huh?"

"That bad."

They were both silent for a moment; everyone wanted family and friends to be happy about their marriage. That was human nature. It felt *uncomfortable* when folks weren't happy.

"I think…" Liam said, "that Sarah believes that my marriage to you means that she's stuck in Seattle and she'll never be able to come home to Montana."

"But that's not true." Kate put her hand on her chest. "At least not on our end."

"I told her that. But words are cheap with Sarah these days. She knows her mom is in control, and her mom wants her to stay in Seattle. Now that I'm married, Sarah figures there's no way her mom will agree with letting her come live with me."

Kate lay back down beside Liam, her hands resting on her stomach. They were both caught up in their own thoughts, not speaking.

"We have got to do something about this mattress," Liam grumbled, shifting uncomfortably.

Kate popped up again. "Let's switch. I'm used to the spring."

Liam reached for her and pulled her back down. "No. Come back here."

She lay back down, but the minute her head hit his shoulder, an idea came to her and she popped back up.

"What are you doing now?"

Kate went back to sitting cross-legged and facing him. "I just had a great idea."

"What's that?"

"We haven't even talked about our honeymoon."

"We've been so busy, with your back-to-back clinics and my exploding practice. I feel real bad that we haven't—"

"No," she said, cutting him off. "I wasn't trying to make you feel bad. I had an *idea*."

"Okay." Liam laughed. "You're so damn cute, Kate. Tell me your idea."

She touched his leg. "I love your laugh. Okay. Why don't we honeymoon here? We can both clear our calendars for two weeks. I'm actually kind of light next month. And, *then*, we can invite Sarah for a special trip to the Triple K. If she's here with us, we'll be able to *show* her that our marriage isn't a bad thing for her."

"You want my daughter on our honeymoon?" Liam sounded surprised and touched.

"Why not? Like you've said, we aren't teenagers. We both have children, and we need this marriage to work for everyone in our family, not just us."

Liam pulled her down playfully on top of him and kissed her. "Have I told you lately that I love you, Mrs. Brand?"

"No." Kate rested her head on his chest, listening to the steady, strong beat of his heart.

Liam ran his hands over her back.

"I love you."

"Oh!" Kate exclaimed. "Itch. Itch!"

Her husband started to scratch all over her back until she stopped squirming.

"Did I get it?"

"Yes! Thank you." She went back to resting on him. "I love you too, Liam."

They lay together, enjoying the quiet of the night, not feeling the need to fill every minute between them with talk.

Sleepily, Liam asked her, "Are we still too tired to fool around?"

Kate rolled off his body and curled into a ball facing away from him. "Yes."

"Okay," he agreed. "Kate?"

"Hmm?"

"We're buying a damn mattress tomorrow."

* * *

"How did you manage to get all of this done so quickly?" Kate couldn't believe that Savannah had managed to transform the main house of Sugar Creek Ranch into a wedding reception extravaganza. There was a band, and catered barbecue, and a photographer there to capture candid moments for a keepsake photo album.

"I was worried you wouldn't like it." Savannah looked around at the decorations with a critical eye. "Is it too fussy?"

"No. Not at all!" Kate was more than amazed, she was touched to her core. The Brand family was showing, by way of this party, that they were welcoming Callie and her with open arms.

"Then, I'm relieved." Savannah smiled, then her expression changed as her hand went to her noticeable baby bump. "My baby just gave me one heck of a kick! Must approve of the music."

Kate laughed feeling lighthearted and safe with her new family. "Do you know if you're having a boy or a girl yet?"

Savannah's face softened, her eyes filled with love for her unborn child. "A girl. We're having a girl."

She put her hand on her sister-in-law's arm. "Girls are so much fun. Any names picked out?"

"Amanda," Savannah told her. "After her great-great-aunt who came here for a visit with her father from South Africa and ended up falling in love and marrying into the Brand family. Family legend has it that Amanda Brand was a hard-as-nails trailblazer with a can-do, never-quit attitude."

"Amanda Brand." Kate tried out the name on her tongue. "I like it. I like it a lot."

* * *

It was moments like these that Liam appreciated his family the most. Yes, they were a large bunch, a rowdy opinionated bunch, with family dysfunction to spare. But the Bozeman Brands could pull together like no other family he'd ever seen. When someone was in need, they circled the wagons.

"Thanks for this, Pop," Liam said. "This is the kind of welcome I wanted for Kate and Calico."

"You've got Lilly and Savannah to thank," Jock said in his typically gruff tone. "I thought we could just throw a couple of steaks on the grill and call it a day."

Jock eyed him. "I was none too pleased to hear that you're abandoning the family."

That comment threw Liam for a loop. "What are you talking about, Pop? I'm not abandoning anybody. Certainly not my family."

"You're movin' right off of Sugar Creek. That's abandonment right there."

Jock wanted all of his children to live at Sugar Creek Ranch. Anything short of that was seen as a failure to him.

"Pop…come on."

"What do you think you're gonna do with that chunk of land I gave you? You're just gonna let it sit there and rot?"

"No." Liam put his empty glass down on a nearby table. "I'll keep it maintained. Sarah may want to live there when she's older."

"What about Cole? That ain't right takin' your son's birthright and handin' it over to Sarah."

"Pop. Cole isn't a rancher. Trust me. Out of the two of them, I think Sarah has Sugar Creek in her blood."

"The girl." Jock frowned.

Liam smiled, half in humor and half in resignation. His father was nothing if not a chauvinist. "Yes, Pop. The girl."

They ended the conversation with Jock handing him an envelope. "That's just a little fun money."

"Thank you, Pop. We appreciate you."

Jock waved off his comment like he was swatting away a pesky fly and then ended the conversation by just turning and walking away.

He was still watching his father when Kate appeared at his side.

"Can you believe all of this?" She looped her arm through his. "They even have a cake. A *wedding* cake. I didn't even realize that I wanted one until I saw it. Did you see it?"

"Not yet." Liam handed her the envelope. "This is from the folks."

Kate stared at the envelope for a moment before she peeked inside. She looked at the number on the check, her eyes widening slightly. She closed the envelope. "There's enough in here to revise the plans on the house *and* break ground!"

"Pop's always been generous with money." Liam nodded, not surprised. His father had always been generous with his money and his land—he just didn't have it in him to be generous with his praise.

Jock could always put him in a weird mood—it seemed that he could never really please Jock, and he wished his father's approval didn't still matter to him.

"May I have this dance?" Liam asked his bride, wanting to shake off his sullen mood. This was a night for celebration, not for an analysis of his complicated relationship with his father.

The moment he took Kate in his arms to slow dance to one of his favorite Trace Adkins songs, Liam forgot about everything as his focus narrowed to his wife's pretty face.

"Are you having a good time?" he asked her.

There was so much love for him, for his family, in her eyes when she said, "This is one of the best nights of my life, Liam. I'll never forget it."

He kissed her lightly on the lips, a promise of better things to come when they were alone.

"You look beautiful tonight, Kate." Liam was so happy to have her in his arms.

"I think you are so handsome." His wife gazed up at him in a way that made him feel completely accepted and loved. "I love looking at you."

Liam kissed her again with a chuckle. "That's good, baby. Because you're going to be looking at this mug for the rest of your life."

They danced and they drank and they ate incredible food together. They mingled with friends and family, and spent special time with Callie. Liam made sure that he had requested one of Callie's favorite songs so they could share their first father-daughter dance. At the end of the evening, when too much food and too much booze was consumed by all, it was time for the cake-cutting ceremony.

"Speech! Speech!" A chant started with the small gathering of friends and family.

Liam put his arm around Kate's shoulders, proud to call her his wife. Proud to call Callie his daughter.

He waved for Callie to join them from the front row

of the crowd. Shyly, she walked to his side, and he put his other arm around her shoulders so he was sandwiched in between mother and daughter.

"Thank you to my family for putting this incredible shindig together to celebrate my marriage to this wonderful woman on my right. And thank you to our friends for supporting us no matter what and for all of the presents I saw sitting on the foyer table." That got a laugh out of the crowd. "But in all seriousness, all I can really say is that my life is now complete with Kate and Calico in it. Thank you for coming tonight. We love you," Liam said. "Now, let's cut this damn cake!"

Chapter Fifteen

"That's the last of it." His brother Bruce stacked the last box in the moving van.

It was moving day for Liam, and several of his brothers had cleared their schedules so that they could help him move his life from Sugar Creek to the Triple K. It was a light move, considering that he was leaving most of his furniture behind. Kate didn't have room in her small ranch, and lately he'd been toying with the idea of renting out his cabin to people who wanted to experience life on a real Montana ranch. Of course, he was going to have to run that idea by Jock. Later.

"Are we ready to go?" Gabe, a long-distance hauler for high-end horses, had loaded both of his horses into the trailer.

"You can go on ahead," Liam told him. "Kate's waiting for you."

"All right, then." Gabe gave him a nod. "I'm moving out."

Bruce pulled down the door on the back of the van and locked it. "I'm heading out too."

"Thanks, man." Liam slapped his brother's shoulder. "Shane and I will be right behind you."

Shane, a veteran of the Iraq War, who rarely made an appearance at any family function, had managed to show for the move. Shane stood beside him quietly, his eyes red from lack of sleep and smoking too much dope.

"I think I'll cut out here," his brother said to him.

There was no sense pushing Shane. The war and too many deployments had changed him; he wasn't the same man who had left, and the family was beginning, slowly, to come to terms with the fact that he never would be again. This, the man that he was now, *was* Shane.

Liam hugged his brother. "Thanks for coming out to help, Shane. I know it's not easy for you."

"I like Kate," his brother said.

"I'm pretty partial to her myself."

After a short minute of silence, Shane changed the topic. "My landlady died."

"I'm sorry to hear that. When?"

Shane scratched his chin through his long, scraggly beard. "Oh, I don't know. About a month or two ago."

His brother seemed to be fuzzy with time a lot these days.

"No one's been around to collect rent. I may be kicked out of my place. Who knows. If I need a place to crash…?"

Liam cut him off. "No problem. You can stay here.

But no drugs, Shane. I don't want you smoking pot on my property."

Shane's lips turned up in the slightest of smiles. "I don't know what you're talkin' about, brother."

"Okay." Liam frowned, but gave his brother another hug for the road. "Sure you don't."

"I'm exhausted! I thought men traveled light!" Kate flopped onto their brand-new mattress after taking a long, hot, steamy shower. She had rifled through her husband's T-shirt drawer and was wearing one of his faded, black Trace Adkins concert shirts.

"It takes a lot of work to look this good." Liam raised one eyebrow and posed for her jokingly.

"Thank you. You do look good, I'll give you that."

Liam had his shirt off; he made his abs ripple for her. "Oh, yeah? Do you like what you see?"

"That's...amazing."

"If you're lucky, you can get some of this later," her husband said as he headed into the bathroom.

Kate listened to the sounds of Liam preparing for bed: turning on the faucet, brushing his teeth, uncapping the mouthwash. They had only been married a short while, and yet she had come to count on those sounds.

Liam appeared in the bathroom doorway naked as the day he was born; the man had never been shy about his nudity. And because the man preferred to sleep in the buff, Kate always checked their bedroom door to make sure it was locked. Callie knew better than to open a door without knocking, but she wasn't taking any chances.

Her husband turned off the lights but opened the

blinds so they could enjoy the light from the moon, as limited as it was. He climbed in bed beside her with a happy sigh.

"I have to admit." Kate turned her head toward him. "I don't miss the old mattress."

"I think you know where I stand on that topic." Liam reached for the remote control and clicked off the TV, which she had on mute.

Her husband leaned over, slipped his hand under her shirt, the palm of his hand on her stomach, his head resting on her thigh.

Kate began to rub his head, something she had discovered early on that he liked for her to do.

"Are you happy, Mrs. Brand?"

"Yes," she said on a sigh. She was happy. For the first time in a long time, she felt happy at her core. Oddly, she hadn't known that she was *unhappy* until she had a chance to know what it felt like to be loved by Liam.

"Are you?" she countered.

He kissed her thigh. "Yes. I am."

"Was it strange leaving Sugar Creek? I tried to imagine what it would be like to move away from here, and I couldn't."

"It was strange," he acknowledged. "A little sad. I never imagined my life anywhere else. Until now."

Kate's breath caught—she had been worried about Liam all day. How would he feel once he moved from his family's ranch? Would he genuinely feel that their marriage was worth that sacrifice? Much like the Triple K was to her, Sugar Creek was Liam's lifeblood. It was his heart.

"I'm sorry," she said.

"No." Liam lifted his head so he could look at her. "I

don't want you to apologize. I don't want you to worry that I have any regrets, because I don't. Not one. *This* is what I want. You. Callie. Our future here at the Triple K. That's what matters to me. Yes, I was sad to leave my home, but that sadness doesn't compare with the happiness I feel being your husband."

Liam moved so he was next to her on the bed, so he could take her into his arms and kiss her. They pressed their bodies together, legs intertwined.

"I'm worried you're going to not like it here."

He looked into her eyes. "Hey. Listen to me, Kate. I'm happy wherever you are."

Wanting to feel her naked flesh pressed against his, Kate broke the embrace to take off her T-shirt and panties. She couldn't wait to get back into his arms.

"You feel good, baby." Liam kissed her neck.

"So do you."

He rolled her onto her back so he could kiss her between her thighs. He enjoyed loving her this way, and she had gotten used to just *receiving* it. He kissed her and licked her until she was squirming and tugging on his arm to relieve the ache he had created.

"You taste as sweet as a sugar cookie." Liam covered her body with his.

She was so wet, so ready, that he slipped inside her until he was so deep that it made her gasp. Liam looked down at her, admiring her. He didn't move, not an inch. Her husband loved to tease her, to toy with her in a playful way.

"How do you want it, baby?" He nipped at her neck.

"Slow." She pushed her hips up against him. "Give it to me slow."

Every inch of Liam's body gave her pleasure. He

loved her slowly, passionately, taking his time, massaging her breasts, kissing her lips, building her up until she was panting and straining and biting down on her lip to stop herself from making too much noise.

"Yes, baby."

Liam already knew her body so well that he could feel her getting ready to climax. She dug her nails into his back and bit down on his shoulder. Her orgasms with Liam were stronger, longer, more powerful than ever before. Usually Liam didn't come at the same time, but tonight, as she shuddered in his arms, her husband buried his face in her neck and groaned. She held on to him, holding him as he held her.

"Oh my God." Kate laughed quietly. "I hope it's always this good between us."

Liam separated their bodies and covered them both with the covers.

"It will be," he said with certainty. "We love each other."

Kate curled up with her back pressed against Liam's warm body. Her husband curled his body behind her like a spoon, his hand on her stomach.

"Good night, baby. Tomorrow is going to be a great day."

The day for the adoption had arrived. Tomorrow, Liam would legally become Callie's father. It would be the first time in her daughter's life that she truly had an active, loving father. And, for her, it would be the first time that she wasn't a single parent. Liam had come in, on his figurative white horse, and fixed parts of her life she didn't even realize were all that broken.

"I'm nervous," she admitted. "But so excited. Good night."

* * *

The lead up to this day had weighed on Liam heavily. Ever since it was in his heart to become Callie's father, knocking down all of the barriers in his way had become an obsession. The first hurdle was getting Lloyd to relinquish his parental rights, then he had to settle the back child support. Next, he needed to marry her mother—that wasn't a hurdle, it was a highlight. Now the final hurdle was about to be leaped—he would sit before the judge, answer questions posed by his attorney and Callie would be his.

"How do I look?" Kate was more nervous than he'd ever seen her before. "I don't know what happened. These pants shrunk, and now they look like highwaters."

"How about putting on your knee-high boots. I like those."

Her features were pinched, eyes worried. "Do you think they're appropriate?"

"Sure. Your feet are going to be under the table."

"Are you being serious or funny right now? If you're being funny, I don't appreciate it. I feel like we're running late."

"Come here, baby." Liam hugged her. "It's going to be okay. We aren't running late. You look great, as always. Just calm down. I'm right here, and everything's fine."

Kate wiggled free of the hug. "I don't even know why I feel so stressed out."

"Because—" he tried to reassure her "—this is a big deal. It's not every day your daughter gets adopted."

His wife disappeared into the closet.

"Any doubts?"

She came out with her knee-high boots in hand, dumped them on the floor and sat down on the bed so she could put them on.

"No." Kate stood and stomped her feet so her toes went down farther into the boots. "I don't have one single doubt. You are the best thing that's happened to Callie in a long time."

His wife came over and gave him a brief "apology" hug.

"I'm sorry I've been a bit off."

He rubbed her shoulders. "Don't worry about it. You're doing great."

Kate watched him carefully when she asked, "Do *you* have any doubts?"

He smiled at her. "Baby, I've got a few of best days in my life." He held up his fingers so he could count them as he went. "The day I graduated from vet school, the days my children were born, the day I married you and today."

They piled into Kate's truck, with him behind the wheel. Callie was with them, wearing a new dress just for the occasion. They had debated for quite a while about whether Callie should be in attendance; in the end, Kate didn't want this to be something that just "happened" to her daughter. It had taken weeks of preparation to get Callie to a place where she understood, on a basic level, what the adoption meant. Her first worry, which they expected, was that she already had a dad. But once they got Lloyd on the phone, and he assured her that he would always be her dad, and that nothing in the world would change that, Callie began the process of making sense of her changing reality.

Liam had to give Lloyd credit—the man had stepped

up, better late than never, and was acting in Callie's best interest.

"Do you remember why we're going to the courthouse today, Callie?" Kate looked over her shoulder into the backseat.

"Yes," Callie said with a smile. "Adoption."

"That's exactly right, kiddo." Her mother smiled back at her daughter. "Today you are going to get a bonus dad."

"Are you still good with that idea, Calico?" Liam glanced at his daughter-to-be in the review mirror.

"Yes." She nodded thoughtfully. "I—I like the i-idea."

"So do I." Kate put her hand on her husband's leg.

They arrived early and took a seat at the back of the courtroom. Callie sat between them, holding one of her mother's hands and one of Liam's. Callie didn't always understand the gravity or complexity of a situation, but she could feel the tension in their bodies, the anxiety in their voices, and now she was tense.

Liam looked over his shoulder every couple of minutes, anticipating his attorney's arrival. Finally, he saw Brad Williams walk through the door. He stood and shook the man's hand.

"Are we ready?" Liam asked, after Brad had taken a moment to greet Kate and Callie.

His attorney leaned forward and addressed all of them. "This is mainly procedural. The judge will swear you in, you'll spell your names for the record and state your address. We've got everything filed with the court. I don't anticipate any hiccups."

Liam tried to stop moving his leg up in down while they waited, but finally gave up. He wanted to be on the back end of this; he wanted Callie to be his daughter, legally and forever. When their case was called, all four of them moved to the table. Liam poured himself a glass of water, drank it and then poured another.

"Relax, Dad." Kate was now the one who appeared to be more at peace.

Judge Ackredge, a heavyset man with thick jowls, rounded nose and thick glasses, addressed the court, "We'll go on the record. This is docket 841-FA-029. Counsel."

When the judge wasn't in his robes, Charlie Ackredge was one of Liam's father's hunting and fishing buddies; it was nice to have a familiar face on the bench during the adoption hearing.

Brad stood for a second to address the judge. "Thank you, Your Honor. Brad Williams representing the petitioners."

The judge swore them in so they could proceed. Under the table, Liam held on to Kate's hand with a sweaty palm.

"Please answer the questions regarding the petition for adoption loud enough for the judge to hear." Brad took out the petition and turned to the signature page.

"Is the signature on the petition yours?"

"Yes."

"Were the facts in this petition true when you signed it?"

"Yes."

"Is the adult you want to adopt named Calico Kathryn King?"

"Yes."

The questions continued, one by one.

"Have you entered into a legal marriage with Kathryn Julia King?"

"Yes." Liam squeezed Kate's hand.

"Would you like there to be a name change?"

Liam looked at Callie to make sure she still wanted to become a Brand. Once Callie realized that her mother's name was Brand, she wanted to be a Brand, as well.

"Yes. Her name is Calico Kathryn King Brand."

It was a strong name; it was a good name.

Brad covered Liam's employment and his ability to support Callie, as well as letting him know that if the adoption was granted, that he would have the same rights and responsibilities as a parent or legal guardian. Which was exactly what he wanted.

The attorney then questioned Kate, asking her if she approved of the adoption by her husband of her daughter.

"Yes." Kate had tears in her eyes as she held on to his hand with both hands. "Yes, I do."

Next the attorney turned to Callie.

"Hi, Callie."

"Hi."

"I asked you earlier if it was okay if I asked you a few questions. Is it still okay?"

Callie nodded.

"Please say 'yes' if it's okay Callie," Brad prompted.

"Yes."

"Do you know why you're here, Callie?"

"To be adopted."

"And what does adoption mean to you?"

"I-it means that I'm going to b-be a part of the B-Brand family."

Brad nodded. "That's all I have, Your Honor."

Judge Ackredge took over the proceeding while Liam had to hold back tears. The last time he had cried was the day his divorce was final. This was a much better reason to have tears in his eyes.

"I have a properly completed petition for adoption for one adult. Based on the testimony I will enter a judgment of adoption today that will establish the same relationship between the dependent adult and the parent as if they had been born to the adoptive parent. Congratulations."

And that was that. After months of preparation and discussions and meetings with his attorney, Callie was *his* daughter.

"Congratulations." Brad shook his hand and then shook Kate's hand.

"Thank you so much," Kate said as she wiped tears from her cheeks. "For everything."

"It was my pleasure." The attorney gathered his belongings. "Congratulations, Callie."

Callie Brand ducked her head and giggled. "Thank you."

Outside the courthouse, Liam felt like a king. He was a husband to Kate and a father to Callie. Life was just about perfect.

"Brand family hug!" Liam opened his arms wide.

Kate and Callie stepped into his arms, and they all hugged each other.

After they broke the hug, Liam addressed his daughter. He put his hands on her shoulders.

"You're my daughter now, Callie. Forever."

His daughter rewarded him with a wide smile.

"You can't call me Dr. Brand anymore," he told her. "What do you want to call me?"

"I—I don't know."

Kate put her arm around Callie's shoulder. "You

already have a 'Daddy.' How about if you call Liam 'Dad'?"

Callie threw herself back into his arms and hugged him. "Dad."

For the last hour, Liam had been holding back tears. When Callie called him "Dad," he didn't even try to hold them back any longer.

Kate wrapped her arms around both of them for a second group hug. She caught Liam's eyes and mouthed, *Thank you.*

"We're a family," Liam said as they headed back to the truck. "Now and for the rest of our lives."

Chapter Sixteen

"Are you all packed?" Kate stood in the doorway of her daughter's room.

This was a day that Kate had been dreading; this was the day that she flew with Callie to San Diego. Liam had offered to travel with them, but she felt that this was something she needed to do on her own. Perhaps it didn't seem like a monumental step for her from the outside looking in; for her, this was a rite of passage for Callie. Her daughter had never been out of state for a day, much less two weeks, without her.

"I—I'm ready to go!" Callie pulled her heavy suitcase off her bed, and it hit the ground with a thud.

"You aren't going there forever, Callie," Kate reminded her daughter. "You're coming back in two weeks."

"I—I know. I—I need to have options."

That made Kate laugh. "Fair enough, kiddo."

Callie had certainly packed options; Kate had been with her daughter to make sure she had packed all essentials, while her fashionista daughter had focused on her wardrobe. Wherever Callie had gotten her sense of style, it hadn't come from Kate.

Callie happily wheeled her suitcase out of the room, past her mother and stopped at the door.

"All right." Kate grabbed her keys off the counter. "Let's go before I lose my nerve."

They would be flying to San Diego with one stop in Salt Lake City. It would take them nearly four hours of fly time and six hours total. Callie didn't like to fly, which hadn't dampened her enthusiasm for the trip… yet. It would, though. Liam insisted on buying first-class seats in order to make the trip easier on the both of them. She resisted in the beginning, but couldn't deny his logic after a couple rounds of discussions between them. Having the extra room, having Callie close to a bathroom, would make the trip go much more smoothly overall.

"Are you all checked in?" Liam asked her when she called him from the airport.

"All checked in," she confirmed. "Callie's anxiety has already started to crack through her excitement."

"Just be careful. I believe in you and I believe in Callie."

They exchanged I-love-yous, and then soon after that phone call, first class was given priority boarding onto the plane. Normally Kate liked to be one of the last on the plane—she wasn't a fan of flying either. But today she took advantage of the perk and used the extra time to get Callie settled in the seat next to the window.

By the time all passengers had boarded, Callie had a ginger ale, called Tony before Kate showed her how to put her phone in airplane mode, and accepted a pillow and blanket from the steward. Callie was snuggled beneath her blanket, looking out the window, when the cabin door was slammed shut. Her daughter jumped, her face registering that familiar panic.

Kate reached for her daughter's hand. "We're going to push back from the gate, Callie. First we'll get in line at the runway for takeoff."

"And then we take off."

"Just close your eyes and hold on to my hand, kiddo. Think about how happy you'll be when you see Tony at the airport."

This garnered a small, nervous smile from Callie. "I—I can do it, Mommy."

"Calico, I know you can."

We are here.

Kate sent a text to Liam the moment they landed in San Diego. She had to admit to herself that she had underestimated her daughter. Callie was growing up, and she was highly motivated to see Tony, and this new maturity and motivation made the trip go much easier than Kate had imagined.

"Do you see them?" Callie had asked this question several times as they deplaned.

"Are we at baggage claim yet?"

"No."

"Where are they going to pick us up?"

"B-baggage claim."

"So, what do you think?"

Callie giggled at herself. "They're at b-baggage claim!"

And they were at baggage claim; Tony, his mother and his father were all awaiting their arrival. Tony was armed with balloons, flowers and a large stuffed bear.

"Hi," Kate greeted Tony's parents while Callie hugged her boyfriend.

Tottie ignored her offered hand and hugged her; she smelled sweet, like candy. Tony Sr. refrained from hugging her, for which she was grateful.

"Callie!" Kate called out to her daughter who was kissing Tony right there in baggage claim. "You need to come and watch out for your bag."

"Young love," Tottie said, her body language saying that she was just as uncomfortable as she was about the kissing in public.

Kate was lucky to get a flight back to Bozeman within a couple hours of landing. The Salvianos took her out for an early dinner, which gave her an opportunity to go over Callie's health concerns and diet restrictions. Tony and Callie sat at a separate table; every now and again, Kate would watch her daughter sitting with her boyfriend. It was hard to admit, it was hard to process, but she could easily see that Tony was smitten with Callie.

The return trip was a tiring, long and lonely event for Kate. She had never left her daughter in another state with virtual strangers. Every fiber of her being railed against it. Yet it's what she had to do. She had to let Callie go. All her life, she had told Callie that she could do anything, be anything. Now those chickens had come home to roost, because her daughter was putting those words into action.

She had a heavy heart when she landed in Bozeman, feeling so worn down that she thought about taking a nap in her truck before making the trip home. Kate sent Liam a text the moment the plane landed; he answered back that he would see her when she got home.

"Hello, Mrs. Brand."

Kate was startled when she heard her husband's voice where she hadn't expected to hear it. There, leaning against a pillar just outside the airport entrance, was Liam.

"What are you doing here?" she asked, but didn't wait for him to answer before she threw her arms around him and buried her head in his chest.

"Waiting for my lovely wife." He ran his hand gently over her hair, holding her tight.

Unbidden, tears that she had been holding back for hours, days, weeks, poured out of her eyes and onto his shirt.

"It's okay," Liam said quietly. "Everything is going to be okay. Let's go home."

Liam had gotten his brother to drop him off at the airport so he could drive her back to the Triple K. It was, by far, the sweetest, and to her, the most romantic gesture a man had ever made to her.

In the passenger seat, Kate leaned back, closed her eyes and periodically wiped the tears off her cheeks.

"I can't believe you're here," she said, her voice choked with emotion.

"I knew this was going to be a tough one for you." Liam shifted into gear and started the journey home.

Kate opened her eyes, put her hand on his leg. "Thank you."

"You're welcome, baby. This is part of my job."

* * *

It had been only two days since he had picked Kate up from the airport, and now he was back to pick up his daughter Sarah. It took some doing, some negotiating with her mother, but eventually his ex approved the unscheduled trip. Liam suspected that his teenage daughter, who took after the Brand side of her family, was making her mother's life hell.

"Hi, Dad." Sarah had her bangs in her eyes and a mopey look on her face.

"Hi." He hugged her tightly even though she tried to resist. "I'm glad to see you."

They gathered her bags and headed out. Liam tried, mostly unsuccessfully, to pry some sort of conversation out of his daughter. There was one subject she *did* want to talk to him about.

"I want to stay at Sugar Creek."

"We'll visit." He told her the same thing he told her on the phone. "But I don't live there anymore, Sarah. I live at Triple K Ranch. With my wife."

That stopped all communication until he turned into the long winding drive that led to the Triple K homestead.

"Look at this place, Sarah. As far as the eye can see. You can ride for miles and never find a fence."

Sarah stared out the passenger window. "It's not as pretty as Sugar Creek."

"Sugar Creek is God's country," Liam agreed. "But so is Triple K."

"She *hates* me," Kate whispered while they were brushing their teeth. It was her idea to bring Sarah on their stay-at-home honeymoon, but it was a suggestion that she seriously regretted. From the moment Sarah arrived at the Triple K, the teenager was a nonstop stream of complaints, "remember when Mom and you did" comments and negativity aimed at everything Triple K Ranch.

Liam didn't deny it because he *couldn't* deny it.

Her husband spit toothpaste into the sink, and turned on the water to rinse out his mouth and wash the toothpaste down the drain.

"She acts like she hates you. But I don't think she does. Not really."

Sarah was bunking in Callie's room; already she had complaints about the mattress and the low ceilings and the fact that there wasn't a bathroom attached.

"No," she argued. "She really hates me. It's like she's been waiting for you to get back together with her mom, even though her mom is *remarried*, and I've come along and screwed everything up!"

Kate yanked back the covers, frustrated. She punched her pillows with her fist, then got into bed, kicking her feet to loosen the sheets tucked in tightly at the end of the mattress.

Liam joined her in bed. It was the first time since they had married that they were disagreeing. It didn't feel good.

"I'm telling you, I know Sarah. She doesn't hate you. She's angry with me, she's angry with her mother…"

"And I'm an easy target," Kate snapped. "Does she even know that I'm the reason she's here? That I wanted her to be with us on our honeymoon?"

"I've told her, baby." Liam turned off the light to signal he was ready to go to bed.

Still sitting upright, and annoyed Liam was shutting

her down by shutting off the light, Kate stared into the darkened room.

"Hey…" Her husband touched her arm. "Come on. Lay down. She's only been here for one night."

Kate looked at Liam. She was tired, he was tired. Maybe she should just drop the conversation and see what the next day would bring.

She scooted down in bed, flipped away from him so her back was to him and pulled the covers over her shoulder.

"Hey…" Liam leaned over for his good-night kiss. "Where are you."

"I'm right here." Kate turned her head enough to accept the kiss.

Liam gave her a quick kiss and then lay back down. "Good night, baby. I love you."

"Good night."

Then, after a minute of silence, she added, "I love you, too."

The Triple K was a big enough ranch for both of them. This was what Kate thought after she left the house after breakfast, with a still moody and unhappy Sarah sitting at the kitchen table. The only thing she could do, the only thing she had control over, was work. There were horses to train, so she decided to get to it.

A beautiful Friesian, a muscular, coal black horse with feathered hooves, had been delivered to the Triple K for training. Kate had been itching to take him for a ride, but first she wanted to earn his respect on the ground.

"Come on, Solomon." Kate led the powerful gelding out of his stall.

She started working with Solomon in the round pen, without a halter or bridle. Kate stood in the center of the ring, putting the Friesian through his paces. First she had him walk, then trot, and then canter to the left and then to the right.

"Good boy." She walked up beside him, gave him a treat from her pocket and then moved him forward by swinging the rope in the direction of his hindquarters.

"Who's this?" Liam asked, hanging over the top rail of the round pen.

"Solomon," Kate said, not taking her eyes off the gelding trotting around the edge of the pen. "Isn't he spectacular?"

"He certainly is," her husband agreed. "I've got to run into town, get a couple of things from the store. Sarah doesn't want to come with me. Is it okay with you if she stays here?"

Honestly, she wished Sarah would go with her father. But that wasn't realistic. She had invited her stepdaughter to the ranch to get to know her—Kate was the adult, and it was her job to break through the attitude and connect with Sarah. She couldn't do that if she was always sending her off with Liam.

"That's fine." Kate nodded. "We'll be fine."

She finished working with Solomon and moved on to the next horse on her list for training. Riding boarded horses, keeping them exercised and making sure they picked up their cues to trot or canter, was a big part of how she made a living.

"What's his name?"

Sarah had been watching her work with the Friesian from across the yard. She hadn't gotten too close to the round pen, but the teen's interest in her work with horses seemed like a possibility to make a connection.

"Solomon."

Sarah pushed away from the wall, her features so like her father's, that the teen tugged at her heart.

"Can I ride him?"

"Not this one." Kate handed Solomon's lead to one of the stable hands. "Rinse him off, cool him down and then turn him out in the north pasture.

"I don't own him." Kate finished answering Sarah's question. "I can show you the horses you can ride. Your father's horses are here too."

That was when Kate first saw a spark in Sarah, a point of connection. She could work with this. Kate saddled up one of her horses and let Sarah ride. The girl had a great seat in the saddle, and Kate told her so over lunch.

"I rode all the time when I lived at Sugar Creek," Liam's daughter reminded her. "I don't get to ride in Seattle. Ever."

The conversation ended there. Kate had never been one to beat around the bush, and she had a feeling that Sarah was someone who appreciated cutting to the chase.

"You don't like me," she said.

Sarah stopped chewing, looked up at her, surprise in those bright blue eyes so like Liam's own bright blue eyes.

"No."

"Because I married your dad?"

Sarah shook her head. "No. I don't care about that anymore."

Kate raised an eyebrow and waited.

"I don't know." The teen frowned into her plate.

"I know you want to move back to Montana," Kate said. "Do you think now that your father is married to me that you can't move back to Montana?"

A shrug was all she got, but Kate knew, instinctively, that this the reason behind a big chunk of the resentment Sarah was feeling toward her.

"Are you finished?" she asked the teen.

A nod.

"Help me clear the table. I want to show you something."

After they cleared the table, Kate rolled out the new house plans on the table for Sarah to see.

"This is the house your father and I are going to build."

Sarah tried to act like she wasn't interested; Kate could see that she was.

The horse trainer pointed to one of the rooms in the house. "Do you know what this is?"

A shake of the head. "Nope."

"*This* is your room."

That got the teen's attention. "My room?"

"That's right," Kate said. "Your father and I want you to have a place with us. I can't guarantee that we can get your mom to agree to let you live with us full time. But we are going to try."

Sarah stared at her, unblinking, and then ran her finger over her bedroom on the house plans.

"We want you to be with us, Sarah," Kate said. "Do you understand? Triple K is your home too."

Liam wasn't sure what he was going to find when he arrived back at the ranch. He had hoped that Sarah and Kate would find some common ground upon which to build a relationship if he gave them some space and time.

He expected to find Sarah holed up in Callie's room on her computer and Kate in the barn with her horses. He did not expect to see the two of them, standing at the top of the hill where they were going to build their dream home.

Liam shifted into Park, turned off the truck and leaned forward so he could get a better look out the windshield.

He wasn't imagining it—his daughter and his wife were standing together on the site where they planned on breaking ground in a month.

"What's going on up here?" Liam had decided to leave his truck parked and hike up the hill.

"Hi!" Kate had a genuine, easy smile on her face. "We're making plans for the new house."

"Kate says I can paint my room any color I want."

"Other than black," Kate corrected.

"Other than black," Sarah amended.

Kate put her arms around his waist, kissed him quickly and then said, "I hope you don't mind that I ruined the surprise. I showed Sarah the house plans."

"What do you think?" he asked his daughter, whose face had lost its scowl.

Sarah gave a little nod. "It's pretty cool."

"Yeah," Liam agreed. "It is pretty cool."

His daughter kicked a clump of dirt, walking in a circle where her room would eventually be.

She stopped, looked at him directly in the eye and asked, "Are you really going to try to get mom to let me live with you?"

Liam caught Kate's eye; he understood why she had talked to Sarah about this before he'd had the chance. The timing was right, and she did it. If it helped heal their relationship, then he was glad.

"Come here." He held out his free arm; when she reached his side, he put his arm around her shoulders. "Do you know what I know about your mom?" Liam asked his daughter. "I know that your mom loves you more than anything else in her life."

Sarah frowned at him, but he persisted.

"It's true, Sarah. And if your mom thinks that it's best for you to live here full-time, or at least for the summer, she'll say yes. And I'm going to give convincing her one heck of shot, Sarah. That's what I can promise. Can you live with that?"

His daughter nodded, and for the first time in a long time, Sarah leaned against him and put her head on his shoulder.

"It's going to be another beautiful day." Liam gazed out at the clear, blue Montana sky.

Standing there with his wife and his younger daughter at his side, Liam realized that all of his wishes had been granted. He was a husband, a father; he was building a home with the woman he loved; one day, they would be surrounded by their children and grandchildren. He finally had a family of his own. Perhaps he didn't deserve it, but God had, indeed, been good to Liam Brand.

* * * * *

MILLS & BOON

Coming next month

BABY SURPRISE FOR THE SPANISH BILLIONAIRE
Jessica Gilmore

'Don't you think it's fun to be just a little spontaneous every now and then?' Leo continued, his voice still low, still mesmerising.

No, Anna's mind said firmly, but her mouth didn't get the memo. 'What do you have in mind?'

His mouth curved triumphantly and Anna's breath caught, her mind running with infinite possibilities, her pulse hammering, so loud she could hardly hear him for the rush of blood in her ears.

'Nothing too scary,' he said, his words far more reassuring than his tone. 'What do you say to a well-earned and unscheduled break?'

'We're having a break.'

'A proper break. Let's take out the *La Reina Pirata*—' his voice caressed his boat's name lovingly '—and see where we end up. An afternoon, an evening, out on the waves. What do you say?'

Anna reached for her notebook, as if it were a shield against his siren's song. 'There's too much to do . . .'

'I'm ahead of schedule.'

'We can't just head out with no destination!'

'This coastline is perfectly safe if you know what

you're doing.' He grinned wolfishly. 'I know exactly what I'm doing.'

Anna's stomach lurched even as her whole body tingled. She didn't doubt it. 'I . . .' She couldn't, she shouldn't, she had responsibilities, remember? Lists, more lists, and spreadsheets and budgets, all needing attention.

But Rosa would. Without a backwards glance. She wouldn't even bring a toothbrush.

Remember what happened last time you decided to act like Rosa, her conscience admonished her, but Anna didn't want to remember. Besides, this was different. She wasn't trying to impress anyone; she wasn't ridiculously besotted, she was just an overworked, overtired young woman who wanted to feel, to be, her age for a short while.

'Okay, then,' she said, rising to her feet, enjoying the surprise flaring in Leo di Marquez's far too dark, far too melting eyes. 'Let's go.'